D0313016

WALLIS:
THE NOVEL

Books by Anne Edwards

BIOGRAPHY

Sonya:
The Life of Countess Tolstoy

Vivien Leigh:
A Biography

Judy Garland:
A Biography

Road to Tara:
The Life of Margaret Mitchell

Matriarch:
Queen Mary and the House of Windsor

A Remarkable Woman:
A Biography of Katharine Hepburn

Early Reagan:
The Rise to Power

Shirley Temple:
American Princess

The DeMilles:
An American Family

Royal Sisters:
Queen Elizabeth II
and Princess Margaret

NOVELS

The Survivors

Shadow of a Lion

Haunted Summer

Miklos Alexandrovitch
Is Missing

The Hesitant Heart

Child of Night

Wallis: The Novel

AUTOBIOGRAPHY

The Inn and Us
(with Stephen Citron)

CHILDREN'S BOOKS

P. T. Barnum

The Great Houdini

A Child's Bible

WALLIS:
THE NOVEL

Anne Edwards

William Morrow and Company, Inc.
New York

It is the policy of William Morrow and Company, Inc., and its imprints and affiliates, recognizing the importance of preserving what has been written, to print the books we publish on acid-free paper, and we exert our best efforts to that end.

Library of Congress Cataloging-in-Publication Data

Edwards, Anne, 1927–
Wallis : the novel / Anne Edwards.
p. cm.
ISBN 0-688-08835-X
1. Windsor, Wallis Warfield, Duchess of, 1896– —Fiction.
2. Great Britain—History—Edward VIII, 1936—Fiction. I. Title.
PS3555.D87W3 1991
813'.54—dc20 90-22735
CIP

Printed in the United States of America

First Edition

1 2 3 4 5 6 7 8 9 10

BOOK DESIGN BY M. C. DEMAIO

To Harvey Ginsberg,
a prince among editors

NEAR ENCOUNTER

April 7, 1920

The late afternoon sun splashed wildly through her bedroom windows. Wallis adjusted the shades. Even in April, California evenings arrived unfashionably late. Jewels and satin were meant to be worn at night. Daylight made them appear vulgar. Here it was past seven P.M. and the day gave no hint whatsoever of fading. They were expected at the Hotel del Coronado in less than an hour and Win was not yet home. Wallis despised being late. Punctuality was an essential part of her personality. Anyway, this party was like no other she had ever attended. The guest of honor was to be England's handsome young Prince of Wales who, en route to Australia, had called in at San Diego aboard HMS *Renown* this very afternoon and would sail out again tomorrow.

Wallis smiled confidently into the mirror. She was not beautiful in a conventional manner. But she was an attractive creature and she knew it. Her sleek dark hair, the luminescent violet-blue eyes set roundly beneath thickly arched black brows and the well-boned aristocratic nose had been inherited from her father's side—the proud Warfields, patricians for two centuries in Maryland, and many more in England. What made her face so arresting was the background and frame for these bold features—the high forehead and broad cheekbones, the pointed jaw with its faint shadow cleft and the smooth pale-white skin so prized by the women in her mother's family, the equally proud Montagues of Virginia.

Because of her heritage she thought of herself first as a Southerner and then as an American. In her youth her Southern roots had always been of life-and-death importance. Baltimore, Maryland, where she had grown to womanhood, considered itself an unconquerable Southern peninsula in an encroaching Northern sea. Something about Wallis, herself, evoked this same impression.

Baltimore was now three thousand miles away and she was married to a Lieutenant-Commander in the United States Navy, which meant she saw her husband only at the Navy's convenience. In the three and a half years since her wedding in November 1916 to Earl Winfield Spencer, Jr. (then only a Lieutenant Junior Grade), they had been transferred three times. Twice, she had felt an outsider to Navy society. When Win had been reassigned to North Island, California, near San Diego, she devised a scheme to change that pattern.

She found a charming furnished house on Flora Drive in nearby, socially prestigious, Coronado, with an enormous studio living room which opened on to a large, brick-walled, Spanish-style patio rimmed by an immense flame-colored bougainvillaea vine. Immediately, she gave a series of small cocktail and dinner parties (ostensibly to honor the steady incursion of top naval officers who came and went at Win's base), to which she invited some of Coronado's most prominent residents, who, of course, would then be obliged to return the invitation.

Wallis was quickly recognized as a talented and witty hostess who not only served superb food but had an undeniable knack for putting together a stimulating guest list. The young Spencers were living above their means and Wallis was always having to ask for her family's assistance. But she felt confident that their new friends would benefit them socially, for there were invitations to polo at Del Monte, beach parties at La Jolla and weekends at Santa Barbara where they met the rich and the powerful. Win was highly critical of her fast-moving social circle and in a constant state about her extravagances. "We are not rich," he would chide her. "And if this keeps up we'll end up in the poorhouse!" She dismissed this easily, for Win never had a good word to say about anything.

After meeting Win—so handsome and high-spirited—she had written her mother, Alice, "I have just met the world's most fascinating aviator!" Alice, who was presently visiting with her, had begged her to wait, but Wallis married her airman only a few months later. She soon had to contend with Win's strange and sudden shifts of temperament, the emotional highs that would often erupt into violence. She had learned quickly how to recognize a coming storm. The laugh wrinkles around his dark eyes disappeared and he became morosely silent. Alcohol was responsible for Win's changes of mood and his violent outbursts. It also increased his jealousy of any small attention paid to her by another man. Wallis freely admitted to being flirtatious. What red-blooded Southern girl was not?

She ran her hands down the smooth plum-satin torso of her gown. She had lied to Win about its price, making up the difference herself with the small check she had received from Uncle Sol. He had meant it to be used to entertain Alice during her visit. But her mother had already received a dozen invitations from Wallis's friends and she did not feel the least bit guilty in appropriating the money to buy a dress which set off her slender figure to perfection and was, at the same time, elegant and distinctive.

She had borrowed Alice's pearls and her chignon was held in place by tortoise combs sprinkled with small diamonds, the pair inherited from Grandmother Warfield. Entering or leaving a room she would make an impression. Wallis laughed at her own theatricality. She accepted many things about herself: her need to impress, her ambition to be more than she was, her fetish for tidiness, and her obsession with perfection in her dress, the flowers in her home, the table she set, the food she served.

She knew some people considered her a social climber, a bit too ambitious and vain. Army and Navy bases had their fill of bored, envious service wives and daughters, and Wallis, not infrequently, was the subject of their catty gossip.

"Well, let them talk," Wallis had decided. "At least they turn their heads when I go by."

Slowly and lovingly she drew on her high-buttoned white satin gloves. The slippery softness against her bare arms, the ritual of massaging each finger into place, of erasing every tiny crease with the tips of the fingers of her other hand, gave her a satisfying sensual feeling. She had practiced a curtsy all morning. Marianna Fulham, Rear Admiral Fulham's daughter, and her good friend, had also assured her that Fiona Bell-Hawkins, the English resident who had arranged the reception, had included Win and herself on the list of guests to be presented to the Prince.

"Bessie Wallis, don't you look jus' grand!" her mother called from the doorway, drawing out her daughter's hated childhood name so that it became even more offensive to her.

Wallis turned away from the mirror. "Thank you, Mama," she smiled stiffly. Her Southern upbringing was apparent in the cadence of her words but not nearly as prominent as in her mother's speech, for Wallis had spent long hours as a child talking in front of a mirror so that she could overcome it. A touch of the Old South could be charming. Her mother's speech, on the other hand, lacked polish.

Time had not dealt too kindly with Alice Montague Warfield Rasin and she was outwitting it the only way she knew how—by covering the age spots on her fragile fair skin with chalky powder, using dark-brown pencil on her gray brows, rouging her cheeks and wearing dresses that emphasized her still-firm breasts and wasp waist. Wallis covertly glanced at the plunging neckline of her mother's black beaded gown. *More the Merry Widow than ever,* she thought, her face flushed with embarrassment, though she did not comment.

Until Wallis's marriage to Win, Alice had been her lifeline and they had been more like friends than mother and daughter. Although not knowledgeable about intellectual pursuits, Alice knew a lot about life. Witty, full of gaiety, she always had the most wonderful stories to tell and defiantly had refused to be daunted by the hard life she and her fatherless daughter had shared. "Don't you evah believe we're poor. We are jus' a mite, temporarily broke" was her most repeated axiom. And somehow she would borrow additional money from Uncle Sol so that Wallis could have a new frock and attend the right schools.

"Well, how do I look?" Alice asked, stepping backward.

"Just fine, Mama."

"Fine? That doesn't sound like much of a compliment to me."

"You certainly look too young to be my mother," Wallis laughed.

"That's bettah," Alice grinned.

Wallis could not help but be amused as she watched her mother preen. She was pleased Alice had come to visit. Her mother was lusty and fun, capable of saying the most outrageous things. Lord, nothing fazed Mama! And she had plainspoken advice for every occasion. "Darlin'," she had told Wallis that very morning, "'course I can see Win's a drunkard. Got a mean temper, too, an' he's jealous to boot. But so far the Navy hasn't caught on. So you make the most of that. An' if a time evah comes when the bad is heaped higher than the good—you jus' dig in as deep an' fast as you can, an' start shovelin' your way out."

Win's drinking had grown steadily worse the last few months. Most nights he came home late, alcohol strong on his breath, his voice thick, his manner aggressive, often threatening. He'd drink himself into a stupor on Saturday nights because he didn't have to fly on Sundays and, before passing out, would become belligerent. Once, when he planned a bachelor evening with his friends, he hogtied her to the bed to keep her home and then, while she was helplessly bound, spread out her framed family photographs on the floor in front of her and shattered and ground the glass with the heel of his boot. Win had a terrible anger within him. She could not admit to herself that he was a sadist although she sensed his violence was not normal. *This is a terrible phase that he will come out of,* she kept telling herself. For sober, Win cast a manly figure, possessed great charm and a sense of humor. They made a handsome couple, a fact that she did not doubt increased the number of invitations they received. To leave

Win at the present time could end her social life in Coronado. And where would she go, and how would she support herself?

Wallis pushed such unpleasant thoughts out of her mind as she turned away from the mirror. "I do look smart, don't I, Mama?" she grinned. She went over to Alice and extended a gloved hand. "These buttons are real nail breakers. Could you help?" Both of them heard the front door slam shut. With a small affectionate squeeze of her daughter's gloved hand, Alice disappeared discreetly up the hall to her own room.

Win stood in the doorway tanned and lean, his close-cropped mustache impeccably trimmed. The gold officer's stripes and the brass buttons on his uniform caught the sunlight that slithered from the sides of the shades. He whistled insinuatingly and then laughed. "We must be going someplace." The undertone of sarcasm in his voice hinted at harsher forces working beneath the surface. He entered the room with an uneven step.

Good Lord, Wallis thought, *he must have stopped at the Officers' Club and had at least two double gins.* He skimmed his hat across the room where it landed straight up in the center of the bed. "You know I hate that. It's bad luck," Wallis admonished.

"I'm not superstitious," he replied.

"Well, like every other Southern girl who had a colored mammy, I am. Never throw your hat on a bed was Ellie's number-one rule." He removed his tie and hung it over the doorknob. "Never hang anything on a doorknob was another. Ellie had a rule for everything. Never sit down thirteen at table, never start a journey on a Friday, never let a peacock feather into your house."

He laughed derisively and she angrily scooped up the hat from the bed, lifted the tie from the doorknob and placed them both atop his bureau. "The Bassetts are coming by to pick us up in twenty minutes; please be ready." Her tone had turned cold.

"How about one for the road?"

"I'll have a chilled martini waiting for you in the living room," she said with an edge that he understood meant quite the opposite. "You'll need to change into your dress uniform.

The occasion is very formal. The Prince of Wales is the guest of honor, remember?" She closed the door before he could reply and then stood there for a moment to collect herself. *I won't let him spoil my evening,* she thought, the words ricocheting inside her head.

Wallis was not without strong feeling for Win. To her humiliating distraction, when he was sober she still found him enormously attractive. Headstrong, hot-blooded, danger-loving—off alcohol Win represented the kind of venturesome man whom women could rely on in the most desperate of situations. Though he had never had to, she was certain he could fight off an attacker, or carry her to safety in fire, flood or war. Win was moved by the most primal forces, and Wallis admired his basic maleness. She also respected his abilities as a pilot and an officer. His men had flown a total of 35,000 hours without one fatal crash, or even a serious injury, or a single scrubbed plane.

The problem as she interpreted it, trying hard to rationalize her feelings, was that Win did not respect his own accomplishments. He was a fighting man who, with the war over, had been left with no way to prove his steel. That was why he drank and turned on her so often she was sure. Nonetheless, this knowledge did not ease the pain she suffered with his abuse.

She joined Alice in the living room and chattered away inconsequentially as she glanced nervously up at the mantel clock. In the bedroom Win could be heard slamming drawers open and shut. This was followed by ten minutes when he could not be heard at all. Finally, Wallis stepped into the corridor, and called, "What are you doing, Win? The Bassetts will be here soon. Do hurry."

The bedroom door opened and he strode down the hallway singing at the top of his lungs, *"I found my love in Avalon—be-side-the-bay,"* then lunged through the archway that divided the front room from the rest of the house. He had obviously located what he had been looking for in his bureau—a bottle of gin.

"Mr. Caruso bettah watch out," Alice commented.

He paused as he came abreast of Wallis and laid his hand

heavily on her bare shoulder. "Oh, Lord, not in front of Mama," she thought. "He wouldn't dare get rough." She pried his hand from her flesh and straightened the straps on her gown. "You're drunk," she said, and then called out, "Mama, help me get him to the sofa." Alice was immediately at her side.

"I left my love in Avalon," Win sang, his voice raised to percussion volume, *"and-sailed-a-way."* He seemed happy enough and allowed the two women to guide him over to the sofa and then promptly collapsed onto it. A car squeaked to a stop outside. "The Bassetts," Wallis said. "Now that's just swell!"

"You get your wrap, darlin', while I stop them from comin' in," Alice ordered. "I'll tell Mr. Bassett that Win's been delayed at the base." She swept up her cape and evening bag from a chair near the front door and rushed out.

If either Rita or Joe Bassett guessed the reason for Alice's surprising appearance on the pathway of the house, good manners prevailed. They returned to the car where, once they saw Alice comfortably seated in the back, they waited for Wallis. When she joined them, they each commented on how charming she looked and kept up a light banter of superficial conversation all the way to their destination.

The rambling, towered, ornate Hotel del Coronado had been designed a decade earlier by the leading architect Stanford White in the style of a Mediterranean palace. Three flags—American, British, and the state flag of California—flew atop the front façade. Palm trees looking like leafy windmills lined the wide circular driveway, already crowded with arrogant limousines, their long noses waxed to a glistening finish. The sky was a dark Prussian blue. A wind had risen and with it the pungent evening water scents from San Diego Bay. Night would momentarily slipcase the day in darkness, but the hotel, every light blazing, would turn the space it occupied into a blur of incandescence.

As Wallis entered the pillared grand foyer—with its Spanish tile floors set gem-like in colors of tourmaline, jade and lapis lazuli, the massive, intricately designed wrought-iron chandeliers, the heavily carved Spanish furniture and urns (large enough to conceal Ali Baba) filled with exotic flowers—

she felt as though she was stepping into a Castilian past where the sound of castanets and the sight of mantilla-crowned women would have been quite natural.

A shiver of excitement shot through her. She had been to a dozen or more gala affairs at the Hotel del Coronado but tonight was somehow different. The electricity generated was like opening night at the opera. Women wore their best jewels. Heads turned with each new arrival and bobbed after each entrant had passed. Over a thousand guests, drawn from society's *crème de la crème,* were due to arrive, many of them having traveled from as far up the coast as San Francisco. The Prince of Wales was not to appear until nine P.M. and Wallis wondered how she could contain her curiosity until then.

Over the grand entrance of the Crown Ballroom, the hotel's most impressive salon, was a gilt crown embossed upon a Spanish coat of arms, presumably that of Queen Isabella. A gilt *fleur-de-lys,* the Prince of Wales's emblem, had been added for the occasion. The magisterial Fiona Bell-Hawkins took Wallis aside as she entered. "My dear, where's Win?" she asked, her gray eyes two pointed stones in her long, narrow face. "He is coming, is he not?" she added, chin jutted forward, her wide mouth twisting out the words.

"He's been delayed at the base. Why? Is there a problem?" Wallis asked, trying to keep her voice casual.

"It's the presentations. All the names have to be submitted beforehand."

"Just give mine. Win won't mind, I promise you."

"I think His Royal Highness would very much enjoy exchanging a few words with Win. He's extremely interested in flying and Win is, after all, one of the finest pilots on the base. If you could let me know as soon as he arrives," Fiona replied, and then loped off.

Wallis surveyed the room. Everyone who was anyone in the San Diego Bay area was there. Win's stripes would have been lost among all the top brass and gold stars. But Wallis was far more interested in the exquisitely dressed woman she sighted talking to Lucien and Andrea Faraday, whose yacht she had sailed on recently. Wallis had studied enough fashion and society magazines to recognize the gown the woman wore as a Worth, bought, no doubt, in Paris, and its owner as the thrice-married Averill Gavin, a member of the Vanderbilt clan.

She made her way over to the Faradays. From the corner of her eye she caught a glimpse of Alice laughing a bit too raucously at something Joe Bassett was saying. Well, her mother was enjoying herself, so that was just fine.

"Why, hello, Wally," Lucien grinned as Wallis joined their small circle.

Averill pushed a blond ringlet back from her pale heart-shaped face and patted it tenderly into place. "Don't you look marvelous, Wallis. However did you find such a stunning gown in stodgy old San Diego?"

"Not easily," Wallis replied. Lucien laughed and she joined in.

"Isn't that Win coming our way?" Andrea said.

Wallis glanced casually over to the entrance of the room, certain that Andrea was mistaken. To her astonishment, Win—his step purposeful, his arms whirling propellers as he winged his way roughly through the throngs of guests, deaf to their sharp asides—headed straight for her. Thank God, he was wearing his dress uniform, although his tie was askew. In moments, he would confront her and she would have to say or do something that would avoid embarrassment. The Faradays and Averill would have had to be blind fools not to notice that he had been drinking heavily. She moved quickly toward him and took his arm in what she hoped appeared to be an affectionate gesture. Speaking loudly enough for those nearby to hear, she said, "Win, darlin', well the Navy does have a heart after all."

She raised herself up on her toes and kissed him lightly on the cheek. His eyes were bloodshot, his face flushed. A bit kittenishly, she straightened his tie. "You certainly must have been in a terrible hurry to get here," she said, and then drew him onto the dance floor.

"I should have handcuffed you to the bed," he muttered, his voice still thick. "Whose husband did you plan on seducing?"

His fingers cut into her back as he held her. He was just sober enough to move in time with the music.

"I'm not interested in other women's husbands and you

damn well know it," she said under her breath. "I came because I thought Mama would like to see the Prince of Wales."

"And you?"

"Well, who isn't curious about a prince? I don't expect he'll ever again be back this way."

The orchestra ended the set and Wallis led Win to the edge of the dance floor where she had just sighted her mother. "I'm sure you want to dance with Mama," she said, and gave Alice a look that indicated she needed her help.

"Let's jus' sit this one out, Win," Alice smiled and linked her arm through his as she steered him away.

"The Prince," a large, much bejeweled woman close to Wallis confided in a husky voice as a low buzz spread throughout the room. "Why, he's standing over by the drinks table!" The orchestra struck up a chorus of Irving Berlin's "A Pretty Girl Is Like a Melody." The woman could hardly contain herself. "They say that's his favorite song!" she exclaimed, "And that he's wild about dancing!"

Wallis's first impression of the Prince of Wales was of a fair, slender figure, short, looking surprisingly more boyish than she had imagined. He was, in fact, twenty-five at the time, two years older than herself. But even in his impressive naval uniform, he seemed more the young man around town than heir to a throne. He was chatting away to Fiona in a pleasant manner, and when the music ended, crossed over to the bandstand to shake hands and exchange a few words with the orchestra leader. By the Prince's side, also in uniform, stood a tall, dark youthful man with a most arrogant air.

"That's the Prince's cousin, Lieutenant Mountbatten," the heavyset woman who had chosen to become Wallis's instant confidante told her. "He's only twenty, I understand, but he could put his shoes under my bed anytime."

Wallis gave her a cool side glance. The dance floor was cleared. Fiona reappeared by the Prince's side with the Faradays, Averill Gavin and the most senior officers (along with their wives). Wallis edged closer, hoping to catch Fiona's eye as she gathered the next group together to be presented to the two royal cousins. At one point in the proceedings, Fiona glanced in her direction, and then deliberately turned away. Wallis's breath caught. She was to be passed by.

"I must find Mama," she told Win, who had come up behind her.

"Alice is doing just dandy on her own," he said. His grasp tightened around her waist as he guided her with unrelenting pressure through the clusters of feathered and sequined guests, too caught up in their fascination at being so close to royalty to give Wallis more than a brief look of irritation as Win bulldozed her toward the door.

She was strong enough to have resisted him. Once, in a drunken state, he had struck her across the face and she had swung back with all her might, knocking him right off his feet. Slight as she was, his size alone did not frighten her. In public when she had stood up to him, he had quit his bullying tactics. But from the moment she had first seen him coming toward her in the ballroom, she experienced a new kind of fear. Something in the hard glint of his eyes, the chill in his voice, had alarmed her. Any wrong move on her part and he would reel out of control. And, more than anything else, Wallis was terrified of a public scene, especially one on an occasion as socially important as this one.

Years later, she would have trouble recalling the events of this evening in their proper sequence. At this time, she had a conscious feeling that the night was especially important. For that reason, she made herself aware of as many of the details as she could. Her most vivid impression was of Win, holding her with one hand, a cigarette between the twitching fingers of the other, brooding, impatient, moment by delayed moment growing dangerously agitated as they stood in the crisp breeze waiting for the parking attendant to bring their small roadster to the front canopy.

She stared across the brilliantly lit hotel driveway, feeling as though a thousand pairs of eyes peered at her from the darkness beyond. From inside came the sound of distant music, a loud and precariously pitched trumpet making it difficult for her to recognize the song. Humiliation overcame her as she replayed in her mind the scene of Win propelling her through the ballroom.

Her body grew slack, her resistance to Win's hold weaker, almost nonexistent. Win was not in her thoughts at all. She was angry that she had not been presented to the Prince and she longed to be back inside the ballroom swaying to the music.

Their car was pulled to a halt before them. A red-jacketed attendant held the door open on the passenger side. "Get in," Win commanded and let go of her hand.

Later, she would question why she had not turned away and run back into the hotel. Now, she just wanted to avoid a public scene, and so she came around the rear of the car and slid into the seat beside him. She had not been given time to collect her cape. Trembling from the cold, she wrapped her arms about herself. Something about the gesture, the touch of her own flesh, brought tears to her eyes.

"I'll never forgive you for this evening," she said as Win revved the motor and the car jolted forward out of the circle of light and into the dark silence of the deserted road that led to their house.

Win's perception had altered. They were driving so close to the edge of the road that twice they careened over the curb. As the car pressed recklessly into the night, a wide grin of exhilaration split open his face. If past history was repeated, he would force himself upon her when they reached home. The thought of him making love to her in his present condition filled Wallis with revulsion. If she could not outwit him, she would have to fight him off and as drunk as he was this could be dangerous.

She clutched her arms tighter around her body. *I must not let him see how frightened I am,* she thought. She slid her hands down into her lap where she clasped her evening bag as though it were a weapon. "I thought he was very disappointing, didn't you?" she asked, her voice amazingly controlled.

"Who?"

"The Prince of Wales. Terribly short. And boyish."

Win didn't reply although his foot eased up on the gas pedal.

She must remain cool, let Win believe her fear had passed. "I suppose he's a real person, in spite of who he is," she said. "It's hard to conceive of a boy like that living with the knowledge that one day he will be King and have all that responsibility."

"My heart bleeds for him," Win jeered as he turned into their driveway and ground to a stop.

She jumped out and headed for the front door. Luckily, he had left it ajar in his rush to bring her back from the hotel. She thought she might make a dash for their room and then lock herself in, but he was right at her heels. She entered the house without comment and went into the living room. "Shall we have a nightcap?" she asked, playing for time. He stood leering down at her, so close she could feel his breath.

"If you need a drink, don't use me as an excuse," he snapped. The violence had crept back under his voice. "You like to get me angry, don't you, Wallis? It excites you. Like a professional soldier. It puts color into that magnolia skin of yours, makes your nipples harden."

She managed to sidestep him, but he grabbed her right wrist. The buttons on her glove cut into her flesh. "Stop this, Win," she ordered, and with all her strength pulled free. Her hand and wrist hurt. She would have to cover the bruises the next day. The only thing that mattered now was to get out of this room, away from the deadly assault his eyes threatened.

"It's you who likes these war games. Not me," she countered. "But you notice you only play them when you're fired up on booze? Maybe you're a real man up there in the sky, or behind the wheel of a car, or in the officers' club with your men. But sex makes a coward of you."

The impact of her words momentarily had stunned him and she continued, "You just aren't sure you have the ammunition and so you drink and get drunk and when the alcohol takes over and fires your courage, you bully your way into a semblance of manhood."

The fury in his eyes made the blood pound against her temples. She turned away and started toward the door. His arm whipped out and he spun her back. A barrage of words was the only defense she could muster. "What I find so contemptible," she hissed, "is your sham, your bold-faced hypocrisy—your nauseating attempts to make me feel less a woman so that you can feel more a man!"

His hand swung out, catching her on the cheek. Wallis reeled, stumbled backward and would have fallen except for the support of a high-backed chair directly behind her. Never had she felt as endangered as she did at this moment. She must get past him to the safety of their room. Whatever had enraged him would remain a mystery until he was sober when, as often happened, he would be miserably penitent for his foul behavior.

He started toward her. When he was only a hand's reach away, she slid down onto the floor, rolled over out of his grasp, and then, half crouching, her dress hiked above her ankles, staggered from the living room into the hallway where, once upright, she ran to their room, securing the lock just as he approached the door from the other side.

Utter darkness enveloped her. All the breath was gone from her lungs. The knob turned sharply over and over. She expected him to break in the door. She could visualize him glaring, his face purple with fury, stepping back, a bullish gesture before starting to ram it. She edged noiselessly away, keeping close to the wall. Her hand slipped down to remove her spike-heeled shoes, a better weapon, at least, than her purse. Several terrifying moments passed. His heavy footsteps sounded in retreat down the hallway. Then—silence. She wasn't sure how long she stood with her back against the wall, too frightened to move, fearing he would suddenly come crashing through the window. Finally, she decided he must have gone back into the living room for a gin from the bar.

A narrow strip of moonlight cut across her bed. She headed toward it and, after carefully folding back the spread, sat down exhausted on the edge, removed the combs from her hair and unclasped the pearls from about her neck, placing them neatly on the side table. One by one she eased her fingers from her gloves and then folded them before putting them down next to the other items. Even in the dimness around her she could see the dark marks on her wrist. She lifted her wounded hand and pressed her lips gently against the soreness. Win had bruised more than her flesh. She knew in this moment that she would never feel the same toward him. Still dressed, she eased herself back onto the pillows, determined to remain awake until her mother had returned.

How, she thought, had she managed to mess up her life so badly? She had no answer, but to stave off drowsiness, she forced herself to remember the past, trying to extricate from her memory that one decisive incident that might have led to her current desperate situation.

PART ONE

BESSIE WALLIS

1899–1916

1

Daylight and shadow had both vanished as Bessie Wallis waited in the vast dimly lit library of Grandmother Warfield's house on Preston Street for her mother to come and take her away. She sat on the edge of the leather sofa with its enticing slipperiness. Many times she had been chastised for bouncing and sprawling on it. "Bessie Wallis," her grandmother would say severely, "how will you ever grow up to be a lady unless you learn to keep your back straight?" Now she sat stiffly, only her large, expressive eyes moving as she watched the elderly woman sway back and forth in the familiar green-velvet upholstered rocking chair.

During the five years Bessie Wallis had lived in the Preston Street house she had spent countless hours in this awesome room on the second floor, the windows almost always closed, the scent of old leather and violet sachet suffocating her as her grandmother rocked and retold stories of Baltimore's brave history during the Civil War or quoted endlessly from the Bible. Despite the old woman's austere nature, the child loved her very much and sensed that her affection was fully returned. And though the house had a forbidding ambience, Bessie Wallis seemed not to notice. She had come to live there when she was five months old, and it was the only home she had ever known.

Baltimore is a city of row houses. The Warfields' was a red-brick, four-story building (not including the basement which held the kitchen). Outwardly, it was identical to its neighbors, with white marble front steps and stoop kept pristine by the daily scrubbing of the scullery maid. But the Warfields, whose home this had been for several generations, had placed their own unique stamp on the interior. Dark woods, dense velvets and brown leather prevailed, giving the interior its ominous air. Paintings were hung in such profusion that there were large expanses where the flocked wallpaper was obscured. A long parlor filled with oversized, heavily carved and darkly upholstered furniture dominated the ground floor. Sofas and chairs were straight-backed and lace-cuffed. A bust of the Widow Warfield's husband commanded the room from a sturdy library table positioned in the center. Deep, wine-colored portieres kept out the daylight and the intrusion at night of a streetlamp that faced the front windows. Bessie Wallis was allowed into the parlor only when company came, at which times she was brought downstairs to be introduced and then ushered hurriedly back to her own room.

Twin mahogany breakfronts—on which gleamed the Warfields' fine collection of Baltimore's famous Kirk silver, baroque and profusely encrusted with design—lined the opposite sides of the dining room, which was across the hallway from the parlor. The most imposing of Grandmother Warfield's three rocking chairs, from which she ruled her world, was situated between two ceiling-high windows. Perched on top of the back of the chair was a fierce, carved, beak-nosed American eagle. From this bizarre, throne-like rocker, each morning, her grandmother gave the servants their instructions for the day.

Grandmother Warfield wore black dresses with starched, high white collars that cupped her narrow chin. A white linen cap with black satin ribbons covered her gray hair, which she drew back into a tight bun. Around one bony wrist hung a black enamel memorial bracelet. The rest of her jewels were kept under her bed in a padlocked iron box that had not been taken out since the death of her husband, Major Henry Warfield, many years before Bessie Wallis had come to live there.

The Warfields, one of Baltimore's most prominent families, had originally come from England where they could trace their roots to the time of William the Conqueror. One of their ancestors, Robert de Warfield, had been a knight of the famous Order of the Garter during the reign of King Edward III. King John had awarded another Warfield a grand estate, Warfield Manor, which sat on former Crown land in Windsor Forest. And the family had ties with the powerful English clans of Neville, Upton and Elye. The Warfields had come to America in 1662, and had helped to settle the state of Maryland. Warfield men had fought courageously and with much honor in the Revolutionary and Civil wars, first against British rule and then on the side of the Confederacy. A Warfield had been governor-elect of Maryland, another, a member of Congress. Such an illustrious heritage imbued the family members—who considered themselves American aristocracy—with a degree of inbred arrogance.

The last of her grandmother's trio of rocking chairs, a simpler, more homely model, sat in the bay of its owner's bedroom. Reposing on a table beside it was the great family Bible, a faded purple ribbon marking the place where she had last been reading. Mrs. Warfield was profoundly religious. "Episcopalian High Church," she would primly say so that there would be no mistaking her position on certain aspects of Protestant doctrine. Since the age of three, Bessie Wallis had sat for an hour each day on a petit-point stool at the old woman's feet, listening to her read from the Bible. Her grandmother smelled of dried violets and her touch—no matter what the temperature—was cool, and the child found both of these characteristics reassuring.

Ellie, Bessie Wallis's black mammy, was afraid of Grandmother Warfield, although she seemed otherwise to be the bravest person in the world, even speaking up on occasion to Uncle Sol, who also lived in the house on Preston Street. Uncle Sol was Mrs. Warfield's unmarried oldest son, Solomon Davies Warfield, head of the family, political hopeful and a banker of means. He had lost a bitter battle to become Mayor of Baltimore and had organized the Independent Democrats, a splinter group of the Democratic party.

A tough adversary, ruthless in his methods, cold of manner, Uncle Sol was in his thirties, a distinguished, rather stern, small-statured man, always impeccably dressed. He wore an ascot and a high stiff collar to breakfast and never sat with one leg crossed over the other, which he claimed ruined the crease in his trousers. His calculating eyes were clear blue and the bone structure of his face strong and punctuated handsomely by a trim mustache that rimmed his upper lip. With all his hard-edged reserve, Uncle Sol was not unattractive and there was whispered speculation (not heard by the child) about his stays in New York where he maintained an apartment and of his passionate interest in the opera, more particularly, its divas.

Attached to his watch chain was a silver nail clipper and when he was concentrating the biting sound of metal on nail would perforate the silence. Bessie Wallis tried her best to love him but he inspired too much fear in her to make this possible. Uncle Sol, she was often reminded, was a very important man. Not only was he the president of a bank and one of the city's strongest political forces, he was Baltimore's Postmaster, a position of considerable esteem and power. Even his younger brothers, Emory and Harry, looked up to him as the patriarch of the family, a man due unqualified respect.

Her feelings toward her grandmother were entirely different from the way she regarded Uncle Sol. Ellie would often grunt, "That woman's don' got ice watah fuh blood," or "That woman don' know nothin' 'bout chillun." But, despite Ellie's grumbling, she never spoke up to Mrs. Warfield, perhaps because she knew that Bessie Wallis had found a corner of warmth and kindness in her grandmother that had not been discovered by many others.

The short passage that led from the library to Mrs. Warfield's bedroom contained a grandfather clock which now struck the hour of six. Bessie Wallis glanced toward the door. Dulcie, the upstairs maid, her Indian features etched boldly on her brown face, entered, as she did every evening at this hour, to turn on the lamp that sat on the carved-wood library table. The petticoats under her black dress and starched white apron made a rustling sound as she moved. She came and went without saying a word, but she managed a flickering smile for the child.

"It's a good thing I had the sense to feed you first," Grandmother Warfield said in the bone-sharp voice that indicated some displeasure. "The only thing Alice was ever on time for was your birth." Her chair did not stop rocking back and forth. "Now you remember when you're with your mother, don't drink coffee. The stuff will turn your skin yellow. And don't you have any words with any of that Northern scruff she knows. Did Ellie pack your Bible?"

"Yes, ma'am," the child replied.

"That was your daddy's, you know, so you treat it well, hear me?"

"Yes, ma'am."

"While he was in this house he never missed a service. Now, child, do you know *why* you're leaving the only real home you've ever had?"

"Because it was mama's decision," she replied, having been told this several times that day.

"It's her Montague frivolousness. She's a widow just like I am, but she won't accept it. Flittin' about Baltimore as she does with all those no-goods and Northerners. And now movin' from this proper home to a hotel, no less! I never knew a respectable woman in my life who lived in a hotel, and most particularly one with a girl child."

Bessie Wallis squirmed uncomfortably, knowing what her grandmother was about to say, for the old woman could be relied upon to repeat certain things as she did her litany.

"Your father, Teackle, was too young and fevered to be held responsible for your mother's lack of good sense and morals. Tuberculosis weakens the mind as it does the body. And so, poor child, you might have been a bastard, but the Warfields have a fear and love of God. Your father did what was right and married your mother so that you would not be illegitimate. You will remember to say a prayer for your dead father every night?"

"Yes, ma'am."

"And you will say a prayer each night for your Uncle Sol who insisted we make a home here for you and your mother?"

"Yes, ma'am."

Back and forth the rocker went as Mrs. Warfield silently studied the child. She was glad that Bessie Wallis looked like the Warfields. Of her four sons, only Teackle had resembled her mother's family, the weak-chinned, myopic Emorys. But, thankfully, the child had the strong Warfield jawline and the directness of eyes that her husband, Henry, and her other sons shared. From birth, Bessie Wallis had displayed the Warfield look (enhanced, she had to admit, by the fair skin and distinctive violet eyes of the Montague women), a fact so obvious that no one could have disputed Alice's word that the girl was a Warfield.

The sound of a horse and buggy could be heard pulling up before the house. The doorbell rang, but Mrs. Warfield continued rocking. A few moments later, Eddie, Uncle Sol's elegant Negro servant, dressed as always in a black frock coat, gray trousers and wing collar, appeared in the doorway.

"Miz Wahfield, someone don' come fuh Missy," he said uncomfortably.

"Am I to understand it is not her mother?"

"He be a—" Eddie suffered from asthma, and at this moment he was seized with an attack of it that caused his breath to come and go in whistles and wheezes.

Mrs. Warfield stood up, slowly took the few steps to the window which overlooked the front stoop, pushed aside the lace curtains, glanced down below and then, her arthritis evident, walked stiffly back to her chair. "The child is not goin' to leave this house for a hotel in the company of a hansom driver," she said implacably. "You will go with her as soon as you're through with your spasm." Still wheezing, Eddie turned to leave. "And you tell Ellie she's to go, too."

Bessie Wallis could not suppress a happy grin. Her mother had said they could not afford to have Ellie come with her, a decision that had propelled the large, otherwise indomitable black woman into a state all week, with sighs, tears and protestations to the Lord.

It would be years before Bessie Wallis would learn the true reason for her mother's departure from the house on Preston Street. But even at this early age she had overheard backstairs gossip. Her Uncle Sol had fallen in love with Alice, whose bedroom on the third floor (which connected with Bessie Wallis's) was just down the corridor from his own. Her grandmother had not wanted her bachelor son to marry, nor did she fancy a scandal. Alice had taken a small journey to visit her cousin Lelia in Virginia while Bessie Wallis stayed with her grandmother, who told her she was now to live permanently with her. The child was desolated by this news. But Alice returned to Baltimore, moved to the Brexton Hotel and demanded that her child be allowed to leave the house on Preston Street.

Bessie Wallis suspected that her grandmother and her mother did not like each other very much, a perception that had made her sad and at the same time stretched her loyalty to the farthest bounds as she tried desperately hard to prove her love to each of them.

"Never forget you're a Warfield," her grandmother said as she rose again from her chair. With a sharp upward gesture of her hand, she bade Bessie Wallis to rise. "The Warfields of Maryland have prospered for generations because they are sturdy, industrious and High Church." She leaned down and cupped a hand beneath her granddaughter's chin. Their gazes met and locked. "You have the Warfield look," she said. "A plain face but well-marked and with eyes that aren't afraid to return a person's contemplation." She kissed the little girl on her forehead and lightly patted her on the head before turning aside. "You better go now," she ordered.

Bessie Wallis stood uneasily. She detected a strange quivering in her grandmother's tone. She had just taken a step toward her when Ellie's voice came in excited spurts and gasps up the front staircase.

"Where is you, chile? Where you be?"

"Bye, Grandmama," she said, and ran out of the library, smack into Ellie's large form. For a moment she considered going back up to her room, which had been a sun porch before her occupancy and was the one bright area in the house. She had purposely left her favorite doll, Sally (which Dulcie had made from a corn husk and Ellie had dressed in calico), under the window seat and wanted to make sure it had not been removed. If Sally remained she somehow felt the room was still hers. But Ellie hustled her downstairs where Eddie waited with a large carpetbag that contained all her other possessions.

Once she was seated in the cab, she looked up to the lighted windows of the library. For a brief moment Grandmother Warfield's slim, shadowy figure could be seen. Then the curtain slid into place and the velvet draperies were drawn. A chill suffused the girl's body and she began to shiver.

"Heah, chile, come closah to Ellie," the black woman said. She covered her with her shawl and drew her near. "You'll soon be with your mama," she consoled.

Bessie Wallis had no memory of her father. Teackle Wallis Warfield had died of tuberculosis when she was an infant. The photograph contained in the locket that her grandmother had given her, and which she always wore around her neck, was of a pale man with dreamy eyes set deeply in their sockets in a gaunt, angular face. Bessie Wallis had a way of scrunching up her eyes to make the picture seem animated, but she was never able to fully visualize her father as a real person. Her mother never spoke about him and whenever her grandmother mentioned his name, it was with a sigh, followed by a comment about his "Christian ways" which her mother had "subverted." Bessie Wallis was not sure what that word meant, but she knew it was one of the reasons why Grandmother Warfield was so angry at her mother. Another reason was that the Warfields did not like the Montagues, "any more," Alice once told her, "than did the Elizabethan Capulets."

Teackle's physical decline and his daughter's birth had, abetted by Sol's persuasion, somewhat broken down Mrs. Warfield's resistance to Alice, and Teackle had come home to Preston Street to die. His widow and child remained in the house under Warfield protection, but Montague-Warfield hostilities had not ceased. A battle raged over Bessie Wallis from the cradle.

Both families shared the Mason-Dixon Line as a common frontier; otherwise they were dramatically opposed in temperament and outlook. For generations Montague women had been celebrated for their spirit and beauty and their men had made reputations as wits, rogues and gamblers. Maryland had been a divided state during the Civil War, the legislature having voted not to secede from the Union, while the sympathy and allegiance of the principal families were with the Confederate cause. Grandfather Warfield had been arrested and held prisoner for over a year for advocating Maryland's secession. Alice's father, Grandfather William Latane Montague, far more romantically, had been a spy for the Confederacy and run guns past Union lines. Now old and twice widowed, his mind gone, he lived in an institution outside Baltimore. Although Bessie Wallis had never seen him, occasionally her grandmother referred to him as "that crazy old man" and her mother told stories of his once glorious wartime adventures along with tales about other brave Montagues during the time of the Confederacy.

Nearly forty years had passed since the end of the Civil War, but as Bessie Wallis still heard her grandmother and most of her older relatives talk about "the damnyankee soldiers" who ransacked their homes, she had come to believe the war had been fought and lost just before her birth. Ellie often spoke about how her mother had been a slave and had once shown her some Confederate money.

Alice was a Montague through and through, daring, with an irrepressible love of life. Bessie Wallis was as much in awe of her mother's beauty and gaiety as she was of her grandmother's puritanical rectitude. She seemed to be the very center of a tug-of-war. When she misbehaved, Grandmother Warfield would cite the Montagues' irresponsibility. Her good behavior, on the other hand, was attributed to her Warfield heritage. By contrast, her mother expressed exactly reversed sentiments.

Despite the house's intimidating aura, Bessie Wallis was frightened to be leaving Preston Street for she had so often been warned of the hostile world waiting to set upon her beyond those revered walls. But she had desperately missed her mother in the six weeks they had been separated. With Alice away, all sound seemed to have been pressed from the house. No games were played, the piano in the front parlor was silent, and guests did not impatiently ring the doorbell. When Bessie Wallis pictured her mother in her thoughts, Alice was always laughing and running, eager to greet people.

She could not help but envy her mother's delicate, yet glowing, beauty although Grandmother Warfield said envy was a mortal sin. Alice had golden hair that framed a softly curved oval face. Her eyes were the violet-blue of the wild cornflowers that grew at the rear of Grandmother Warfield's otherwise cultivated gardens. But perhaps the features Bessie Wallis envied most were her mother's small retrousée nose (for hers was of a disconcerting length), her graceful hands and her tiny, narrow feet. Once she had seen Uncle Sol hold one of her mother's slippers in the palm of his hand. Nightly, Bessie Wallis prayed that her feet would not grow. But every three months or so Grandmother Warfield would have to take her in her grand victoria drawn by Gadfly, the carriage horse, to the Emporium for a new pair of next-size shoes.

As the cab carrying her to her mother jogged through the early darkness a dog ran out into the road and barked at the wheels. She put her arms as tightly as she could around Ellie's ample waist, pressing her face against the large cushion-like breasts. Despite the rough-textured fabric of Ellie's dress that made her cheeks itch, the child clung tighter. The black woman, touched, returned the embrace and smoothed the girl's hair with her free hand.

"Don' you worry none, chile. You gwine to lak it fine bein' with Miz Alice," she consoled.

"An' a sight bettah 'an *Woe*field House," Eddie, who was seated opposite them, commented.

"Hush yo' mouth," Ellie commanded.

Bessie Wallis pulled herself upright and raised her chin. Her violet eyes flashed in the moonlight. "I shall have two homes like Mary Beth Howard," she said, recalling the daughter of the Warfields' next-door neighbors, who also had a country house where they spent every summer. The idea pleased her and thus resolved, she moved over to the window and peered through the darkness, now anxious to arrive at her destination.

* * *

The Brexton was a quiet family hotel, but Bessie Wallis's first impression was of a far more glamorous structure. To her eyes and in the soft blur of the streetlamps, the little white building with paint-chipped columns was a grand plantation house, the kind her mother described when she told stories about the Montagues' former stately home, Wakefield Manor, in Virginia. ("That plantation has fallen into even worse neglect than when the Yankees stripped it bare," Grandmother Warfield had sneered. "It's been mortgaged and remortgaged; parts of it sold off. The Montagues never have been ones to hold on to things.")

As Eddie helped her down onto the bricked path that led to the front door, Alice came flying out to greet her. Tears filled her mother's eyes as she grabbed her hands and then drew her close, but when she broke away she was laughing merrily. "Oh, we are goin' to have such a wonderful time!" she exclaimed and then pulled Bessie Wallis after her and into the warm, bright, firelit front reception room of the Brexton.

What intrigued the child even more than her first excursion inside a hotel was the sight of her mother out of mourning clothes. Except for nightdresses and morning wrappers, Alice had always worn black at the Warfields'. She now was resplendent in a pale robin's-egg-blue silk frock that outlined her generously rounded bosom and tiny waist. In her golden hair a matching bow was tied. Bessie Wallis thought she had never seen anyone quite so lovely.

"Say 'how-de-do' to Mrs. McConnell, Bessie Wallis," her mother instructed.

As though bestowing a favor, Mrs. McConnell, the apple-cheeked proprietress of the Brexton, leaned down and extended her hand for the child to shake. The large woman exuded a sour odor which caused Bessie Wallis to draw back. A disapproving glance from Alice propelled her to thrust her hand forward into Mrs. McConnell's grasp.

She was not to see much of Mrs. McConnell during the three months that she and Alice lived at the hotel, because her mother insisted they keep to themselves. On her part she might have enjoyed foraging in the great old basement kitchen and storerooms of the Brexton, or sitting in the reception room just watching the people come and go, for what she did see of the establishment's residents was fascinating. There was a Reverend Peabody who carried an ivory Bible and dressed completely in white even to his stockings and shoes. He was a preacher who had lost his flock, Alice said; and there was Rosa Dellaporta, a friendly lady who spoke with a strange accent, had blue painted on her eyelids and dressed in the bright feather colors of Mrs. McConnell's parrot that sat on a perch behind the registration desk and squawked all day long.

Her new home was a pleasant double room that she shared with her mother and in which they ate all their meals on a tray although food was served to the rest of the guests in the dining room. Bessie Wallis sensed an undercurrent of unhappiness in her mother, but Alice's blitheness of spirit prevailed at most times. Their room often rang with laughter and all tasks were turned into small games. Although independence exacted its price, Alice explained, it was worth it. Uncle Sol's monthly contribution seemed never to be enough. Few jobs were open to women and these were for the most part closed to ladies of her class and gentle rearing. Uneducated except in the decorous graces, she had, however, been taught, like most Southern women, how to sew, and quickly put her one useful talent to work by making children's clothes for the Women's Exchange.

Bessie Wallis would sit at the one table in the room and hold a paper pattern while Alice cut bright pieces of cloth. She taught her daughter to thread a needle and make little cross stitches and gave her scraps on which to practice. And as they both worked she told her stories she had made up about the adventures of Smudge the Cat who lived in one of the chimneys of Windsor Castle and who one night hid in Queen Victoria's giant fur muff and became the Queen's constant companion.

There were outings together—to Aunt Bessie's, her mother's older sister, rather forlorn excursions to the house on Preston Street, where she was suddenly and mysteriously treated like a visiting guest, and on Saturday mornings to

Richmond market, an exciting adventure, worthy of any engaged in by Smudge the Cat. The market was open on all four sides and crisscrossed by aisles flanked with stalls heaped with every imaginable kind of produce and provender. The market bustled with people and smelled of fresh country foods and fish still carrying the sharp, briny scent of the sea, and of the sweet odor of chewy yellow taffy.

Although Ellie had her own small house off Pennsylvania Avenue in the black section of town and did not expect to reside at the Brexton, Alice was firm in her decision that she could not afford a servant. Uncle Sol, who believed a white child without a mammy was unthinkable, insisted on paying her salary. Still, Alice remained adamant. And after an emotional and teary farewell, Ellie departed, much missed by Bessie Wallis, especially on afternoons when she was left alone while her mother delivered her work to the Women's Exchange.

There were also nights when, believing Bessie Wallis was sound asleep, Alice would dress in her most rustling clothes, and slip out for a visit with friends. When this happened a shivery feeling came over the child as she lay in the dark for hours, her eyes wide, filled with dread that her mother might never return. This loneliness and fear were painful for her to endure, but endure them she did, not knowing what else to do, not daring to displease her mother, especially now that her grandmother's love seemed somehow to have diminished.

She feigned sleep when Alice opened the door upon her return. The dim light from the hallway would trail into the room; and the dancing steps her mother took as she undressed, and the little song she hummed as she climbed into the large feather bed that they shared, gave her a warmth of reassurance. But there remained an unsettling fear that next time Alice might not come back.

2

Something about Uncle Sol disturbed Bessie Wallis. His presence engendered a sense of personal guilt in her. Suddenly, it would happen, like the click of a camera. She would be happy and content and he would enter the room and she would experience a sharp catch in her heart and the air would seem to leave her body. Uncle Sol made her feel as though she had just done something shameful and been caught out. And yet, there was no denying his generosity.

"Thank Uncle Sol for your new shoes, Bessie Wallis," her mother would urge when they had returned from shopping to Preston Street before they had moved to the Brexton. This required obeisance occurred often enough for her to understand that Uncle Sol's gifts to her were not without strings.

Bessie Wallis could not help but observe that he did not treat her mother with the same dismissive, lording attitude that he did her. And, even before they had left her grandmother's house, she had a child's suspicion that her Uncle Sol was in love with her mother. It would have been the union of the sun and the moon, of fire and ice. And Bessie Wallis never believed in her heart that her mother could love Uncle Sol. Once, she had overheard Aunt Bessie say that her grandmother would never allow her bachelor son to leave her home, much less to marry. The child received the news with great relief.

No secret had been made of her uncle's contribution to Bessie Wallis and her mother's support. Every month he deposited a sum of money in Alice's name at the Continental Trust Company where he headed the bank's board. However, the amount was ever-changing. The first month it was enough to cover all their expenses; the next, barely enough to pay Mrs. McConnell the rent; and the third, increased only a tad above starvation. "A banker's way of remindin' a frivolous widow of the hazards of independence," Alice's older sister, Bessie Merryman, sniffed when they went to call on her in her modest home on Chase Street. Aunt Bessie tried to convince Alice to move into the two small top-floor rooms. But for the time being, Alice chose to remain at the Brexton.

One humid summer day, she dressed Bessie Wallis in her best cotton frock and walked with her all the way crosstown to Uncle Sol's bank which occupied the lower two floors of the Calvert Building. Flushed, hot and exhausted, Bessie Wallis was content to be planked down on the hard wooden bench in the reception room while her mother disappeared into Uncle Sol's private office, the thick-paneled oak door shut tight after her. Five minutes later, Alice reappeared in such a distracted state that she almost went right past the child without recognition.

"Mama . . ." Bessie Wallis called, still afraid to rise from her perch.

Alice grabbed her hand and pulled her after her into the street. "We're moving to Aunt Bessie's," she announced, "and there's lots to do." She started off at a pace too difficult for Bessie Wallis to match, but feeling the tug of the child's hand she stopped.

"I'm afraid we haven't got money for a cab," she confessed. "Let's make it a game. Every time we cross a street let's pretend it's a big ocean and when we reach the other side—why! we'll be in another country. Now, where would you like to go first?"

"Africa," Bessie Wallis replied. "That's where Ellie said her folks came from."

"Ellie was born right here in Baltimore and so were her

mama and papa," she paused. "But, I 'spect at least one member of her family came from Africa."

Her mother never spoke of what had transpired in Uncle Sol's office, but Bessie Wallis felt it had something to do with the move to Aunt Bessie Merryman's. However, her new surroundings did not displease her. The house was built of gray stone with a parlor, dining room and kitchen on the ground floor, two bedrooms on the next landing, and the small, dormered rooms that were to be theirs—a front bedroom and a servant's room—at the top. Chase Street was paved with hard cobblestones and the impact of iron wagon tires on its rough-hewn surface was almost like that of a hammer on an anvil. From the child's small window could be heard the fearful clatter of the milk wagon and other such regulars.

Bessie Wallis did not mind the noise, the airlessness of her boxlike room or the invasion of flies, no-see-um bugs and mosquitos that on warm summer nights made their way through the netting around her bed. Aunt Bessie had a hearty laugh, her mother was happy and Ellie had returned to work for them. Aunt Bessie employed only a maid and a laundress, short staff by fashionable Baltimore's standards, where the large black population afforded an abundant supply of domestic help at pitifully low wages. Row houses in the best residential neighborhoods were thought to require the care of a minimum of five servants. Grandmother Warfield had a staff of eight—a cook, a downstairs and upstairs maid, a butler, a driver who cared for Gadfly and the buggy, a laundress, a handyman who looked after the furnace, and a scullery maid, who, among other duties, daily washed down the front steps.

More was expected of Bessie Wallis at her aunt's house than had been at the Warfields'. She had specific household duties. She helped in the kitchen shelling peas for dinner and cracking nuts for the cakes her mother or Aunt Bessie made. After meals she wiped the table silver and returned each piece carefully to its special niche in the tall mahogany silver chest in the dining room. But Ellie took care of her room and of her clothes and fussed a lot over her manners.

Baltimore was the largest city in Maryland and the seventh largest in the United States. It was situated on the Patapsco River estuary, an arm of Chesapeake Bay and a great seaport with extensive docks. From these aging wooden piers and wharves, giant sailing ships, banana boats and freighters often packed with immigrants unloaded their goods and human cargo, and then embarked again for exotic, faraway ports. Shipbuilding and shipping were among the city's leading industries. Baltimoreans were proud of their association with the sea and its oceangoing vessels and fascinated by the men who sailed on them. Uncle Buck Merryman, Aunt Bessie's dead husband, had been no exception.

Bessie Wallis remembered Uncle Buck taking her to a large badly lit tavern on the dock one afternoon when she was about four and he had come to bring her to his home for a visit in a handsome black buggy with bright yellow wheels. Once inside he hoisted her up on a high stool before a counter. "I feel a need to cut the dust in my throat," he confided as he gulped down the first of three or four shots of whiskey. When Grandmother Warfield heard about the excursion, Uncle Buck was never again allowed to take her out in his buggy.

Uncle Buck's death had put Aunt Bessie in short funds and she had been forced to sell the rig. A framed photograph of him sat atop the high bureau in her bedroom, and Aunt Bessie would clasp it to her breast on occasion and say, "Poor man, he liked to tip the bottle too much!" Uncle Buck was from an old Baltimore family and had worked as an auctioneer for an estate company, but because of his "drinkin' sickness," as Ellie called it, Aunt Bessie had to live modestly and put money aside or she would "mos' prob'ly been destituted."

One evening when Bessie Wallis was returning the table silver to the chest, she noticed two iced-tea spoons were missing and ran, much distressed, into the kitchen to tell Alice.

"Never mind, darlin'," Alice soothed. "The set was a weddin' gift from Uncle Buck's family an' there are twenty-four twelve-piece settin's. Next month they'll probably be two oyster forks gone, sent along to the pawnbroker. The silver is what Aunt Bessie calls her annuity."

"What's an annuity?"

"Well, sort of like the nuts the squirrels hide for winter," Alice explained, "so that they never have to go hungry."

Alice and her sister Bessie bore little resemblance to each other in appearance, character, or speech (for Bessie had taken dramatic lessons once and lost her Virginia accent). They did share a strong sense of pride in their Montague ancestry. Montagues had been among the earliest English settlers in Virginia, several of whom had claimed descent from titled aristocrats. The Civil War had all but bankrupted them and it had now been forty years since any of the Montagues had enough to support themselves in the style they considered theirs by heredity.

Along with many similar families, they had undergone the humiliation of genteel poverty, which their friends knew all about but which they pretended not to: darning a shawl to make it last through another laundering, taking in distant relatives or the friends of relatives as boarders who pretended they were family visitors.

Alice and Bessie had lost their mother as children. Their father, William, had remarried and moved to Baltimore with his second wife, Mary, and the girls, hoping through family connections to rebuild the Montague fortunes. The pace and competition in a large metropolitan city was entirely too much for a man as arrogant and effete as he. Except for the kindness of fellow Virginians and the swiftness of Mary Montague's needle, his daughters would have lived in dire poverty, for the small two-bedroom home they occupied could not accommodate a paying guest.

To William's despair such social requirements as the right address and coming-out parties for his daughters were impossible. Bessie, who was neither a beauty nor possessed of dazzling charm, had compromised and at thirty years of age had married the happy-go-lucky but rather common Buck Merryman. When he died after six years of marriage and left her with only enough to scrape by, she had felt terribly cheated.

A place in society demanded social connections, one's name in the society columns, and the wherewithal to dress well, travel to other cities and entertain lavishly. These amenities were out of Bessie's reach. A woman of strong sensibilities, she recognized her situation. She was a genteel but poor widow, in her late thirties, portly and plain of face. Alice was—and always had been—the beauty in the family and, as well, was endowed with wit and vivacity. The Montagues had maintained high aspirations for her future. William had dreamed of her marrying into one of Baltimore's great families. But Alice had always been headstrong and somewhat wild. At seventeen she had run off with a touring actor who had been appearing at Ford's Theatre. William had followed her to Philadelphia and brought her home within a week's time. By then, whispers of the incident had swept like brush fire through the parlors of Baltimore's elite. Alice had seemed to have lost any chance of making a good alliance.

Mrs. Warfield had been well aware of the scandal attached to Alice's name, and when Teackle had informed her of his intent to marry her, she had fought with her every weapon: the church's views on such a woman, his illness, his duty to his mother. Finally, she cut off her dying son without a penny. But then there had been the child to be considered; and in the end she had relented. The scandalous Alice Montague became a respectable Warfield.

Of the two sisters, Bessie was the more ambitious. With some cause she had believed that being a Warfield widow could work to Alice's favor in brokering an advantageous second marriage. Of course, she should have known better than to think her sister would cooperate. The problem with Alice, she finally decided, was not that she was a rebel, but that she was too great a romantic and in her position could ill afford such emotions. Bessie had given up on Alice, who never took heed of her warnings or was swayed by her advice. But the child was quite another matter.

And so the aunt's aspirations had been transferred to Bessie Wallis. Fortunately, her niece carried the Warfield name. That should open some doors. And then there was an inheritance that would be certain to be hers upon old Mrs. Warfield's death. Aunt Bessie was determined that she would have all the advantages that she and Alice had missed. Not only would she learn how to dress stylishly, be a gracious hostess, a lively conversationalist, and an interested listener, she would attend the best private schools and make her debut at the prestigious Bachelors' Cotillion when she reached seventeen.

Only one thing stood in the child's path to social success. Her birth certificate, which would have to be produced at various stages in her life—the start of school being one—clearly showed she had been conceived several months before her parents were married.

Autumn was in the air; a hint of brisk days and chill nights rustled the yellowing leaves of the maple tree in the backyard and the sky had turned a metal gray. The day had a quality of temperance to it, as if it were applying all its restraint to holding back a wind that might prematurely whip the leaves from the trees and shake up the stolid citizens of a city that for generations had lived by the book and the calendar. Leaves did not traditionally fall before the fifteenth of October and here it was early September and that constancy was being threatened.

Alice got up from the kitchen table and closed the window over the sink. Still feeling a chill, she wrapped her shawl more tightly about her shoulders and stood looking across the room at her sister.

"I don't know why you are so concerned. Wallis's birth certificate proves she's a Warfield," she said.

"No one doubts that, I'm sure," Bessie replied. "But they still aren't certain when you married Teackle. The wedding was such a private matter that even poor Papa and I weren't invited. Well, no need to go back over that. But no announcement was ever made in the papers—"

"Under the circumstances," Alice interrupted, "you could hardly expect us to place a sign on top of the Calvert Buildin'!"

Noting the tense expression on her sister's face, Bessie softened and went over and put her arm around her shoulders. "Don't you worry, honey," she comforted. "I'll think of something so that the child's birth certificate does not have to be presented." She steered Alice closer to the stove where it was warm. A gleam shone in her heavily lidded eyes. There was nothing Bessie Merryman enjoyed more than directing other people's lives.

"Bessie Wallis will come down with scarlatina," she announced.

Alice looked at her aghast. "Why, Bessie Wallis is as healthy as a child can be," she protested.

"Of course she is. But I always liked the sound of that malady. It has a sort of ring to it and it's not nearly as bad as scarlet fever."

"What are you gettin' at, Bessie Merryman?"

"Certainly we wouldn't want to have anyone think she had something of her daddy's malaise. They might consider that hereditary. And a heart complaint could be difficult to dismiss later on. No, scarlatina is just right—and it's sudden. She'd have to delay the start of school for six weeks at least. By that time, I am certain I can convince the school board that they were sent the certificate and most carelessly must have lost it but that I will sign a paper saying I was witness to the date of her birth."

Alice could hardly believe what she was hearing. "Are you suggestin' that Bessie Wallis pretend she is ill, that she remain a prisoner in this house for six weeks, an' then lie about her physical condition?"

"I'm bein' more specific than that. I'm insisting that we follow this course and that Bessie Wallis be made to understand that folks must believe her spell of sickness is the God-almighty truth."

"I won't have it!"

"Alice, honey, I know how much you want the very best for Bessie Wallis," Bessie wheedled, "but this is the only way. If any of Baltimore's best should see or hear about the unfortunate dates on the child's birth certificate, it will be the end for her, the absolute end. You might as well leave Baltimore if that happens."

"You are involvin' the child in a conspiracy an' I won't have it!"

"I'm afraid, Alice, this is the one and only course we can take. We'll have Ellie move in for the duration of her convalescence. It will pinch the budget some, but it will look more convincing." She turned toward the stove and slid the teakettle onto the fire. "Let's have some fudge brownies for tea," she offered. "Bessie Wallis does so love fudge brownies."

Shortly after the sun came up over the Patapsco the next morning, Bessie Wallis woke to see Ellie's large form seated in the one straight-back chair in her small room.

"Ah gwine fix yuh breakfuss." Ellie offered as she rose to her feet with a mighty sigh.

"I'll come with you," Bessie Wallis said, throwing back the covers and swinging her legs over the side of the high bed.

"Oh, no, you won't. You is sick. Didn't yuh mama tell you?"

"I'm not really sick. It's a pretend game."

"Nevah min' what you calls it. Yuh mama an' Miz Bessie says you is sick so you is sick. Now you gets yuhseff right back under them covers an' wait there 'til ah comes back with yuh breakfuss. No use you squawkin' an' complainin'," Ellie insisted as she lifted the child back into the bed. "That's the way it am an' that's the way it be."

"Don't I even have to brush my teeth?"

"A'course you has to, and whatevah else peoples mus' do. But in bed when ah comes back with yuh breakfuss an' a bedpan."

As she sat propped up against her pillows waiting, Bessie Wallis thought about the puzzling predicament she was in. Grandmother Warfield had always warned her that to lie was a mortal sin and that if you lied you had a defective character and that, next to Christian Principle, character was the most important thing in the world. She had also told her that children should mind their elders, and her mother and Aunt Bessie had said she must follow their instructions, which, although she might not understand them, were to stay in bed for so many weeks, even though she didn't feel sick at all.

The window was closed to keep out the early morning chill but she could still hear the street noises. In the four weeks she had been living at Aunt Bessie's she had learned how to distinguish between the different wagon sounds. The milkman had only one horse and it always neighed when it came around the corner and the racks for the milk bottles rattled. The iceman had a team, and before it turned cool, children could be heard gathered about begging the driver for ice chips. The vegetable and scissors men both had strange calls that echoed up the narrow street, and the junkman's horse had a cowbell that hung around its neck and made a terrible jangle.

She could hear a pair of horses high-stepping up the cobbled road and then doing a little double step as they came to a halt across the street. That would be Mr. Willoughby's grand black victoria come to take him to the funeral parlor that he owned. She giggled nervously as she thought about Mr. Willoughby. He always wore a black suit and a tall black hat and, peeking over his jacket pocket, a white handkerchief arranged with little points that, Ellie said, was kept there for "grievin' widows."

Bessie Wallis crawled out of bed and ran over to the window. The ledge was just above her head and she had to stand on her tiptoes to see out. There was Mr. Willoughby coming down the steps from his house. My goodness! she thought, he certainly is a long, skinny man. Once she had passed by him on the street and he had given her a sad look.

"Chile! What you doin' at that window?" Ellie stood in the doorway holding a tray with a steaming bowl of oatmeal. Bessie Wallis scurried back to the bed and jumped on top. "Ain't I tol' you an' tol' you it's the baddes' luck to look on that fun'a'rul man? No ways a knowin' what could happen you do that! Now you cross yuhseff three times heah? An' this very minute too."

Bessie Wallis immediately did as she was told.

"Now heah's a bowl an' yuh brush. You wash yuh mouth an' then you gwine to eat yuh cer'rul."

She sat straight up in the bed. "Ellie, what's a bastard?"

A scowl burrowed across the black woman's face. "You wash yuh mouth good aftah sayin' that word! Where you heah it?"

"Grandmother Warfield said it once."

"No suh, she nevah said no such thin'!"

"Yes, she did and it set me to wonderin' what it meant."

"Well, ah ain't gwine to tell you an' that's that. You hadn't oughta a'looked at the fun'a'rul man! That's why you is talkin' lak you done." She worked furiously to smooth out the covers. "Now Miz Alice done make rennet custard fah lunch. Ain't that a treat! An ah done got a s'prise fah you."

She stood at the foot of the bed, her scowl slowly dissolving into a broad, toothy grin. From the deep pocket of her muslin skirt she brought forth Bessie Wallis's corn-husk doll. "Dulcie found this heah li'l lady in yuh room at Miz Wahfield's."

"Oh, no! Sally!" Bessie Wallis cried as she rolled over and sobbed into her pillow.

"Why, chile," Ellie said gently. Coming around to the side of the bed, she sat down on the edge and rubbed Bessie Wallis's back. "Ah thought you'd be happy to see Sally agin. An' Miz Alice done give me a mighty pretty piece of cotton cloth to make Sally a new dress."

"You don't understand. No one understands!" Bessie Wallis continued to cry. A short time later she was helping Ellie cut a pattern for a doll's outfit, but her heart was heavier than it had been. She was frightened that, with Sally no longer there, she might never return to Preston Street, to the sunny room with its window seat and the parlor with a piano, where tea was served on a grand silver tray, in cups so delicate you could see right through them. Ellie had been right. She should never have looked at Mr. Willoughby.

The first snow had fallen before she was allowed to roam around the house. Before then, Aunt Bessie was too worried that an unexpected caller might wonder why a child with scarlatina was up and about. Her mother had conducted daily lessons in reading and writing so that when she attended Miss Ada O'Donnell's private lower-grade school, she would be up with her class. Every morning she would wake up and pretend that she was in the classroom and that Sally sat at the next desk. She thought she wanted nothing more than to be able to attend school and wear the gray serge uniform that was required.

One morning she came down to find that Aunt Bessie had made buckwheat cakes and sausage for breakfast, which was always looked upon as a special treat. Her hand trembled as she poured maple syrup all over her plate. She had come to learn that whenever anything terrible was about to happen she was served something special—fudge brownies or buckwheat cakes. An hour after breakfast her mother told her that she had decided there would not be any lessons that day.

"But, darlin', what we're goin' to do is to play beauty shop." Suddenly Alice turned to her sister. "I can't do it, Bessie. I just can't do it," she said and ran from the kitchen where they had been sitting.

Ellie came and stood behind Bessie Wallis and placed her hands comfortingly on her shoulders.

"You have to have a haircut," Aunt Bessie explained. "I don't know why that should be such an emotional thing."

Bessie Wallis wore braids that reached almost to her waist and she hated to have her hair brushed every morning. "A haircut? How short?" she asked. "To my shoulders? Will it tangle less?"

"Well, child, I might as well be straightforward with you. We have just learned that when you have scarlatina your head has to be shaved. I asked Mr. Vazuzzi, the barber around the corner, how fast hair grows, and he said about a quarter of an inch a week. That means that your hair would be one and a half inches long by now. And in another six weeks, when you're able to return to school, it will be long enough to make curls all over your head."

It had just dawned on Bessie Wallis what her aunt planned to do, and she got up from the kitchen table and hurried to follow her mother out of the room, but Ellie reached out and stopped her.

"Chile," she said, "it ain't gwine to hurt."

"They'll laugh at me. All the girls will laugh at me. No one has short hair and curls like a baby's. I won't let you do it!"

"Bessie Wallis, you were named after me and that gives me certain privileges," her aunt said in a stern voice. "I have to ask you to go sit down at the kitchen table. Ellie will put a sheet around your shoulders and you may hold my silver looking glass to see how I'm progressing."

"I won't!" There were no tears or even a catch in her voice. It was now the child's will against her aunt's.

"Bessie Wallis, you will sit down as I tell you. If you don't let me cut your hair, everyone at school will know you did not have scarlatina. Your classmates will call you a liar and that would be far worse than if they laughed at you."

Bessie Wallis walked slowly back across the room and dropped into a chair. "You can cut my hair but I won't wear any curls."

"All right. That's a deal."

The sheet was placed around her shoulders and Aunt Bessie took her sewing shears and began to snip away. Ellie let out a cry followed by an exclamation of "Lawd, Lawd!" as cuttings of the girl's dark hair fell onto the white sheet and then feathered out. Bessie Wallis sat stiffly, her hands poked through the bottom of the sheet as she held the mirror and stared into it. When it was almost done, Alice peered around the corner of the door. "Oh, good God! She looks like a porcupine!" she exclaimed and then disappeared.

Only then did Bessie Wallis begin to cry.

3

Mr. Vazuzzi, the barber, had calculated incorrectly. Her hair was no more than a stubble when Bessie Wallis turned up at school for her first day. She survived the ridicule of the other students by wearing a knitted cap pulled down over her bare ears.

Unbeknownst to her, the matter of producing her birth certificate had been successfully avoided, and her plight had allowed her special privileges at home where Aunt Bessie and her mother could not have been more solicitous. Alice had made her an elegant blue velvet dress, collared with Irish lace and sashed with blue taffeta to wear on her Sunday visits to Preston Street. And Aunt Bessie had bought her a pair of white kid gloves and a blue velvet bonnet with ribbons that tied beneath her chin. Though a few of her classmates had snickered at her appearance, all of them, without exception, had taken note of her. She had, in fact, become something of a celebrity. People she had never met stopped her on the street and asked after her welfare. Being different, she had learned, could hurt, but it also made you stand out from the crowd.

The estrangement between Bessie Wallis and her grandmother had dissolved with the advent of the child's "illness."

Alice no longer accompanied her on her visits to Preston Street. Eddie collected her and brought her home in her grandmother's victoria. She still harbored a deep distrust and fear of Uncle Sol, but she very much looked forward to these Sunday excursions. A sense of great pride filled her as she sat, as tall as her back would stretch, in the rear of the elegant carriage with its dark-blue plush seats, aware of the admiring and curious glances of pedestrians and the passengers in other vehicles as she passed. The trappings of wealth, she decided, were equally as exhilarating as being different.

Another child might have found these weekly excursions to the Warfields' trying; not Bessie Wallis. So pleased was she to be back in the good graces of her grandmother that she did not mind the strictly kept ritual of Preston Street. No sooner did she arrive than it was time to attend church services. Sunday supper was served punctually at three P.M. in the dining room. Uncle Sol and Grandmother Warfield sat at opposite ends of the long table built to accommodate sixteen, with all the chairs in place. Bessie Wallis, three empty seats on either side of her, sat facing the breakfront containing the Kirk silver.

Despite Uncle Sol's solemn presence, Bessie Wallis much enjoyed being in a house where the silver was on display and where she knew it would not have to be sold, where three servants waited on them at supper and a handsome victoria would speed her home. And she reveled in the knowledge that Mary Beth Howard, in the house next to the Warfields', could always be caught watching from an upstairs window as she arrived and departed in her fine new Sunday outfit.

One cold November week, Aunt Bessie had gone up to Washington to visit cousins and she and her mother were alone. On Saturday afternoon, Alice had hired a cab to take them to Druid Hill Park where the ice had already hardened on the boat lake and winter skating was in full swing. Bessie Wallis took her first wobbly steps on rented skates amid squeals of terror and delight. Though she was not a good athlete, the brilliant panorama of the brightly dressed skaters as they glided on the ice and the cold *whooshes* of air they stirred as they passed invigorated her so that within an hour she had managed, with Alice's strong support, to circle the lake.

Dusk had fallen before she would let her mother hire a cab to take them home. Seated in the back seat, her face flushed a robust crimson, she had devoured the bag of roasted chestnuts that had been a bribe from Alice to get her to leave. But it had been the additional promise that they would stop at the Rennert Hotel for hot chocolate, tea sandwiches and cakes that had done the trick.

The Rennert was the city's leading hotel, famous for its teatime delicacies, its dining room, and the fact that it housed the headquarters of the local Democratic party and its controversial and colorful boss, Isaac Freeman Rasin, one of the most powerful and popular politicians in Baltimore. Alice and Bessie Wallis were seated at the rear of the lobby where the tea was served; an adjacent door led to the rooms of the Democratic Party Headquarters where much fevered activity was taking place. The Republicans had occupied the White House for five years, but Baltimore remained stridently Democratic.

Politics, or perhaps, more aptly, politicians, intrigued Alice. Baltimore and Washington were separated by a mere eighteen miles and happenings, trends and crises in the capital city were of vital interest to Baltimoreans. While most young girls followed the adventures of *Alice in Wonderland,* her mother read Bessie Wallis reports of the activities of the President's daughter, Alice Roosevelt. "Princess" Alice, as she was dubbed by the press ("Jus' like your mama's name, darlin'," her mother liked to remind her), had attracted attention because of her good looks, forthright personality, unconventional ways and acid tongue. Her debut a number of years before had been treated as a national event. No party could have launched a more spectacular career and no princess was ever more feted and admired. Her adventures in and out of Washington society were served to the reading public in the dailies, and every morning at breakfast, Bessie Wallis would hear from her mother about the "Princess's" elegant tastes, her choice of clothes, friends, beaux, and the lavish parties she attended.

"In Europe there are real princesses and princes, of course," Alice would comment. "But here in America I'm afraid we have to make do with the President and his family.

Politicians are our royalty." Then she would sigh. "But they come and go so fast. It can never be the same thing."

The sound of bellowing voices and raucous laughter filtered through the door of Democratic Headquarters, distracting Bessie Wallis as she tried desperately hard to sip her hot chocolate in the ladylike manner Aunt Bessie had taught her: no slurping, of course, pinky outstretched as she held her cup, the other hand in her lap, and sitting in such an erect position that she looked as though she had a broomstick poked between her shoulder blades. Her mother's attention had been diverted by her interest in the men going in and out of that door. Suddenly, it bolted open and a large man with a bush of red hair exploded into the lobby. His collar was too tight for his thick neck and he tugged on it as he strode back and forth behind the tea tables. A smaller, slimmer, and considerably younger man was trying, with difficulty, to keep step with him. They were arguing about something. Then, the slighter man turned furiously away and walked back into Democratic Headquarters.

Heads inclined as a buzz of low voices spread across the lobby. The red-haired man was Rasin's son, John Freeman Rasin. Free, as he was known, had a reputation as a gambler, womanizer and layabout. The other man had been his younger brother, Carroll, their father's confidant and aide, who shared the widowed political leader's manorial estate which boasted one of the largest private ballrooms in Baltimore. Bad blood existed between the brothers, and the tea guests at the Rennert were speculating on the possible cause of this current disturbance.

"Money, for sure," a woman at a nearby table whispered to her companion. "'Bout time Carroll an' Mr. Rasin refuse to pay Free's debts."

"I have to go to the powder room, darlin'," Alice told her. "You sit here like a good girl an' finish your chocolate. I'll be right back." Alice rose gracefully from her chair and, smiling, walked in the direction of the man. Bessie Wallis watched her mother with a new kind of fascination, as though for the first time she was seeing her as others did and it made her squirm in her seat. Alice's tightly corseted figure was outlined in her bright blue dress; her full high bosom, slim waist and curvaceous hips became even more accentuated as she sinuously threaded her way through the nearby tables.

Her mother and the man were talking. Both of them laughed: Alice demurely into a white handkerchief; the man, with his leonine head thrust back, loud enough to make people glance uncomfortably away. Only a short exchange took place and then Alice passed on to her destination which was discreetly hidden behind a painted screen of women in powdered wigs and voluminous pastel dresses.

Alice was exuberantly happy on the ride home, humming remembered snatches of the skating music that had been played by a five-piece band in the cupola at the lake. She held Bessie Wallis close to her and gave her affectionate hugs from time to time, but otherwise seemed to be wrapped up in her own pleasant thoughts. Her buoyant spirits prevailed throughout the evening rituals of her daughter's bath, bedtime stories, and prayers (which she held down to the obligatory "God-blesses").

On arriving home, Alice had started the fires in the parlor and the kitchen stove, and the pungent scent of burning wood filtered up the staircase, adding to Bessie Wallis's sense of well-being. As she settled down in the dark of her room under the thickness of her quilt, she heard the rustle of her mother's skirts and the steady *click-clack* of her tiny high-heeled boots as she descended the staircase. Her mother must have gone down to put out the fires before going to bed herself, she thought, and then Bessie Wallis promptly fell asleep.

The house was still warm when she awoke. She was not in the habit of getting up in the middle of the night and had only done so once or twice in her memory, but the sweets she had eaten along with her hot chocolate had been too rich and some small waves of pain were passing across her stomach. The light from the streetlamp came through the blinds as she made her way to the door. Her original intention had been to go into her mother's adjoining room, but once she was standing in the dark at the top of the staircase, she could see that light glowed from below. Sleepily, she made her way down to the floor below, where Aunt Bessie had her bedroom. She could now hear voices. Her mother was talking to a man. Slowly, cautiously, she began to descend, not really knowing why she felt so apprehensive. When she was about halfway down, the acrid smell of cigarette smoke caused her eyes to tear. She held her hand tightly over her mouth to keep from coughing and leaned over the banister to see who was there.

Through the archway from the front hall to the parlor she could see the room within. The fire was higher than when she had gone to bed, but none of the lamps was lighted. The voices were a little louder now, although still muffled. Alice and whoever was with her were in an area of the room out of Bessie Wallis's vision. She held her breath, went down another two steps and then squatted on the lower one, looking through the wood rails of the banister. Directly to the far side of the fireplace, her mother, her boots off, was stretched out on the settee; the man with the red hair was kneeling beside her. The voices stopped. The house was silent except for the crackling of the logs. Crouched in the great yawning silence, dark, slithering shadows from the flames streaking across the parlor ceiling, she was certain her heart would burst and that she would drop dead, like Mary Beth Howard's pet canary had done when it fell from its perch onto the floor of its cage, stiff and on its back.

Suddenly her mother jumped up, almost knocking the man over. He rose instantly to his feet and grabbed her around the waist.

"Let me go!" her mother commanded as she attempted to free herself from his grasp.

"Alice, Alice," the man cajoled as he turned her about so that they faced each other.

"No, no!" her mother repeated with an unfamiliar wildness as she managed to pull away, stumbling as she did, the uncalculated movement causing her golden hair to slip its bonds and cascade loosely over her neck and down her back. The man scooped her up in his arms and held her until her body stilled. Then his hands moved upward and became entangled in her hair.

"Free, you mustn't," her mother cried in a quivering voice.

They were standing sideways to Bessie Wallis so that she could see both figures in profile. Behind them soared the flames of the fire. The man called Free was holding out her mother's hair and golden strands caught the light of the fire. Bessie Wallis's heart pounded furiously. Her mother had suddenly become the young woman about to burn at the stake in a picture in Grandmother Warfield's book of the martyrs. For an instant she considered jumping down into the hallway and running to her mother's aid. But, to her surprise, Alice went limp in the man's arms. He lowered his hands to grasp her shoulders and as he did, the image of the burning female dissolved.

The man was supporting Alice with one arm as the hand on the other worked to undo the buttons on the back bodice of her dress. Alice rested her head against his chest as he fumbled awkwardly with the buttons.

"Undo your stays, darlin', undo your stays," he ordered.

Alice raised her head and, straightening, reached behind herself to help him unlace her waist cincher. The bodice of her dress slipped down, falling into bright blue waves about her waist; and two rounded, perfectly formed breasts rose pridefully like foamy whitecaps above them.

"Step out of the dress, darlin'," he commanded. To Bessie Wallis's amazement her mother did as he said.

Alice stood in the glistening aureole of flames, naked, except for her garters and stockings. Bessie Wallis could not recall ever having seen her mother with so few clothes before, even when they had shared the same room at the Brexton, and the sight fascinated her. So magnetized was she by her mother's nudity that she had not seen the man unbutton his trousers.

"No, Free, no!" her mother warned and then swooped down in a quick gesture and grabbed at her dress in an attempt to cover herself. The man pulled the cloth out of her grasp and then, his hands on her bare shoulders, pushed Alice down onto her back on the floor and swung his body over hers. Her mother flung her arms about him and was making strange noises. But she was not struggling to force the man off her.

Bessie Wallis wanted to scream out for them to stop, but she was too terrified at being discovered to do so. Then, as though she had been able to hear her thoughts, her mother called out, "Stop! Stop!" The man, his rufous hair mane-like around his head, his massive shoulders heaving, raised himself up on his arms and to one side of Alice and then, shaking mightily and with a great cry, as though he had been wounded, collapsed onto the floor beside her mother's prostrate form.

The tall Seth Thomas clock in the front entrance struck, the suddenness of it seeming to absorb all other sound. Her mother sat up and drew her dress about herself. Bessie Wallis rose speculatively and as quietly as she could and began to feel her way backward up the stairs. In a matter of three steps all sight of the parlor was gone and she turned and raced up to the first landing. The clock was still striking. She had been too alarmed to count the strokes but from the number of them she had realized that it must be eleven or twelve in the evening and not the middle of the night as she had originally thought.

Just as she went to cross the landing to the second floor, the front door opened in with a great gust of cold air that shot straight up to where she stood. Looking down from where she was she could see only the hemline of a woman's outer coat and then a carpetbag as it was lowered to the floor, which she immediately recognized as belonging to Aunt Bessie.

"My God!" Aunt Bessie exclaimed.

Bessie Wallis moved around the corner of the landing where she could hear but could not be seen.

A great commotion followed as her mother and the man obviously got to their feet and covered themselves.

"John Freeman Rasin!" Aunt Bessie shouted in a voice that would have sent most people scurrying. "You get out of my house! This minute, heah me?"

"I would 'spect, ma'am, that the President up in Washington could *heah* you," the man replied.

"If he did I have no doubts that he would know how to deal with scum like you! Out! Out!"

The voices became unintelligible but in a few moments another blast of cold air hurtled up the stairway and the front door slammed shut. Bessie Wallis could imagine her mother standing frightened and alone in the parlor entrance, her clothes clutched tightly to her as Aunt Bessie continued to shout.

"Alice, how could you? How could you? That man has a scandalous reputation."

"You're always preachin' the importance of family background," Alice interjected. "Free Rasin's daddy was a close friend of President Cleveland an' his momma, Julia Claypoole, was descended from Edward the First, King of England."

"There's nothing wrong with Mr. Rasin's *background,*" Aunt Bessie countered. "It's his foreground that's *awful*! Everyone knows he's a lazy no-account who does nothing but make trouble for his father."

"Bessie, dear," Alice cajoled, "please don't be so harsh on Free." She paused significantly. "I think I'm in love with him."

"You thought you were in love with a Warfield as well and look where that got you! Pregnant. Well, if you want Baltimore to call you a whore, you're doing your best to spread the word, that's for sure! But I won't allow you to ruin the child's future. She can be everything I had no chance to be, and that you have spoiled for yourself."

Her mother had come out into the hallway and her voice was clearer. "I agree, Bessie, I did an unforgivable thing this evenin'. This is your home, not mine. I had no right havin' guests unknown to you."

"Well, I can only thank the Lord that storms in Washington made me decide to take the late train home tonight instead of tomorrow morning as I had planned. Now, go up to bed, Alice, I'm disgusted at the sight of you, your hair all unbound, your face still red from the rub of that man's beard. We'll talk tomorrow when I'm more collected and able to pound some sense and some shame into you."

"There's nothin' to say, Bessie. My daughter an' I will leave as soon as I find a suitable accommodation." She started up the stairs and Bessie Wallis moved quickly to escape being seen.

"No need to be rash," her aunt countered, "or self-centered. It's the child who must be considered. She's not to be moved back into that hotel, understand? And without money, where on earth would you go?"

"I'll get money. I'll go see Sol Warfield."

The last words Bessie Wallis heard before she pounced underneath the covers of her bed and pulled them up over her head were spoken by her Aunt Bessie from the second-floor landing. "You have no shame, Alice. No shame!" Aunt Bessie was sobbing as the door to her room slammed shut.

"Darlin'?" her mother called from Bessie Wallis's darkened doorway. "Are you asleep?"

Bessie Wallis held her breath and tried not to move. A moment later she could hear Alice crying softly in the hallway. The house was cold and silent before Bessie Wallis fell asleep. What had warmed her in the last moments of wakefulness was the image of her mother standing naked, her fair hair loose around her shoulders and down her back and the firelight creating a halo all around her. Never had she seen anything, she thought, that was so astoundingly beautiful.

4

Three weeks after this traumatic episode Alice and Bessie Wallis moved to the Preston Street Apartments, situated just six blocks from the Warfields' house. The building had only recently been completed and they were the first to occupy the ground-floor front apartment. The scent of plaster dust and fresh paint hung in the air, and Bessie Wallis hated the idea that almost everything in the flat was new.

"Ain't nothin' good that ain't been 'round a spell," Ellie grumbled in agreement.

Bessie Wallis truly missed Aunt Bessie. But Alice seemed happier than ever. Uncle Sol had advanced her a sizable loan to furnish and decorate the apartment which in part was intended to be used as business premises, her plan being to cater small private luncheons and dinner parties. The two reception rooms were soon turned into public areas. A narrow hallway led directly from the front entry to Bessie Wallis's rear room. This meant she did not have to pass through the front parlors when she came in after school. Alice let her choose her own fabrics, a sunny yellow floral pattern for curtains and coverlet. Grandmother Warfield had given her the brass bed from her old bedroom. It was her first real possession to take pride in and she herself polished the golden metal until it gleamed.

As soon as Chez Alice was ready to receive guests, Bessie Wallis slipped printed cards under the front doors of the occupants of their building and of the other prosperous-looking apartment houses nearby. Within two weeks Alice had several reservations.

The kitchen, with its massive, new, gray-enamel cooking stove, became the center of Alice's household. Ellie was employed as cook's helper and waitress, the latter activity requiring her to wear a starched white cap that she regarded with great repugnance. The accursed object was always askew and in danger of falling into the stockpots. "Ain't nat'rul! Jus' ain't nat'rul," she would growl and then complain to Bessie Wallis in a voice loud enough for Alice to hear, "Since yuh mama cain't 'ford no mammy no more, dis am de only ways ah kin keep mah eye on you."

Despite her lamentations Ellie trailed willingly behind Alice on their shopping excursions, carrying a large wicker basket for their purchases, and worked enthusiastically in the kitchen. The winter of 1904 was the coldest Baltimore had experienced in over a decade, and Bessie Wallis was content to spend her afternoons in the kitchen's steamy warmth inhaling the aromatic smells of her mother's fine soups and sauces and the pungent odor of rising yeast from Ellie's breads and sweet rolls. Whenever Alice served terrapin or Smithfield ham, Ellie made Maryland biscuits, considered *de rigueur* as an accompaniment. The large black woman, her broad face skewed in concentration, would roll up her sleeves to the elbows as she let Bessie Wallis flour the biscuit board.

"Now you keep the time," she ordered her young assistant. "Ah's got to pound dis here dough zackly half a' hour. No mo', no less. Zackly. Unnerstan'? Ah's gots ta wuk 'em till dey pops."

"Yes, Ellie. Thirty minutes," said Bessie Wallis, as her eyes fastened on the large kitchen clock that hung over the sink.

"Ain't no good to try to sho'tcut de time, or dese here biscuits will be hard as a ter'pin's shell." She dumped the pale yellow, doughy mixture onto the board, sprinkled it with flour and began pounding and then flattening it with a rolling pin. With each bang of the pin, the muscles in her thick forearms flexed and unflexed, the rhythmic, even beats of the action so hypnotic they disallowed conversation.

"Time!" Bessie Wallis called out when half an hour had elapsed. Then came her favorite chore, to help Ellie form the dough into the size and shape of pullet eggs and set the unbaked biscuits out on a cooking sheet.

Ellie also prepared the spoonbread and shortcake that Alice served, but the proprietress herself supervised the plates of stuffed oysters, deviled crabs, broiled shad and shad roe, Smithfield ham, and her two "specialities"—wild duck and diamondback terrapin. Her endeavor met with enthusiastic response. By all odds it ought to have been a financial success, however modest. The problem was that Alice insisted she serve only the finest quality of the foods hardest to come by.

Since she knew no hunters who might share their daily quarry with her, she bought her wild duck from one of Baltimore's most elite poultry stores. "The secret," she confided to Bessie Wallis as she basted a brace of roasting ducks with a generous lashing of port wine, "is not to cook the ducks too long. They simply hafta fly through the oven, an' nevah, evah be stuffed. An' they should be served with wild rice an' currant jelly, nevah mashed potatoes an' hominy grits as some unknowin' folks do. Now, when you become a grand lady, you remembah to tell your cook all this."

Alice purchased only the most expensive diamondback terrapin for her guests, for only the flavor of that extravagant breed met with her exacting taste. She bought them live (at an exorbitant five dollars apiece) from a burlap bag the terrapin man carried over his shoulder as he walked through the streets, calling out in a high-pitched, singsong voice, "Terrrrr-a-pin! Terrrrr-a-pin!"

Unfortunately Bessie Wallis did not share her mother's enthusiasm for terrapin or for wild duck, especially when they ended up in her school lunchbox. "This isn't just terrapin, this is *diamondback* terrapin," she would say archly as she set out her exotic fare at the school lunch table, and then creatively add: "The King of England prefers this kind to all others and he has them shipped *live* to England in a great tank filled with seawater and has them fed the best cornmeal on their journey."

Taking a morsel in her mouth with deliberate gusto, she would roll her eyes suggesting ecstasy. Secretly she hungered for a plain jam sandwich. To her chagrin the remains of Alice's charlottes, meringues and cream puffs were doled out sparingly and with a warning by Ellie that if she ate too many sweet things all her teeth would fall out by the time she was twenty and she would be an old maid.

All in all, she was not unhappy about the move to the Preston Street Apartments. The preparations for her mother's catered affairs exhilarated her. On nights when they were given, she would lie in bed with the door open just a crack so that she could hear the soothing buzz of the voices and the warm sparkle of laughter. Then, too, Ellie was once again in their employ, she owned a brass bed so shiny it caught and spun the moonlight and the man with the red hair no longer came around.

Uncle Sol's money was soon gone; Alice did whatever she could to keep Bessie Wallis from realizing the precariousness of their finances. But Mrs. Warfield always managed a grim reminder spoken to Sol over her granddaughter's head at the Sunday supper table. "The child looks like a sparrow and eats like a crow. You know what that means? Not enough nourishin' food for her to eat at home, I suspect. And why doesn't she have a proper winter coat and some heavy woolen stockings when it's bitter cold? Alice isn't fit to mother, if you ask me."

Despite these jabs, Bessie Wallis always looked forward to Sundays, but this particular Sunday was to be even more of an event for it was her grandmother's seventieth birthday and all of the Warfield relatives would be gathered at supper for a celebration. That meant that her two aunts and their husbands would come down from Philadelphia, along with her Uncle Emory and his wife, and Grandmother Warfield's youngest surviving son, Uncle Harry, and his family. Uncle Harry lived in Baltimore, but he and Uncle Sol did not get along too well and he appeared only on the most important occasions.

Church bells pealed as she made her way early that morning, alone and on foot, past the red-brick houses built wall to wall, up the six blocks on Preston Street that separated her new home from her grandmother's. A stiff southwesterly wind caused her to hold in place the great blue taffeta bow her mother had attached to the top of her new pompadour hairdo. Her hair had finally grown to a length where something could be done with it. Her spirits were high and she was much amused to see men in high wing collars clutching their derbies and women tugging at their full sweeping skirts to avoid anyone's glimpsing of their high-buttoned shoes and the tops of their cotton stockings.

She kept a cautious eye on the horses and carriages as she crossed the cobblestone streets. Overhead the maze of telegraph and telephone wires strung on wooden poles reverberated in the brisk wind which had risen the previous night and showed no sign of letting up. Bessie Wallis enjoyed the sensation of being propelled forward at an accelerated pace by its momentum despite the sharp lashes it delivered to the back of her legs as she was swept along to her destination.

She pushed her hands deep into the pockets of her coat to reassure herself that the gift packets for her grandmother—a hand-embroidered handkerchief from her and a needle case from Alice—were snug and secure. Mrs. Warfield was waiting in the sitting room, bonnet tied, her cloak wrapped about her, when she arrived.

"Happy birthday, Grandmama," she sang out as she entered the room. She desperately wanted to give the old woman the two small, beribboned packages, but had been instructed by Alice to do so only along with her cousins' offerings.

"Let me look at you, girl," Mrs. Warfield squinted up at the child's new coiffure. "A bit too showy for my taste," she said. "That ribbon is large enough for a five-pound box of chocolates!" She leaned heavily upon Bessie Wallis as she rose to her feet. "Come along now," she ordered and, when they had reached the hallway, called out hoarsely, "Sol?"

He appeared from the dining room where he had apparently been eating his breakfast, for a large white napkin remained tucked into his vest and he was holding the Sunday papers, which he always read while drinking his second cup of coffee.

"It's all this upsetting news about Russia and Japan," he said as though continuing a conversation with an unseen companion. "War is damn certain."

"Sol," Mrs. Warfield warned, "not on Sunday, and do hurry or we'll be late for church."

"Church? Yes, yes, of course." He folded the newspaper in neat quarters and removed the white damask square at his front, handing them to Eddie who, grinning widely, had seemed to have materialized from under the stairs where the door leading down to the kitchen was located. Eddie then disappeared to return in moments with Sol's coat and derby.

"Mark Hanna's gravely ill," Sol continued. "Seems whenever we elect a good man to the Senate, death marches in and steals him away. I've come to believe God votes Republican!" He stuffed his arms into the coat Eddie now held for him.

"Sol, do you have no respect for Sunday?" his mother chided. "And you haven't even said 'good day' to Bessie Wallis."

He nodded his head in lieu of a greeting, but in a moment a smile rippled across his face. "That pretty bow, of course, would be Alice's doing." His hand brushed Bessie Wallis's cheek in a manner that conveyed his approval and she felt her face flush in embarrassment. She had always become awkward when Uncle Sol displayed even the most remote affection toward her.

They drove the three blocks to church in the victoria, allowing Bessie Wallis to sit near a window so that she could see out. Reverend Parr's sermon dealt with the evil permeating a thrill-seeking society speeding at twenty miles an hour in one of the new high-powered automobiles, threatening the life and limb of carriage riders and pedestrians. His frizzy white hair seemed to fly from his head as he shouted in a rasping voice, "The vehicle is the devil's own carrier!" He raised his long arms, hands clenched, and then lowered them suddenly to his chest as though he had just been struck a paralyzing blow.

Shortly before eleven o'clock, the congregation—kneeling in silent prayer—was brought to its feet by a jarring clang of fire-engine bells passing by. The sound of more than one team of fire horses indicated a four-alarm fire raging nearby. A few moments later, a deafening explosion shook the church windows. Danger seemed imminent and members of the congregation rushed up the aisles shouting, "Fire! Fire!" Mrs. Warfield grabbed Bessie Wallis's hand to keep her from following their lead. "We are in the Lord's house, child," she admonished.

Reverend Parr tried to keep order but the church was nearly emptied in a matter of minutes, the Warfields being among the last to leave. Outside, great flames billowed in the distance and the sky was a pall of thick black smoke. People ran in the street; shouts mingled with the hoofbeats of the teams of galloping fire horses. Bells and sirens sounded in all directions. The entire downtown of Baltimore was afire. Huge flaming embers streaked through the air and fell over the city. To Bessie Wallis's horror, one came down nearby and a horse's tail went up in flames.

Mrs. Warfield had not let go of her granddaughter's hand. The carriage was nowhere to be seen, having apparently been made to move by the blue-helmeted police who were out in force. "You don't think those damned Yankees," Mrs. Warfield began and then stopped, having realized she had cursed on a Sunday.

"Good Lord, Mother, this is 1904," Sol managed, his arm protectively about his mother and niece as he hurried them away from the flames and in the direction of Preston Street. People were pushing them from all sides—some in a rush to get to their homes, others to get a closer glimpse of the wild conflagration.

"It's moving towards Charles Street!" a man shouted as he raced past them, brushing Bessie Wallis so hard that the force spun her around and knocked her to the ground. For the first time she could see what was behind them. Windswept waves of flame, eight to ten stories high, engulfed blocks of the nearby downtown district where the fire had started. The sky was a smudgepot of black smoke and the air so acrid that, as she breathed it, she fell into a fit of coughing.

Uncle Sol reached out his hand to help her to her feet. To

his surprise, Bessie Wallis jumped up, drew back and, stumbling, ran in the opposite direction. The man had said the fire was near Charles Street, which was at the corner of the Preston Street Apartments where she had left her mother asleep only two hours earlier.

Above all the clamor she heard her uncle screaming at her to stop, but she knew he would not leave her grandmother to come after her. She ran as fast as she could, the wind lashing her face and the fronts of her legs. Twice, she fell to the sidewalk. Passing people helped her back onto her feet. But no one stopped her.

The strong wind carried ash and debris. Finding it impossible to run in the face of it, she slowed to a brisk walk, her arm crooked and raised protectively over the lower half of her face, her eyes fixed on the brick facade of her apartment building as she drew closer, each step such an effort as to be physically painful. Then, suddenly, through tears she could not control, she sighted Alice standing on the front stoop. Drawing from a miraculous reserve of energy, she lunged forward, ran up the path and into her mother's arms, where the two of them clung for several moments.

"Let me look at you," Alice finally said, as she pried her daughter loose and held her at arm's distance. "Whatever happened to your bow?" she exclaimed, noting the unraveled ribbon hanging down the side of the youngster's head. "An' your stockin's? Why, child," she said with alarm, "your knees are bleedin'!"

Bessie Wallis looked up into her mother's eyes, and an intense feeling of well-being pervaded her as she saw the love and concern in them. She started forward to grasp Alice again, when something suddenly struck her as odd and she stepped back and stood staring dumbly at her mother. Alice was wearing a man's greatcoat. Bessie Wallis's teary glance traveled past her mother's figure to the doorway of the building. There, to her utter surprise and instant resentment, stood the red-haired man.

The fire, which devastated seventy-three city blocks and emptied Baltimore for weeks, put a dramatic end to Chez Alice, which could not sustain a forced closure. Although the Preston Street Apartments had escaped the inferno, Bessie Wallis suspected that she and her mother would have to move back to Aunt Bessie's. To her surprise, Alice informed her that they were to have—for the first time—a home of their own. A week later they moved into a small but comfortable red-brick row house at 212 Biddle Street, not far from the Preston Street Apartments, although in a less fashionable area. Her room was on the top floor. The brass bed was moved in. Alice, however, purchased a new bedroom suite for her larger accommodation on the second floor. Bessie Wallis never thought to ask where the money had come from for all this new splendor, assuming that Uncle Sol had once again been their benefactor.

One afternoon she returned home from school to find the red-haired man seated in their front parlor. As she came into the room—called by her mother to join them—he stood up. He appeared heavier and jowlier than she had recalled. On the table next to him was a small bowl containing a bright orange goldfish swimming about in water. He picked up the bowl and, crossing to her, set it carefully in her hands.

"I'm not very good at knowing what little girls like," he said, "but I figure everyone needs something living to care for." He paused, wanting to say more, but when Bessie Wallis stood stone-faced and silent, he was unable to continue. He laughed nervously. "Well, I didn't do *that* too well, I guess," he said over his shoulder to Alice. "You'd better help me out."

Alice came to her daughter's side and placed her hand gently beneath her chin. "Darlin', what Mr. Rasin wants to say is that—after long reflection an' with your welfare always in mind—I've accepted his kind an' generous proposal of marriage."

Bessie Wallis stared at her mother in dismay. She had long ago refused to consider the idea that Alice might one day remarry. She wanted to scream out for Mr. Rasin to leave their house, but she suddenly realized that the house was probably bought by him. The thought of sharing her mother with anyone else, of living in *his* house, of Alice sleeping in her new bed with *him,* filled her with uncontrollable rage.

Quite without realizing what she was going to say, she screamed, "I won't let you marry him, I won't! He's fat and carrot-haired and bulgy-eyed, just like this goldfish, and he's ugly!" And then, as though it was a ball in her hand, she threw the fishbowl across the room. The glass shattered. Water splattered on the newly papered wall and the small, bright metallic fish floundered helplessly on the dark wood floor that rimmed the patterned rug.

"Bessie Wallis, go to your room, this minute!" her mother ordered.

"It's not my room, and I'll never, ever sleep in it or in this house!" she cried as she started to the door.

"Bessie Wallis, where are you going?" her mother called.

"To Aunt Bessie's," she replied and, unable to suppress them anymore, burst into tears.

"Please, darlin', please," Alice begged, her tone quickly changing, her own eyes misting over.

Through the blur of her tears Bessie Wallis caught sight of John Freeman Rasin as he scooped up the writhing goldfish in his hands and deposited it in a vase of flowers. The gentle action sent a perverse and fresh wave of hatred through her and, turning sharply on her heel, she ran from the room and the house.

5

Three days later she returned home, where Alice Montague Warfield and John Freeman Rasin were united in the front parlor; Bessie Wallis wore a white organdy dress with a purple sash that had once belonged to an older Montague cousin, the beautiful Corrine Montague, who was now married to Lieutenant Henry Mustin. Corrine was only nineteen, had golden hair, dazzling blue eyes, the smallest waist that Bessie Wallis had ever seen and a wildly coquettish nature, undiminished by a year of marriage. Bessie Wallis was fascinated by her and was just gathering the nerve to go over and speak to her, when her great-uncle, the boldly mustachioed and balding Powhowtan Sinclair, sat down at the Pianola and struck the powerful opening chords of the wedding march.

While the service was in progress, Bessie Wallis slipped out of the parlor and made her way cautiously to the festively decorated dining room. In the center of the flower-bedecked table stood Ellie's five-layer wedding cake complete with a miniature bride and groom perched on the top and, as Bessie Wallis had been told, a lucky golden charm hidden inside. The room was empty and Bessie Wallis tiptoed up to it, studied it for a moment, and then, with one powerful chop of her bare hand, split it open. So involved was she with her task that she was unaware that the service had ended. A collective gasp could be heard from the dining-room doorway, through which Alice and her new husband were just that moment leading their guests.

"I found the ring," she cried out, as she whirled around holding the small unrecognizable object in her smeared hand. Alice stood stunned at the sight of the destroyed wedding cake. An uncomfortable silence was finally broken by a roar of laughter from Free Rasin as he hoisted the culprit into the air in his strong arms.

"If that is the ring—you'll be the next bride; but you'd better wait a few years!" he said good-naturedly as he set her down again. "The champagne is about to be poured!" To his stepdaughter's surprise he left her standing there without one word in reprimand as he went to pop the cork of a bottle of champagne from a full, open case.

In the whole of Bessie Wallis's life, no one had been as nice to her as Free Rasin turned out to be. Despite her frequent sullen moods and rudeness, he never chastised her. He bought her a small bulldog, whom she loved and named Bully. He paid for piano and dance lessons and gave Alice money to buy fabric for new wardrobes for the two of them. Now, her mother's life was considerably easier. Her husband had no job, but a family trust inherited after the recent death of his father insured that he received what should have been an adequate income. However, Free Rasin liked to host extravagant parties for his family and friends. And he gambled.

Evenings, the Biddle Street house rang with laughter and high spirits. A weekly poker game was held on Wednesday nights; and although Alice was the only woman present, she was allowed, when she chose, to take a hand. Being good at cards she often retrieved at least a part of what her husband lost.

On poker nights, Bessie Wallis would creep to the top of the stairs in her nightgown, listening to the voices of the men and her mother seated about the dining-room table playing their mysterious game. Once, when Mr. Rasin (and she never called him anything else) caught her out, he carried her into the smoky room and sat her down on the top of the sideboard (to Alice's expressed displeasure) so that she could watch.

"Now, take note," he whispered into her ear. "It's not always what's in your hand but what the other players *think* you've got in it that makes the difference."

The next morning he gave her an old set of poker chips and, laughing in the face of her mother's objections, taught her stud and twenty-one. She was an able student and a running account that he kept of their winnings and losses charted her growing aptitude for cards.

The elaborate dinner parties that Alice once catered were now given solely for Mr. Rasin's political friends and family. He had three married sisters and a host of other relations who often came to call. His younger brother, Carroll, who had inherited the largest share of their father's estate, had refused to attend the wedding. The two brothers, such opposites in their personalities, had irreconcilable differences. Once, Bessie Wallis overheard her mother inquire of one of Rasin's sisters, "Why won't Carroll accept our invitations?" To which her sister-in-law answered boldly, "I don't really know if you want to hear this, Alice, but Carroll says he's simply fed up with Free's gamblin' debts and extravagant ways."

"Nobody seems to understand Free but me," Alice had replied. "I guess we are both mavericks."

Nonetheless, her mother appeared to be exuberantly happy. Usually, she and Mr. Rasin were still in bed when Bessie Wallis left for school. On her return, she would find Alice busy in the kitchen with Ellie preparing food for the evening's festivities and Mr. Rasin in the library reading the newspaper and chain-smoking cigarettes. Except for an occasional afternoon spent at the corner saloon with his poker friends or political cronies, he seemed to want to do nothing except loll about the house.

Aunt Bessie came by some days and the sisters would retreat into the small back bedroom and close the door. "Ain't no place for chillun." Ellie warned her when she once wanted to follow them inside. "Dey's talkin' woman talk."

"What's that?" she asked.

"Dat's when things am bein' 'cussed chillun ain't s'pose ta heah," Ellie replied, "an mah lips am sealed. Yuh ain't gwine heah nothin' frum me."

"About what?"

"How's yuh mama gwine pay fuh yuh sculin' what wid all dis hip an' hoorayin' 'roun' heah! Dat's what!"

Bessie Wallis continued to spend her Sundays at the Warfields'. Neither her grandmother nor Uncle Sol made a secret of their disapproval of Mr. Rasin. She had been told by her mother that Uncle Sol now refused to contribute a cent to her support. But since Bessie Wallis had a chest full of new clothes and all other comforts, this did not seem to be a deprivation.

However, her stepfather's constant presence made her feel uncomfortable about bringing friends home with her from Arundel, the school she now attended. The situation became even worse late one Saturday morning when Sally Mae Everly, a schoolmate, came by unexpectedly to find Alice, still in a chiffon negligee, and Mr. Rasin, in his bathrobe, breakfasting at half past eleven on quail and champagne.

After she reported this incident to her mother, Sally Mae was never allowed to speak to Bessie Wallis again. To make matters worse, details of the scene ("the gown was so sheer you could see *right through it*!") were whispered from girl to girl and often not out of Bessie Wallis's hearing. Within a short time she had been ostracized as other mothers heard about the Rasins' scandalous behavior. The incident was finally brought (by a concerned parent) to the attention of Mrs. Warfield, who acted immediately.

The very next day, which happened to be a Sunday and less than a week away from her summer break, Bessie Wallis had been asked to sit down in the parlor after lunch; her Uncle Sol had something of great importance to discuss with her. He then informed her of a new plan for her holiday. She would divide the time between Wakefield Manor, the newly restored and renovated Montague homestead in Virginia, now occupied by Alice's first cousin, Lelia Montague Gordon, and Pot Spring, her Uncle Emory Warfield's farm in Timonium, a suburb of Baltimore.

"Afterward, you shall return to live here," he said.

"No, I won't," she replied defiantly.

"Well, you have time to think about it. But if you refuse, I shall insist that you be sent off to boarding school."

"Mama will never let you do that!"

"We'll see," he had calmly replied. As she rose to leave, he reached out and took her hand. "Bessie Wallis, if you change your mind and decide to live here, I will make you my heir."

"What's that?" she asked, pulling free.

"Well, when I die a major share of what I own shall be yours."

"And all I have to do is come and live here?"

"You must never enter that lowlife Rasin's house again."

"But that's Mama's home, too," she protested.

"Yes. But you may never again see her *there,*" he added sharply.

"Nobody has the right to tell me I can't see my own mother!" she countered.

"I did not say that. I said . . ."

"I don't want to be your heir and I won't go away to school!" she insisted.

"We'll see, we'll see," he repeated ominously.

A few days later Alice told her that in the autumn she would be sent to Oldfields, a boarding school fifteen miles away at Glencoe, Maryland. "Uncle Sol has generously offered to pay the bills," her mother added with a small, contrite smile.

After a great deal of crying, she gave in, believing that, when the year had ended, she would return to Biddle Street. Not until much later was she to realize that her life with Alice and Mr. Rasin was over and that for the next four years she would be packed up at the close of each school semester and shipped off to an accommodating Montague or Warfield relative in alternating order. During the shorter school breaks she remained in Baltimore with Aunt Bessie or her grandmother. Alice visited her at her own family's residences. She was not allowed to take her beloved dog, Bully, with her, which was a great wrench. However, when she was at Aunt Bessie's, secret visits to Biddle Street were arranged. The gaiety in that house was a welcome relief, and she realized that it was not only her mother and Bully whom she missed, but her high-spirited stepfather.

Wakefield Manor was situated not far from Fredricksburg, where so many thousands of Civil War soldiers were led to bloody slaughter. Though the estate had been in the Montague family since early Colonial days, it had, as Grandmother Warfield often repeated, fallen into serious disrepair until Cousin Lelia, recently widowed and left a large fortune, had it restored and refurbished to its original grandeur, its stately white columns and two long wings that flanked the main hall a commanding sight. Formal gardens distinguished by fine boxwood and well-manicured lawns had replaced the haphazard but gracefully redolent former grounds. A new rose garden boasted forty-two different varieties.

Cousin Lelia had three children: the ebullient, irascible Basil, who—although a foot taller—was just Bessie Wallis's age, and two daughters—blond, giggly Lelia, Jr., called Lee-Lee, and the much younger but exceedingly precocious Anne, who claimed at times to be a kidnapped Indian princess and at others a descendant of the Moon God, the hero in an Indian tale. Despite Basil's strident presence, Wakefield Manor had a distinctly feminine aura. Rose-patterned fabrics and bowls of the real flowers abounded in all the reception rooms. Ruffles and bows protected peekaboo lace curtains. Display cabinets were filled with delicate porcelain shepherds and shepherdesses. Tradition and pride of ancestry were stressed. Gilt-framed portraits of even the most insignificant of Montagues were hung in profusion, one above the other, their aristocratic faces full compensation for possible ignominious pasts. And everywhere the sweet and spicy scents of verbena (worn by Cousin Lelia) and fresh roses pervaded the house.

One wing had been given over to the children, Mr. Fenimore (called "no chin" by Basil behind his back), who took care of Basil and organized all outings and competitive sports, and Miss Lucinda Merriewether, the sisters' governess. A spinster in her middle years, Miss Merrie, as she was known, had retained the gay insouciance of a Southern belle. She dressed her graying hair with fetching velvet bows and sashed her cambric dresses in bright ribbons. Although the dour-faced Mr. Fenimore was more than a decade her junior, she appeared to defer to his judgment on most matters concerning the children. In truth, she nearly always won her way.

"That truly is a clevah ideah," she would declare, her amber eyes glazed in admiration, her hand fluttering in ladylike enthusiasm. "I surely would nevah have thought of that mahself." In fact, it had been her initial scheme, presented in what one might call a rear-flank approach: "Ah do recall you once said (or suggested) that (whatever she had in mind)."

"You see, a Southern girl mus' train for her job jus' as rigorously as any man trains fah his," she confided to the girls one especially warm day when they were preparing for an afternoon rest amid unanimous complaints that Basil was swimming in the nearby lake and making such a "whoop an' hollah" that he could not be ignored. "Basil mus' grow strong an' that comes from exercise," Miss Merrie explained. "You all mus' have fine complexions an' be refreshed when men are fatigued an' that comes from gettin' plenty of rest."

Miss Merrie's contention was that a Southern woman simply must have charm, and to attain it, all she had to learn was to understand men. The girls were thus instructed to watch Basil and Mr. Fenimore and study their foibles and find out what they liked best to talk about.

"All Basil likes is to talk about himself," Bessie Wallis snipped.

"Well, Precious," came the reply, "you jus' encourage him to do that. But don't think you can be a namby-pamby. You also have to be able to assert yahself an' shine, shine, shine! Otherwise men will find you a loathsome bore. So jus' when your gentleman swells out beneath his fancy vest an' is convinced he has met the mos' wonderful girl in the world—then you have to show yah spirit, put him off balance a bit, you know? Be both a coquette an' play the devil."

Despite her unmarried state, Miss Merrie's advice was well heeded by her young female charges, for their governess had a romantic past. At the age of twenty she had fallen in love and become engaged to a visiting British nobleman. Plans were made for a wedding that following summer when her fiancé was to return with his family. But this was the time of the Boer War and the young man was killed in action that same spring. Miss Merrie kept his photograph in a locket she always wore on a gold chain about her neck and, when asked, she was more than pleased to display it, accompanied by a great trembling sigh.

Alice came to spend the Fourth of July at Wakefield Manor and remained until midway through the month when she and Bessie Wallis took the train back to Baltimore, where she had spent the night surreptitiously at Biddle Street. The following day she was delivered to Pot Spring, her Uncle Emory's farm.

Where Wakefield Manor had burgeoned with roses and was framed in verdant lawn, Pot Spring had beanpoles, a tomato patch, a cornfield and some marigolds planted to keep out the rabbits. Uncle Emory did not approve of flowers unless they had a good use. The contrast was startling. Although the main building was a large antebellum structure surrounded by wide verandas and graced in the front by tall columns which supported a balcony, the house had never risen above its farming past.

Emory Warfield, spare in build and hawkish of countenance, was Sol's younger brother, a pious, humorless man who had never reconciled himself to his position as the middle son in the family, nor accepted Sol's unsubscribed patriarchal domination. He made much of the fact that his wife, Betty, was a great-grandniece of President Monroe. A sewing basket which had belonged to Mrs. Monroe was displayed with much reverence beneath a large glass dome in the austere front parlor.

Bessie Wallis found it almost impossible to make the transition from the free and easy ways of Wakefield Manor to the sobriety of Pot Spring where life was regulated by daily reminders of Christian responsibility. Her Aunt Betty, a birdlike woman with dark, piercing eyes and a voice that bore the rasp of an underfed crow, was even more religious than her grandmother. A family ritual was made of morning prayer held in the front parlor, attended, as well, by the house servants. The floor had no rug and the hardwood planks hurt her knees as she kneeled to listen to Aunt Betty read a chapter from the Bible and Uncle Emory deliver the daily prayer. The longest grace Bessie Wallis had ever learned had to be said before each meal.

Uncle Emory had two sons: Douglas, a law clerk who was seventeen years older than Bessie Wallis and had long since left his parents' home for life in Philadelphia, and Henry, who was nine years her senior, tall and lean, with sloe eyes that mocked as they smiled. Henry Warfield was Bessie Wallis's first crush. To her despair he seemed to be unaware of her existence. An expert horseman, he kept a number of fine horses and had erected jumps to practice with them behind the old stables.

Life at Pot Spring was lonely. Lacking the companionship of her Montague cousins and the warm supervision of Miss Merrie, Bessie Wallis was forced to find her own amusements. Her favorite pastime was to sit on the fence behind the stables and watch Henry jump his horses. Since he did not like to do so in the heat of the day, this usually took place late in the afternoon or after supper, when the shadows from nearby trees and outbuildings made Henry, dressed in black form-fitting breeches and matching high leather boots, seem welded to Erebus, his ebon mount. She imagined her cousin Anne's Moon God would look like Henry, his body dark and fluid as he flew with Erebus through the air.

For several weeks Henry made no note of her presence, but then he began to do things that seemed to be motivated by a need to scare her away. He rode Erebus at *whooshing* speed, nearer and nearer to where she was perched, letting out a loud cry, his riding crop chopping the air as he passed. She was certain he would eventually crash right into her, so close did he come. Yet, she did not flinch. By now, it had become an act of defiance on her part and a challenge on his.

Instinctively she understood that he wanted to see how far he could push her before she reacted and that his attempts to terrify her filled him with unusual excitement; for, afterward, eyes glowing, he would energetically stroke Erebus amid words of praise about the animal's splendid performance.

Her own reactions to Henry mystified her. The closer he pushed her to the edge of danger, the more hypnotized she was by him and determined not to lose the contest he had elected to run.

"Hey, Moo," he called to her one evening as she sat, her

ankles clasping the rail of the fence. "Moo" was a name he had invented, he said, because "Bessie Wallis sounds like a cow." She loathed and despised it. Still, she climbed down from the fence and stood nervously waiting as he slowly and deliberately walked his sorrel jumper toward her. "How'd you like to learn to ride?" he asked, looking down at her, a smile curling his mouth, his yellow-flecked dark eyes like two tiger stones in the half-light.

"Now?"

"Right now."

Dismounting, he took her hand and led her into the stable where he untied a giant gray animal with huge doe-like eyes and a thick black mane, and lifted her onto its broad bare back. Her neatly pressed gingham dress had hitched up around her hips and she could feel the animal's unsettling warmth against the insides of her thighs. She dared not look down because the distance was more than her own height and reinforced her initial fear. Yet, terrified though she was, she managed to stay on as Henry led the animal by a rope into the field. A dense smell of horseflesh assaulted her nostrils. Instinctively she felt the horse was equally frightened. As soon as they reached the open air, he neighed and shook his head, almost causing her to lose her balance. She held on tenaciously, her arms wrapped tightly about his thick neck.

"Sit up straight," Henry ordered. "Let him know you're in control." Bessie Wallis stiffened and slowly relinquished her hold. Henry handed her the rope. "His name is Major. Tell him to go forward, and pat his neck."

She suddenly recalled hearing that Major was the most difficult horse in the stable and that Henry had not been able to get a saddle on his back, which explained why she was bareback. She glanced down at Henry. The smirk on his face shot a flash of fury through her. "Too scared to ride him, Moo? Want me to help you off?" he asked.

"G-g-go on, Major," she commanded the horse, who moved slowly forward.

"If you're frightened he'll know it," Henry warned in a shrill voice.

"I'm not frightened! I'm not!" she lied.

"You will be!" he shouted. At that moment he gave Major a resounding crack on the right flank with his riding crop. The horse bolted, front legs up, head high into the afternoon dusk.

She pulled the rope about Major's neck and then grabbed his coarse mane and yanked it, meaning to give the animal a command to stop, but instead he jolted forward. She hung on for about ten seconds, then lost her hold and fell, luckily, into a ditch, which seemed to have caught and cradled her in such a way as to protect her from serious injury. She was not sure how long she lay there unable to move, too terrified of discovering all her bones were broken; but as soon as she saw Henry's leering face above her, his hand extended to help her out, she grabbed hold of him and pulled herself to her feet. Except for bloodied elbows and knees, she was unharmed.

"I thought you would have the sense to ask for help," he said, his voice revealing a sincere quality of concern.

"I never was frightened," she replied in fury. "And if you can't treat your animals better than that you don't deserve them!"

She stalked back across the field as fast and straight as her bruised body permitted, never glancing over her shoulder to see if Henry was following. The next morning she came down for prayer and refused to wince or cry out as she knelt. Henry smiled kindly at her. To her amazement she realized she now possessed a certain power over him. She assumed he thought she would complain to his parents, but she did not. She enjoyed the conspiratorial aspect of the situation. Although she knew she should have hated or feared Henry for what he had done, on the contrary, she found his presence even more exciting than before. But she no longer went out behind the stables in the afternoon to watch him jump, an omission that seemed to distress him.

"I missed you today," he would say. She never replied, nor let him know that she had been watching him stealthily from behind the lace curtains of the dormer windows of her third-floor bedroom.

* * *

As a treat before her daughter's departure to boarding school that autumn, Alice had taken her to the nickelodeon. The movie she saw had something to do with an Arab sheikh, and as she accustomed her eyes to the flickering movements of the players, she found herself able to superimpose Henry's image on the leading actor as he swept a young woman (curiously wearing a garden frock in the desert) onto the back of his camel.

Now, all she had to do to create an erotic phantasmagoria was to close her eyes and concentrate hard on something she remembered. Alice partially undressed and framed by the firelight with Mr. Rasin leaning over her would become Henry and herself. And she would open her eyes in alarm when, in another "vision," Henry fell into the ditch on top of her instead of pulling her out. *Sex* was not a word she had ever heard spoken, although she had seen it printed several times in one of the newspaper tabloids Mr. Rasin read. Still, intuitively, she knew these were sexual fantasies that she conjured up and that if anyone at all, even her new best friend Mary Kirk, was to learn of them, she would become a social outcast as she had at Arundel.

Oldfields housed forty girls between the ages of twelve and seventeen. It had an impeccable record for conducting its charges across the threshold of adolescence. The school was strictly run by the Reverend McCulloch and his puritanical sister, Anna G. McCulloch, Miss Nan to her pupils. Advanced in years, Miss Nan wore her iron-gray hair brushed into a severe pompadour held in place by several long-toothed black tortoise combs. Her black dresses were made of bombazine, a rough-textured heavy cotton fabric that exuded a vinegarish odor. Tall, angular and precise of movement and speech, she reigned inflexibly over her teaching staff and their students.

A rule existed for almost everything and infractions were dealt with harshly. Excluding the regular school holidays, the girls were allowed only two weekends at home during the entire school year. Even a death in the family could not alter this. Except for one's relatives, there was to be no exchange of letters with anyone of the opposite sex.

A gray stone, ivy-covered parish church built in 1782 was nestled into a gentle curve on a grassy slope at the rear of the extensive grounds and was reached by a gracefully winding path of old brick that circled the apple orchard. The Reverend McCulloch strove to inject a reverence for God in the same autocratic fashion as his sister. Daily, before dawn and breakfast, the girls were marched down to the chapel for lengthy prayers; and evenings, after supper, hymns were sung until the nine o'clock bell to retire rang out. Sundays were devoted almost fully to instilling in the girls "the obligations of the Christian faith."

Yet, despite all its stricture and restraints, Bessie Wallis quickly came to like her life at Oldfields. For one thing there was the grandeur of the school itself, which had once been the stately home of Maryland aristocrats. Set on the crest of the highest hill in the county, it commanded lordly views over all below it. Except for the new addition of a dormitory wing, the main house had been kept architecturally pristine. The auditorium had been the original ballroom, very impressive, with French doors that opened on to terraces on three sides and a chandelier of French-cut crystal weighing several hundred pounds. On sun-filled days the refractions from the glass were so dazzling that they caused eyes to tear.

Portraits of the former owners hung on the walls of the magnificent double stairway and the marble balustrades were topped by baroque carved griffins which were said to have been part of their family crest. Some books on the area claimed the original owners of Oldfields were descended from two English kings.

"So am I," Bessie Wallis confided to Mary Kirk. And once, when she caught her finger on the corner of her gymnasium locker she cried out, "Oh! I'm bleeding blue blood!," and she and Mary dissolved into uncontrollable laughter.

She insisted that Mary and the other girls call her Wallis, although Miss Nan, the Reverend McCulloch and the teaching staff still referred to her as Bessie Wallis. But Henry's demeaning nickname, "Moo," had made her feel that Bessie did indeed sound like a cow's name. Then, too, *Wallis* appealed to her. There were in fact, two other Bessies at Oldfields, many

Marys, Sarahs, Janes, Susans, Patricias and Annes—but she was the only Wallis.

Mary Kirk quickly became her confidante. When they had met, Wallis instantly recalled the magnificent Kirk silver displayed in her grandmother's dining room. The Kirks had been a revered, affluent family of master silversmiths for generations. Mary was the daughter of one of the heirs and directors, enough reason for the newly self-christened Wallis to single her out. Wallis had by now tasted several modes of life—and it was the gracious and luxurious Wakefield Manor in which she felt the happiest. The Kirks had old money like the Warfields, but their name appeared consistently in the Baltimore society columns as hosts at grand parties given in what was described as their "baronial mansion."

A normally shy youngster, led at home by her older siblings and a charismatic mother, Mary followed Wallis enthusiastically, reveling in her ingenuity and audacity. Only Wallis could have shown the girls in her dormitory how to play the absolutely forbidden game of stud poker by moonlight after lights out.

The school sports uniform consisted of middy tops, green serge bloomers, while ribbed-cotton stockings and green and white "sweat bands" worn on the forehead and meant to keep the girls' long hair in place. To her roommates' delight, Wallis would slip a long chicken feather, taken surreptitiously from the refuse in the back kitchen, beneath the band. "Besides two kings, I am also descended from an Indian princess," she avowed, echoing her cousin Anne's claim.

To the blue-eyed, freckle-faced, chubby Mary Kirk, Wallis was the very height of sophistication. Wallis had, in fact, matured considerably over the summer. Slim, almost willowy, she had a special grace not usually associated with adolescence. She loved to dance and was the best student in her eurythmics class. Her violet eyes, fair skin and dark hair gave her an exotic look, considerably older than thirteen, a fact that local teenage village boys were quick to note. During each of the few school excursions to Belmore's Sweet Shoppe in town, Wallis received covertly delivered, impassioned letters from several youths as she sipped a cherry phosphate at the soda fountain. Inevitably, they asked her to meet them, and she managed several times to do so.

She told Mary the truth, that she only exchanged a few words in the apple orchard with these village boys, adding: "People should be allowed to see who they want."

Mary admired her friend's courage and principle, but some of the other girls now called Wallis "fast." Among the boys, she was known as a tease and each one elaborated on reality to make it appear that he had succeeded in: holding her hand (which she swiftly withdrew), kissing her cheek (Wallis had pushed him over backward), or receiving a torrid love letter (the only letter sent by Wallis read: "I would burn in hell before kissing *you*!").

At times she believed she would rather be Mary Kirk than anyone else in the world: Mary was rich and had both her parents and the Kirks were an integral part of Baltimore society. In addition, Mary possessed a natural warmth and sincerity that made everyone—students, teachers, even the McCullochs—like her. But then, Wallis would recall with great pleasure the look in Henry's eyes when she refused to be terrorized and the envy displayed by her roommates when she defied Miss Nan's rules and slipped out to the apple orchard to meet a young admirer.

At heart she knew she was a maverick. But understanding only made her agonize more. For she realized that her mother's indiscretions would—as long as Baltimore was her home—keep her from ever entering on equal footing the world Mary Kirk was born into. It was a reality she could never accept.

6

As Wallis sat alone in her dormitory room waiting for Miss Nan to escort her back to Baltimore, she recalled the childhood game, find-the-penny, she used to play with her mother. Alice would close her eyes while her daughter tiptoed cautiously about the front parlor searching for a secret hiding place for the coin. Wallis's favorite spots were such small dark recesses as the hollow center of china figurines or underneath the candle snuffer on the mantel. If, when her mother opened her eyes, she could not, after six guesses, say where the shiny copper penny was hidden, it was hers.

The playing of the game was exhilarating, but it also contained an element of dread for the child, who did not want the penny to be found—not so it would be hers, but so that it might remain in dark seclusion where she alone knew its refuge. She felt that way now about her real feelings, wanting desperately to keep them safely hidden, deep inside herself. Miss Nan was the last person to whom she wished them exposed.

The pleasures of her third year at Oldfields had been overshadowed from the start of the term by "family problems." Mr. Rasin had been forced to sell the Biddle Street residence and most of its contents to cover his gambling debts, and he and Alice had moved ignominiously into a rooming house near the boardwalk in Atlantic City, ostensibly for the benefits of the good sea air since Mr. Rasin had not been well.

Wallis sensed what was indeed the truth: that her mother's cheerful letters were a cover and the move had been made to avoid their creditors. She could not bear the idea of Alice confined to someone's back room. To add to her unhappiness came the disturbing news that Aunt Bessie had to sell her home and was acting as the paid companion of a rich Washington widow, Mrs. Griselle Smith. These changes in family status had a very great effect on the ambitious sixteen-year-old girl whose aspirations were now concentrated on her own future. The day was drawing nearer to the time of her debut and proposed entry into Baltimore society. Cousin Corrine had found a husband at nineteen, but how would she ever find a suitable man in three years if things continued to go so badly?

Then, the day before the Easter break, Miss Nan had called her out of the classroom and to her office, where, with unaccustomed compassion and over a cup of tea served in Miss Nan's best fragile bone-china cups, she was told that Mr. Rasin had died and that her mother was bringing her stepfather's body back to Baltimore for the funeral. In view of the tragic situation, Miss Nan would be accompanying her to Baltimore where she was to be met at the train station by a family representative. Her stepfather's death did not immediately seem real to Wallis. Perversely, all she could think about at that moment was how obliging it was of Mr. Rasin to die at school recess.

Having Miss Nan as a chaperone on her short journey meant she was the last girl to leave school, all the others having departed directly after breakfast. The emptiness and silence of a room always brimming with girlish laughter and clutter was unsettling. As though to fill the void, she conjured up an image of Mr. Rasin, recalling the first time she had ever seen his robust face and massive figure as he took giant strides across the hotel lobby where she and Alice had stopped for hot chocolate. She knew that her stepfather had not been the most respected of men, and that he had brought her mother as much grief as happiness, but somehow her memories of him were warm and loving.

She had, she realized, cared for Mr. Rasin to a degree she could never feel for Uncle Sol. That was not something she would tell anyone. "I'm a self-centered, terrible person," she thought with alarm. "I don't want anyone to know that I think Mr. Rasin was a kind, good person because they might think less of me!" Tears rose in her eyes, but when Miss Nan entered the long narrow room with its two rows of neatly made-up beds a few moments later, she felt more terrified than unhappy.

Standing in the blare of light from the strong midday sun, the principal's countenance could not be clearly seen. But with her shrunken face and long black garments she seemed to Wallis to be a messenger of death sent to collect her and escort her to hell.

Ellie met them at the station and took Wallis to the house of one of Mr. Rasin's sisters. Wallis could not contain her happiness at seeing the aging black woman and clung to her in the cab as she had done once before as a small child when being delivered to her mother. Because Alice could no longer afford to employ her, Ellie had been forced to accept day jobs which took a great deal more out of her. "Dey's 'spect a week's wo'k in one day," she told Wallis, "but ah ain't los' mah house an', chile, yo' ain't too big ta come ta Ellie iffen yo' feel de mis'ry bad, unnerstan? 'Cou'se, yo' mama, she be needin' cheerin' up ruther'n leavin' be, an' dat yo' am big 'nuff ta unnerstan', too!"

She paid the cab driver with some change she had tied up in a black hankie. "It am powahful bad luck fah a colored person ta see a dead white man on Sunday," she said as she stood with Wallis on the front stoop of their destination. The whites of her eyes were veined with red. She looked as if she might burst into tears. It suddenly occurred to Wallis that she had never seen Ellie cry. "Now yo' be good ta yuh mama, heah? Dat poor lit'l thing gwine need someone." She rang the doorbell. As soon as the handle of the door could be heard turning, she left Wallis without looking back and hurried off down the street in the direction of the trolley stop.

A maid showed Wallis into a dark front room and then quickly withdrew. The curtains were drawn and there was only the light of two candles burning on the mantel. At first Wallis thought she was alone. Then, in a far corner, a shadow moved.

"Darlin', is that you?" her mother asked in a trembling voice.

"Yes, Mama," she replied.

Swathed in a black crepe veil that reached her knees, Alice glided phantom-like toward her. As Wallis strained her eyes to accustom them to the blackness, a sound of muffled weeping made her turn toward the other side of the room. There, on a window seat, all in a row before the drawn blinds, she could make out three more shapeless shadows; Mr. Rasin's sisters, draped alike in heavy black veils and sobbing softly in unison.

Her mother's arms were now about her and after a tearful greeting they made their way out of the suffocating darkness to the door that led to a back parlor: a room, Wallis was grateful to find, with open blinds that allowed a gentle twilight to filter in.

Alice appeared so tragic in her widow's weeds that Wallis was shaken. "Oh, Mama," she cried and held her in her arms in a rare reversal of roles. A few moments later they had both controlled their emotions sufficiently to talk.

"We were married such a few years," Alice said as she lowered herself stiffly into a Gothic-shaped chair near the window. It was still difficult for Wallis to see her mother's face through the scrim of black gauze and she concentrated on Alice's delicate, pale white hands which were clasped gracefully in an attitude of prayer. "I had not thought that it was possible to hurt so much," she sighed.

Wallis was not sure if her mother meant she was suffering from Mr. Rasin's death or his actions before he died, but she thought better of questioning her.

"I'll have to return to Atlantic City to settle matters there. Not that there is much left to pack up. I think you should know that I made a premarital agreement with Mr. Rasin's family. I don't get anythin' but the corpse an' the law doesn't allow me to keep that more than three days. Free's annuity goes back into the family trust. I was to have the house an' furnishin's. But, of course, that's all gone. We have nothin', darlin', nothin'. I'm sorry." At last, Alice lifted the veil and the sadness in that fragile and beautiful face moved Wallis once again to tears.

"What's this?" Alice asked with a small uneasy flickering smile. "Now, you remembah you're a Warfield, positive an' clear. An' I'll make sure that your Uncle Sol nevah forgets it. So you don't have to worry about what's goin' to happen to you. You'll graduate Oldfields *an'* you'll have a debut jus' like I promised."

"But what about you?" Wallis asked. "What are you going to do?"

"I'm goin' to stay at Aunt Bessie's apartment in Washington. It's a trifle small for the two of us, but Aunt Bessie plans to take a European tour with Mrs. Smith an' so I shall have it to myself for the time it takes for me to re-situate."

Wallis stared at her mother, unable to comment. Suddenly she had become aware that with Free Rasin's death her life, as well as that of her mother, threatened to be even more insecure.

After the funeral, Wallis stayed with her grandmother until it was time to return to Oldfields. Uncle Sol was in New York, where, she was told, he now kept an apartment to use for his increasing trips to that city on bank business. Mrs. Warfield was bedridden with arthritis and was growing senile. Often she thought Wallis was Alice and was cold and cutting in her remarks and manner. Once she called her a "whore and harlot," another time, "Montague trash." Would the war between the Warfields and the Montagues never end? Wallis wondered.

The first weeks following Free Rasin's death and funeral were difficult, but soon Wallis put the tragedy behind her to once again become the school daredevil. She spent the summer with Corrine in her lovely home on Boston's North Shore, near to where her husband, Henry, was stationed as an officer. Boys were constantly on her mind and Corrine encouraged her interest. "No girl can be too popular, you jus' remembah that," she would wink when a young man came by to visit.

She loved parties and recalling Miss Merrie's advice did all she could to *shine*. She had an easy way that young men liked, a peppery tongue that made people laugh, and she knew all the latest dance steps. Corrine taught her how to play bridge and gave her daily lectures on the difference between fashion and style. The latter, Corrine insisted, was what one sought to achieve. Style made the woman stand out; fashion, the clothes.

Aunt Bessie was still traveling in Europe and Wallis corresponded religiously, prodding her for full details about everything she saw and everyone she met. She asked for rotogravure pictures of all the great European society events, kept them in a scrapbook and became familiar with the participants' names, titles and accomplishments. Her dream, she confided to Aunt Bessie in a letter, was to one day tour the Continent with her. Her aunt wrote back that she was saving money for that very purpose.

"After my graduation, I plan to go with my aunt, Mrs. Merryman, to Paris," she would say to a young admirer. "My aunt knows all the best people there." She never added that Bessie was a paid companion and that most of her connections were through her affluent employer. The proposed "grand tour" was also somewhat in the far distant future because of the state of Aunt Bessie's finances. For her aunt had generously turned over her savings to Alice to enable her to refurbish a boardinghouse in Washington to a standard suitable to rent rooms to government employees.

A further blow came in February. Grandmother Warfield died, leaving most of her large fortune to Sol and the church. Her other children and grandchildren (with the exception of Wallis) received trusts of $25,000 each. Wallis was willed the smaller sum of $5,000 and a pair of diamond and tortoise combs, a tintype of Teackle Wallis Warfield and her grandmother's Bible with the purple ribbon marker. To make matters worse, the $5,000 would not come to her until her twenty-first birthday. It was not that her grandmother thought less of her, Sol explained, but that she feared Alice would end up the beneficiary.

The unfairness of the will cut deeply. She had truly loved the old woman and had spent more time with her and under her roof than any of her Warfield cousins had, and she had always been led to believe she would benefit equally with them. The disappointment was severe and as the Easter holiday approached again, her grandmother's death proved to deprive her of more than a just share of the inheritance. With only a bachelor uncle in residence, no longer was it proper for her to stay at Preston Street. Yet to go to her mother's boardinghouse or remain alone in Aunt Bessie's small apartment was equally unfitting. Mary came to her rescue and Wallis was invited to spend her school recess with the Kirks.

Mrs. Kirk was a handsome woman who bore a striking resemblance to the recently crowned Queen Mary of England. Like her, she had a great passion for jewels. Sitting across from Mrs. Kirk in the room called the "grand salon" and being served afternoon tea from an elegant Kirk silver urn, Wallis wondered if Buckingham Palace could possibly be any more impressive, or Queen Mary more regal. Her hostess, her gray hair swept up in an elaborate hairdo, was dressed in soft blue lace. Five strands of creamy, perfect pearls caressed her long neck, and a pear-shaped diamond, the largest Wallis had ever seen, glittered blindingly in the light as she poured the tea.

"Mary tells me you have been mos' kind to her at school," she said, her Southern heritage apparent in her voice. They were having tea alone because Mary was being fitted for some new reading glasses. Wallis rather suspected that Mrs. Kirk had arranged the appointment so that she could speak privately with her, but about what, baffled her.

"It's not a case of being kind. Mary is my best friend."

"I'm sure she would be mos' pleased to heah that. Good friends are not easy to come by." She smiled benevolently and then leaned slightly forward, her china-blue eyes fastened on Wallis. "In fact, that is why I am so happy that we can have these few moments together. You see, I worry quite a bit about Mary?"

"Goodness gracious, why?" Wallis asked. The terrible thought flashed in her head that perhaps her friend was suffering from an incurable disease and had not yet been told the tragic news.

"Well, Mary is rather *impressionable,*" Mrs. Kirk explained.

The stress Mrs. Kirk put on this last word alerted Wallis to approaching danger and she carefully set down her teacup and saucer. She needed just a moment or two to gather her forces. "Have you heard stories about me that have displeased you, Mrs. Kirk?" she asked, having decided to take a bold approach.

"*Displeased* is too strong a word. Let us say some of the things Mary tells me about your activities are *disconcerting*. She seems to find it mos' admirable that you don't abide school rules, that you meet boys secretly and that you have been known to smoke a cigarette. Now, I attended boarding school myself once, and I understand the need to buck authority from time to time, to assert one's own personality, so to speak."

A fire blazed in the marble hearth. Wallis was wearing her long-sleeved navy-blue-wool sailor dress; yet a sudden chill stabbed at her. She felt awkward and curiously aware of the largeness of her hands and the slim gracefulness of Mrs. Kirk's as her hostess refilled the teacups. Wallis surreptitiously pushed her hands behind her in an effort to conceal them, a movement that also served to extend and brace her body so that she was at once eye to eye with the swan-like Mrs. Kirk.

"But you see," the woman continued, "one has to learn early wheah to draw the line. Back orchards and village boys are quite *common*—and I chose that word uneasily. I don't mean to imply that *you* are common, just your actions. You are, after all, a Warfield, an ancestry to be proud of. I remembah meetin' old Gen'ral Henry Warfield when I was a child. What a distinguished man! And your grandmother—a fine woman. How distressed we all were to heah of her passin'. But I digress—"

"Village boys, you were saying—" Wallis reminded her, a hard edge to her voice.

Mrs. Kirk flushed. Her disapproval of her young guest's deliberate prodding was revealed by a narrowing of her nostrils, followed by a small sharp intake of breath. It did not pass by Wallis unnoticed. "Well, the point is that my Mary is in awe of you and your daring. Don't misunderstand. I do think spunkiness is an admirable trait but I would not like to see my daughter take a false step that could damage her reputation in any way."

Wallis dug her clenched fists into the back of the chair. Her face, fixed in an expression of attention, did not reflect her rising anger and bitter feelings at being placed in this unjust and humiliating situation.

"Mrs. Kirk, did you invite me here for the recess to tell me this?" she asked in a controlled voice.

"No, no, of course not. Mary did so want you to come and it is so nice to see her happy and spirited. She has always been such a shy, introverted girl. But I also thought we might, as indeed we have, find a few private moments to—well, exchange some ideahs."

Not that I've been allowed to express my opinion! Wallis thought. She was aware, as she knew Mrs. Kirk was, that she had no place else to stay in Baltimore for the Easter holiday if she left the Kirks'. "Mrs. Kirk," she said as she rose to her feet, "I'd like to be excused."

"I'm terribly sorry if I've hurt your feelings. I know what it's like to get your feelings hurt," her hostess apologized.

"Oh, for God's sake!" Wallis exploded.

"There's no need to swear."

"I'm not swearing, although I promise you I could if I chose to. I just had to say something—*shocking*—to stop you from going on so. I just think you are being unfair to Mary, talking to me behind her back, making her seem such a cream puff. I've been listening to you go on about how gullible and soft-bellied she is and it's made me so embarrassed that you think so little of your daughter, I wanted to stop you, that's all. Now, please, excuse me." She turned and moved quickly to the door.

"Bessie Wallis—" Mrs. Kirk called out imperiously.

Wallis paused, her hand on the heavy brass knob.

"You are a mos' remarkable girl and I think Mary is indeed lucky to count you as a friend," she said, in a manner that indicated Wallis had won this round but this round *only*.

"But you must understand that as her mother, I feel responsible for her best interests. You have obviously—shall we say—matured faster than Mary and your background has not prepared you for restraint. I merely want you to *recognize* the difference that exists between you and Mary and to"—she paused in her search for the right words—"to ask you to *distance* yourself accordingly."

Wallis opened the door and left the grand salon without a word. What distressed her most had been the element of scornful rejection implicit in Mrs. Kirk's words. Wallis had endured much in her young life, but she had never had to confront scorn. The irony was that she had so wanted to make a keen impression on Mary's mother, who was such a strong social force in Baltimore. It did not help that she now considered her a prig and a snob who had made up her mind that her daughter's friend was a bad influence even before inviting Wallis to be a guest in her home, obviously with the sole intention of confronting her privately.

She might have told Mrs. Kirk that though she did enjoy shocking people she had never truly misbehaved. But no one as self-righteous and socially secure as Mrs. Kirk would have understood her desperate need to *shine* (as Miss Merrie had advised) and to stand out from the crowd. Poor puddling Mary, shallow and silly as she was, shared the very same desires and that was what had sealed their friendship. At school and away from her mother, Mary felt rudderless. Wallis had given her direction and pride in being the best friend of the most outrageous girl in their class.

"It's so unjust! So mean!" Wallis cried once she was safely behind the locked door of her room. She vented her anger by pummeling the bed pillow. Intuitively she knew what Mary's mother would never admit—that Mrs. Kirk was to blame for her daughter's weakness. Mary was always telling Wallis that, no matter what she did, she never seemed to please her mother who was forever reminding her, in what she thought were subtle ways, that she was not as pretty, as clever or as promising as her older sisters, who were both now married to suitable husbands. Wallis strongly suspected Mrs. Kirk spoke the truth. Perhaps she even recognized Wallis's lack of real affection for Mary and the questionable motives for her side of the friendship. Still, that did not excuse her perfectly awful, snobbish behavior.

"She'll be sorry one day," she sobbed into the pillow she now held close to her body. The threat was empty. After all, whatever could she, Wallis Warfield, do that could affect Mrs. Kirk's life? Nothing.

Wallis stumbled into the bathroom and applied a cold washcloth to her eyes to make sure they would not look red or puffed. That night when she dressed for dinner she slicked back her hair and twisted it into a bun, securing it with her grandmother's tortoise and diamond combs. This would be the first time she had worn them. Alice had suggested she put them away for a year or two at least since diamonds were not appropriate to be worn by anyone quite so young.

"Just the trick," she grinned, as she studied her image. Her grandmother's recent death would have called for her to wear dark colors. Instead, she had chosen the jade-silk dress that had once belonged to Corrine, and which perhaps fitted her a bit too sleekly, but no one could say it did not become her.

Mary met her in the upstairs hallway and they descended the wide, curing central staircase together. "Oh, Wallis," Mary gasped. "Mother will simply *die* when she sees you!" She giggled approvingly and linked her plump arm through her friend's.

Shortly after the Easter holiday Wallis received a letter informing her that she was one of over six hundred young women whose names had been submitted to the Cotillion Board. Only forty-seven girls would be approved and it would be six months before their names would appear on a formal invitation. Between graduation in June and Thanksgiving, all Wallis could think about was being one of those chosen. Making one's debut at the Cotillion not only lent a girl a certain cachet; if she did not appear there, her future in Baltimore society and her chances of making an advantageous marriage were considered ruined. Mothers were known to whisk their daughters immediately off to Europe if a Cotillion invitation was not forthcoming, their only alternative to ruin seeming to be a large dowry to attract an impoverished foreign nobleman.

The Cotillion operated like any private club. Young men who wished to join it had to be proposed and voted upon by older members, who also had the right to submit the names of prospective debutantes to the Cotillion's Board of Governors, who eventually made the final selection. Family background counted far more than wealth and a girl's deportment overshadowed her ability to charm. That was not to say that money or looks did not matter, simply that they were not given top priority except in a close decision.

Aunt Bessie had always envisioned the Bachelors' Cotillion as the final goal for her niece and she never allowed Alice to forget what she considered her sister's duty to her only daughter. Sol Warfield was a Cotillion member; at Bessie's prodding, Alice wrote and asked him to submit Wallis's name. He replied that he did not feel a proper period of mourning for her grandmother had transpired. Aunt Bessie, refusing to put off her niece's debut, importuned a distant male Merryman relative and Wallis's name was added to the list. Immediately after this occurred, Wallis received a long letter from her aunt.

> *Dear Child—what wonderful news! Your mother and I celebrated with a bottle of French champagne, given us by Mrs. Smith, who also wants to extend her congratulations. You must be flying high and I do not want to say anything that might deflate your spirits. But you must remember that even though your name has been placed on the list, we have not yet reached our goal. There remains a great deal more to accomplish before that time comes. So please heed carefully what I have to say.*
>
> *Firstly, do try to be the best girl ever. Hold your tongue no matter how provoked you may be. Things have a way of being exaggerated and ears are* everywhere.
>
> *Although the Cotillion is not until Christmas, and invitations of those lucky girls who are chosen do not go out until November, a proper wardrobe must be put to-*

gether, fitted and ready in the event (and of course it shall *happen) that you are selected.*

I cannot see how you could manage this on less than $1,000 and as you know neither I or your mother has anywhere near this amount left in savings (although I could manage $200 if necessary). There are only three other people who I think could be helpful: Sol, Corrine and Cousin Lelia.

Corrine (and don't breathe a word of this) is having some marital problems, so I think it best not to burden her further at this time (other than a request to borrow some pearls and that lovely sapphire necklace and earring set which would so beautifully set off your own strong coloring). Cousin Lelia's new marriage to Major Barnett has added to her fortunes and I doubt if she would miss the money. But as she is the only person I can think of who could afford to pay the expenses usually borne by a sponsor (a debut party for one thing), I do not think we should ask her to also advance you money for a wardrobe.

That leaves your Uncle Sol whose opinions you already know. But I have prevailed upon your mother, who has won him over before with even greater obstacles in her path, to try again. She has written such a letter and will let you know as soon as he replies. So all we can do is wait on that score.

Poor darling! Mother and I hate to have to involve you in all these boring financial details. But it is best you know the true situation and for you to understand at the same time that we both feel it of the utmost importance for your future for you to do as we ask. We will be in close touch.

How nice Mary Kirk also made the list. Did you ever doubt she would?—All my love, Aunt Bessie.

A week later, Wallis received a short note from Alice.

My Darling Girl, I can't believe that life has chosen to be so cruel to you, who have always been such a loving child and daughter. Uncle Sol flatly refuses to have anything to do with your debut if it is scheduled for this December. This is all terribly dispiriting. But Aunt Bessie says not to give up hope. She has yet another plan. All this makes me feel so helpless and guilty. Your loving Mother.

P.S. Uncle Sol is spending the month of June in New York. He has an apartment in a beautiful building at 623 Park Avenue. Perhaps if you *write him, you could be more persuasive.*

Not only was her future in society in doubt, Wallis had no idea where she would go after her graduation in June. Corrine's husband had just been transferred and they were in the throes of moving to Pensacola, Florida. She was unlikely to receive an invitation to Wakefield Manor from Cousin Lelia who had so recently remarried. Pot Spring without Cousin Henry, who was in England for the summer, was too desolate an idea to even consider, and she did not want to spend the time in her mother's Washington boardinghouse.

After putting a great deal of thought into the matter, she decided on what she thought was a grand scheme: She would go to New York and ask Uncle Sol to help her find a summer job, perhaps as receptionist in the New York branch of his bank. The Barbizon Hotel for Women would be an acceptable place for her to stay. She was positive she could talk Uncle Sol into advancing her the funds for such a practical plan.

She was the only girl at her graduation not represented by a family member. Mrs. Smith had decided to leave early for her summer home in Newport and Aunt Bessie was obliged to accompany her. Alice could find no one to look after her boardinghouse. Uncle Sol remained in New York but remembered with a lovely bouquet of roses. She had lied to Mary and told her the card that had accompanied them was signed "a secret admirer." In Mary's eyes this made Wallis the most romantic and lucky graduate in their class. But, until the hour before her final departure from Oldfields, she did not know where she was to go. Alice had kept a small back room in her boardinghouse available for her. Aunt Bessie had immediately rejected this idea as "simply unacceptable for a young woman about to make her entry into Baltimore society."

In truth, Wallis was no longer a resident of Baltimore. For that matter she had no residency anywhere. Whatever she had accumulated in possessions during her years at Oldfields had been sent the day before graduation c/o the station master's office at Baltimore Depot.

Aunt Bessie had written to several family members who, she assured her niece, "are certain to have your interest at heart." No one had come forward with an invitation for Wallis to spend the summer with them. It looked very much as if she would have to redirect her suitcases to Washington after all.

"Damn," she thought, "why on earth did Mama sign a premarital agreement!" Her self-centeredness instantly struck her. Whether Alice lived in a mansion or ran a boardinghouse, she was her mother and she loved her. Of course, she would not have loved her *less* if Mr. Rasin had left her well provided for and with the Biddle Street house still in her possession.

7

Pinned to the collar of Wallis's pale-yellow graduation suit was her mother's present: an antique, blue-enameled lapel watch with a delicate diamond bow. She felt very smart, indeed, seated in the first-class compartment of the early morning New York City *Commuter Express* with a ticket purchased from her own savings. At the last moment Cousin Lelia had extended an invitation for her to spend the summer at Wakefield Manor. Wallis had sent her acceptance by return telegram, adding that she would arrive a day late since she had already planned a visit with Mary Kirk in Baltimore. In turn, she asked Miss Nan if she could remain for the night at Oldfields because her family was delayed in Washington.

The ease with which she had pulled off her deception greatly pleased her. Opposite her in the compartment were two ladies who told her they were embarking that very evening for a summer abroad.

"Are you visiting family in New York?" asked the more affluent-looking woman as she removed an enormous straw hat mounded with elaborate bunches of artificial cherries and placed it on her considerable lap.

"My uncle, Mr. Solomon Warfield," she replied.

The second woman (whom Wallis instantly recognized as

the paid companion of the first, for she was dealing with the expensive luggage and had taken the seat away from the window with a touch of deference) picked up on the mention of Sol's name. "Oh," she cooed, "Mr. Warfield is most distinguished." She adjusted her glasses on the narrow bridge of her long nose. "I do hope he has not moved away from Baltimore."

"No, but he keeps a well-staffed apartment on Park Avenue for business reasons. I'm going to help him host a dinner for the mayor," she lied with a smile, and then opened the copy of Upton Sinclair's once-controversial book, *The Jungle,* that she had brought with her. "Mr. Sinclair is my cousin," she said, before seeming to immerse herself in the text. This, in fact, was the truth. Sinclair was Alice's first cousin, the son of her mother's sister, and Wallis had met him once as a child when he visited Alice on Biddle Street.

Her traveling companions duly impressed, she settled back into the faded red-plush train seat and closed her eyes, the opened book raised to conceal her face. The privacy allowed her to give herself over to thoughts of what was before her. She was confident that everything had been taken into consideration, even the possibility that Uncle Sol might be so furious that she had come to New York on her own that he would refuse to listen to her scheme. But if this did occur, she would have lost nothing more than a day in New York.

"Nothing ventured, nothing gained," Wallis had decided. "Must have, can get," Alice would have added, knowing her daughter well.

The *Commuter* was scheduled to arrive at 9:05 A.M. at Pennsylvania Station. By 9:30 she would be at Uncle Sol's apartment. If he had already left for his bank's office in the city, she would ring him there and make an appointment for lunch. Recalling her Uncle Sol's repeated assistance to her mother through the years bolstered Wallis's confidence. Forgotten in her enthusiasm was the number of times her uncle had refused to help.

"He won't say no! He won't say no!" she repeated to herself.

"Were you saying something, dear?" the corpulent lady with the fruited hat asked.

"Trains aren't what they once were," Wallis sighed enigmatically. "Just look at the shabby upholstery of these seats."

"She's quite right," the woman's lean companion chimed in and, running her hand along a frayed edge of the armrest, set her prim mouth into a hard line of disapproval.

As soon as Wallis entered the imposing lobby at 623 Park Avenue, her childhood discomfort at an impending confrontation with her uncle returned. She had twice visited New York with Alice and they had lunched at the glamorous neighboring Delmonico's with its gilt-framed mirrors, bright-green plush carpets and massive floral displays. The contrast was extraordinary. The reception area of this building evoked the ambience of an expensive but staid gentleman's club. Walls were paneled in dark mahogany. Shiny brass spittoons monitored the corners. In lieu of flowers, two enormous rubber plants stood in giant wrought-iron stands on either side of the double front door.

"Can I be of any assistance, miss?" the concierge, a touch of Ireland in his voice, asked as she approached his desk.

"I've come to see Mr. Solomon Warfield," she said.

The man's round, ruddy face was inscrutable as he lifted the telephone receiver. "Who shall I say is calling?"

"Miss Warfield," Wallis replied smartly.

"A good morning, sir," the man said into the telephone. "It's Patrick at the front desk. A Miss Warfield is at the reception." He placed his hand over the mouthpiece. "Which Miss Warfield is it?" he inquired indifferently.

"Wallis," she replied, and then amended it with some irritation to "Bessie Wallis," for Uncle Sol might not recognize the shortened name.

"Miss Bessie Wallis Warfield, sir," the man repeated into the mouthpiece, then he turned the instrument toward her and handed her the receiver. "He should like to have a word with you," he said.

"Bessie Wallis?"

"Yes, Uncle Sol?"

"Whatever are you doing *here*?"

He had phrased the question in a way that indicated his

annoyance that she was not only in New York but in the lobby of his apartment building.

"Well, I wanted to thank you for the lovely flowers for my graduation," she said none too brightly, "and"—now she began to gather her courage—"and talk to you about something of—immediate importance."

"Is your mother well?" he asked, concerned.

"Yes—quite."

"I've just awakened. Let me speak to the concierge. I'll have him let you up in five minutes or so."

The man had been standing at a discreet distance, but as soon as Wallis glanced up, he stepped in and took the telephone from her. "Yes, sir. Yes, of course, Mr. Warfield. Ummm. Yes, I quite understand." He disconnected. "There is a settee by the fireplace, miss," he suggested, a wide gap between two of his front teeth revealed as he smiled for the first time.

She positioned herself instead in a leather wing chair by the elevator and watched with fascination as the openwork wrought-iron cubicle ascended and then descended to disgorge its passengers: a well-dressed woman with two beribboned Pekinese, a gray-haired man with a silver-handled cane, and a uniformed nursemaid behind an enormous navy-blue pram, its sides too high to see the baby inside. Wallis studied her new lapel watch. Nearly ten minutes had passed. She was about to go over to the concierge and ask him to ring her uncle again when the elevator doors cranked open and a woman enveloped in a pervasive scent of jasmine stepped out and in front of her, for the moment barring her path.

Wallis was struck by the woman's exotic good looks: the alabaster-white skin, the heavy-lidded dark eyes and the thick black hair arranged in two great snake-like coils behind her ears. A large woman with an extremely curvaceous figure, she was dressed (really *costumed,* Wallis thought) most inappropriately for the hour in flowing red chiffon, an enormous black and white fringed Spanish shawl flung dramatically about her shoulders. As she neared the front door, she tightened the shawl about herself. Wallis moved over to a side window to watch as she entered a sleek black limousine with the help of a grandly uniformed chauffeur.

"Miss Warfield," the concierge called. "Mr. Warfield will see you now. The apartment is on the eighth floor, number Eight-C, that's C—for Carmen."

Carmen! Of course! Wallis thought. Even the concierge had caught the resemblance. The woman had, indeed, looked like an idealized version of Bizet's Carmen; in fact, she had reminded Wallis of the diva in the framed poster of that opera that Uncle Sol had hung in his study just after Grandmother Warfield's death.

Not until he opened the door and she entered the vestibule of his apartment, which held the distinct scent of jasmine, was she sure. The woman in red chiffon *was* the diva in the opera poster, Lydia Landamoor, and the only valid explanation of her leaving a bachelor's apartment in evening dress at half past nine in the morning was that she had stayed the night. This shocking thought put Wallis momentarily off balance. Only when she was seated opposite Uncle Sol in the elegant, antique-appointed sitting room was she able to regain her composure.

As she glanced around, she could scarcely believe what she saw. The walls were covered with photographs of actresses and opera singers, and all of those she could make out were affectionately autographed to her uncle by their donors. Something stirred in her memory—a much younger Uncle Sol sitting in the austere parlor at Preston Street raptly listening to operatic arias issuing from the horn of the Victrola.

Uncle Sol nervously pulled at his small mustache. He was attired in a black morning suit, his pocket handkerchief bordered in black. "Well, now, what is this all about?" he asked in his usual condescending manner.

Wallis forced her attention back to her uncle who was looking at her as if he had caught her cheating on a school test. His cold, hard gaze made it difficult for her to reply. Sun streamed from behind him through the trio of windows at the far end of the well-proportioned room. The brightness of the light hurt her eyes and she turned her glance away and around the room to the drinks tray on a handsome ivory-inlaid cabinet. The richness of the floral brocade that covered the upholstered pieces and the many ornate and fascinating bibelots led her to suspect that, aside from the picture gallery, her uncle had not decorated and furnished this room.

Only a moment had passed since he had spoken, but it had seemed much longer. "A curious thing just happened," she finally replied with a burst of new confidence, fully aware that she was not only evading his questions, but could be heading into dangerous waters. "I saw Lydia Landamoor in the lobby—the great Italian diva, you know? Well, of course you do, because you have a huge picture of her in your study on Preston Street. Does she live here?"

"Here?"

"In this building?"

"I'm sure I don't know." An expression that Wallis interpreted as indignation settled on his face. Uncle Sol had strong objections to his niece playing the inquisitor. She had started on the wrong foot and she knew she must step fast to avoid an unfortunate collision. "I haven't answered your question, have I?" she smiled.

"No, you have not."

"Well—" she began. His hostile attitude had unnerved her. It simply had not crossed her mind that Uncle Sol might be living a double life and that he expected his privacy to be rigidly honored by his family. She should, of course, have been more cautious. He had once loved her mother, that was true, but she had come to believe that by now he was a confirmed bachelor, no longer interested in women. Otherwise, why would he have devoted the past twelve years so entirely to his mother? Her grandmother's fortune was the answer. For, had it not, in the end, come to him?

So lost was she in her observations that she had forgotten for the moment why she was there. Her uncle waited impatiently for her to speak. She stood up, a new scheme brewing. "I'm afraid I suddenly feel rather—queasy," she said in a faint voice. "Could I have a glass of water, please?" She swayed, and then leaned down to grasp the armrest of her chair. He was instantly to his feet, his arm under her elbow as he eased her back into her seat before going over to the cocktail cabinet to pour her a glass of water from a silver carafe. "Drink it slowly," he ordered, when he returned with it.

She took a few obedient sips. "I've made you angry at me," she said in a vulnerable voice. "And I'm awfully sorry. I never would have come uninvited, except Mama insisted. She said I could not have lunch with my friend Mary Kirk and her mother in New York and not see you. That it would be terribly rude—hurting—and since they were shopping this morning, I decided not to go along and to come here instead. But I see that was wrong."

Her wide violet eyes flashed. "Mama would not have known—and, of course, I won't tell her—I mean about Madame Landamoor. I once saw a picture of her husband, a rich Scotsman, I believe, in the rotogravure." She placed her water glass on a Chinese dish on the table next to her and rose uneasily from her chair. "I'm all right now. I think I'd better go." He stopped her when she had taken only a few steps.

"Perhaps you should rest here for a while," he urged. "The building has restaurant service. I'll order breakfast for the two of us."

Wallis walked slowly over to the bank of windows and gazed out on the sun-hazy city skyline as he telephoned. Her plan to have him finance her summer in New York would have to be abandoned. But he might be very happy, indeed, to pay her *not* to be close at hand while he was conducting an affair. If Uncle Sol would advance her money for a debut wardrobe, she would not have to take a job. What she had in mind was blackmail, bold and simple. However, her guilt was quickly assuaged by the pure excitement she felt at attempting to outwit her uncle.

By the time the food had arrived and she was being served, she was talking animatedly. Wallis had a way of telling a story that brought it completely to life, tailoring her tales as she spoke to her audience's response. Confabulation, Henry had called it. She had looked up the word and quite liked the definition. She was not lying, merely embellishing the truth, making it more interesting to her listeners.

When her uncle inquired as to when she and Alice were last in New York, she immediately replied, "During the Christmas break. Mama came up from Washington and we had lunch at Delmonico's and then went shopping. She was still in mourning, of course, which got us the most *wonderful* table and the *very best* service. We decided she should always wear black when we really wanted an elegant lunch! Waiters spoke in hushed voices and the maître d' sent glazed fruits and bonbons to our table.

"After lunch," she continued, "we went to Tiffany's to look at the beautiful Christmas displays. Well, right in front of a counter where dozens of silver boxes were on show, Mama tripped on the edge of the carpet and landed flat on her back with a terrible *kerplunk*! She never cried out and just remained there perpendicular on the floor, her black veil askew as she looked up startled. Before I could even kneel down to see if she was injured, the floor manager materialized from somewhere and was by her side.

"'Madam,' he said, 'I am so sorry.' Meaning, of course, that she had fallen.

"'Oh, it's all right,' Mama answered. 'While I'm down here, though, you can fit me for a silver coffin.' Oh! the poor man! He didn't know what to say! There she was, shrouded in black, flat on the floor in front of a case full of silver boxes and small caskets. She could have been a rich eccentric or a madwoman, but he never could have believed she was a widow with a somewhat macabre sense of humor who preferred to be thought of as crazy rather than clumsy!"

"Was she hurt?" Sol asked with sincere concern.

"She was stunned, but, thank goodness, unharmed. We both helped her to her feet. And then the manager insisted on having the company limousine, a long, sleek black vehicle ('Good Lord! they're driving us in a hearse,' Mama said) take us back to the railway station." The fact that the incident actually had taken place in the five-and-dime before the ribbon counter, and that the store manager had merely hailed Alice a cab, did not seem to Wallis to alter the truthfulness of the story.

"Mama really is terribly brave. It's been very difficult for her since Mr. Rasin's death. He left her penniless. Well, of course, you know that."

"She never should have married that bounder," Uncle Sol commented, the red rising in his face.

"I suppose not," Wallis agreed, covering her own warm feelings about her late stepfather. She had decided that it was now time for her to introduce the matter she had come for. She crossed over to the window, her back to the room. "As I told you on the telephone from the lobby, I have something important to tell you," she confessed rather dramatically, tossing the words over her shoulder.

"Yes?"

She turned back to face him and took a deep breath before beginning. "I've been offered a position as a salesclerk in the silver department at Cartier's," she lied. "Mr. Kirk arranged it. I'm going this afternoon to talk to the personnel manager and then to the Barbizon Hotel for Women. Aunt Bessie says it's the safest place for a young, unmarried woman to stay and, of course, it's not far from here."

This was considerably more than a confabulation, but when she observed the nervous twitch that flickered across her uncle's face and the cloudy expression in his eyes, she pressed on.

"I don't quite know how I really feel about it," she sighed. "I suppose it will end any hopes that I might have had—well—for a place in society—although Mama doesn't think being a salesclerk is the end of the world for me. Still, it doesn't seem to be a fair exchange for all the sacrifices *everyone* has made to give me such a good education, does it?

"But, you see," she continued without giving him a chance to reply, "if Mama is penniless, then so am I, because Grandmama's inheritance won't come to me until I'm twenty-one, and that's a whole three years away. I don't see how I can remain in Baltimore, anyway. I have no home and no funds."

"I thought you were going to Wakefield Manor," he said, surprising her with this knowledge which she herself had gained only at her graduation. That meant either her mother or Aunt Bessie had been in touch with him.

"That could only be for the summer. It's almost completely unstaffed the rest of the year. I couldn't stay there alone. And even if it was possible, I would have to have *some* money on which to live. Well, anywhere that would be true. I really need to be in a city where I can get a job. Mama would have to sacrifice the needed income from my room if I went to live with her in Washington. That's why Aunt Bessie thought—"

"Bessie Merryman!" he exploded. "If Teddy Roosevelt had conscripted her, she could have defeated the Mexican Army single-handedly! For years she's been putting nonsense into your mother's and your heads!"

"Aunt Bessie thought," she continued unperturbed by his outburst, "that since you were in New York so frequently I would not feel so alone here, and that, perhaps, I could save up enough in a year's time—"

"Bessie Merryman thought that if you came here as you have, I could be coerced into giving you money for a debut this December. It was the height of irresponsibility and greedy ambition. That you have learned that I am but a mortal man with male appetites will, perhaps, at least teach you a little more about life. I long ago concluded that banking, while a convenient way to make a living, can be extremely dull." His glance swept appreciatively over his gallery of beauties.

"That I chose to conduct this part of my life away from Baltimore should also bring you to understand the sacrifices one must make for propriety."

Wallis fastened her eyes on a purple vein pulsating in the side of his neck. She recalled some of her uncle's strange habits: the twice-daily cold baths he had taken even on the most frigid winter days; his insistence while she lived on Preston Street that no dessert be served except at Sunday lunch. Sol Warfield was a highly disciplined man who had been able for years to keep his life cleanly and neatly divided into two separate worlds. Her Aunt Bessie had obviously discovered his dual existence and he hated her for it. That was why, Wallis reasoned, her mother was always the one to appeal to Uncle Sol for assistance. And she had learned one more useful fact. Uncle Sol was a terrible hypocrite.

"I don't mean to imply that you are in any way to blame for your aunt's actions," he continued. "You are still a very young woman and apparently quite impressionable."

(*Oh, no!* Wallis thought. *Not impressionable—not like Mary Kirk!* But she said nothing.)

He was pacing back and forth across the room, his hands clasped tightly behind himself, his steps measured, and he pivoted always on the same place on the Persian carpet where the design showed a dragon's head. After a few moments of this he came to an abrupt halt and faced her.

"Bessie Wallis, I want you to tell me here and now what it is *you* want to do with your life, not what your Aunt Bessie or your mother have insisted that you should want."

The question was so unexpected that Wallis was stunned. "Well, I—" she began slowly, "I—I," she stuttered, "I want to get married, I guess."

"Why?"

"Why?" she repeated.

"Yes, why?"

"To have a home of my own," she answered, the honesty of the reply surprising even her.

"And—" he prodded.

"And what?"

"What else besides a home of your own?"

She paused, breathing deeply. "I want to make everyone in Baltimore look up to me," she said quickly.

He had been strangely moved by her rush of words, though she could not comprehend the reason. Immediately his attitude softened.

"You have not had an easy life," he said in a gentler voice and sat down, stretching his short legs out before him, his hands resting on his flat abdomen. "Perhaps your mother could have made things different for you, but it is not possible to erase our pasts any more than we can hide our iniquities from the Lord. Each of us, in the end, must be responsible for his own actions. Until now, you have been an innocent. You should not have been made to suffer for your mother's mistakes—or for that matter—your father's. But, where is it written that life is fair?"

He studied her with such intensity that she had to turn aside. "You are not beautiful," he said, as though to himself. "Yet, you are most striking and cunning. A Warfield to your fingertips." He stood up and walked over to the mantel, apparently trying to work out something in his mind. Wallis sensed that it was best for her to remain silent. "I would like that, too," he said almost beneath his breath. Then louder, "For Baltimore to look up to you."

He drew his gold watch from his vest pocket in an unconscious act, held it for a moment and then replaced it without ever looking at its face. "I do not approve of your having a debut so near to your grandmother's death. Baltimore is a city of traditional codes. Mourning is observed for a full year; in the case of a widow, often longer. Most citizens of my generation would share my need to respect such traditions. You should know that I did not refuse your mother's request for money for your debut because I am hardhearted. I feared that you would be severely criticized and more doors would be closed than opened to you."

He went over to a magnificent Regency desk. "You assumed correctly," he said. "Madame Landamoor was here last night. You are also right to think that it would be—inconvenient—for me if you remained in New York City. Not, however, for any of the reasons you might suppose. You already know of my liaison, so I would hardly be risking discovery. Nor would your presence curtail my activities. But you see, Bessie Wallis, I do not believe this city is the right place for a girl like you. In truth, I don't completely trust you and would therefore have the added worry on a day-to-day basis of your comportment."

He opened a drawer of the desk and took out a leather-bound check ledger. "It is unconscionable that a granddaughter of Henry Warfield's should not have a place to live in Baltimore as long as the Preston Street house remains in a Warfield's possession. I will be in this city for most of the coming year. You go to Wakefield Manor as planned. At summer's end, you may stay at Preston Street. When I come to Baltimore I will reserve an accommodation at my club. Far more convenient for a bachelor anyway. You may have the use of the house for one year. It is somewhat understaffed. Ellie can perhaps be called back into service. I will take care of her salary and all the other household expenses."

He wrote out a check, blotted it, tore it from his ledger and held it in his hand. "This is for one thousand dollars. If you put aside plans for a debut this year, it is yours free and clear. If you go against my wishes and what I think is best for you, it shall be deducted from your inheritance when that comes due." As he crossed to her, he folded the check in half and then slipped it into her hand.

"I wish you liked me a little better, child," he sighed. A small, cynical smile ticked at the corners of his mouth. "Or disliked me less," he added.

"But that's not true!" she protested.

"Hush, girl! You have what you came for. Leave now, so that I can retain what I have paid for—my self-esteem." He turned away, cleared his throat and then went over to the telephone. "Patrick, Mr. Warfield here," he said into the instrument. "Would you please see my niece safely into a cab? Thank you."

As she walked to the door she passed close to him. "Was that your mother's?" he asked, as he lightly fingered her lapel watch.

"Yes. It was a present for my graduation."

A rare, almost tender expression touched his face. "I gave it to her—years ago."

For a brief instant Wallis considered kissing him on the cheek, a gesture she thought might not be unwelcome for his hand rose slightly toward her—as though he had been seized with a similar desire for contact. Then he stiffened and stuffed his hand into his pocket. The old look of condescension had returned. "Good-bye, my dear," he said coolly.

"Thank you, Uncle Sol," she managed.

Not until she was seated in the back of the taxi and on her way to Fifth Avenue where she thought she might do a bit of window-shopping, did she realize she still held the check. She opened her purse and slipped it securely into a side pocket. The day had turned hot and sticky and the air that came through the open window was stifling.

"Why," she thought angrily, "why must I always be made to feel so—so *wanting*!"

In November, Wallis was notified that she was one of the forty-seven young women selected to debut at Christmastime under the Cotillion's auspices. She had been very careful with the money Uncle Sol had given her, spending only half on her wardrobe, carefully reserving the remainder for the time when she would have to leave the house on Preston Street, for she knew Uncle Sol would remain bound by his word and that she could not expect to receive a penny more from him. Her premonitions were correct, for he lost no time in displaying his disapproval of her actions, first in a letter to Alice, then to Wallis. ("You have deliberately gone against my wishes. I remind you that we struck an agreement. It would be useless for you to look for any further assistance from me.") And not only had he withdrawn support, he flatly refused to appear at any of the festivities in her honor.

"Your absence from Bessie Wallis's debut will be impossible to explain," Alice wrote him, pleading, "Baltimore will interpret this as a total rejection of her by you and will trigger their own disapproval of her not observing the strict rules of mourning. Dear, dear Sol, you cannot, and I know you will not do this."

That August, war had erupted in Europe. After Germany invaded Belgium, Great Britain and France came to that small country's defense and the death toll had been enormous. Sol Warfield, along with most Baltimoreans, was strongly pro-British. Never able to entirely refuse a plea from Alice, he inserted the following notice in the society column of the *Baltimore News:*

> MR. S. DAVIES WARFIELD WILL FORGO THE BALL THAT HE MIGHT OTHERWISE BE EXPECTED TO GIVE FOR HIS NIECE, WALLIS WARFIELD, AND WILL NOT ATTEND THE COTILLION BALL, FOR THE REASON THAT HE DOES NOT CONSIDER THE PRESENT A PROPER TIME FOR SUCH FESTIVITIES, WHEN THOUSANDS OF MEN ARE BEING SLAUGHTERED AND THEIR FAMILIES LEFT DESTITUTE IN THE APPALLING CATASTROPHE NOW DEVASTING EUROPE.

Despite this public statement (or perhaps even because of it), Wallis's refusal to withdraw her name for the season was condemned behind closed doors, a situation finally confessed to her by Mary Kirk.

"It's about time Baltimore came into the twentieth century," Wallis countered, "and I'm proud to be dragging them into it on my ball skirts! Men fight wars so that their lives at home will be the same when they return. And I don't know what good it will do my dead grandmother, or those poor men in France, if I don't have a debut this year."

Nonetheless, the gossip had its impact on Wallis. For a time it looked as if no one would sponsor a debut ball for her. As always, Cousin Lelia finally came forward. She wrote Wallis:

Sol Warfield's actions are intolerable. I don't mind admitting I have never liked that man! Too pompous for my taste!

Dear girl, what we shall do is have the ball at our Washington residence. I am aware that it means you will have no official private function to honor you in Baltimore like the other girls, and that the city (and specifically the local press) may look at that askance, but the Major and I are prepared to hire a fleet of limousines if necessary to transport Baltimore guests back and forth. You can compensate yourself with the knowledge that you will have the most dashing and available officers in Washington attending your affair.

Quite frankly, Baltimore is not the world, although it may seem so to you now. Compared to the Capital it is downright parochial. And although your Uncle Sol's indifference must be a disappointment, there are great advantages in having it here, not the least of these the chance to meet some splendid young men, and to see one's name appear in society columns here and in New York.

I have also informed your mother and Aunt Bessie of my plan and they agree that it is the only course to take. I think you will need only two really spectacular gowns—one for the Cotillion and one for the party here. Since white is de rigueur for the Cotillion, perhaps a more vibrant color—jade or sapphire or amethyst—for Washington? You do look good in jewel tones. Let me know what you select and I will decorate the ballroom accordingly.

Alice made almost daily excursions to Baltimore to help her daughter prepare her wardrobe. Most of the other girls ordered their ball gowns from Feschal's, the city's most fashionable shop. Wallis's budget excluded any such thought. She found a magazine photograph of the famous dancer Irene Castle dressed in a spectacular white Grecian gown and Alice, with Ellie's help, copied and hand-embroidered the dress, which had a white satin bodice with an overlay of white chiffon that covered her shoulders and fell to her knees in a cascade of sheer fabric banded on the bottom with seed pearls. The satin gown beneath this tunic flared to the ground where it was also edged with pearl embroidery. For the second gown, Wallis chose a combination of deep-blue taffeta and velvet with a heart-shaped neckline, copied from the very latest in Vogue patterns. Though she was only five feet four, her neck and torso were long and slender, an advantage both dresses dramatically emphasized.

Since the debutantes were expected to choose their partners for the ball from Cotillion members, Wallis invited her cousin Henry Warfield, who because of the war in Europe, had returned from England and gone to work for Uncle Sol at the bank. She had to wait several days for his reply, but finally, to her delight, he accepted. The fact that he was her cousin meant they did not need to have a chaperone.

The month preceding the Cotillion was a whirl of lunches, tea dances, suppers and late parties. "Honey Pot," Henry called her privately, "because, my beautiful cousin, you attract men the way molasses draws flies." There were many reasons for this. Wallis had a natural gaiety, a sense of humor, the ability to laugh at herself when necessary, and she always had a captivating story to tell.

She had many admirers. Charm, personality, a romantic mind and an undeniable earthiness about her provided an aura of the femme fatale. But none of the young men met her expectations. Wallis set her standards high. She refused to fall in love with anyone ordinary. He must be unique, attractive and powerful enough to make all Baltimore sit up and take notice.

Ellie and Alice helped her dress for the Cotillion. To

heighten her color, Alice brushed her cheeks lightly with rouge, the use of which was considered a little fast. But the end result seemed just right.

"You look like a real lady,' darlin'," Alice said as she stood back to admire her daughter.

Wallis studied herself with satisfaction in the long pier glass. "I love the gown, Mama," she replied, and embraced her mother warmly.

Henry arrived punctually at half past seven, shortly after Alice's departure to catch the train back to Washington. The rules of the Cotillion demanded that all the men who attended wear white tie and tails. Henry seemed to have stepped off the pages of *Vanity Fair.* His slim, dark good looks were well suited to evening attire. "Am I grand enough?" he demanded, preening in a half-arc so that his tails undulated at his sides.

"Until you compliment me on how I look, I won't tell," Wallis snapped.

He took her hand and held it at arm's length. "Turn for me. Uh-huh," he crooned as she did as he asked. "Honey Pot, I can assure you that you will be the most enchanting, most exquisite creature at the Cotillion." He gave her hand a sharp tug, which pulled her abruptly close to him. "A beautiful woman in virgin white," he whispered in her ear, "is a powerful aphrodisiac."

"Miz Wallis, the car am waitin'," Ellie announced from the doorway, her round face hard set in an expression of disapproval. She held Wallis's evening wrap, purse and gloves. "Now, you be careful how you treat dat dress," she mumbled under her breath as she handed the items to Wallis, and then stood back as Henry guided her out the door, Wallis's laughter trailing behind her like brightly colored ribbons.

The car was Grandmother Warfield's old black Pierce Arrow, usually kept garaged when Uncle Sol was in New York. Eddie, now pensioned, had come out of retirement to drive Wallis and her cousin to the ball.

The Cotillion was held at the Lyric Theatre. The gilt and crimson interior had been transformed for the occasion; seats were removed and replaced by a dance floor polished until it shone; a solid wall of boxes, one for each debutante—banked with flowers of her choice—formed a crescent around the room. A red velvet curtain backed the stage which was edged with bowers of red and white roses. Gold satin cushions were heaped along the sides of the steps leading up to it.

Wallis entered the auditorium, her breath short, one hand resting lightly on Henry's arm. She was struck instantly by the attractiveness of the gowns worn by those debutantes who had arrived before her. The sudden specter of being outshone flashed before her and she leaned close to Henry to whisper, "Don't leave me for one moment. If no one asks me, you will just have to dance every dance with me."

"Honey," he replied with an easy smile, "you will be the belle of the ball."

They were directed to the reviewing stand where they exchanged greetings with the Board of Governors and their wives and then made their way across the congested ballroom to Wallis's box, festooned with American Beauty roses that matched the bouquet (stretched across two gilt chairs) that Henry had waiting for her. Moments later, the band struck up the first one-step and he led her onto the dance floor. The Cotillion had begun.

Henry's prediction proved correct. Wallis was not only lovely to look at, she was an excellent dancer and she was a much sought after partner. Soon she was caught up in a dreamy haze of music, male voices and laughter. Near midnight, a whistle sounded, the orchestra stopped playing and the dance floor was cleared. Led by the Senior Governor, each of the forty-seven debutantes with her partner slowly circled the ballroom. Because this had been ordered alphabetically and there were no XYZ's, Wallis was last. A loud burst of applause followed her appearance. It was meant for all the debutantes, but Wallis smiled and curtsied. The orchestra began the romantic "Parfum d'Amour," the final dance on the program.

Wallis had made a successful debut. Yet, she felt oddly unchanged and she wondered if she might not have missed something in the excitement. What mattered was that Henry had seen how popular she was; that he was—that very moment—helping her on with her wrap, and that he had agreed to accompany her to the Country Club where most of the young people were going to continue their celebration. Once there, she danced until dawn, silently resenting the male attention that kept her from spending more time in Henry's arms.

"Well, Honey Pot," he said as he saw her to the door. "I was right. You were the belle of the ball." He kissed her lightly on the forehead. Wallis raised her chin and looked up at him.

"Too bad we're cousins," he smiled wryly and stepped back. "And that Sol Warfield is both our mentor and our uncle. You're quite a girl, Wallis. I've known that ever since I watched you ride Major. You should know, however, my future at the bank means a lot to me and Uncle Sol trusts me—which is why an old man nine years your senior got to take you to the Cotillion. But Uncle Sol would definitely not approve of my being more than a chaperon. Neither would the ladies of Baltimore society, who, I might add, have an extremely strong influence on the eligible young men in that same society."

All the exhilaration Wallis felt collapsed. "You only escorted me because Uncle Sol asked you," she accused, a sharp edge to her voice.

"Now, come on," he grinned, his dark eyes glinting. "I find you damned attractive but still too young."

"You owed me the truth *before*, not *after*," she said, unable to conceal her bruised feelings.

"Kiddo, nobody owes anyone anything, least of all the truth. *The truth* are the two most libeled words in the English language. There is, after all, *my* truth, *your* truth, *Uncle Sol's* truth, *ad infinitum*." He stood studying her, admiring the way she had not averted her eyes and thinking how splendidly defiant she was. "Don't hate me, Wallis. My only crime is not wanting to see you end up in seduced circumstances."

Despite her pique, Wallis could not suppress her laughter.

Cousin Lelia gave a coming-out party for Wallis in Washington the following April in the flag-festooned Marine Barracks; the Marine Band, some sixty strong, in gala red coats, provided the dance music. Mary Kirk, Emily Lisson and some of her other friends traveled from Baltimore for the affair. And, of course, her cousins Lee-Lee and Anne also attended.

"I've made sure no girl will be a wallflower," Cousin Lelia

informed Wallis. "If there is an unmarried Marine officer stationed in Washington who is not here, it must be somebody who has just reported in from the Fleet. I've rounded up all the rest."

Wallis wore the deep-blue gown made for her by Alice and Ellie, and with it the sapphire necklace and matching earrings that Corrine had let her borrow. The overall effect was quite striking and brought out the extraordinary color of her blue-violet eyes. She danced every dance with a different partner and had a fine time; and as Cousin Lelia had predicted, the event was vividly described in the social column of *The Washington Post* the following day. But she returned to Baltimore not having caught the eye of any one particular Marine officer.

All the festivities she had so looked forward to and hoped would change her life had come and gone. She remained at Preston Street until the agreed time of her occupancy had lapsed, when she had no choice but to accept her mother's offer of a room in her boardinghouse. Once there, she was shocked by her mother's struggle to make ends meet, cleaning the rooms herself and preparing the meals single-handedly.

After six months, Wallis was in a state of despair, certain she would never find a suitable husband in her current circumstances. Without her knowledge, Aunt Bessie had consulted Cousin Lelia. A week later, Wallis received an invitation to visit Corrine and her husband, Captain Henry Mustin, who had recently been appointed Commandant of the new Pensacola Aeronautic Station.

PART TWO

WALLIS WARFIELD SPENCER

1919–1926

8

"God, I'm glad you're here," Corrine said as soon as Wallis stepped onto the train platform in Pensacola. "You can't believe how deadly borin' this town can be. Of course, there are scads of men, but as the Captain's wife I dare not flirt no matter how harmless it might be." She paused and pursed her small mouth as she studied Wallis in the new navy-blue suit that Aunt Bessie had given her as a going-away present. "My! don't you look stylish—and slim." Concern shadowed her fair, heart-shaped face. "You don't think I've gained too much weight, do you?"

"You look marvelous," Wallis said honestly, for Corrine's voluptuous figure had always added to her striking good looks. Her softly wavy blond hair was brushed into a stylish high pompadour. She had enormous blue eyes and a soft, lazy, caressing voice that instantly evoked mental images of porticoed plantation houses, drowsy afternoons, enchanted evenings and beautiful women in crinolines. For years Wallis had been envious of Corrine; her strongly feminine aura, her natural beauty, the small hands and feet that gave her such grace. Corrine was nearly ten years older than Wallis, which meant that she was thirty, difficult to believe when faced with her youthful appearance.

Corrine's golden hair shimmered in the strong sunlight of

the warm April day as she and a porter led the way to the front of the station where a car and a driver stood waiting. She wore a softly draped white dress and carried a wide-brimmed straw hat with red ribbons; so right did she look for the balmy day that Wallis instantly regretted that she had not worn a less severe outfit.

"Let's take the shore road so that Miz Warfield can see the best of Pensacola," her cousin told the young uniformed man at the wheel of the car.

Corrine had written Wallis that Pensacola "with its white sand beaches that rim the blue-blue Gulf, is the American Riviera." Untraveled as she was, Wallis knew that her cousin's claim was fanciful. Pensacola was not a city one read about in society columns. The *beau monde* had winter homes in Palm Beach, on the Atlantic seacoast clear across the state of Florida. But she had expected a more progressive and bustling metropolis than she now saw. Pensacola's streets were nearly deserted. Stores displayed provincial merchandise. No great homes rose along the waterfront. Roads were rocky and unpaved. Pensacola was, in fact, a city much behind the times and it did not look to Wallis that it would ever develop into a resort to rival the likes of Palm Beach or any other popular Southern city. Train routes were circuitous and there were no surefire tourist attractions such as the French Quarter in New Orleans or the antebellum plantations and historic Civil War sites in Mobile, Savannah and Charleston.

"The town fathers an' their snooty ol' aristocratic wives aren't keen on the Navy bein' here," Corrine sneered. "Although they were fallin' on their backsides 'til they came. The noncommissioned men are mos'ly young fellas, far away from home, lonely, lookin' for a girl to fill their off-duty hours, an' too many of them whoop it up to please the old guard."

They were driving along Pensacola's waterfront, the brilliant blue sky reflected in the calm waters and garlanded by the swoop of seabirds above. A section of white beach was rimmed with saucy, red-and-white-striped canvas cabanas. No one was swimming and only a scattered few sat in beach chairs enjoying the sun, but atop a platform at the water's edge perched a bare-armed, bronzed life guard. Wallis turned her head as Corrine talked on and watched until he was only a gleaming dot on the horizon.

Corrine's house was on a knoll near the bay, a short distance from the Navy Aeronautic Station. In former times it had belonged to an affluent farmer, and although it was a modest dwelling, it possessed an Old World charm. A railed veranda banded the front and sides of the ground floor. The heady scent of oleander perfumed the air and large shade trees, at least a century old, spread their elegant leafy branches like great feathered wings over the path that led to the front door.

A soft wind rose and parted the branches, so that long shafts of sunlight fell over Wallis as she stepped onto the veranda. It seemed a sign of some sort, a portent that she was about to enter a new and marvelous world. But the interior of the house did not support this premise.

Corrine's hand could be seen everywhere. She had brought her furnishings with her from Boston, and the fine-turned legs of the antique side tables, the pale-gold brocade sofas and petit-point pillows were at odds with the hardy simplicity of the house's architecture. Wallis was given a large upstairs room under the eaves, prettied up by Corrine with delicate lace curtains and several vases of brightly mixed garden flowers. The lace canopy on the four-poster bed scraped the ceiling and the full-length pier glass, set in a corner, tilted uneasily because the floor was on a slight slant.

As with Corrine's house in Boston, Henry Mustin's influence was not visible. No leather club chairs or hunting prints proclaimed a masculine presence. On the hour in every room, clocks, kept in excellent repair, made an alarming sound as they struck in harmony. Henry was a taskmaster about punctuality and one reason he was so fond of Wallis was her ability always to be on time. Henry sat down at his dinner table at exactly 7:05 every evening (five minutes being allowed for predinner chitchat). If guests arrived late they were ushered directly to the table and served the same course their host was eating, which might mean they missed soup or were served only dessert.

Punctuality was only one of Henry Mustin's idiosyncrasies. He gave the appearance much of the time of being absorbed in a private world of his own, always wrestling with some deep problem. He had retained his youthful good looks: the well-carved features and ruddy complexion, the athletic build, the thick, dark-brown hair that, even at forty-two, showed no trace of gray. But inside Henry was an old man who seemed never to have known youth. He had been in the Navy all of his adult life and believed the world—and certainly his own home—would be a better place if run like a ship. However, Henry had spent very little time at sea. Early in his naval career he had proved himself to be a genius as an inventor. Trained as an engineer, he designed the famous Mustin gunsight. His interest had turned from the sea to the air while he was stationed in Boston, and he was the first man to be catapulted off a battleship in an aeroplane, an enterprising act that had brought him to the attention of the Navy's top brass and eventually to Pensacola as Commandant of the air station.

The Mustins were an old, respected Southern family. Henry proudly told heroic stories about his two uncles who had been wounded in the Civil War. "Don't you pay a bit of mind to my husband," Corrine would say, her blue eyes sparkling. "Those old gents got their wounds by slippin' on the floor suds in a Baltimore saloon." In Boston, Henry had smiled indulgently at his wife's small jokes. Wallis now detected hostility between them. She knew, of course, that Corrine and Henry had nearly separated a couple of years back. They had reconciled before coming to Pensacola—or so Cousin Lelia, Corrine's older sister, had informed the family. *It seems more an armed truce than a reconciliation,* Wallis thought as Corrine led her guests (two officers and their wives and the station's rather elderly, widowed doctor) back into the sitting room after dinner.

"I'm afraid there'll be no coffee," she announced. "Henry believes it's fit only for A-rabs an' Turks to drink. We have some camomile tea for the ladies an' port for you gents. Although it seems to me the gents are gettin' the best of it."

Later, after her company had left and Henry had gone up to bed, Corrine poured port into two empty teacups and—quoting something she had read—confided to Wallis: "When love dies, there is no funeral; the corpse remains in the house."

"Oh, Corrine, what are you going to do? You can't go on like this," Wallis replied.

"Well, not forever, I grant you. But a separation has to be well planned. A woman has to have foresight. An', anyway, I couldn't leave Henry here in such a one-horse town as Pensacola. The scandal would be dreadful. There has to be honor even among couples who have fallen out of love. That's really what our problem is. Henry doesn't love me anymore. When I thought he did, I was able to endure *anythin'*—all his irritatin' habits, his silly prudery. Why, would you believe I have nevah seen Henry in the altogether? He claims it's indecent for a man an' wife to expose their bodies to each other. Good thing I have such cat's eyes or I'd probably nevah know what a man looks like! Once I said 'Now, Henry, let's be devilish an' leave the shades up an' do it by moonlight.' He didn't talk to me for a week!" she laughed merrily.

She drained her teacup and refilled it. "Come on, take your port an' follow me." She turned out the sitting-room lights and they walked around the dark shadows, faint moonlight slipping into the house around the edges of the drawn curtains, to the kitchen where she lit a candle on the stove.

"You hafta keep a candle handy because we're forever havin' power failures," she complained. "They might as well nevah have invented electricity. It always happens when I've invited the mos' interestin' people for dinner." She motioned Wallis to sit down at the kitchen table and placed the burning candle between them.

"Wallis, I'm goin' to ask you a very pertinent question. You don't hafta answer, of course. But I'm askin' it for your own good." Her eyes glinted cat-like in the candlelight. "Wallis, are you a virgin?" she whispered.

The color rose in the younger woman's face. "Yes," she said with a nervous laugh. She had spoken the truth but she knew if circumstances had been different and Henry Warfield less principled, this would not be the case.

"Good! Now, you stay chaste until you get yourself a husband, heah me? 'Cause men only marry for money—which you haven't got; position—which you also lack; or sex—an' where that's concerned they want to believe they're the first *real* love in your life." Corrine's eyes flashed. "My God, Wallis, do I envy you! This town is brimmin' with good-lookin', eligible young men an' there's nothin' stoppin' you from havin' the best time of your life as long as you remembah that if you lose your virginity you'll be ridin' on a duck's back without a paddle!" A smile slid across her beautiful face as she lifted her tea-cup. "Bottoms up!" she said, and then, giggling, changed her mind. "Or should I say—*legs crossed.*"

Wallis awakened the next morning to a terrible grinding sound. She grabbed her bathrobe from the foot of the bed, made a dash to the window and flung back the curtains. A spiral of white smoke snaked through the blueness of the sky. She caught sight of an aeroplane, the first she had ever seen so close, its silver wings blazing in the sunlight. A moment later it was gone. She pondered with amazement at the almost incomprehensible idea that a man—someone she might meet—was right now flying through the clouds. Certainly that pilot must be one of the most courageous and exciting men in the world. All pilots must be, she decided, as she hopped back into bed to think about it, for today she knew she would be introduced to three airmen.

Several times a week Henry had some flight officers for lunch so that they could discuss the business of the air station in relaxed surroundings. Corrine casually had remarked that three officers would be coming that day. "We'll eat together, of course," she said, "but then Henry will expect us to get up discreetly an' leave as soon as dessert is finished."

Shortly before noon, as Wallis sat on the front veranda talking with Corrine, a car pulled up to the gate. She glanced up to see Henry coming toward them, deep in conversation with a young officer and followed closely by two more. At that distance there was little for her to distinguish among the young men. They were all tanned and lean, dressed in uniform, walked in step and bore themselves with that indefinable erectness that is the hallmark of an Annapolis graduate. But as they drew closer, the man to Henry's right caught her eye. He was laughing while the others were not. Something in his deportment—the way he thrust his shoulders back, the lack of restraint in his laughter—suggested an inner force and vitality that appeared lacking in the other men.

"Wallis, I want you to meet Lieutenant Spencer," Henry said when they were on the front porch a moment later. And then, not giving her time to acknowledge the introduction, added, "and Lieutenant Gardener and Lieutenant Robertson." Wallis shook hands with all three but her eyes were drawn back to the first officer. He returned her glance with a candidness that should have made her blush but curiously did not. There was something bold and arresting about his face: the amused look in his keen dark eyes, the neat close-cropped mustache that called attention to his wide mouth and square, purposeful jaw.

He was seated to her left at lunch and as the meal progressed she became increasingly aware of him. Whenever she turned away to talk to Corrine or one of the other officers, the gold stripes on his shoulder-boards, glimpsed out of the corner of her eye, acted like a magnet and drew her to him.

The conversation at the table centered around flying, a subject Wallis knew nothing about. But she managed to turn her lack of knowledge to her advantage. By the time dessert was served she had learned that Pensacola was the Navy's only air station, that there were fewer than two dozen pilots in the service, and that Lieutenant (Junior Grade) Earl Winfield Spencer ("Please call me Win," he had asked) was the Navy's twentieth pilot to win his wings (worn over his left breast pocket).

"My," she had replied, "that means you must know almost one twentieth of all that the Navy knows about flying."

"Not quite," he laughed. His knee touched hers under the table. A lingering moment of mutual awareness passed between them. Over peach pie and vanilla ice cream she discovered that Win Spencer was twenty-eight, the eldest of four brothers and two sisters. A brother who was two years younger had the odd name of Dumaresque, their mother was British, from the island of Jersey, and their father a Chicago stockbroker. Of the other two airmen at the table she still knew little except their names and the fact that they did not have a speck of the charisma possessed by Win.

Too soon for Wallis, Corrine rose and said, "Well, I expect you men will want to talk about business now." Wallis followed her out of the dining room with the excuse, "I really must write some letters."

Indeed, she sat right down at the small kneehole desk in her room and, on a sheet of Corrine's creamy-white embossed stationery, wrote her mother, "I've just met the world's most fascinating aviator."

Late the following afternoon, Win appeared at the Mustins', apparently uninvited, looking—Wallis thought—handsomer than before. Corrine seemed uncomfortable with his presence, a curious reaction for her flirtatious cousin who so much enjoyed male companionship. She remained on the veranda with Win and Wallis and then insisted they join her inside to wait for Henry's return. Wallis finally decided Corrine was just playing the diligent chaperone and felt awkward about it.

Henry arrived, dinner time approached and Win made no move to leave. Unable to do otherwise, Corrine asked him to stay. He was amusing and attentive. His smile insinuated; his gaze flattered. By the evening's end, Wallis had fallen completely and helplessly in love.

Early the next morning she and Corrine took a walk down toward the beach. "No doubt you're attracted to Win by the glamour of his bein' a flyer," Corrine conjectured. "Pilots seem to belong to another race of men—God-like creatures, I suppose, descended to earth from some mystical kingdom. I even feel that way about Henry sometimes. What they do is so thrillin' an' dangerous. But Wallis, you keep your head about you. Win Spencer is nothin' like the boys back in Baltimore, or the young men you met in Boston. There's somethin' wild about him, untamed. I've heard that off duty he can get violently drunk an' there's been talk about his ways with women."

"What exactly does that mean?"

"Let's jus' say that he has a bit of a reputation."

They had reached the warning sign that barred civilians from the flying area of the station. Straight ahead was the bay, its clear waters glass-still. To the right of them was a barbed-wire fence. A hundred feet or so beyond this barrier, flight preparations were in progress. The flimsiness of the box-like, fabric-covered aeroplanes with their bamboo outriggers shocked Wallis. The engines were mounted on a metal rack just behind and over the pilot's head. If Win's plane ever crashed he would be crushed in the cockpit by the weight of all that metal tearing free from its fastenings.

She shivered at the thought. No wonder men like Win,

who took such risks, drank off duty and sought solace in a woman's arms. How could Corrine be so insensitive to the feelings of these young officers?

As they stood watching, one of the small aircraft took off, struggling and bouncing across the bay in an effort to gain the air. "Have there been crashes?" Wallis asked apprehensively.

"Two fliers were killed jus' before you arrived. An' there have been several other crack-ups." Corrine's voice grew serious, her expression pained. "I hope you nevah hafta to heah the awful sound of the crash-gong. I pray I'll nevah heah it again."

Win came by to collect Wallis every afternoon. He gave her golf lessons on a small sunbaked course midway between the station and the town. Or they walked along the water's edge, racing the tide as it came in. These were the only times they found to be alone. In the evenings they went to the movies in town, to the Country Club, or dancing at Pensacola's fashionable San Carlos Hotel, always with Corrine and Henry in attendance.

One day as they strolled along the beach, Win pulled her close to him, his hand under her arm. They continued walking in this intimate manner, their knees touching, their steps slow. The sputtering motor of a plane in takeoff broke the spell. They drew apart, staring upward until the small aircraft was safely on its way.

"We'd better go back," she said.

He stood facing her. "Wallis," he replied in a deep furry-gruff voice, "you know damned well we can never go back." He grasped her narrow shoulders between his large hands. She did not flinch. "You're like a small bird," he mused, "a rare, exotic variety. Unusually strong. It would not be easy to clip your wings."

"Why would you want to?" she replied.

He laughed and slipped his arms around her, lifting her slightly and then kissed her with a passion she had never before experienced. "You're a virgin," he said as they drew apart. The color rose in her face and he gave her a broad, reassuring smile and gently tousled her hair. "Well, don't worry, little bird, I find virgins most attractive."

"Too bad I don't feel that way about your male ego!" she

snapped, her recovery so immediate that he was momentarily stunned and stood frozen as she started back up toward the house. He soon caught up with her and reached for her hand. Wallis did not pull away, and they walked, hand in hand, silently until they reached the front gate where he left her with a jaunty salute and a tip of his officer's cap.

9

Corrine stood waiting for Wallis when she entered the living room. There had been a strain in their relations over the past week. The original month that Wallis had planned to stay in Pensacola had extended to six weeks. For Wallis it could have gone on and on. She had never felt so happy. Now as she faced Corrine, her cousin's fragile face and delicate mouth noticeably tense and drawn, she blamed herself for being so wrapped up in her own emotions that she had not observed Corrine's state of mind. Something must be wrong between Corrine and Henry, she thought.

"Don't see Win anymore," Corrine said as she clenched her hands in front of her and then dropped them sharply to her sides.

Unable to contain her surprise, Wallis asked, "But why, Corrine? What is this all about?"

"I told you. Win Spencer has a bad reputation an' here you are in my house, in my care—an' Lord knows where it all will end!" She walked over to the front window and stared out. "Lelia will have herself a chicken fit. So will Bessie an' your poor mother. An' you'll be ruined."

"Why will I be ruined? I've never let Win any more than kiss me."

Corrine whirled sharply to face Wallis, and her blond hair loosened from its pins and billowed around her small pinched face. "You haven't? You swear to me that's the truth?" she asked.

"Of course it is."

"Oh, God!" She clasped her hands to her head. "Why have I made such a scene, goin' on like a preacher hot-footin' the devil. It's jus' my nerves. I'm uncommonly nervous today." She started past Wallis on her way out of the room.

"There's more to this than nerves," Wallis observed. "What is it?"

Corrine paused and looked straight at Wallis. "Win has had an affair with several of the married women on the station, and I'm one of them," she replied candidly. "And I'm not sayin' these things because I'm jealous. It was over almost before it started with Win an' me. He's got a cruel streak. I saw it an' I wanted no part of it an' I can't jus' stand by an' watch you jump headfirst into a growlin' volcano when all the Montague ladies have done so much—an' sacrificed so much—to keep you out of the fire." She brushed the loose wisps of hair back from her face.

"An' I can't say a word to Henry," she continued in a strained voice. "He thinks Win is an admirable officer an' one of the air station's best pilots. Anyway, unless I confessed the truth—which I'm not about to do—Henry would say I'm listenin' to gossip I have no business hearin'. So, I'm tellin' you. Forget Win Spencer. Go back to Washington for the time bein'. Summer's only a short time away an' I'm sure Lelia would be pleased to have you at Wakefield Manor."

It had genuinely shocked Wallis to hear that Win and Corrine had been lovers. Corrine must be exaggerating about there being a violent streak in Win. He was strong and masculine, that was true. But he had always been tender and gentlemanly to her. Corrine was just saying these things to make her break off with him. Or maybe she had made up the story because she wanted him. "How was he cruel, Corrine?" she pressed. "Did he ever hit you?"

"No, but I don't doubt he could be moved to strike a woman." She turned to go. "I better freshen up for dinner.

You, too, Wallis. You're all windblown an' frowzy. Lieutenant Robertson is joinin' us. Later, it bein' Saturday night an' all, the four of us are goin to the Club for some dancin'."

"Win and I planned . . ." Wallis began.

"Plans can go skitterin' on a Navy post. Tonight Lieutenant Spencer, I'm told, is to be the first pilot to take one of the new Curtiss N-nine planes up for a patch of night flyin'."

A feathery breeze blew across the bay that evening; the moon was full, the stars brilliant, the sky as light as dawn. Lieutenant Nigel Robertson was attractive, attentive and a good dancer. Still, Wallis could think only about Win as she strained to hear the sound of his plane above the brassy music of the Navy band.

The air station had been an old Navy yard, long inactive, before it had become a seaplane base, the officers' club, a boathouse used for storing small gear. It had the advantage of a picturesque location directly on the harbor and of having a space large enough for dancing. Some care had been taken in its conversion, the old beams preserved, the remnants of its former life not entirely done away with, although the rough plank floors had been replaced and the walls paneled and painted white. By midevening the main room, which tended to be overcrowded on a Saturday night, was uncomfortably warm, the windows of the building being small and the ceiling fans, attached to the tall rafters, too high to do much good.

"Are you all right, ma'am?" Lieutenant Robertson asked Wallis, noting her sudden distraction.

"A bit warm," she replied. She had paused midstep, for coming through the doorway was Win, wearing a crisp uniform, a smile slapped across his broad face as he caught sight of her. "If you'll excuse me," Wallis said and, leaving her partner standing rather awkwardly alone, made her way to the edge of the dance floor.

Win motioned to the door and then disappeared through it. A few moments later he greeted her on the front porch, took her hand and pulled her over to a secluded corner.

"How on earth did you manage this?" she inquired. "I thought you were testing night-flying conditions."

"The moon was too bright. You're not sorry to see me, are you? It seemed to me I rescued you from Dante's inferno in the nick of time."

He slipped his arm around her waist. The scent of roses and oleander nearly overwhelmed her and for the moment she felt as though she might suffocate. He pulled her closer to him, tracing her backbone with his fingers through the sheer organza of her dress and then settling his hand on her bare neck. He was pressing against the hairpins that held her chignon in place and she pulled slightly away to ease the tension.

"I never thought I was the marrying kind, Wallis. But I'll be damned if I don't want to marry you!"

"Is that a proposal?" she asked nervously.

"Yes, it is," he said.

She could hear voices on the porch but Win was blocking her view. The band was taking a break and the sudden ending of the music had magnified all other sound. Win eased her farther back into the corner. She was now wedged into a narrow space. He leaned over her, raised her face upward and kissed her soundly. For a moment she felt as if she were losing all the air in her body. She found it impossible to pull away although she could easily have done so. In truth, her airlessness was a new and exhilarating feeling.

"Do you love me, Wallis?" he asked as they finally broke apart.

"Yes . . ." she whispered.

"We can still have a June wedding," he said. "I believe women like such romantic trappings."

"It's already June," she laughed. "That's impossible! Anyway, I can't agree just like that to marry you. I have to discuss it with my mother and my Uncle Sol."

He stepped away. His dark eyes were dead serious and his voice hard-edged. "Don't keep me waiting too long, Wallis," he cautioned.

Over the next two weeks Wallis saw Win every day and learned a great deal about him. "Deeply imbedded in his nature," she wrote in her diary, "under the surface layer of jauntiness and gaiety, is a strange brooding quality that verges on bitterness and even cynicism. A word or gesture can change his manner in a flash. The laughter that crinkles the lines around his dark eyes will disappear as if a blind has been drawn across his mind, and he becomes silent and morose. I can understand now how Corrine could have said what she did about him. Still, I'm convinced she is wrong. Win needs love and security. Something in his past life is haunting him and must be exorcised."

She did not tell Corrine or write Alice that he had proposed, although her letters to both her mother and Aunt Bessie were filled with news about him. "He is very mature for twenty-seven," she told Alice. "Henry believes he is an officer of unusual promise." And to her aunt she proclaimed, "His brother fliers say he is the best at the station, that he has an intuitive, natural feeling for planes and flying that gives him an edge over all the other airmen."

Only to her diary was she able to admit that neither his expertise as a pilot nor his undoubted good looks were the basis of her attraction to him; that it was "his strange and sometimes bewildering alterations of mood" that fascinated her. "He is the most subtle, complicated and dramatic personality I have ever known," she confessed.

He escorted Wallis to the San Carlos Hotel the Saturday night following his proposal (with Henry and Corrine as chaperons, of course), and they danced for hours. He was extremely graceful and knew all the new dances. He taught her the tango, which he claimed to have learned from a Brazilian lady. "We exchanged lessons on other subjects on which we had expert knowledge, as well," he grinned.

"Flying?" she asked.

"You might say so," he laughed.

On such evenings, and always in the company of others, he would be charming, great fun and mysteriously intriguing. When he was alone with Wallis, his dark side would surface. By now, she could sense it coming—the brooding look that would glaze his eyes, the silence that followed. With her gentle prodding he told her stories about his family. "We're all living under some sort of ill omen," he confided late one afternoon as they sat on the top of a grassy slope that overlooked the bay; large and small boats moved lazily about in it, their masts and sails shimmering in the haze of the sun.

"Grandfather Spencer fell in love with my grandmother's youngest sister. And one day he shut himself in his study, put a gun to his mouth and fired. The problem was he didn't kill himself as he had planned. He destroyed one whole side of his face and went through the rest of his tortured life in reclusive disfigurement. The horror of it has never left my father—or any of us Spencers, I guess."

When he finally looked at Wallis, tears had welled in her eyes. "Thank you," he whispered as he kissed her lightly on the forehead and then, jumping up, pulled her to her feet. "What would you have done if I had ravished you right here?" he asked as he held both her hands tightly in his own. "Screamed for help? Given in? Enjoyed it?"

"I'm not one for speculation," she replied.

"Too bad. It's a flaw in your character. But I'll overlook it." He released his hold and they started down the hill, running after only a few downward steps. Wallis lagged farther and farther behind as they neared the bottom where he stood laughing, waiting for her. Behind him, in the distance, standing on the veranda of the house, Corrine was watching. Wallis slackened her pace even more.

"Hey! Slowpoke!" he shouted.

When she reached him he took her arm but she pulled away. Corrine had not moved from her post and Wallis felt uneasy.

"Don't *ever* reject me like that," Win said, his words hard-clenched. He took her arm again and held it tightly in his grasp.

Wallis looked up at him with surprise. "You're hurting me," she said.

For a long moment Wallis thought he might not release her, that he might even throw her to the ground. His eyes had clouded with anger, his chin set in defiance. Then he let go his hold and stepped back. Wallis continued on alone. When she reached the house, he was still standing where she had left him.

The next day he was the old, charming Win. Wallis was

troubled. Time, she thought, was needed to explore Win's sudden moods. No longer able to prolong her stay without feeling she was imposing on the Mustins, she took up the dreary task of packing to return home. Corrine drove with her to the railroad depot. Win stood waiting on the station platform, handsome in his uniform, his officer's bars gleaming in the sun. He helped her board the train and then pulled her back into the open vestibule. Indifferent to Corrine's presence at the foot of the metal steps, he kissed her full on the mouth.

"I'm taking a short leave in August," he said, "and I'll expect an answer before then. In two weeks."

"I promise," Wallis replied, and fled back into the train where she sat down at a window seat. Win stood watching as the train ground its way out of the station.

"Two weeks!" he shouted, and although she could not really hear him through the window, she understood that he was giving her an ultimatum.

Wallis was in love—or at least she thought she was. Once her mind was made up to accept Win's proposal, nothing could shake her determination, not even Aunt Bessie's seductive promise that, while Europe was out of the question because of the war, they could travel to the Orient the following summer. The life of a Navy wife, especially of a pilot at such risk, was not what Bessie wanted for the niece on whom she had pinned such hopes. Alice was equally discouraging and pointed up to Wallis the Navy's notoriously low pay and the loneliness and apprehension that were sure to be hers when Win was on duty or flying. Then there was the danger that the United States might enter the war and he was already an officer and bound to be one of the first men to be sent overseas. Uncle Sol was far more cold and calculating in his comments.

"Why should I care whom you marry, Wallis? You will never heed my advice, whatever I thought about your Lieutenant or his suitability as a husband. But once you are married, be aware that you cannot expect any assistance from me." Wallis did not allow Uncle Sol's ultimatum to discourage her. She wrote Win that she accepted his proposal and he arranged a meeting in late August at his family's home in Highland Park, a suburb of Chicago.

She made the train journey to Chicago alone, but while in the city she was to stay with the Bryan sisters, Iris and Lavinia, well-to-do spinster friends of Aunt Bessie's who were distantly related to the Merryman family. The two women could not have been more pleased about being involved, however peripherally, in a youthful affair of the heart. Wallis was given a large front bedroom with windows on the lake.

"Alice Roosevelt once occupied this same room when her father was on a campaign visit here," Lavinia boasted. "Our father was a great supporter of Mr. Roosevelt." The sisters, who both wore curled brown hairpieces that came down onto their high foreheads, an effect that only emphasized their long, narrow noses, looked enough alike to be twins. In fact, it was impossible for Wallis to discern which one was the younger.

The sisters had been waiting at the depot with Win, whom they had not met until the moment when Wallis stepped off the train. The engaged couple, therefore, had not yet had any time alone.

"It's a charming room," Wallis said, her eyes on Win, who had just set down her suitcase. She had almost forgotten the vibrant darkness of his eyes, how tall he was, how broad were his shoulders. The sisters discreetly excused themselves shortly after they had tea in the front parlor.

"You're a skinny bird, after all. Maybe I was blinded by the Florida sun," he teased, when the door was closed and they were finally alone. A moment later he drew her into his arms and held her close. "Well, you're not *so* skinny. I can feel flesh," he added and then kissed her before taking a small jewelry box from his pocket. "It cost me a month's pay. I had to sign a pledge to pay three more equal payments so I hope to hell it fits." He opened the box, took out a pear-shaped diamond ring of two carats. Holding her left hand, he slipped it onto her third finger.

"It's splendid, Win! Just beautiful." She brought it close to her face, pressing the hard, cold surface against her lips. It was much more tastefully expensive than she had expected, and she was genuinely thrilled.

That evening she dined with Win's family. They lived in a large frame, turreted house that had been built about twenty-five years earlier in what was now called the Victorian style. Neat hedges bordered a well-kept lawn, as they did most of the other similar houses on the street. The Spencers were a middle-class family of comfortable means. Large oak pieces, lace curtains and rounded fringed lampshades formed the decor of the house.

Wallis was not prepared for the overwhelming array of unique prospective in-laws who ranged themselves about the circular, pedestaled dining-room table. Win had three brothers and two sisters, none of whom resembled him—or for that matter, their father, mother or each other. They appeared, on first meeting, to be lacking a single common family characteristic. Dumaresque was blond, almost Viking-like. Another brother, Egbert, was dark and lean, an aesthetic young man. The youngest brother, Gavin, had a Gallic look. One sister, Isobel, was fair, soft-featured and insipidly pretty. The other, Ethel, had mousy hair and brown eyes too small for her large face. Yet, as the evening progressed, Wallis concluded that the Spencers were strangely all of a piece, displaying the same tense nerves, the same erratic hand gestures, and—except for Win—the same lack of levity.

As Wallis turned her attention to Mr. Spencer's stern countenance and then to his wife—who, though softer, possessed a most disturbing haunted look—she was struck by the total unreality of the scene. Win and she seemed to be inadvertently a part of a stage play in which his relations were performers. Of one thing she felt sure. Win was as much an outsider to his family as she was. Certainly he was the most spirited. He tried hard to keep the conversation light and appeared undaunted that he did not succeed. Dumaresque held center stage throughout the meal, talking about the war in Europe, reeling off casualty statistics and castigating President Wilson for not going to the aid of England and France.

"You must be aware of the precariousness of the situation you propose to enter, Miss Warfield," Mrs. Spencer warned Wallis. "All our sons must live on their own earnings. Your husband will have only his Navy pay. You cannot count upon assistance from Mr. Spencer and myself. The size of our family has already overtaxed our resources." Her small dark eyes were fastened ferret-like on the face of her future daughter-in-law.

"I'm sure we won't need your help, Mrs. Spencer," Wallis replied uneasily and smiled across the table at Win, who rose instantly to announce that he must drive her back to Chicago. Although tense when they set out, by the time they reached the door of the Bryan sisters' he was his old self again, joking, teasing and, as he kissed her good night, as daringly romantic as ever.

Wallis did not return to Highland Park. Win came daily into Chicago. A brooding Dumaresque joined them for dinner at the sisters' one night, an edgy Egbert another. Ethel and Isobel, a bit restrained yet passably sociable, came to tea. Wallis did not see Mr. and Mrs. Spencer again. The Bryan sisters thought it very odd indeed. Acting on their sense of moral obligation, they wrote Aunt Bessie of their feelings. Wallis received a letter from her aunt suggesting she give serious thought about marrying into such an odd, antisocial family. But Wallis was determined.

Perversely, the curious natures of her future in-laws brought a better understanding of Win's moodiness, which, she was cheered to note, had not recurred during all their time together in Chicago. She reasoned that he had wanted her to see his family as they were, to be sure it made no difference to her. When he saw it had not, a great load seemed to have lifted from his shoulders.

Their wedding date, three months hence, was formally announced. Neither Wallis nor Alice had money for a trousseau or a wedding. Aunt Bessie dug into her savings but they were not sufficient to cover the kind of send-off she felt Wallis should have and Uncle Sol had made his position clear from the outset.

Wallis still had four thousand dollars remaining of her inheritance, although it was not due to be paid over to her until her twenty-first birthday the following June. With no alternative, she went to see her uncle. For a strenuous hour he soberly impressed upon her the fact that, if she used these funds in what he considered a frivolous manner, she would have nothing to fall back upon should times prove difficult. He recommended a small, private wedding with a maximum guest list of fifty. Wallis would have none of it. In the end, he agreed to advance her the money from her inheritance.

Christ Church, in Baltimore, where Warfields had always worshipped and where Alice had been denied a wedding to Teackle, was decorated with huge white chrysanthemums in profusion. Wallis had spared no expense on her own behalf. Over three hundred guests, there, she knew, because this was a Warfield wedding, sat waiting for her to enter.

"Well, this is it, Corrine," she said as she peeked through a narrow slit in the door with a view to the altar.

Corrine, who was her maid of honor, pressed her hand affectionately, "Wallis, I hope you will be truly happy, I really do." In her soft, feminine face was a genuine warmth.

"Oh, Corrine, I hope so, too!" Wallis answered.

She felt every inch the elite bride. There had been very few refusals, and to her delight, Miss Amelia Love, the society editor of the *Baltimore Sun,* wearing her trademark—a heart-shaped gold locket—was seated in a front pew.

Wallis stroked the sleeve of her white panne velvet gown so extravagantly embroidered with pearls, certain now that the exorbitant cost had been worth it. Corrine straightened the long court train. The door through which the bride was to enter was opened. Uncle Sol, who had agreed to give her away, stepped stiffly to her side.

She carried a magnificent bouquet of white orchids and lilies of the valley. Her dark hair was drawn into two soft nests of curls over her ears. She had not wanted a veil to cover her face and so yards of tulle were held in place by a coronet of orange blossoms set tiara fashion in her hair. Corrine walked behind the bride, making sure the elaborate train was in position. Mary Kirk (sans glasses and aglow), Cousin Lelia's two daughters, Lee-Lee and Anne, Ethel Spencer, and two other bridesmaids who had attended Oldfields, followed in their orchid-colored bouffant gowns, their small nosegays with long yellow ribbons held high.

Wallis was aware of the stir of excitement her striking appearance created among the assembled guests and she was relieved that Uncle Sol was giving her away. She knew Baltimore society would believe he was responsible for the wedding and that he had, therefore, approved of the bridegroom. Win, striking in his full-dress uniform, waited at the altar for her with his best man, Dumaresque. Win was calm, almost offhandedly so. A wave of apprehension flooded over her. What if this was a mistake? What would she do then? But when she took her place beside him and he reached down and clasped her free hand momentarily in his, her doubts faded. At the end of the ceremony he kissed her with unrestrained passion.

"Hey, boy, you got a whole lifetime for that," Uncle Harry joked.

The reception, in the grand ballroom of the newly refurbished Stafford Hotel, was a buoyant affair. Alice had supervised the menu and was enjoying the festivities even more than their guests. Wallis had insisted on the selection of her mother's conservative French-blue velvet gown, worn high at the neck and tight at the wrist. Alice looked more dignified than Wallis had ever seen her. But as the evening progressed, the champagne that was being served liberally released her usual high spirits. Her mother became a bit louder, more giddy, and finally, to Wallis's horror and the dismay of Mr. and Mrs. Spencer, she got up on the bandstand and sang an animated chorus of a provocative song performed by the Dolly Sisters in a new theater revue.

"Mama, come off the stage," Wallis whispered from close by.

"What's that, darlin'?" Alice laughed. "Say it loud enough for everyone to heah."

"You should have been on the stage," Wallis said with embarrassment.

Alice promptly began a second chorus. There was nothing for Wallis to do but endure.

Mary Kirk caught the bride's bouquet, and half an hour later, Wallis, wearing a deep-amethyst going-away ensemble, and Win, still in his uniform, drove off to Washington with Cousin Lelia and Major Barnett, who deposited the bridal couple at the Shoreham Hotel where they were to begin a two-week honeymoon.

"It seems all wrong to leave you with this strange man," Cousin Lelia said, after she kissed Wallis in parting.

As Wallis stood waiting for Win to tip the bellboy and settle the luggage in their room, she pondered Cousin Lelia's words. *Strange* had many meanings. Cousin Lelia must certainly have meant that Win was simply not yet well known by the family.

Finally, they were alone. Win crossed over to her. "Have pity for me, Wallis," he said in a husky voice. "I love you as I have never loved a woman before."

"I love you, Win," she said softly. She was standing by the side of the bed and he moved close to her and deftly undid the buttons on her jacket.

"Get undressed," he said.

He stood, fully clothed, watching as she obeyed his command. His hands moved to her small, bared breasts and slid down her narrow torso. The throbbing sounds of the city outside clashed with the pounding in her ears. He left her there and turned off the lights and pulled up the shades so that the room was lighted only by the moon. As he advanced, he undressed, leaving his clothes wherever they fell. Wallis was struck by a flash of memory. She was standing concealed on the staircase of Aunt Bessie's house on Charles Street and a man was kneeling over her mother's partially nude body.

As Win came within reach, she threw her arms around him, not knowing if she was propelled by some wild and new passionate desire or if she just wanted to hold him in her arms, be held by him, and reassured that she had made the right decision, that he was not strange at all, that he would be her protector, her lover, her dearest friend.

The strength and passion of her apparent surrender drove Win into frenzied action. He pushed her down on the bed and buried his lips in her neck, her bosom, her navel, while his hands groped between her legs and his fingers moved up and inside her body.

Wallis felt choked, terrified. She would be torn apart by his hands, crushed by the weight of his body as he lifted himself on top of her. A state of dementia overcame her. She could see her mother's naked image, flames rising behind her, and herself, a small child wanting to scream but knowing that if she did it would not save her mother from the flames or herself from the disgrace of being where she should not have been.

A searing pain coursed brutally through her. She let out a cry. Win pressed his mouth hard on hers to silence her. A few moments later he rolled off her. She felt sore and bruised and yet she was experiencing an extraordinary sense of ecstasy. Her ears rang. His hand brushed her side and a wave of unendurable sensitivity swept over her.

He had not been a tender, gentle lover as she had fantasized. Perhaps this is what Corrine meant when she had said Win could be cruel. No Southern lady could have forgiven the forceful lovemaking she had just experienced. But Wallis felt no anger, nor did she feel the pity he had asked for earlier, for the frenzied passion she awoke in him gave her a sense of power that she had never known before.

10

The next day Win and Wallis went by train to White Sulphur Springs, West Virginia, where they were to spend a week at the Greenbrier Hotel before ending their honeymoon by taking in the sights and a few shows in New York City. As a child, Wallis had once been brought to the Greenbrier, a short journey from Wakefield Manor, by Alice. The memory of the idyllic weekend she had spent there with her mother had lingered, and she had chosen to return for what she had anticipated would be the happiest time of her young life.

They arrived in the late afternoon. Early twilight had settled on the surrounding hills, turning their grassy slopes purple. The giant willows that graced the grounds swayed in a biting wind, their yellowing leaves making a crackling sound as they fell. Wallis had been a summer guest before, and things looked entirely different in the autumn. Now, there was scarcely anything about the place that seemed familiar. Where it had previously been brimming with guests and gaiety, the Greenbrier was nearly empty, November not being a month when many people holiday.

Their room was cheerful enough, dominated by a huge old brass four-poster bed and decorated in bright chintz and white wicker furniture. Wallis breathed a sigh of relief. She was lost in her own thoughts, trying desperately to recapture even a fragment of that long-ago weekend with Alice. She could see herself crying, not wanting to leave, knowing she would go back to Wakefield Manor and her mother to Baltimore. "Now, darlin', we'll both have these two days to remembah, won't we? An' they belong only to us. No one else has a share in them," Alice had comforted.

"Goddam it!" Win exploded.

Wallis turned sharply, her memory abruptly severed. Win was leaning over the dressing table, reading something under the glass top.

"Whatever is it, Win?" she asked.

"West Virginia is a fucking dry state and there are no alcoholic beverages sold in the hotel! Imagine that happening to a man on his honeymoon," he laughed, but from the harsh tone of his laughter, Wallis knew he was in no way amused. "Well, that does it! We certainly can't stay here."

"You don't really mean that," she began.

He stood frozen for the moment and then flung open one of his suitcases, where, from under the shirts, he pulled out a small flask. "Just enough left to get up flying speed until I can locate a source of supply," he said, bucking up a bit.

Although Wallis was not sure how he had managed it, a bottle of gin wrapped in brown paper was waiting in their room when they returned after dinner. She had been more alarmed by his nautical oaths than by his need for alcohol. Mr. Rasin had also liked his gin and his consumption of it never had become threatening; in fact, he was especially lively and good fun when he "had a few under his belt," as he would say. Win did not become better company, but during the rest of their honeymoon he never became drunk or abusive and he appeared not to drink before sundown—a sign, Wallis rationalized, that meant he was no more than a social drinker.

Nonetheless, a shadow of discontent clouded her thoughts, dimming the happy times they did share. Living with Win was not at all the realization of her fantasies. Despite his moodiness she had imagined him a sensitive and romantic companion. Instead, she found him distant, an invisible wall separating them. She knew little more about him at the end of their honeymoon than she had known before. Yet, the unexpected excitement she experienced during their lovemaking compensated for his remote behavior at other times. The first few days of their return to Pensacola were filled with parties given for her as the newly arrived bride by Corrine, who seemed genuinely pleased to see her, and several of the officers' wives. Then the reality of her new life set in.

Designed for fifteen hundred men, the air station housed three thousand. Conditions were primitive. Noncommissioned men lived in tents; sanitation was nearly *au naturel*—trench latrines and washing by hand buckets.

Her own living conditions were far more civilized. The officers' houses were situated along a street leading from the main gate down to the waterfront. Since Win was sixth-ranking officer at the station, their house, a small bungalow identical to its neighbors, was the fifth on the street. (Henry, as Commanding Officer, was allowed to be housed off the base.) The front door opened directly into a narrow living room. No more than six could be seated in the small dining room. The entire house could easily have been put in her grandmother's parlor on Preston Street. Wallis instantly had the walls painted white and hung flowered-chintz curtains at the windows in fond imitation of the decor at the Greenbrier. Black servants cost a pittance and she was able to employ a cook and a maid, although she tried to leave the house when they were both at work since it became suddenly overcrowded.

Her life was confined to the mile-square perimeter of the station and the town of Pensacola. She played bridge with Corrine and fellow Navy wives in the afternoon, and poker (which Mr. Rasin had taught her) for modest stakes in the evening when the husbands joined them. She was the only woman in these after-dinner games, but Wallis took up poker in earnest and was as a player superior to most of the men. This forward act of hers quickly alienated many of the wives. Still, Wallis persisted. The alternative was to spend her evenings with the women in another room, discussing domestic issues while embroidering. The truth was that after they had welcomed her so hospitably, the naval wives turned somewhat chilly, and but for Corrine's efforts, her social life would have been bleak.

"Wallis, you really should bite your tongue sometimes," Corrine advised her. "You're far too outspoken for these ladies. A Navy station is a very conservative world. When you join the men at poker or talk about politics an' writers like Upton Sinclair, the women bristle a bit. An' they think you're high-hattin' them when you repeat all that social news you read in *The Washington Post,* which you shouldn't have sent to you, anyway, 'cause it makes you seem even more uppity."

None of this advice did Wallis heed. She liked playing poker and she found the men far better company than their wives. She also won consistently and Win did not appear to object.

As far as she knew, Win did not drink when he was on duty or scheduled to fly. On Saturday nights they would descend on the San Carlos Hotel to dance and, in Win's case, to drink without restraint. By the end of the evening, he was usually drunk enough to render, in front of the bandstand, impromptu impersonations of famous Broadway vaudevillians, his favorite being George M. Cohan. These exhibitions embarrassed Wallis, as Alice's Dolly Sister routine at her wedding had done. Still, she preferred Win in this exhilarated state to the spells of moodiness he often fell into and which she attributed to the tensions in his job.

Flight conditions were unsophisticated. Planes were in short supply. Seaplanes lacked radio equipment and were supplied with carrier pigeons instead. The wives always were attuned for the first sound of the crash-gong. Then there was the uneasiness that war was around the corner. The activity at the station escalated at an almost impossible tempo. Every train into Pensacola brought more cadets. Win drove himself and his men, who had to be trained, qualified pilots if war arrived. The dread, awaited day came on April 6, 1917. A week later Win received the news that Dumaresque, who was also a pilot, had been shot down in France, one of the earliest of America's wartime casualties.

Wallis helplessly watched Win decline into frequent spells of deep depression. His drunken moments, though still confined to his off-duty hours, took on a more threatening, angry tone. He would deride her, swear at her and once struck her across the face when she told him to stop his badgering. "I'll be the one to give the orders!" he had shouted as she grabbed hold of a table to keep from falling. Although she could not find it in her heart to forgive him, she attributed his abuse to his own frustration at somehow not being able to take vengeance for Dumaresque's death. Against her wishes, he requested an overseas assignment. Instead, and to his great disappointment, he received orders to proceed immediately to Squantum, Massachusetts, near Boston, to take command of a new naval air station. Wallis kept her silence at her delight in this transfer. She knew she would never miss Pensacola.

With Wallis's prodding, they took an apartment in a hotel in the Back Bay section of Boston, a considerable distance from Squantum Naval Air Base. This often meant that Win was gone from seven in the morning until after nine at night, when they would have a quiet dinner in the hotel dining room before going up to bed.

Win was working harder than she had ever seen him, and he was not drinking. He was responsible for producing a new crop of aviators every eight weeks. To do so meant running the base on a highly accelerated and superbly organized schedule, which Win succeeded in doing, although he would complain to Wallis, "I need an eight-day week to produce my 'Eight Week Wonders.'"

Wallis had hoped that in a city the size of Boston, where she already had met members of several influential families, her social life would greatly improve. However, she had placed herself in an awkward situation—too distanced from the other officers' wives to be included in the life at the air base, her connections with Bostonians too tangential and in the past to be of much use. Five years had passed since she was last in Boston, and then she had been a teenager. Corrine's friends were considerably older than she was, and—she reasoned—they most probably felt they had little in common with a twenty-one-year-old bride.

Whatever the cause, Wallis quickly discovered that Bostonians did not take well to outsiders; and with the war and so many officers coming in and out of the city, they had become especially clannish. People were pleasant enough to her on the telephone, interested in news of Henry and Corrine, offering assistance if Wallis needed help in locating household staff, a milliner or a dressmaker. But no one extended an invitation for lunch or dinner or even bridge. If, like Corrine, she had been able to afford a house where she could entertain, no doubt some of the ice could have been broken. With her two rooms at the hotel, this was impossible, and people did not entertain in hotel dining rooms unless they were giving a large, gala party.

In the beginning, Wallis kept herself busy by taking streetcar excursions to the city's historical landmarks. After these were exhausted, she embarked on a new and rather bizarre source of diversion. Local newspapers were filled with lurid details of a sensational white slavery–murder trial of an eighteen-year-old girl, accused of shooting a man moments after he had enjoyed her favors. One morning Wallis went along to the courthouse where the case was being tried and sat in the gallery. She had never before been in a courtroom. Her fascination held her there until the end of the day's proceedings. After that, she came back daily as a spectator until the case went to the jury. (The young woman was found not guilty after it had been proved that she had been sold into a white-slavery ring at the age of thirteen.) Within a week Wallis was back in the gallery following the trial of a man who had shot his wife's lesbian lover. (He, on the other hand, was declared guilty of second-degree murder.)

"I may not be getting to see the insides of many of the stately homes of Beacon Hill," she wrote Alice, "but I am becoming quite an expert on some of Boston's sleazier characters. In the evening, when Win comes home, I describe the fine points of the day's proceedings, tally the score and render my judgment on the defendant's innocence or guilt."

She did not confide in Alice her growing unhappiness with her marriage. She had thought that if Win would curb his drinking, their problems would be solved. This had not occurred. He seldom had free time and even worked late Saturdays at the air base. When he was home, he had little energy for more than dinner and bed. His sex drive had almost totally disappeared. If she had been honest with Alice and herself, she might have admitted that her retellings of the salacious details of the trials she attended were an overt provocation on her part to sexually arouse Win. They nearly always failed, but even when they did not, his passion was quickly spent and with little regard for her own emotions.

Win was a devilish contradiction, sliding like the valve of a trumpet between the high and low notes without any awareness of what he was doing. No officer was tougher on his men or on himself. He had not given up his pleas to the Navy Department to be sent overseas. The answer was always the same: his services were needed more at home. In late October he was notified that he was being transferred again, this time to organize a naval air station on North Island, near San Diego. He was to supervise the construction of a base several times the size of Squantum and the training of hundreds of pilots and mechanics.

A week before they were to leave, his youngest brother, Egbert, an expert rider, was thrown and killed while jumping a horse recklessly over a hurdle. Only days before, he had been turned down by the Cavalry. Suicide was possible, but not discussed. Wallis agreed she would pack up and move them to California while Win attended Egbert's funeral in Chicago. When Win arrived he learned that his sister Ethel had taken a lethal dose of barbiturates the previous night, for what reason no one in the family seemed to know.

Their first home in California was two rooms at the palatial Hotel del Coronado. Wallis soon found a Spanish-style house nearby that suited her needs if not her pocketbook. The living room of the stucco and brick bungalow on Flora Drive, with its picturesque red-tiled roof and arched doorways, contained an impressive cathedral ceiling and gave entry to a charming patio. With California's warm climate, she would be able to entertain on a gracious scale, both indoors and out.

The house was fully furnished, but she unpacked her wedding gifts for the first time. The magnificent chased-silver bowl Uncle Sol had given them in place of the check she had hoped for was placed on a low table before the sofa and kept filled with fresh flowers. Her mother's Lenox china, bought when they had lived in the Preston Street Apartments, was displayed in a cabinet of distinctive Spanish design. On top of a dark oak sideboard was Cousin Lelia's present, a Kirk silver tea service, and Corrine and Henry's gift, a Tiffany cut-glass decanter and six matching glasses. Wallis filled a shelved niche with books she bought at a jumble sale, and a bay window with large terra-cotta pots planted with greens. She had a true talent for turning a new place quickly into a home.

Win, on his part, immediately set to work with a vengeance at the air base. He had returned from Chicago in an appalling state and she had feared he was heading for a nervous collapse. He managed somehow to stay sober on duty, driving himself as he had at Squantum, putting in twelve- and fourteen-hour days. But he was drinking heavily on his own time. His depression intensified, erupting often in acts of threatened violence toward her.

One night when they had returned from a party he broke an empty bottle of gin against the kitchen table and advanced with it toward her. "You ever even *look* at another officer with those cow eyes as you did that pansy captain tonight and I'll rip your face ugly. So don't test me, Wallis!"

He lowered his hand with the jagged glass only a few feet before reaching her. Strangely, she had not been terrified. Yet Wallis understood neither Win's often outrageous behavior nor her reactions to it.

On occasion they still shared good times together; and when he was sober, he was a responsive lover. His sadism increased with his drinking. He had become unreasonably jealous. Wallis was a self-liberated woman and spoke as easily—perhaps even more easily—to men as she did to her own sex. She could exchange a slightly off-color joke and relished being the center of attention. She was young, a good dancer, slim and attractive, and men enjoyed her company. Win accused her of trying to seduce every man to whom she had been talking. She did not recall exactly when the accusations began, but after the first few months in California they were the harbingers of angry scenes that threatened violence.

On Armistice Day, November 11, 1918, a wild celebration took place in the streets of Coronado. Later, there were to be bands from each branch of the service, dancing and a parade, and Wallis had looked forward to these events. Shortly before noon she went into the bathroom to freshen up and turned the water on in the sink. The door was reflected in the mirror above, and as she glanced into it, she could see the doorknob turning. The lock clicked. She crossed the small room to try the handle. The door was locked. "Win," she called.

There was no reply.

"Win! Open this door!" she shouted.

The house was still. If Win had not gone out and left her locked in the bathroom, he was not moving, in order to further torment her. She pounded on the door and shouted until her hands were sore and her throat raw. Finally, she collapsed onto the floor, feeling an unreasoning terror at the touch of the cold tile against the bare flesh of her legs. The small, high bathroom window overlooked the patio which was enclosed by a brick wall. She could never squirm through the window, nor hope to be heard by anyone if she called out for help. She took a nail file from the medicine cabinet and tried unsuccessfully to pick the lock.

She decided she must concentrate on something pleasant. Make believe this was not a terrifying situation, that Win might not return until the next day. He had been gone overnight before without telling her where he was going. Or he could be stretched out on the bed in the room beyond her prison cell. In either case, she had to turn her thoughts elsewhere. She would plan a dinner party for the Christmas season. Crunching a towel beneath her legs, she leaned back against the cold enamel of the tub and began to concentrate on names for a guest list.

It was a ridiculous exercise, but the situation was equally ridiculous.

"Let's see," she said aloud. "I'll have Rear Admiral Fulham, and his two daughters, Marianna and Rhoda; Maurice Heckscher—he has a string of polo ponies and knows a lot of good people, and Benny Thaw, who'll soon be going as second secretary to the embassy in Warsaw. That's eight, the right size for a small dinner." She thought a little more about it. No, Win wouldn't appreciate their being the only married couple present. She would include her new friends, Katherine and Tom Bigelow.

Her fear mounted despite her attempt to control it. Silence claimed the rest of the house. Win had obviously gone out. It might be days before help came. She must not think about that. *The dinner party.* She could make her mother's recipe for oyster loaf as a first course, then roast beef and gravy, roast potatoes, artichokes with hollandaise sauce, and ice cream with chestnuts and brandy. She went over the recipes in her head. Oysters might be a problem in December. Better serve something simple and elegant. Maybe melon and port wine or grilled grapefruit with sherry.

Rain slashed against the window. The day had darkened. The bathroom was streaked with shadow. She wondered what was happening in town. Well, no one ever stopped a war for rain, so why wouldn't the Armistice celebrants continue in their festivities? A war had ended. The fighting men—at least most—were coming home. *Dumaresque.* Yes, of course! How foolish of her not to have realized that the Armistice would reawaken all of Win's fury over his brother's death. A street party would seem outrageous to him when Dumaresque was buried in an unmarked grave on some muddy, deserted patch of foreign soil.

This grim image blocked out the distress of her current predicament. And so the long hours of her confinement passed, filled with thoughts that would block her fears. Day faded into dark twilight. She flicked on the light and sat on the edge of the bathtub, the towel around her shoulders to ward off the evening chill. The heat was controlled by a thermostat and would not come back on until eight P.M. She had no watch but she could assume that would only be a short time off. The rain was steady. Her anger grew. How dare Win rob her of her personal rights? Why should he cause her pain and suffering because the war had claimed Dumaresque's life?

A burst of what sounded like gunfire brought her to her feet. Through the window she could see what looked like a shooting star. Then the sky was filled with an explosion of stars. She had forgotten about the scheduled fireworks display.

A snake of light slithered under the door. Win was in the bedroom. The door handle turned, and when he found the door still locked he apparently decided to let it remain so. Wallis held her breath, controlling her urge to shout at him, to bang the door again. No, she would not do that. Two could play the same game.

She ran a bath and poured in some fragrant bath crystals. She would pretend nothing was amiss in the hope that out of curiosity he would unlock the door. She undressed and stepped into the warm water. Immediately she felt reassured. She trailed her hand back and forth through the bath water, making a *whooshing* sound that she wanted him to hear. Several minutes passed. The lock clicked. The handle turned.

Win loomed tall in the doorway, his shirt opened at the neck, his hair disheveled. He stood staring down at her nakedness beneath the water and yet she had the feeling that he really did not see her, that his mind was distracted elsewhere.

"If you're coming in," she said, surprised at how steady her voice sounded, "close the door after yourself. There's a terrible draft." She scooped up the soap and clasped it tightly. He had not noticed her movement.

"Hand me a towel from the shelf," she said, and rising, the soap concealed behind her, stepped over the rim of the bathtub and onto a small mat. He did not move. His dark, brooding eyes were sharp flint, as though a deep, interior anger had been struck. She reached for a towel, wrapped it around herself, tucking in the end to secure it. Win remained motionless. *Now!* she thought, and with the bar of soap in her hand, lashed out at him, pushing it hard into his mouth, and then took his off-guard moment of sputtering surprise as he spit out the soap to slip past him, into the bedroom, moving as fast as she could toward the bedroom door. It was locked and she whirled back in fury. Win held the key so that she could see it.

"Got you this time, Wallis," he sneered.

"Win, this has been a difficult day for you, I know," she said, grasping the towel tightly about herself. "Our boys are coming home and Dumaresque won't be with them. I understand more than you realize. You were the oldest brother. You were the one who was expected to fight for the others. And you never had a chance and now they're dead—Dumaresque and Egbert, and even poor Ethel, and you have this belief that somehow you're responsible. Well, you're not." She had regained her composure and looked him straight in the eyes as he advanced slowly toward her.

"I'll try to forget what happened today," she said. "You should not have locked me in a room. You know that was wrong, Win. And I am sure you will unlock the bedroom door. Not to do so would be sick and perverse and very wrong. And I know you couldn't be like that." She was talking to him as though he were a small boy. "I know you were really beside yourself with grief today. It must have seemed to you that the whole world was celebrating—even me."

He was only an arm's reach away. She stepped back. He reached out and grabbed her arm. "What the hell do you really know about me, Wallis?" he asked, his voice underscored with bitter sarcasm. "Or for that matter, what the hell do I know about you? Just that you drive me mad because I can see you really don't love me. Not that it should matter, because you aren't capable of the kind of love I require. I need to be so deeply a part of you that you don't exist without me." He was holding her bare shoulders vise-like between his large hands. "All you can think about is dinner parties and polo games. It's not enough for you to be my wife. You have to prove to the world that you're better than that. If I were a general you'd want to be First Lady. No one will ever be good enough for you, Wallis."

His hands tightened their hold on her shoulders. A sharp pain seared down Wallis's back.

"You're hurting me. Let go," she shouted. To her amazement, he did as she asked.

"I could have crushed all your bones," he said.

She stepped cautiously away. She must remain cool, not do anything that would agitate him. "I'll get dressed," she said, as she crossed to her wardrobe closet. "We'll go out to dinner. Not to the Club. Maybe that Mexican restaurant you like so well. I'll put on something casual." She pulled out a simple dress, smoothed it over the back of a chair, took out fresh lingerie and stockings from her chest of drawers and dressed quickly but methodically. All the while, he stood watching her with rage in his eyes. "Do you think we'll need a reservation?" she asked. "With all the excitement in town it might be a good idea. The number is in my address book in the living room, right by the telephone."

"You're not going anywhere," he said.

"Well, there's not much in the house for dinner. I wasn't able to get out to the market today." The moment she said it she regretted the hard tone in her voice. He took a threatening step toward her. Except for her shoes, she was dressed. Her mind whirled. She needed time and something to defend herself with. She made a casual motion to retrieve her shoes from the inside rack of her wardrobe. Win reached out, pulled her back and swooped her up in his arms.

"Put me down!" she shouted. "Put me down!"

He dropped her on the bed and when she tried to get up, he pushed her down again, holding both her hands in one of his while he undid his loosened tie and, using it as a rope, bound her hands to the rear of the bed.

"Win, don't—don't you *dare*!" she screamed, certain he was about to rape her.

She kept thrashing the bed with her feet, and he took two ties from his tie rack on the rear of his closet door and tied her legs, spread-eagled, to the two bottom posts. Wallis was silenced by her terror, pushing her body as deep as she could into the mattress as if she thought she might be able to escape that way.

But to her surprise, Win walked away, toward the door which he now opened. "I'm not sure when I'll be back, Wallis. At least I can count on your being here to greet me," he said as he left the room. Moments later the the front door slammed shut. She was alone. Her fear subsided. He would not return for hours. By then he would be well and truly drunk. When he had sobered he would become a small, repentant boy. He would buy her a gift. He would try to do all he could to please her. That was his usual pattern. The bonds were too well secured for her to break. She lay there, staring up at the ceiling, and vowed she would never let Win or any man humiliate her in this manner again.

11

The following spring Alice came to visit for a month. Although Wallis had been careful not to mention her marital problems in her letters, her mother had read between the lines and, once in Coronado, was quick to note the flickering expression of disdain when something Wallis said to Win did not please him.

For a year Alice had been head housekeeper at the fashionable Chevy Chase Club in Washington, a fact that Wallis had told no one in Coronado. It rankled her that she did not have the means to give her mother a better life and she nurtured a long-festering resentment against the Warfields (including Uncle Sol, who always made her mother come begging) and the Rasins, who she believed had treated the widow of their kin in an abominable fashion. When she thought about it, she knew that, in the event of Win's death, the Spencers would not do well by her either.

Wallis could not understand, after her terrifying Armistice Day experience, why she had not left Win. She had been more humiliated than bruised. She supposed she would never be able to find it in her heart to forgive him, but there had not been another such incident since. She had also seen Win's faith in himself, despite a promotion to lieutenant colonel, disintegrate rapidly as men under him transferred to more stimulating jobs than chief officer of a training center in peacetime. He was convinced that he was being passed over for younger, less experienced men.

A temporary cessation of hostilities between them was maintained for the first three weeks of Alice's visit. Then, on the night of the gala in honor of Britain's visiting Prince of Wales, Win returned home drunk from the Officers' Club. After that night, when he dragged Wallis away from the dance before they had been presented to the royal guest and terrorized her after they had arrived home, his conversation consisted only of pointed jabs at Wallis. A remark by Alice as innocent as: "I thought the Bassetts most gracious to invite Wallis an' me on their boat for Saturday lunch" evoked the reply: "Poor Rita, they say the wife is the last to know when her best friend has eyes for her husband. Right, Wallis?"

By now she was accustomed to Win's unfounded jealousy. Alice was not. "Wallis," her mother said the morning of her departure, "the thing that worries me most about you an' Win is how little tenderness you show for each other. Anger that can be expressed is not always a bad thing. Lord knows, I got angry at Free from time to time, an' he wasn't always pleased with me. But we did as much touchin' an' lovin' outa bed as in. In four weeks I have nevah seen Win take your hand, or put his arm about you, or look at you in that special way people do when they love someone. An' what concerns me is that you don't exhibit much affection for him either."

"I know, Mama. We're just having a rough patch. Win doesn't know what his future will be in the Navy with the war over and the need to train pilots so diminished." But Wallis knew in her heart that her mother was too perceptive not to see the irreparable differences that were mounting between Win and herself.

After Alice left, their life together became a succession of bitter quarrels. Win's drinking continued but at least he did not lapse into violence or display the appalling sadism of which he was capable. Wallis desperately cast about for some solution to their difficulties. His distress over his disappointing naval career led her to suggest he leave the service for the newly born field of commercial aviation. She knew this notion was motivated by her own needs. She had seen enough of the Navy mode of life—gypsy pilgrimages to new stations for brief sojourns in rental bungalows or tasteless government housing—to conclude that it was not for her.

When Win refused even to consider a civilian career, Wallis was forced to put the idea out of her head. Later that year, after he was transferred to March Field, Riverside, California, she remained in Coronado, a drive of many hours from his new air base. This meant that he came home only when he had two days or more of leave, which left her to attend social affairs on her own. Her invitations increased. Win's drinking had become a public encumbrance. She did not hesitate when asked to spend a weekend up the coast at the large seaside estates of the prominent and very rich. In such lavish settings, Wallis could nourish her growing fantasy of one day becoming the chatelaine of a great house. Unlike Win, she was comfortable in such lavish settings, and her welcomed visits—for she was always good company—helped her to overcome the residue of anger she still retained about the indignity of her youthful visit to the Kirk home in Baltimore.

After only a few months of marriage, Tom Bigelow had died suddenly of a heart attack, leaving Katherine a young and beautiful widow. "Kitty" was tall, blond and willowy. The two women made a striking pair as they met for lunch to exchange confidences at the Hotel del Coronado. Their shared laughter caused the curious to glance toward their table. During the war Kitty had served with the Red Cross in France, an experience that gave her a certain cachet in Wallis's eyes. She had recently met Herman Rogers, the heir to a railroad fortune. His family's magnificent estate on the Hudson, Crumwold Hall, adjoined Hyde Park, the Roosevelts' impressive home. "Herm" was not only rich but spectacularly good-looking, with the dark wavy hair and distinctive profile of a matinee idol. Kitty was deliriously in love.

"He says when he was a major with the armed forces in France that I served him coffee and a doughnut at Amiens when his company was on their way to the front and that he told another officer, 'That's the most attractive girl I've ever seen! If I ever find her again, I'm going to marry her!'" Kitty beamed.

"Sounds like a good line," Wallis said skeptically.

"Oh no! I think he's sincere. He's asked me to marry him."

"Oh, Kit! Will you?"

"Well, of course, it's only been five months since Tom's death. I couldn't possibly consider his proposal yet. But I'm not going to let him slip through my fingers either. I've arranged a trip to New York in two weeks. He only came out here for the big party that Benny Thaw threw." Kitty paused significantly. "The one you missed when Win came home for the weekend."

"Win is away so much that we needed the time together," Wallis explained. "And he's on the wagon."

"I'm glad to hear that, Wallis. I'm so happy, I want everyone else to be happy, too."

Kitty and Herman Rogers were married in a small ceremony that November and then went off to the Orient for an extended honeymoon. Win was ordered back to Pensacola for a short tour of duty. Wallis refused to accompany him. She viewed the separation as a temporary split, a chance for each of them to discover how they felt living entirely apart. Coronado, the winter of 1920 to 1921, was bleak; the California coastal regions experienced the coldest, dampest season in forty years. Those residents who could departed for sunnier climes or took advantage of the lack of sunshine at home to travel to the Continent, South America or, like the newlywed Rogerses, the Far East. With Kitty gone, Wallis was dependent for companionship on the very group of women—the service wives—whom she had alienated. Only a few extended her invitations and those women she found depressingly boring.

Spring finally arrived and with it a letter from Win telling her that he had received orders to report to the Navy Department in Washington as assistant to Rear Admiral William Moffett, who was preparing to set up a Bureau of Aeronautics in the capital. He wrote that he missed her, that he had not been drinking and that he wanted desperately for her to join him in Washington, where he was certain she would feel more at home than at any of their former assignments.

* * *

The point of no return had been reached. If they did not reunite, she would have to admit her marriage was over, which she was not ready to do. There had never been a divorce in either the Montague or Warfield families. Cousin Lelia and Uncle Sol both had deep-seated religious scruples against it, and it would be those relations to whom she would have to turn for financial assistance until she was able to support herself or had remarried. On Win's naval pay she could not expect more than a skimpy settlement. Out of vindictiveness, he might even cut her off without any funds.

Wallis had seen too many relatives who had been forced to live in reduced circumstances. She also vividly recalled the humiliation her mother had to suffer when Uncle Sol had given her a monthly stipend. Unable to see herself placed in that position, she therefore wrote Win that she would pack up all their possessions in Coronado and move to Washington. His reaction was one of delight and she boarded an eastbound train with the hope that the winter's separation had brought him to his senses. She was also looking forward to being reunited with her mother and Aunt Bessie, although, in those moments when she allowed her true feelings to surface, she felt a sense of shame and resentment that Alice was a housekeeper and her aunt a paid companion.

Win had rented a two-room service apartment in a small hotel called the Brighton. Their wedding presents remained in packing boxes and most of her wardrobe in suitcases in the basement storage room. Despite the apartment's cramped quarters and grim decor (mustard walls and brown mohair furniture), they enjoyed a two-day honeymoon. Win was in especially high spirits and had taken a short leave to help Wallis settle in. To Wallis, Washington was a vital city, inhabited by people of many cultures. Spring washed dazzlingly over the monuments and the government buildings. The streets of the capital were alive with the spectacle of cherry-blossom time. She and Win walked beneath the pink extravagance of the flower-laden boughs, hand in hand. His gentle grasp brought a soft, choking sensation to her throat. This is what Alice meant when she spoke about tenderness between couples.

Their steps quickened as they neared the Brighton. A

mutual desire had enveloped them and they began to run toward the hotel, Win just slightly ahead of her, although their hands remained interlocked.

The gold bars on his uniform caught the sun and furred out, almost blinding her. She was reminded of Pensacola and her first view of him coming up the path to Corrine's house. Her eyes teared. Win was laughing and the music of the sound jingled joyously in her ears.

Once in their rooms they made love. There was no violence, no sadism, no wish by Wallis to have it end. Win whispered kisses around the rim of her mouth, the edges of her ears, the nape of her neck, the curve between her small breasts. He was a gentle, *tender* lover. Wallis, at that moment, was as madly in love with him as she had been shortly after they had met and her ecstasy was what she had fantasized for her wedding night.

Neither of them had taken the time to adjust the shades and as they lay quietly, legs and arms still entwined from their spent passion, warm tentacles of sunlight stretched sensually across their naked bodies. For a long time both were silent.

"Win?" she finally asked in a hushed voice, believing he might have fallen asleep, so still was he.

"Yes?"

"Let's start all over, here and now, pretend Boston and Coronado, all the anger between us, never happened."

"Life isn't like that, Wallis," he replied. "When you love someone you have to take their past, their aberrations, all of what they are. This was a moment in our lives. But that's all it was. Don't count on it changing me. I know damn well it won't change you. The sun will go down and you'll turn on the electric lights in here and you'll look at this room, which will then carry the stale scent of our lovemaking, and you'll say to yourself, 'This place isn't good enough for me.' And when I see you watching me with your oh-so-holy, judgmental eyes, the arrogant brows raised, I'll see clear enough what is really passing through your head: 'It's not good enough. *He's* not good enough.'"

She swung her slim, tanned legs over the side of the bed, pulled a coverlet around herself and, rising, went over to the window and drew up the blind. "We might as well have all of the light we can get," she said. No reply was forthcoming and when she turned around his back was to her. She crossed over to the bed. Win appeared to be asleep. She had to clasp her hands together to keep from shaking him awake and forcing him to talk to her, to thrash out what he had just said.

Okay, so much for tenderness, she thought. It could be as menacing as detachment or intimidation or the threat of violence. She took a warm bath and then dressed for the evening. They were to take Alice out for dinner. After an unsuccessful attempt to rouse Win from the bed, she left him a note and went to meet her mother on her own. When she returned to the hotel later that night, he was gone. He came in around three in the morning, reeling drunk.

"Where were you tonight?" he asked in a slurred hostile voice.

"With mother, of course. We had a dinner appointment, or have you forgotten?"

"Never do that again," he warned.

"Do what?"

"Leave me to go out."

"Really, Win, you're being an ass! I told you I was with my mother. And anyway, you don't own me."

"Alice, the merry widow," he sneered. "You're both sluts. Don't think I can't see what you two are up to." He started toward her, stumbled, swore unintelligibly under his breath and then collapsed onto the foot of the bed, out cold.

The next morning when she awoke he was sitting in a chair, staring at her, still dressed in the rumpled clothes he had slept in, his eyes bloodshot.

"God, you look awful," she said. "Shall I order some coffee?" He remained silent, his eyes narrowing as he continued to scrutinize her. "All right, Win, if you want to play the ridiculous role of the injured husband, have it your way." She got up and tying her robe around her went into the bathroom and closed the door. "Oh, no!" she thought, a moment later, and turned to open it again, but the lock clicked in place before she had time to do so.

"Win! Open this door!" she shouted. There was no reply.

She called out to him again and again. Then she took his razor and tried to spring the lock. She nicked her finger. Blood spurted, staining her dressing gown and spotting the white tile floor. "Damn! Damn!" she cried. The finger kept bleeding and she had to wrap it in a washcloth. She butted the door with her shoulder to no avail. A toilet flushed in the room above, a distant door slammed closed. She considered breaking the small window and screaming for help but the consequences of such an action kept her from doing so. The hotel was a temporary home for several other Navy couples. Her private life would instantly become squalid gossip.

The reconciliation had been a terrible mistake. She had misinterpreted his actions. Worse than that, she had not recognized that Win was really deranged. No sane man could do such totally irrational things. She could not waste her life with a crazy person, no matter how repellent divorce was to the members of her family. She was young, good company, and she was also part Warfield and part Montague. Win was right. This was not good enough for her. *He* was not good enough for her.

All she could think about was getting out of this white-tiled sterile box with the acrid scent of disinfectant clinging to the damp walls; out of the apartment, away from Win; to be able, as she had hoped earlier, to start anew. But not with Win. No! not with him!

She had no idea what outrageous act of violence he might be plotting against her. She had not heard him leave the room and was certain he was planning some mad revenge. Nonetheless, she could not allow him to have the advantage. If she could get out, she would make a run for the door, or grab the telephone and call for help. With Win's razor, she managed to unscrew the clothes hook from the back of the door and then twisted it between the frame and the wall with all her strength. The door gave so suddenly that she lunged forward into the room and fell to the floor.

Win only stirred in his sleep. Barefooted, she cautiously skirted the bed, hardly breathing as she made her way to the chair where she had placed her clothes the night before. Win had not moved. She dressed as quickly as she could and then, carrying her shoes, tiptoed to the door of their small suite. Her hand shook as she went to open it. She was too frightened to look back as she rushed into the hallway and took the steps, two at a time, to the lobby.

The doorman got her a taxi. She went directly to her mother's and asked whether she might move in until she could find an accommodation for herself.

"You are absolutely sure this is what you want?" Alice asked.

"Absolutely sure," Wallis repeated with emphasis. To her chagrin, her mother was not in the least encouraging.

"There's never been a divorce in our family," she reminded Wallis.

"Yes, I know, but I can't go on being terrorized. He's crazy."

"A woman alone—a *divorced* woman—it won't be easy, Wallis."

"Life seldom is, Mama."

Alice managed a small smile and, putting her arms around her daughter, she pressed her head to her full bosom. Wallis felt a child again. She remembered the nights at the Brexton, her tremendous sense of loneliness until the moment when her mother entered their room. She had a fragmentary image of Alice standing in the doorway framed by the light that had come in from the hotel's hallway.

"I wanted so much more for you than I was able to give," Alice sighed. "An' in my heart I feel maybe I'm to blame. Not for Win. You made up your own mind on Win. But for only bein' able to pass some dreams of mine on to you, dreams, maybe, that weren't always practical."

Wallis straightened and drew back. "Mama," she said, "my leaving Win has nothing to do with dreams. He's a drunk and a sadist, a dangerous man. What you gave me was more than dreams. You taught me how to survive. Right now, that means leaving Win, eventually divorcing him. I deserve a second chance. You had one. So did Kitty Rogers and look at her life now."

"We were widows."

"Well, of course," Wallis grinned, "I could always murder my husband."

She sat up long after her mother had retired. She had left Win, but now, what was she to do? She could not stay with Alice in this insufferably humble housekeeper's quarters. Aunt Bessie no longer had an apartment of her own. Wallis needed money and, because there was no one else she could think of whom she could ask, she decided to swallow her pride and write to Uncle Sol. She composed a long, emotional letter confessing the sordid details of her marriage (although not the *worst* of them) and asked him for a loan that would help her pay for an apartment until she could take care of the rent. Her intention was to find work and she listed a number of occupations that might suit her limited abilities and help her to maintain the necessities: shopgirl, receptionist, anything in fashion.

It was nearly three A.M. when she had finished. She slipped out and went down to the corner to post the letter before going to bed so that she would not have time to change her mind.

For three nights she slept fitfully on the sofa in her mother's small sitting room. To her shock, Win did not come looking for her. Finally, Uncle Sol's reply arrived. "Any divorce action that you contemplate," he wrote, "including the rental of a separate abode from your husband, must be undertaken entirely with your own resources. I advise you here and now that no help of any kind will be forthcoming from me."

Wallis had no choice but to remain for the time being with Alice. She had only the few dollars that Win grudgingly sent to her from his Navy pay. Fate stepped in very quickly to help her. Despite his stature as a pilot, Win was ordered to the Far East as commander of a gunboat based in Hong Kong. His foreign post meant that his wife was sent a monthly allotment check by the Navy of $225. The amount was modest but it made Wallis independent for the first time in her life.

Washington was a haven and she adored it for having saved her. Almost all its people came from elsewhere, their ambition palpable. Tense young men grasped the tailcoats of power. And those at the top never looked back over their shoulders. The women, single or married, harbored their secrets as well as any seasoned Washington diplomat. Unless you were running for political office you could live in Washington without a past, or you could create one that suited you best.

There were always new people—from all over the country, all regions of the world—who would never have heard of the Warfields, the Montagues or the Spencers. Win's monthly naval stipend had soothed her anger toward him. She was free to be young again, free to enjoy the company of men. Win had given her a second chance. This time she meant to be wiser. She had learned that a woman could be made or ruined by the man she married. "Just look at Kitty," she reminded herself. "And then look at Mama."

She hated staying with Alice in her two backstairs rooms and would have her friends and dates pick her up at the Jefferson Hotel, where a doorman then sent her home in a taxi. Her plan was to find an apartment she could share with a friend. This took time, because *who* the friend was, was important.

Marianna Fulham, the Admiral's daughter from Coronado, was also separated from her husband and living in Washington. She shared a small attractive apartment in Georgetown with a soon-to-be-divorced former Oldfields classmate of Wallis's, Ethel Noyes, who had been one of Wallis's bridesmaids and whose father was president of the American Press. The three women were about the same age, had similar interests (clothes, the social set and a search for attractive, unattached men) and liked the same people.

Ethel was dating Willmott Lewis, the distinguished correspondent of the London *Times,* and Willmott invited Wallis to attend one of the special luncheons given by the *Soixante Gourmets,* a famous Washington club composed of sixty of the city's most eligible bachelors. They met weekly at midday at the elegant Hotel Hamilton, which had a dining room noted for its cuisine, with a lady of their choice, or one whose charms had been approved by another member. Willmott suggested that

Wallis come along one week as the luncheon partner of Don Felipe Espil, First Secretary at the Argentine Embassy.

As Wallis entered the vast Old World dining room, a table extending the length of one side, she glanced hastily around, her eyes darting quickly from one man to another in an attempt to pick out Espil, whom she had seen only in a published press photograph. A dark-haired man in his early thirties, sleek, almost swarthy, was staring at her through a monocle. She had never seen one used before and it held her attention.

"Who is the man with the monocle?" she asked Willmott.

"That my dear, is Señor Espil."

"I rather thought so."

Espil stood up and started toward them. "What a gorgeous man," Wallis whispered to Ethel.

"You bet!" Ethel replied.

He walked with swaggering assurance. The navy pinstripe suit he wore was impeccably tailored for his lean, six-foot frame. A large diamond ring adorned the little finger of his right hand and, as he adjusted his monocle, it refracted light from the brilliant chandelier. Wallis felt uneasy as he drew near. She recalled a time as a child when Ellie had taken her to a healer to cure a shoulder wrenched when she had fallen on the ice. The man had held his hands just above her injury, not touching her, yet she had sensed his energy pass through her. This was the reaction she had as Espil stood alongside her, the musky scent of an exotic men's cologne clinging to him.

"Miss Noyes," he said in a heavily accented voice as he reached across Wallis, took Ethel's hand and brushed it lightly with his lips. "Willmott, you old fox. You have the corner on beautiful women, yes?" He was smiling down at Wallis, his eyes magnetized by her own.

"This is Mrs. Spencer, Felipe, one of America's Southern belles," Willmott replied.

Wallis felt Espil's warm breath as he kissed her hand. "I have never before seen a woman with purple eyes," he smiled in wonder. "They are most ravishing." He placed her hand on his arm as he escorted her to the table. "I find young married women especially attractive. Like the flower when it comes to full bloom, yes?"

Wallis laughed, the sound a bit harsh but very infectious. It was a way to cover her nervousness but Espil assumed she was politely admonishing him and he was pleased with her spirit.

The key to Washington society was the word *precedence.* It firmly dictated who would be included in the most prestigious party lists and who sat next to whom at those events. Because Washington was the nation's capital, government and embassy officials ranked first. The wife of a Navy officer was at the bottom of any list. If Espil was her escort, she could, in effect, "jump the queue." She must, she decided, play this moment shrewdly. Not too pushy, not too helpless; appealing and yet mysterious.

Of course, Espil was only a First Secretary to the Argentine Ambassador, but she knew he was viewed with special distinction for his broad range of abilities and his high visibility. Some of Washington's richest and most notable women had been escorted by Espil. Society editors doted on his social appearances. Washington hostesses, always pleased to have their parties reported in the press, made sure he was included in their guest lists. As lunch progressed, however, Wallis realized there was much more to Espil than her first impression.

Although he spoke with a strong accent, his English was fluent, his vocabulary extensive and his knowledge—of everything from American baseball and the musical theater to his guest country's constitutional law and esoteric economics—impressive. "I am a diplomat by accident," he told Wallis. He had come to the United States six years earlier as an attorney in an international law concern and had been asked four years later to join the staff of his embassy by the Ambassador, who was a close friend.

Throughout lunch, Wallis was aware of the envious and appraising glances of the women who sat near them. If she was to hold Espil's attention and get him to extend her a future invitation, she would have to sparkle as she never had before. Someone mentioned the new short haircuts called "bobs" that were being worn by so many young women.

"Never by me," Wallis declared and then launched into the story of her "bout" with scarlatina and how she had to cut off her hair due to her "illness."

"The barber *vowed* it would grow back in three weeks," she told Espil, not confessing that she had never really had the fever. "Three weeks came and went; a month, six weeks, passed. I resembled a porcupine who had got caught in a revolving door!" She laughed at her own joke and he quickly joined in.

"You are a very honest woman," he said. "I like that. And you can laugh at yourself, a rare quality."

"Did Willmott tell you my husband is in China and that we were separated before he left for the Orient?"

"He did, indeed."

"I do accept invitations," she said under her breath. This time he initiated the laughter they soon shared.

"You are quite remarkable," he said.

She leaned over and whispered in his ear. "On our next meeting you can kiss both my hands."

He laughed again. "Dinner, tomorrow night?" he asked.

She went to bed with him that first evening. This was, after all, the 1920's, the time of the hip flask, short skirts, the "It" girl and anything goes. At twenty-six and separated from her husband, Wallis felt she was old enough to do whatever she wanted. Her dues were paid. After Win's abuse she had the right to self-fulfillment. Espil aroused all her latent sexuality. Under his sensual touch her boyish bosom seemed near bursting. In his glamorous bachelor penthouse apartment at the Wardman Park Hotel she learned from him how to pleasure a man and, for the first time, to be pleasured in return. Espil not only had scientific knowledge of all the erogenous zones, male and female, he was a master of techniques.

Whatever the hour she arrived home, Alice would be waiting for her, sitting up in bed reading or sewing. She never failed to ask Wallis where she had been and what she had done and with whom. Wallis did not exactly evade the truth, but she did not reveal that she and Espil were lovers, and if Alice guessed, she did not press. Then, one night, her mother could not control her censure.

"It is now two-fifteen in the mornin', Wallis. When I was your age no self-respectin' woman stayed out past midnight with a man not her husband. Now, what I wish you'd explain to me is exactly what you do when you stay up so late night aftah night."

The lamp that was attached to the back of Alice's bed cast her in a yellow glare of light. Although not yet fifty, without makeup she appeared much older. *I won't let life do that to me,* Wallis thought. A lot of good being a proud Montague of Virginia had done for her mother. She had ended up a housekeeper living in two basement rooms.

"I'm a grown woman, Mama, quite able to take care of myself and I find it truly humiliating to punch a time clock!"

"It would be a lot more humiliatin' if you should get pregnant with one man's child while bein' married to another! 'Specially since your husband is in China an' couldn't possibly be the daddy!"

"I never said I was having an affair," Wallis protested.

"An' I wasn't born yesterday!"

"Well, if you're going to worry about me whenever I stay out, and if I have to worry about you sitting up to wait for me—"

Alice pulled the chain on the overhead light. Her voice rose disembodied in the darkness. "As long as we are under the same roof, Wallis, I shall continue to tell you what I think is right."

Things had come full circle. Wallis had a vivid memory of the night Aunt Bessie returned on Chase Street to find Alice and Free Rasin in a compromising situation. And like Alice in that long-ago time, Wallis knew she would have to move out as quickly as possible.

Arrangements were made for her to share a little house in Georgetown with Dorothy McNamee, a friend of Marianna Fulham. Dorothy was the wife of a naval officer who was currently on duty in Panama. Wallis was once again able to give dinner parties. Espil was duly impressed at her social and culinary talents, but if Wallis thought this would bring him close to a declaration of love, she was wrong.

He continued to escort her to the weekly luncheons at the Hamilton, attended her dinner parties and took her to those given by members of Washington's diplomatic world. He acted as both a teacher and model in the art of living. An excellent golfer, a superb bridge player, a dedicated horseman and a connoisseur of wine, food and art, he somehow managed a demanding social life without slackening up on the obligations of his career.

His prodigious attention to his work amazed Wallis. No matter how late his hours, he rose early to read at least seven international newspapers and *The Congressional Record* for the previous day. To keep up with him she had to put in a lot of reading time herself so that she could contribute to his conversations with friends. She learned some Spanish and French, became knowledgeable about fine antiques and mastered the proper protocol for foreign gatherings. He took her to theater—anything from *No More Blondes* to *Hamlet.* She was fond of movies and they saw Norma Talmadge in *Within the Law* and Thomas Meighan and Lila Lee in *The Ne'er-Do-Well.* On her own, she would sit in the gallery during open sessions of Congress so that she could discuss the day's proceedings with Espil that evening.

Later, they made love at his apartment. Wide terrace windows overlooked the city lights. She felt above everyone and everything. She dared to believe that he was as wild about her as she was about him and that the only reason he had not declared himself was because she was, of course, still a married woman. But the minute she discussed the idea of her filing for a divorce, Espil drew back. Wallis learned that he had been seen with another woman and she was sick with jealousy.

"I'd move to Argentina with him or anywhere else," she confessed to Ethel Noyes. "I'd even convert to Catholicism. I'm *that* mad about the man."

"With or without marriage?" Ethel inquired.

"With, of course," Wallis replied without a pause.

One warm June night in the summer of 1923, after they had been seeing each other for over a year and only moments after they had made passionate love, he stood on the balcony with his arms around her lightly clad figure as they both stared out over the rooftops of the city. "Perhaps we should not see each other so often," he said in an intimate voice.

Wallis broke away from his embrace and peered up at him with disbelief. "Why would you say that, Felipe?" she asked, deeply shocked.

"We have always been frank with each other, yes?" he asked.

"Yes, of course."

"One day I wish to become Ambassador from my country to the United States. To do so I must have two things I have not got—a wife and money. Now, *querida mía,* as much as I desire you, as much as I love you, I can never marry you. You see I need money and you are poor. I also come from a Catholic country and you, when you are divorced, shall have a living husband. That would make it difficult for the government to appoint me Ambassador. So—it is my ambition against my passion." He took Wallis's shocked face between both his hands and kissed her lightly. "There are other women, just as for you there will be, I am certain, other men. But only one chance for me to fulfill my ambition. In my world a false move—and *pffft,* one more career has ended between the bedsheets."

If he had assaulted her or knocked her to the ground, she could not have felt more stunned or in greater distress. Despite the warmth of the evening, she was suddenly icy cold. And when she saw the glaze that had come over his eyes she knew that Felipe was telling her their affair was over.

"You are one hell of a louse," she said.

"I hope someday you will understand why that has to be."

Wallis walked back inside, into the sitting room she so admired, with its shiny black baby grand piano, the paintings of famous race horses and the bright colors of the upholstery. She had felt safe and loved in this room. Now she had been told she was no longer welcome.

"I will never forget you," she said in a brittle voice, "or this evening."

"*Querida* . . ." he began.

"Never," she repeated, and with the dignity inherited from both the Montagues and the Warfields, she went into the bedroom to dress.

12

Corrine clutched a white lace handkerchief as she sat across from Wallis in the elegant living room of Cousin Lelia's Washington townhouse. Henry Mustin had died suddenly during the summer, felled by a heart condition that even the Navy had not known about. Corrine, now a very attractive widow in her mid-thirties, wore a tight-fitting black cloche hat with a narrow white band, to which was attached a flowing black crepe veil that touched the shoulders of her stylish mourning dress. She had lost considerable weight and with her pale face unrouged, her blond hair curled about the edges of her hat and her big blue eyes wide with emotion, she looked, thought Wallis, simply ravishing.

"I've been in mournin' jus' three months," she was saying to Wallis, who had come to pay her condolences to Corrine as soon as she had received word that her cousin was in Washington. "But I don't think Henry would want me to bury myself for a whole year. He understood my nature more than anyone."

She lifted her veil and pushed it back over the top of her hat as she dabbed at her tear-filled eyes. "Oh, Wallis, I was such a bad wife. I really was. I never appreciated Henry, an' now that he's gone, it's too late an' I'm sure God will somehow punish me for it."

"I'd count on Henry putting in a good word," Wallis said and was immediately contrite. "I'm sorry, Corrine," she apologized. Cousin Lelia had gone out on an errand, and once alone, their former intimacy had returned without a trace of awkwardness.

"Don't be," Corrine protested. "I so wanted to see you, Wallis. You're such good company even durin' the meanest of times. I've been so heavyhearted, all woebegone an' low down. An' then at the back of my mind this notion kept naggin'. I've always dreamed of seein' a bit more of the world, broadenin' my experience. Henry had promised for years that he would take me to Paris one day, an' it seemed like since he won't ever be able to do it, I should take myself an' this might be the best time to do so."

"Why, Corrine, that sounds like a marvelous idea," Wallis agreed.

"Of course, I couldn't go alone an' Leila has too many responsibilities here to go with me. An' my nieces, Anne and Lee-Lee, are both such ditherin' wimps I jus' couldn't consider travelin' abroad with them. So when I heard about you an' Win—not with any surprise I hafta admit—an' then about that cad Espil—" She paused as she caught the surprised look on Wallis's face. "Now, you can't be shocked that I know about your lover from the Pampas an' his beastly behavior! Washington is basically a small town where everybody knows everythin' about everyone."

The idea that she had been feeding the gossipmongers with juicy morsels had not occurred to Wallis until this moment. She had told Ethel and Marianna that she had been the one to end the affair. Obviously, Espil had told the truth. This thought now made her feel almost physically ill. "He loved me, Corrine. That's the worst part of it," she said. "Only his career meant more to him than I did."

"Well, you can't jus' keep hangin' on to a loose rock on top of a mountain 'cause sooner or later it will come right down on you, Wallis. An' that's exactly why I thought you should come with me to Paris."

Wallis was overwhelmed at the suggestion. Paris! Wouldn't she *just* love it! With Espil's ungallant exit there had been a yawning void in her life. She still shared the house with Dorothy McNamee, but Dorothy's husband, Luke, was due to return home soon, which meant Wallis would have to look for a new accommodation. It had not helped the low state of her ego to learn almost immediately after their parting that Espil was escorting an attractive young American heiress on the same rounds he had taken her and to hear that they might soon marry. Corrine's offer was most fortuitous.

"It would be wonderful, simply wonderful, Corrine. But where would I get the money for such a trip?" she asked.

"Henry's will hasn't gone through probate yet," Corrine replied, "so I can't pay for everythin'. However, I'm quite prepared to take on the price of the boat tickets an' our hotel. You'd only need money enough for your personal expenses."

"When do you plan to leave?"

"This comin' January. That's ten weeks from now an' means I'd at least have put in six months of mournin'. I think that's sufficient, don't you, Wallis?"

"I think even Henry would approve," she replied.

"Well?" Corrine prompted.

"I'll have to let you know in a week or so," Wallis said, and then wondered how, on her tight budget, she could even contemplate Corrine's offer.

A week later, she swallowed her pride and went to see Uncle Sol in New York. "Good God!" he said, after she had told him about Corrine's offer. "Why Paris? Paris, of all cities!" He jumped to his feet and launched into a denunciation of Parisian morals that led Wallis to reflect fleetingly that he seemed very well informed on the subject. At the height of his outburst, he came to a halt directly beneath a particularly provocative photograph of one of his alluring divas.

"Any city can be immoral if one chooses to make it so!" she countered. "You're a hypocrite, Uncle Sol, a terrible hypocrite!" she shouted and slammed angrily out of his apartment.

Before she reached the street she regretted her hasty action. She considered returning to apologize. Ever since Corrine had mentioned Paris, she knew she must go, that nothing would stop her. Still, she could not eat humble pie from a man who had so ludicrously given a morality lesson in front of the blatant evidence of his lecherousness. Ironically, the inscription on the photograph, under which Sol Warfield had stood while lecturing her, had said something about "remembering torrid nights beneath a tropical moon," a reference, she was sure, to a winter he had spent in Florida.

She took the first train she could board back to Washington and on arriving went directly to see Aunt Bessie. Her aunt was still employed by Mrs. Smith, who, every October, traveled down to her home in Palm Beach for the winter. Aunt Bessie was left in charge of her Washington townhouse with its fine art collection and museum quality antiques. Her aunt's position was not servile. She enjoyed the freedom of the house and the service of the domestic staff.

Aunt Bessie had long ago given up her apartment and now occupied a pleasant suite of rooms in her employer's home, consisting of sitting room, bedroom, dressing room and bath on the first floor that adjoined Mrs. Smith's considerably grander apartments. Florida was the only place where Aunt Bessie did not accompany the elderly Mrs. Smith, for her stepdaughter and heir annually made this pilgrimage with her. Aunt Bessie joined Mrs. Smith only in her foreign travels which, the previous year, had taken them on an extensive tour of China. Carved ivory and Chinese porcelain, souvenirs of this exotic journey, decorated Aunt Bessie's sitting room along with a jumble of expensive bibelots from the countries of their other travels.

Wallis did not come often to visit her aunt in this house, which she found unbearably depressing. With its ivy-covered brick walls and overhanging trees, it had a forbidding aura and an indefinable melancholy brooded over the interior. This had been the home where Mrs. Smith's husband had died over two decades earlier, and it remained a mausoleum to his memory. His carved-ivory and silver-handled walking sticks had not been removed from their position in a large urn in the front entry; his various hats, from early stovepipe to later bowler, occupied a shelf above. His pipe rack was on display in the library and his bedroom had been kept exactly as it had been on the day of his death, the shades still drawn, the windows closed. No wonder Mrs. Smith traveled so extensively,

Wallis thought, as a maid ushered her up the stairs to Aunt Bessie's sitting room. A musty odor of rooms kept shuttered and free from light permeated the house.

Aunt Bessie's apartments were much more cheerful. Her fondness for bright colors and good reading lamps had been indulged. She had never been a neat housekeeper and tables, desk and niches were a jumble of memorabilia. Photographs of Wallis at various ages were lined up on the mantel. Her aunt warmly referred to them as her "Wallis Collection." Scrapbooks stuffed and overflowing with rotogravure clippings and postcards from her travels were piled high on the floor. The disarray went against Wallis's sense of order. Yet the homeliness of Aunt Bessie's quarters gave her a warm glow and made her sorry she did not visit more often. For she knew she was loved sincerely in these rooms, that she was the daughter Aunt Bessie had never had. Wallis kissed her and then looked around for an empty chair in which to sit.

"I'm sorting through my winter wardrobe," Aunt Bessie explained. A recent small stroke had caused one side of her mouth to turn up in a perpetual half-smile, but she apparently had no other ill effects and was as spirited as ever. "Nothing seems to fit anymore. Just toss that pile of mending on top of the rest of the stuff on the wing chair and sit down on the sofa," she said. She turned to the young uniformed girl still waiting in the doorway. "Tea and some ginger cake, please, Bridget." The maid disappeared, closing the door after herself.

"Now, Wallis, what is it? I can tell by your expression that some scheme is brewing in your head."

"Well, Corrine is going to Paris and has asked me to go with her."

"That sounds like a fine idea. You need to go away for a while and let the dust settle."

"What dust?"

"The stories about your Argentinean lothario. Your mother told me." Aunt Bessie came over to the sofa and sat down beside her. "Wallis, you know how I feel about divorce," she said, and took her hand. "When you first told me you were leaving Win, I believed that if you persisted in this folly your future would be less than uncertain. As a divorced woman you would be entering a shady area and I did not see how you could achieve any of our hopes for you."

"But, Aunt Bessie, you don't understand about Win—" Wallis began.

"I understand more than you would like me to. I never did trust Win Spencer, and his family are simply not our sort. You just had to marry him. No one could have stopped you. *Must have—will get!* your mother always says about you. Now that it's over, I think you should see if you can get a quiet divorce somewhere. When I considered the facts, you see, I realized that there would be, after all, a life after Win. A better one, let's hope."

They were silent as Bridget brought the tea tray and set it down on a low table before the sofa. "Thank you, Bridget," she said as the girl left. "One must always show good manners to staff, Wallis. Remember that. It's a sign of good breeding." She poured the steaming tea into the cups. For a few moments there were only the outside sounds: tree branches scratching at the windows, the ominous drone of wind coming down the chimney. Aunt Bessie's glance moved off into space. "It's important to make the most of what you've got," she said. She put her teacup down and turned her gaze on her niece.

"Wallis, I know you have always thought I was the pushy one in the family," she said. "God knows your mother isn't. If it was up to Alice you would be taking Bridget's job. You have to understand that what I tried to do for you was also done for your mother. You are all she has. Alice's dreams have been put aside long ago. Heaven knows mine should be, too. Lord, here we are—the two Montague sisters, both in domestic service. It's almost incomprehensible. And we can't blame a war fought sixty years ago. The fact is, neither of us had the courage to stand up as women and be counted.

"We are victims of a society in which the men in your life are what matters—who your father was, whom you marry. That's the key to a woman's well-being and future. And in America we are not allowed to make a mistake unless we happen to be very, very rich and very, very beautiful. You are neither, but you have a certain aura about you, and I believed you were a star who would one day lead your poor mother and me out of bondage—make us feel like we matter." She glanced over to the pile of scrapbooks. "People who matter get their names and photographs in the papers. The only time they printed mine was when I married your Uncle Buck and when he died.

"Not that my life is so bad," she continued. "It just never seemed to be *my* life any more than these rooms are really *my* home. This wasn't meant to be my fate. I chose the wrong man, Cousin Lelia the right one. If that hadn't been the case I might have taken over Wakefield Manor and been the one to bring it back to its former grandeur."

She rose heavily from the sofa, walked a few steps and then turned back. It was strange, Wallis thought. She could clearly recall her mother as a young woman, but in her memory her aunt had always been middle-aged. Had Buck Merryman not married her she would no doubt have been a spinster. Wakefield Manor and all it implied would always have been out of her grasp. If Aunt Bessie wanted somehow to live *through* her, the knowledge did not make her in the least bit resentful for it validated her own sense of worth.

"I often imagine myself as a rich widow like Mrs. Smith," Aunt Bessie continued, "that we are two rich ladies traveling to all the best places together. It's not so hard to visualize. You see, Mrs. Smith was nursemaid to Mr. Smith's daughter from his first wife when she came to this house. When his wife died, she stayed on to take care of the girl. Eventually, she married her employer. Ah, yes! Dreams can become reality. At the same time truth cannot be avoided."

She sat down again and refilled her teacup. "Mrs. Smith is eighty this year. I can't expect the good life I lead now to continue much longer. And what can I do when that time comes? I'm sixty years old. My father died in a mental home and my husband left me almost impoverished. Before I came here, the house on Chase Street, even the family silver, was gone."

Her eyes suddenly brightened. "Once Mrs. Smith and I went to see a psychic, a woman who, we had been told, might be able to communicate with the dead. They seemed reluctant to speak up that day, but the psychic kept shouting, 'Who's Wallace? Who's Wallace?' I asked, "Could you mean *Wallis*?'

"'Tell her the King waits!' she said.

"It sounded crazy—but then she did know that Wallis was a woman. Tell *her,* she had said. I've been thinking about that incident ever since you left Win. Maybe she was saying your real love has yet to appear in your life."

"Or maybe that he's already dead," Wallis laughed.

"Well, I think you should go with Corrine to Paris," Aunt Bessie continued. "Wherever your future is, it can't be here. You have to break with the past. I always wanted to take you to France with me—but maybe—"

She got up from the sofa. "I'll be right back," she said and disappeared into her bedroom. "Pour yourself another cup of tea," she called.

Wallis was suddenly aware of why she had come to see Aunt Bessie to tell her about Corrine's offer. She had thought she wanted advice. But no, of course, she had expected financial assistance. The realization made her feel ashamed. All these years she had been accepting money from Aunt Bessie without any thought as to the real cost to both of them. In her heart she knew that the Merryman silver must have gone to finance Alice's schemes and several of her own *must haves.* She had no doubt that her aunt had vanished into her bedroom to retrieve some money from her savings concealed in a secret hiding place. At Chase Street, Wallis remembered that Aunt Bessie had kept her money in a red rubber water bottle in the ice compartment of the wooden refrigerator. Once she had given Wallis two twenty-dollar bills that had been there so long they smelled of rubber. Aunt Bessie did not trust banks. "Not as long as scoundrels like Sol Warfield run them," she was fond of saying.

Aunt Bessie reappeared. She had aged considerably in the last few years. Her hair had gone gray, liver spots blemished her skin. She could never have been pretty, Wallis thought. That must have hurt. Her drab flyaway hair was the kind that would not be held in place no matter how large the battery of hairpins. A considerable gain in weight had given her a paunchy double chin. Still, she had retained her proud carriage. Back erect, shoulders squared, head held high. Alice had been the beauty in the family. Bessie had inherited the Montagues' Southern aristocratic air. Since she began traveling with Mrs. Smith, she had also worked to overcome her Virginia accent and her speech was perfectly articulated.

"Is anyone else going with you two girls?" she asked.

"We're accompanying each other. After all, Corrine is nine years older than I am. She'll be my chaperone."

"Young widows aren't regarded with much more respect than young divorcees."

"Well, of course, I'm not a divorced woman yet."

"Yes, that's right," her aunt said, brightening considerably. "I've made a list of people for you to contact, the American Ambassador and so forth. I'll send some letters ahead. You are escorting your bereaved cousin as your husband is stationed in China." She went over to a table where Wallis had left her pocketbook and slipped an envelope inside. "Next time you meet a man you think you want to marry, first be sure you can get him, and second, if you hook him, make sure he's big enough to bother with or toss him right back," she warned.

When she was out on the street Wallis opened the envelope. Aunt Bessie had given her five one-hundred-dollar bills.

In January, Wallis and Corrine sailed to France on a small American ship. The crossing was rough and Corrine took sick and had to remain, for the most part, in their cabin. Wallis wandered around on her own after finding the other passengers a lackluster group. Next time, she promised herself, she would travel on one of the great ocean liners.

The boat train arrived in Paris after dark. Corrine had not made reservations and they taxied all over the city in heavy rain in search of rooms that they could afford, finally arriving at a comfortable and inexpensive pension on the rue Pierre Charron, recommended by their driver. Wallis's small knowledge of French came in handy and Aunt Bessie's letters of introduction were a godsend. The very next night they dined with the fair-haired, impish "Imp" Eberle, the Assistant Naval Attaché at the American Embassy, and his friend the

First Secretary, Gerry Green, who was a small, dark, vital young man, wiry and compact with a great sense of humor. Both men were bachelors, good companions who were only too pleased to play guide to two attractive American women.

Despite the January chill and the fact that all of Paris society was elsewhere, Wallis loved the city. Its charm lay in the sound of the language, the insouciance of the French, the *Ancien Monde* architecture of the houses and the public buildings. There were no skyscrapers. The view of the city from any of its bridges at the close of day was breathtaking: the narrow facades of the structures lining the Seine; the magnificence of the palatial Louvre to the west and the imposing gray-stone silhouette of Notre Dame to the east.

Their Embassy escorts took the two women to lunch in small cafés where tumblers of deep-red wine and crusty bread accompanied their meal. Seated close to a coal-fired brazier to keep warm, they had aperitifs on the terrace of the Deux Magots. In the evenings they danced *le fox-trot* at the *bals musettes* in Montparnasse. Lack of funds made the exclusive restaurants with their *haute cuisine* out of bounds, but they did attend *Le Revue Nègre* at the Théâtre des Champs Élysées and saw Josephine Baker make a spectacular stage entrance, upside down and nude except for a pink flamingo between her legs, doing a split on the shoulder of a giant black man.

As soon as Corrine had stepped onto French soil, she stopped mourning for Henry. Suddenly, she was young again, the Corrine Wallis remembered from her mother's wedding to Free Rasin. Win was never discussed, Pensacola seldom mentioned. They went shopping together and although neither had much money to spend they were as extravagant as they dared be. On weekends, they drove into the countryside with their Embassy escorts, not caring in the least where they were going or how long it would take to get there. Corrine was unable to learn a word of French. One day, when they passed the sign RALENTIR (which meant "Slow Down"), she whispered to Wallis, "Are you sure these men know where they're goin'? This is the third time in an hour we've been through Ralentir."

Wallis was having the time of her life. But Aunt Bessie's money was running out. She was dejectedly packing to return with Corrine to the States when Ethel Noyes showed up with another friend. They had rented an apartment for a month and asked Wallis if she wanted to share it with them. She saw Corrine off on the boat train, traded in her ticket for a later passage and moved in.

She was, of course, delaying the inevitable. Doubts and confusion about her future plagued her. After Paris, where was she to go? What was she to do? If she returned to Washington, she would have no choice but to live with Alice. And if she *did* divorce Win, her Navy allotment would cease.

As much as Wallis wished to be independent, she had no concept of how this could be achieved. She had been brought up without any thought of a career other than to be someone's wife, preferably that of a comfortably situated man. What good now were the social benefits of attending Arundel and Oldfields, of her debut and the ball given in her honor by Cousin Lelia? One mistake in judgment—her marriage to Win—had destroyed all her chances for a good life.

Her anger built. It was Win's fault. She had tried her best to make a go of their marriage but he had abused her body and her spirit. In her account book he owed her much more than the $225 a month she now received from the Navy as his wife. And then, just when she was feeling the strongest loathing for him, he wrote begging her to give him one more chance to rebuild their life together. He was lonely, repentant. He still loved her. If she returned to the States, she could board the USS *Chaumont* at Norfolk, Virginia, with a large group of Navy wives, disembark in the Philippines six weeks later and transfer to the *Empress of Canada* and be reunited with him in Hong Kong in a matter of days, all through the courtesy of the U.S. Navy.

In the same post had come a warm and chatty letter from Kitty Rogers postmarked Peking. She and Herman had decided to remain in China after their honeymoon and had a lovely house and many interesting friends. "Of course, China is not exactly around the corner," she wrote, "but if you ever do come this way, Herm and I would be delighted." She added that a good friend of Cousin Lelia and her husband, a Colonel Louis Little of the U.S. Marine Corps, was the Commanding Officer of the American Legation in Peking "and he recalls meeting you at the time of your debut."

That evening at a dinner date with Gerry Green, she told him about Win's offer and about the Rogerses. "How very curious," the young man commented. "I've just received word that I am to be transferred to the American Legation in Peking under Colonel Little. I leave a week from next Tuesday." He leaned across the table in the small bistro where they were dining and peered at her with earnest dark-brown eyes. "Maybe it's fate, Wallis. You and me in China. You must have noticed that I'm pretty crazy about you. I've never known another girl quite like you before."

"Well, of course, if I do go to China, it would be to be reunited with my husband," she said rather primly.

He straightened. "Yes, I can see that. Am I out of order then?"

"Oh, Gerry, how could you be?" she smiled, the Southern flirt in her surfacing. "A girl would have to be a nun not to be flattered by such a confession and I'm *nun*-such thing."

He laughed and took her hand. His grasp was strong and there was an unsparing honesty in his eyes. "How about seeing what you might be missing, Wallis?" he grinned.

"Sure thing," she said, and then as his hand tightened his hold, she added, "When I get to China."

The next morning Wallis wrote Win to book passage for her on the USS *Chaumont,* and added, "I can't promise anything but I'll give our marriage one more chance." This was an outright lie. She had no intention of trying to make a reconciliation work. Win owed her this one, she reasoned.

13

Wallis stood on the top deck as the great white liner *Empress of Canada* steamed into the murky green waters of Hong Kong harbor late in the cool September afternoon. Her first impression of the island of Hong Kong was the lack of symmetry and order, the babble of high-pitched voices, the pungency of the smells. The scene that stretched before her was totally alien. Along the wharves, wooden shacks tumbled one upon the other while, rising on a succession of hill slopes above them, houses seemed to be placed higgledy-piggledy on the zigzags of the mountain roads. Fishing junks with high sterns and giant colored sails and single-oared sampans had come out to greet the ocean liner, the men in the smaller, scraggly boats shouting what she supposed were greetings, but the language was incomprehensible. Young, nearly nude boys dived into the clouded waters for coins tossed from the decks by her fellow passengers.

Although the dock was crowded, she immediately sighted Win—tan, lean, handsome in his impeccable summer-white officer's uniform. She recognized in him the fascinating young naval aviator she had once loved. But *that* Win was lost to the past. She thought to herself, "Oh, yes, I knew that man once." He rushed up the gangplank, shouldering others aside, and swept her into his arms. Feeling her body tense up in his embrace, he quickly released her.

"What is it, Wallis?" he asked.

"It's just all so strange, this land, *you*—we've been separated for a long time, two years." People and rickshaws were pushing past them. There were cries of joy as other couples reunited.

Win stepped back to study her. "You've changed, Wallis. It's in your face and your voice."

"I told you. Everything is just so strange and the trip was *endless.* The *Chaumont* was packed. There were four other women in my cabin and there was no cooling system. I was sick when we landed in Panama. Thank God I transferred to the *Empress of Canada.* At least the ship had a doctor and other passengers besides Navy wives." She could feel the intensity of his gaze.

"Well, you are here and looking good." Noting the chic French-print dress she wore, the stylish accessories, he added with a hard edge to his voice, "If extremely prosperous for a Navy wife."

A coolie followed with her luggage as Win led the way to a waiting passenger ferry. "We have an apartment in Kowloon, on the mainland," he said, and then described it in a manner that could have given passersby the impression that he was merely an envoy sent to escort an officer's wife (certainly not his own) to her new home. "It's small but comfortable. There is a manservant. The building has a dining room run by an Englishwoman. You shouldn't have to do much cooking. I'll have to deposit you and then return to my ship. I'll be back later tonight. It will give you a chance to rest. In the morning I leave for three days on river patrol. But there are several Navy wives in the building and they have offered to help you get acclimated."

Now that she was in China, Wallis doubted her wisdom in coming as she had under false pretenses. She felt hesitant to tell Win that she had tricked him, that she had no intention of trying to make a go of their marriage, that she had used him to help her secure a new life in which there would be no room for him.

Before she departed from the States, she had made sure that the Navy provided her with a two-way ticket. During the long crossing she had rehearsed a small speech. The journey, she would say, had given her time to reconsider her decision to join him and now she thought it would be impossible; that she could not go home with him and would stay in a hotel for a day or two. Further, as long as she was in China she would continue on to spend a few weeks in Peking where her cousins, the Barnetts, had a good friend, Colonel Louis Little, who headed the U.S. Legation.

This scheme became unfeasible when, on the last day of the voyage, she learned that China was on the brink of civil war. Trains to Peking—a rugged four-day journey from Hong Kong—were being threatened by the militia and terrorized by bandits. Now she wasn't sure what she should do. Her resources were limited to the money she had been able to save from her allotment checks during her stay in Paris.

Setting things straight with Win as soon as possible was critical. He could say what he liked; she would not be stopped from leaving Hong Kong. Yet, why did she feel so strangely ill at ease? Why had all the painful memories of Coronado and Washington been haunting her? Had she come to China for some terrible destiny? She wiped the perspiration from her forehead with a French-scented handkerchief and pulled herself together. She was being *une hystérique,* as the French might say. The best thing for her to do was to go along with Win until she had formulated a viable plan.

He pointed out various landmarks to her as the passenger ferry crossed the narrow water channel separating the walled city of Kowloon from Hong Kong. He was trying hard to overcome her distraction, for clearly her thoughts were elsewhere. Finally, he gave up his attempt at interesting her with the novelties of the sights. They remained silent for much of the remainder of the short ferry ride.

His car was parked at the dock at Kowloon. "I'm grateful you came, Wallis," he said, when they were seated in it and on their way. "The loneliness had gotten to me. Most of the other officers have their wives with them. Except for missionaries, there aren't any single Caucasian women, and decent Chinese girls are guarded like vestal virgins. That leaves the singsong whores."

Her eyes flashed angrily but she made no comment.

"I've said it all wrong," he apologized. "It's not sex but your companionship I've missed the most. We once had a good thing. Remember how we laughed together at the club in Pensacola, the fun we had, the dreams we shared? I don't know what happened to us after we were married. But I thought—no, *I now hope*—that we can go back to those early days. I've had the idea that we were somehow like a scratched gramophone record and all we needed was to get beyond the spot where the record sticks."

Wallis glanced away, certain that if he could see her face he would know that his suggestion was impossible. As he had said earlier she was different. So many awful things had happened since they first had met and fallen in love. And she had experienced so many new feelings in her two years or her own that she was not the same woman he had married. Anyway, nothing could ever be right between them after her affair with Espil. She knew now that she could be physically attracted to another man. She also knew that when Win held her in his arms on the dock, the old sexual excitement he once aroused in her was gone.

Another time she might have found Hong Kong, Kowloon and the building he brought her to fascinating. The manservant Ti Pei, who spoke pidgin English and whom Win called his number-one boy, was waiting in their apartment to greet her. He drew her bath, scented it with lotus perfume and unpacked for her all in cat-footed, smiling reticence. The apartment was cool, immaculately clean and monochromatic in its bamboo furniture, sand-colored blinds and fabrics. A photograph taken of Win and her at the time of their engagement stood on a low chest in the bedroom. A gin bottle in the bathroom turned out to contain sterile drinking water.

They dined well: soup and fish and a sweet custard. Win did almost all the talking. She was surprised at his affability. He discussed only the present—his job, which for once he liked, the civil war, which he believed would end shortly, and a plan for them to take time, once the war was over, to see the rest of China.

She was grateful he did not attempt to make love that night. The next morning he was gone before she awoke. Attached to the mirror in the bathroom was a note written in his large, childish hand: "I *do* love you. I'll show you how much when I return." She had three days to explore this new strange world and to prepare a plan that would get her safely away from Win, to Peking and to the Rogerses.

She considered writing Kitty and Herman, but there was always the chance they might say, "Don't come," that with the war, traveling alone to Peking was too dangerous, a fear she knew had much validity. She could also contact Gerry Green at the American Legation. But he might assume that she was prepared to accede to his overtures. Her best bet would be to throw herself on Colonel Little's Southern chivalry. She was an American woman from the South, kin of good friends, in distress and alone in a foreign country. Although against her nature, this seemed the best thing to do considering the state of unrest in China and the Colonel's position.

Her Chinese adventure now seemed sheer madness. Well, Aunt Bessie and Mrs. Smith had traveled through China without any mishaps. Surely she could cope with the journey.

The extended crossing had given her much time to think. It was evident that her life until now had been totally unstructured. She had no foundation to stand on. She had spent the last decade as a commuter with neither home nor office at either end; leaving Pensacola for Boston, Boston for Coronado, Coronado for Washington, Washington for Paris, Paris for China. Now what? She desperately felt the need to become a person of consequence. That is what drew her to people like the Rogerses. The combination of money and position provided a secure place in society. She had stepped onto the gangplank of the *Empress of Canada* determined that one day she would have everything that Kitty now possessed—and she would not be deterred by a civil war, bandits, Win's pleading, or her own guilt.

She stood by the window of the sparsely furnished flat in Kowloon with its small, square rooms—mats on the floor instead of rugs—and stared down at the swarms of people scurrying along, one looking just like the other. Everything inside Wallis screamed to be different. "Well, when I was in

China," she could say. But that would never be enough. She had to be able to add, "When I was in Peking at the home of Herman Rogers, the millionaire railroad scion," and not have it be *confabulation*. Admittedly, this was a character flaw. Or so Grandmother Warfield would have thought.

The muscles in her face tightened as they always did when she thought of her grandmother.

Nancy Armstrong, the Navy wife who, with her husband, occupied the next apartment, came by to greet her later that day. A plain, dumpy woman who nonetheless had a bright twinkle in her eye and a touch of Irish somewhere in her ancestry, she told Wallis she was the daughter of a midwestern, small-town minister. When the formality had worn thin, Wallis noted that her companion had a heroic capacity for gin. For from a flask originally in her pocketbook, Nancy refilled her teacup with sizable quantities of its contents.

"Gin is cheap, companionable and effective," she confessed to Wallis, "and since it looks like water, and is frequently mistaken for water, it makes a very satisfactory drink for a respectable woman."

Wallis made no comment. Instead, she asked hopefully, "Do you know anyone in Peking?"

"I've never been there myself. But I hear it is a good city for Westerners." She poured more gin into her half-empty cup. "It's the capital, of course, so there are legations from all over the world."

"Friends of my family live there," Wallis said casually.

"If you find you need a change, I'd try Shanghai. The trip to Peking would be pretty dangerous now. I'm very fond of Shanghai," she added wistfully and then explained that her husband had been stationed there for over a year. "A nice long spell to stay in one place. We had rooms at the Palace on the Bund along with several other naval couples. And when the men were away on their ships, the women all went shopping together. If you decide to go to Shanghai, I could give you some letters of introduction."

By the time Win came home three days later, Wallis had the letters in her possession. She was uncertain how she would approach Win on the subject of her leaving. Her discovery that she was no longer attracted to him had made her ability to be in his company easier. She knew now that they had no more to give, or to take, from each other.

As Ti Pei mixed their evening cocktail she watched Win from across the room. He seemed tense and she suspected he had already had a drink while she was dressing. "One drink only," she warned when the servant had left the room.

"It's all right, Wallis. I've learned how to control it," he protested.

"Of course."

"Don't be sarcastic. It doesn't become you." He was facing her now. An unaccustomed softness came over his face. "I've made some big mistakes, Wallis. I've treated you badly. I can't forgive myself for some of my actions, so how can I expect your forgiveness? But I think there's another person inside me desperately working to destroy all the good things that come to me. If you help me, I can crush him. Would you do that, Wallis?" His voice was pleading but there was a hardness underneath his words.

"Why must everything be violence with you? Crush—destroy—even your vocabulary is filled with it." She caught something troubling in his eyes and changed the subject. "Have you made any friends since you've been here? I mean other than the Navy brass."

"You know I've never been one for the social life." He had not wanted this evening to begin this way. By coming to China she had led him to believe she cared for him after all, and he planned to make up to her for all the rotten times of the past.

"That's what's always been the matter with us, Win. We never liked the same things." Her voice rose harshly.

"I suppose that's right. Hope, however, burns eternal. Even now, as I look at you, in my heart knowing damned well you did not come here to be with me, I can hope. All our married life, you've been scrambling for a means of escape. Maybe that's why I've had this compulsion to lock you up, to clip your wings. I remember the first time I ever saw you on the veranda at the Mustins' house in Pensacola. You had on this neat little blue dress and your white, manicured hands—the kind of hands that never had done a lick of woman's work in their life—flapped restlessly at your sides. You looked like a blue bird standing there. And I thought, 'She wants to fly, to lift right off the ground and soar.' It seemed to me you would understand my own passion for planes, that maybe we could soar together."

He finished his martini and crossed to the bar and poured himself a second.

"We have never been as one, even in our lovemaking," he continued. "Hell, I'm not blaming you. I've been a lout at times and I admit it. But damn! I have loved you. I still love you." His dark eyes swept over her face, trying to uncover something that was not there. "Okay, Wallis, why are you here?" he asked.

"Because I had nowhere else to go," she said impulsively. Instantly, she was sorry. She started out of the room. Win grabbed her roughly by the arm and twisted her around to face him. The cynical eyes flickered. The hard lines around his mouth cut deeper. His protestations meant nothing. Win had not changed.

"No other man to go to, you mean," he said between tightly drawn lips. "Don't you think I've heard about Señor Espil? A friend even sent me clippings—DON FELIPE ESPIL AND MRS. WALLIS SPENCER AT A CHARITY BALL—as though I were dead." He drew her closer; his face contorted. "I was enough out of my mind with loneliness to hope that maybe his dumping you had knocked you off your high horse and whittled you down to my size."

He held her chin vise-like in the palm of his hand, his thumb and forefinger pressing hard. She was alarmed and her expression showed it. "Do I frighten you, Wallis?" he leered, his grasp so firm, she could not reply.

Her old fear crept back over her, this time with greater force. The game of cat and mouse would no longer intrigue him. She struggled to keep herself as aware as she could. He must not catch her panicked or off guard.

"You know why I couldn't make love to you the first night?" he continued. "Because I have the clap and I didn't want to give it to you!" He released his hold with a sharp push, the suddenness of the movement sending Wallis reeling. She fell onto the bed and then slipped down to the floor.

"Oh, God, Win, you disgust me!" she said as she picked herself up with tremendous dignity. "How can you sit in judgment of me when you have been doing who-knows-what?"

"Screwing around is the phrase; singsong houses am the place. Where a woman will look up to *me*. They're honest sluts, not like you."

"I don't have to listen to this. I'm going next door to the Armstrongs until you come to your senses." She started past him.

"You're going noplace!" he shouted, as he reached for her.

Wallis swung out with a closed fist. The strength behind it surprised even her. It caught Win in the chest. His stunned surprise gave her a momentary advantage. She tried to slip by him and was almost out of his reach when his arm pulled her back and in close to him.

"You're crazy!" she gasped. "Just like the rest of your lunatic family!"

She saw the blow coming, but she did not have time to avoid it. He held her with one hand as he punched her hard in the stomach. Something exploded inside her. The pain was paralyzing. He held her in his grasp and hit her a second and third time. She stared up at him, beseeching him with her eyes to stop. She wanted to ask for mercy. Instead, she repeated, "You're crazy!" She crumpled to the floor, almost numb, her vision blurred, but she could make out spots of red blood on his shiny black shoes. Nausea gripped her. Then, gratefully, she passed out.

The room spun around her and when she finally awoke, a searing pain stabbed her from stomach to back. Her mouth was dry. Something was flapping nearby. She turned her head slightly, the motion making her feel suddenly queasy. The blinds were drawn. Even so, she could tell it was night. A moth was trapped inside the lighted lampshade on the bedside table.

Her vision was clearing. She was in bed and Win was sitting in a chair by her side, unshaven, his shirt collar undone, his eyes red, looking thoroughly exhausted, as though he had not been to bed for a long time. "I'm sorry, Wallis," he cried softly. "I'm sorry. I injured your kidneys. I got the doctor to come here. You've been delirious. I thought you were going to die," he confessed, cold terror in his voice.

I should loathe the sight of him, she thought. Yet, somehow his crumpled state, his distraction, his fear were reassuring. "That shouldn't make you cry," she said, the effort of speaking so painful that she winced. He leaned in closer, tenderly touched her hand. It took enormous effort on her part to draw it away. She remembered him hitting her now. "How long have—I—been like this?"

"Two days."

"Two days?" she repeated in amazement. The flapping sound had ceased. She wondered if the moth was dead or if it had flown away.

"You were right. I'm crazy. I don't know what comes over me at times. If I had killed you! Oh, God! What if I had killed you!" he cried.

Everything in her heart screamed for her to tell him to stop his wild torrent of self-pity. It was she who had come close to death and at his hands. She glanced away, unable to look at him. The stabbing sensation seared through her again. "Is there anything—I—can take—for the pain?" she asked.

"Ti Pei!" he shouted. "The powders!" Win raised and pillowed her head as she took a few sips from a glass of chalky white liquid that Ti Pei brought.

She managed with difficulty to keep the medication down. "Maybe he's trying to poison me," she thought with alarm. The room was growing hazy again. If she was so sick—what did he say? he had injured her kidney?—then why was she not in hospital? Where was the kidney, anyway. Her stomach felt as if it had been cut with a blunt knife.

"I want to make everything up to you, Wallis, if you'll just let me," he said softly, almost to himself.

"Stop—babbling," she whispered. All emotion left Win's face. He stood up, staring down at her. He said nothing, just kept looking at her with blank uncomprehending eyes before he turned and walked away.

Thankfully, her pain wavered, blurred, somehow moved into the distance. A short time later, sleep mercifully released her.

For the next week, with Ti Pei's help, Win nursed her night and day, hardly leaving her side. Finally she was able to get up and walk around the apartment. Nancy Armstrong came in to look after her when Win returned to his boat.

"He told me you had slipped getting out of the bathtub," Nancy smirked, her pudgy face screwed up in disbelief. "Hell, I've heard better stories from a deaf-mute. Why do you stay, honey? I tell you, if my Fred ever raised a hand to me I'd be gone so fast he'd think I had vanishing powers." She had Wallis's hand in hers and rubbed it gently in a soothing maternal gesture. "Why don't you report him to the naval authorities?"

"I couldn't do that. It would ruin his career," she replied, knowing full well she did not want word of the degrading incident to spread.

"Wouldn't that be just too bad!" Nancy said. She got up, poured a tall drink and brought it to Wallis, who refused it. Nancy shrugged her shoulders and downed it herself. "You've had a serious injury. I think you should check into a hospital and get yourself another doctor. The one that bastard husband of yours brought here works in the singsong houses."

"I can't do that either."

"Well, what the hell *can* you do, honey?" Nancy asked, the red deepening in her florid face.

"Get better fast so that I can leave him," Wallis told her.

With Fred Armstrong on duty, Nancy almost moved in so that she could supervise Wallis's care and Ti Pei was always close at hand. Each day Wallis felt stronger and the pain finally began to diminish. When Win returned the following week, her suitcases were all packed and she was preparing to leave.

"This time for good?" he inquired. He was cool, detached, but she could see from the taut muscles in his face that he was having to struggle to give this impression.

"Forever," she replied.

Pain etched his face. His mouth quivered. "Where are you going?" he asked in a brittle voice.

"Shanghai. I've booked passage today on a steamer. I'll be leaving shortly. I've asked Ti Pei to get me a driver."

"And then?"

"I'm not sure. I just need some time on my own."

"I'll arrange for your monthly allotments to be sent to you." He reached into his pocket and gave her all the money he had. She hesitated for a moment and he stuffed the bills in her hand. "Let me see you off," he insisted.

They rode in silence to the dock and said good-bye at the gangway. "Pensacola, Boston, Coronado, Washington and now Hong Kong—we've come a long way, only to lose what we began with." He smiled wryly. The youth had faded from his face. Gray shadows circled his eyes. Hard lines pulled at his mouth. Win was a bitter man. *He'll die a drunk,* Wallis thought. *He's dead-set to kill himself, but he hasn't got the guts that the other members of his family had.*

She looked at him in final loathing. "Good-bye, Win," she said, and walked straight up the gangplank and into the steamer without glancing back. The only thing she was sure of when she stood on the deck watching the jumbled rooftops of Hong Kong disappear into the distance was that she would never see Win again.

14

As Nancy Armstrong had suggested, Wallis established herself in Shanghai at the Palace Hotel on the Bund. Shaded by ancient trees that guarded the proud façades of China's largest banks and business houses, the Bund rimmed the waterfront and was crowded at all hours with an amazing variety of vehicles—tram cars, buses, automobiles, rickshaws, bicycles, handcarts and wheelbarrows—all noisily contending for the right of way.

Her room was small and just adequate, but the hotel and its service *grand luxe,* and Shanghai was a far more sophisticated and heterogeneous city than Hong Kong. The streets teemed with Chinese in national dress from every province. Thousands of White Russians who had fled to China after the Revolution had settled here. The foreign community, which made up half of the population, was of a highly social nature. Nancy had told her about the wealth and the magnificence of the homes grouped about Bubbling Well Road, and of the private clubs and gay, glittering parties hosted by their rich members.

Wallis lost no time in sending a personal note along with Nancy's letters of introduction to people Nancy knew in Shanghai. Only one, a widowed Englishman, Sir Robert Bamber, because of his title, seemed likely to produce her hoped-for entry into Shanghai society. The others were a White Russian woman, a naval couple and a Chinese lawyer, a Mr. Ku Ling Yong, who, Nancy suggested, might be able to help her—if she was so inclined—with a divorce.

Shanghai, above all else, was a place to get rich quick (although money could be lost as fast), and many of the Bubbling Well set, who lived like royalty, had arrived in the city with little more than what Wallis currently possessed. Life was cheap, and labor, including children who were chained to their machines in factories, was seemingly inexhaustible. Great fortunes could be swiftly built on their toil and suffering, and equal wealth on the foibles of the newly rich. Gambling was open, drug dealing common and gangland murders frequent. Shanghai was an adventurer's paradise, but one with danger lurking at every turn. Now, added to its dragon-lair streets were the hazards of rebellion and terrorism caused by China's political chaos. An epic power struggle had begun among the nationalists, the communists and the Japanese, but Shanghai's American, British and European society was confident of its survival. Wallis had stumbled into one of the wealthiest, most frenetic, desperate, exciting and wicked cities on earth.

A day after she had sent her letter to Sir Robert Bamber, a large basket of mangoes arrived, followed by a telephone call. The voice was unique, an Englishman who spoke in measured meter; a droll, well-educated, upper-crust voice. Would she care to meet him in the bar of her hotel for a cocktail at six P.M.? She accepted without hesitation. The question arose of how they would recognize each other. On impulse, Wallis said she would wear a single red camellia on her shoulder.

She was expecting a Colonel Blimp character, sixtyish, widowed, stodgy, very correct; and she had dressed accordingly in a navy-blue dress that Aunt Bessie would have approved—high at the neck, simply cut; a strand of jade beads (her first Shanghai purchase) and the flower its only other decoration. A navy-blue pocketbook and matching shoes completed her outfit. She looked trim, neat, conservatively stylish. Only a bright crimson slash of lipstick betrayed her rebel spirit. To her surprise the man who came toward her when she entered the dimly lit bar was no more than forty, attractive in an aristocratic, overbred way with a long narrow face, high forehead, aquiline nose and a chin that thrust slightly forward. He was tall and spare, his vested suit expensively tailored.

"Mrs. Spencer?" he inquired, the voice immediately recognizable. He had pale blue eyes and flaxen hair, a lock of which fell carelessly onto his forehead.

"Sir Robert?" she ventured.

"My dear girl, please call me Robbie. Everyone does." He placed his hand beneath her elbow and guided her through the dusky interior to a small red-lacquered table in a fairly private corner of the crowded room.

"Ever had a Shanghai Sling?" he inquired.

"No, never."

"Dry gin, cherry brandy and Benedictine. Lethal, but guaranteed to crack the ice." He raised his hand to a waiter. "Although American women, I've discovered, are marvelous conversationalists."

"I hope I don't disappoint you," she laughed.

"Cheers!" he said, lifting his glass when their cocktails had appeared rather magically, for he had not actually given an order for them, unless he had done so in advance.

"Cheers," Wallis replied and took a cautious sip of the tall drink.

"Ah! I can see, dear girl, that you won't be easily misled. Pity. Will you tell me about yourself or shall I speculate?"

"The latter would be more interesting."

"Divorcee?"

"Not yet."

"On the way?"

"Yes!"

"I denote quite a stuffed packet of hostility. Was he beastly to you? Or just beastly boring? No, don't reply. Women with hidden pasts are far more titillating. Sheltered background," he continued in his assessment. "The Dixie accent," he explained. "Rebellious spirit," he added, a finger lightly tracing the scarlet line of her lips in the air. "Enough of this gibberish. Tell me what you're really about." He leaned toward her, eyebrows arched, a smile on his thin mouth, and waited for her to speak.

She told him that she had come to China to reconcile with

her husband, who was a naval officer, but it had not worked; that she had lived in Washington, just spent two months in Paris and that she hoped soon to go to Peking to join her good friends, Katherine and Herman Rogers, "the American railroad heir. Have you met him?"

"'Fraid not. Look, I know a splendid place for dinner. You free?"

"Not much is," she laughed. "But if you are inviting me to dine with you—well, yes! I would love to."

He took her to Hang Fa Lau, which, he informed her, had "the finest Cantonese food in Shanghai." The street it was on, Foochow Road, was ablaze with electric lights and huge fantastic signs of lighted dragons spraying fire. As they entered, Wallis adjusted her eyes to the soft candlelight of the restaurant interior. Robbie seemed to know almost everyone in the elegant establishment from the service staff to the guests, to whom he briefly introduced Wallis as they were being escorted to their table.

"See the heads knock together," he grinned when they were seated. "'Who *is* this American Mrs. Spencer?' they are saying. 'Do you suppose she's out to nick our Robbie?' A widower has to put up with friends who think a single man is prey to every unknown designing woman when he should be evening up the statistics of their little group by pairing off with one of their own unmarried ladies or young widows."

During the course of their dinner, he told her that his wife had died in London of influenza six years earlier. He had no children, and since he was at that time with the Foreign Office, he had requested a distant assignment. He was now a partner in an export company.

"You will allow me to give a small party for you at my home?" he suggested later, and she delightedly accepted.

He made no further mention of this but was extremely attentive over the next few weeks, which was fortunate, for it turned out that Nancy's naval friends had been transferred, the White Russian woman was recently deceased, and Mr. Ku Ling Yong sent only his card. Wallis asked Robbie how he had met Nancy, for they seemed odd companions. "At the Race Club," he replied and quickly changed the subject.

With Robbie as her escort, Wallis was drawn swiftly into a totally new and different world. "There are scads of garden parties," she wrote to Aunt Bessie, "race meetings at the Shanghai Race Club, and the most elegant dinner parties in the lovely old Majestic Hotel on Bubbling Well Road. Last evening, Robbie and I danced in the sunken courtyard by the light of colored lanterns to 'Tea for Two.' The combination of that melody, the moonlight, the perfume of jasmine, not to mention the mystical illusion of the courtyard, made me feel that I had really entered the Celestial Kingdom."

She did not write her aunt or her mother the curious turn the relationship had taken. Robbie had finally entertained for her in his handsome home, filled with European antiques and expensive artworks. And she had met Mario Farranti, a good-looking Italian, who was Robbie's business partner and who, it turned out, shared both his stylish home and his bed.

Wallis leafed with disappointment through the morning post which had been brought to her with her breakfast tray. She had written to Colonel Little requesting his assistance in obtaining travel documents to Peking where, she had suggested, because of daily outbreaks of violence in Shanghai, she would be safer.

The past week had produced numerous clashes between British-controlled police and Chinese demonstrators in Nanking Road, just one block from her hotel. The foreign colony in Shanghai was becoming less sure of their personal safety. Robbie and Mario had received crude and vitriolic warnings through their letter box. Anti-foreignism had been exacerbated by political events. Banditry had increased and kidnapping was rife. Several Europeans had been held for ransom, and two were slain. Wallis did, indeed, feel the time had come for her to move on.

Shanghai, she now realized, was the political center of China. The Chinese Communist party had been formed there at a secret meeting in 1922, just two years before her arrival, and was collaborating with the larger, stronger Nationalist party of Sun Yat-sen. A Central Executive Committee had been created recently, and violent conflicts between right- and left-wing elements had followed. At the same time resentment grew over the many foreigners who were exploiting the Chinese people. Peking, with the United States and many other legations located there, seemed a viable alternative.

The potential dangers of traveling bandit-ridden and war-torn China, from Shanghai to Peking, could not be underestimated. Her travel route would be dictated by the railway. The train to Peking went through areas of open hostility. The only fairly secure way she could make the journey would be on the expensive *Shanghai Express* (and even that presented potential danger), and her funds were running extremely low. At the moment she was not sure how she would manage the trip on her meager finances, and Colonel Little's late reply added greatly to her anxiety.

She slipped into her bath, leaned back and closed her eyes. She still had recurring pain in her abdomen and found the warmth of the bath water soothing. How she had reached her present state of insolvency and rootlessness plagued her. She felt easier about the civil war that raged around her than about the rebel thoughts that invaded her mind. Once her conscience had been her safety latch; now it seemed less and less to be controlling her actions.

Wallis did not have a strong religious belief but she considered the way she had come to China dishonest and that she had been punished accordingly. She gazed down at her stomach, the water making small ripples on her bare flesh. After all this time there remained a yellow discoloration to remind her of the harrowing beating she had taken. She wanted desperately to trust her judgment, the decisions she would make that would affect her future. But her bruised body seemed proof enough that she could not rely upon her own instincts. This disturbing thought brought tears into her eyes.

Instantly she straightened and vigorously began washing herself with a soap-filled cloth. She must not allow herself such maudlin relapses. Her doubts would imperil her and become a self-imposed sword of Damocles over her head. She had nothing other than herself, her own grit and perseverance—and, yes! belief that she was entitled to expect as much from life as the women she most admired had received. The so-called "good life" had always been dangled before her like a carrot before a horse's nose. Why had this been done if she was not meant to run the full course and, in the end, enter the winner's circle?

Her thoughts shifted to her mother. In her reveries she saw Alice with a soft expression in her eyes that made her appear exquisitely feminine and vulnerable. When Wallis pondered her mother's fate more closely, she realized that Alice was a natural victim, her apparent defenselessness always attracting disaster. She could see a parallel between herself and her mother, although she could not point to a specific feature in her own looks or personality that they shared. Still, she considered herself the victim in her marriage to Win and in her affair with Espil. Perhaps her Achilles' heel was her inclination to allow her libido to rule her head.

She rinsed the soap from her body, stepped out of the tub and observed her nakedness through the steamy bathroom mirror. She rubbed the glass with the palm of her hand to clear it. Within a few months she would be celebrating her twenty-ninth birthday. Soon she would be thirty. Her figure was, perhaps, a bit too boyish—her breasts too small, her hips too narrow—but her skin was taut, her legs shapely, her overall figure slim and youthful (although more attractive clothed than naked, she thought). Still, time was of the essence.

In Hong Kong there were ten men to every Occidental woman. Shanghai's population was almost reversed, perhaps because it was not a U.S. or British naval base. Wallis had not met many available men since her arrival and she was grateful for Robbie and Mario's companionship. They had shown her Shanghai's many faces. Last night they had gone to The Great World, a pleasure house, an eye-opening experience for Wallis. The six-floor establishment was entered through a tall white pagoda. Once you were inside, the rest of the world was quickly forgotten.

Each floor was packed with people seeking every variety of entertainment Chinese ingenuity could devise. Smiling singsong girls lured people to the gambling tables and slot machines. Magicians and acrobats performed. A heavy scent of incense filled the air. The many restaurants were housed on the second floor, sharing space with barbers, earwax extractors and a dozen different groups of actors. Pimps moved in and out of the crowds, and girls in sleek Chinese dresses slit to the hip flashed their thighs. On the floor above were shooting galleries, fan-tan tables, ice-cream parlors, jugglers and storytellers. The top story featured massage rooms, peep shows, nude girls walking through a mirror maze while others, with the briefest costumes, loitered outside the pleasure rooms.

"No one seems to care much about pleasuring women," Wallis commented drily.

"Dear girl," Robbie replied, "this is Shanghai. It is presumed that pleasuring men pleasures women."

Robbie and Mario were taking her to the Shanghai Race Club that afternoon. It was the day of the season's best attended championship race, the entries all being native Chinese horses. Wallis had not been a great horse-track enthusiast before coming to Shanghai. But here the riders were amateurs, many of them prominent businessmen of the city who maintained stables. The betting, which Robbie informed her would run into large figures on this special day, was on the parimutuel basis, all the money wagered, except for a commission charged by the Race Club, being divided among those who held winning tickets. One horse was named Nanchang, which translated into English as "Southern Prosperity," and Wallis had set aside twenty dollars to bet on what was a longshot and a nostalgic hunch.

As always, she was strikingly dressed for the occasion when Robbie and Mario picked her up at the hotel. Her wardrobe was not large or expensive but she possessed a fashionable flair and wit in her costumes. For today's outing she wore her French-print dress and with it a cape and hat, bought in Paris directly off the back of a gendarme, on a bet from Gerry Green that he would pay for it if she had the nerve to carry out the purchase. They had spent hours looking for a short gendarme, so that his cape would fit Wallis.

"Have you come to arrest me?" Mario laughed when he saw her, his Latin eyes flashing with humor.

"You don't think it's too outlandish?" Wallis asked.

"Yes, of course. But so are you."

She found Mario's company amusing and rather liked the idea of being escorted places by two attractive men. After her initial shock, she had accepted the relationship between the two men. She and Mario, in fact, had become good friends. "I don't mind Robbie's women," he confided to Wallis one day. "But the young men, ah!" And then, his English failing him at such a treacherous idea, he lapsed into Italian, which she did not understand.

The afternoon was crisp, a hint of snow in the air. It was November, *Lee tung,* the beginning of winter. The racing oval and the club's extensive grounds were overflowing. They had seats in the exclusive Enclosure. To her chagrin, Wallis had not yet been accepted in the inner circle of Shanghai's international society. She was not sure of the reasons for her exclusion, but suspected that—although Robbie and Mario knew everybody—her close association with them might have been the cause. Nonetheless, she was not willing to turn her back on the only reliable friends she had made in Shanghai.

Also, to her relief, they did not inquire too deeply into her history. ("People can be extraordinarily testy about their pasts," Robbie had said when she pressed him about Mario's background. "It can bring to an end an otherwise amicable friendship.") She need not (and, indeed, never did) discuss Win's abuse, Espil's rejection, Alice's lowly position or her own difficult childhood. Instead, she told amusing stories about the socially prominent in Paris, Washington and California and could be wickedly funny about the people they met in Shanghai.

In an exaggerated Chinese accent she now announced, "Ah, so! Here come Lady-long-in-the-tooth and Sir Short-in-the-crotch," at the approach of an English couple they knew. She maintained a polite banter during a brief interchange. But, as the husband shifted nervously and pulled at his trousers, Mario had to walk away to conceal his laughter.

The odds on Nanchang, ten minutes before post time of the big race, were eighty to one.

"That proves you should not bet hunches," Robbie declared.

"How do you arrive at that?" Wallis asked.

"Dear girl, longshots almost never win," he warned.

"But when they do, one can make a killing, right?" she argued.

"One can but seldom does," he countered.

"Well, I have a hunch *and* I am going to wager twenty American dollars on it. If I win, what will I make?"

"It depends how much was bet on the race," he explained.

"It could be a large sum, though?"

"Considerably."

"I will bet a *hundred* dollars then."

"You're mad."

"I think it is very exciting," Mario interjected.

Wallis took out her wallet and counted the bills and proffered them to Robbie. "Place the bet for me," she commanded.

"I'll do nothing of the sort! I *know* Bill Hodgkins, who owns and is riding Nanchang. He's an absolute *dolt*! Couldn't lead a thirsty horse to water!"

Mario whipped the money from her hand. "Let me," he grinned and quickly disappeared as he wove his way through the crowds, making it impossible for her to withdraw her wild gesture.

Wallis had no idea why she had acted so rashly and taken such a needless risk when her finances were so low. Yet, she did have this incredible hunch. She had awakened with it that morning and it had remained with her the entire day. The name *Nanchang* kept repeating itself over and over again in her head, a prayer-like chant, a declaration, *an entreaty*. If only she *could* win a bundle; *if only* she had three or four thousand dollars, she could take all the time she wanted in Peking and then she could return to the United States, perhaps New York, or maybe even Paris. Win and Espil would be far behind her by then and the exoticism of her time in China would be an added lure to attract a wealthy, well-connected husband through whom she could enter her Valhalla—the heavenly kingdom of the rich society world.

The Roaring Twenties were passing Wallis by. She remained only conventionally unconventional. Beneath her flamboyance was a strong sense of propriety. She could dismiss love, and the idea of children lacked appeal. But her views on romance, marriage and security were strictly in accord with Aunt Bessie's standards. She had small empathy for the current "flaming youth," and found speakeasies, most contemporary fashion and the popular new concept of free love distasteful and quite irrational. Love could never, and should never, be free. For there to be order in the world, everything must have a price.

She glanced up at Robbie as he studied the racing program. He had brought her gaiety and laughter, a surcease from her bitter memory of Hong Kong. She watched him as his gaze followed Mario's lithe figure as he approached. "Wild about that boy," he said, not quite under his breath.

"Done," said Mario when he returned. There was no time for her to think about her bet. The race, which had twenty-four entries, was about to begin. Nanchang was a smallish black horse, very restless, and his owner and rider had difficulty keeping him from a false start. This encouraged Wallis to believe her hunch was correct.

"Go, Nanchang!" she shouted when the starting gun sounded. She was on her feet and straining to find the animal's position among the bunched horses at the crowded first lap.

Beside her Robbie cried out, "My God!" and Mario screamed something in a pejorative manner in Italian.

"What is it?" she asked. Then she saw for herself. Nanchang remained close to the starting gate, neighing loudly as he pawed the ground in an effort to dismount Hodgkins, who miraculously remained in the saddle. Her hundred dollars was lost. Wallis felt a lurching in her chest. She had this unaccountable fear that her loss was an omen, that she might, also, never make it past the starting gate.

When she returned to the hotel she wrote Colonel Little another letter. Maybe he had not received the first one. Perhaps the train on which it traveled had been intercepted by bandits or, worse, blown up by soldiers. She repeated her request and her reasons for wanting to go to Peking.

There was a polite knock on the door. Before she could reach it, an envelope appeared from underneath. It was a telegram from Peking. She tore it open and glanced first at the sender's name. Then she read the contents.

> DEAR MRS. SPENCER STOP TRAVEL BY LAND TOO DANGEROUS AT THIS TIME STOP ADVISE YOU RETURN TO HONG KONG STOP THE EMPRESS OF CANADA SAILING

NEXT THURSDAY STOP I HAVE TAKEN THE LIBERTY OF WRITING THE BOOKING AGENTS TO EXPECT YOUR CALL STOP YOURS SINCERELY STOP COLONEL LOUIS LITTLE

She crumpled the telegram in her hand and tossed it into the wastebasket. "How dare he order me about!" she said angrily. "I *won't* go back to Hong Kong." Her fury took hold of her. Colonel Little had no right to tell her what she should do, what was good for *her* from *his* point of view! There was no question of her returning to the States now. What on earth was there for her to return *to*? She could manage in Shanghai, but *just,* on her monthly allotment check. Shanghai was more expensive than Hong Kong and she was at a first-class hotel that catered to wealthy tourists. She wondered now how Nancy Armstrong had managed a whole year in the place. Then there was her poor reception by the Bubbling Well set. She needed people with the Rogerses' social influence to pave the way.

Her initial plan was the right one, of that she was now sure. Peking was the place for her. Damn the Chinese for being at war! Foreigners were not allowed to travel to the interior without proper documents. An American passport was not sufficient. One had to be going to something or someone specific and for good reason; like missionary, Red Cross, or legation personnel, or foreign residents caught in Shanghai who had homes in other areas of China. Such papers could be purchased but she had little money. Now, because of her idiotic loss at the track, she had even less than before.

If she wrote home for funds to Aunt Bessie or Cousin Lelia or Uncle Sol, it would be weeks before she would receive a reply. If she cabled them they might panic and insist upon her return. Robbie and Mario were her only real friends in Shanghai, and she briefly considered asking them for a loan but immediately dismissed the idea as being too humiliating.

Suddenly, she recalled the Chinese lawyer recommended by Nancy. What was his name? She went over to the desk and rummaged through her papers for his card. She had almost given up when she glanced down to the floor. A small slip of white paper had fallen at her feet and she picked it up.

His name was Mr. Ku Ling Yong.

His offices were in Nantao, the Chinese area of Shanghai, which had its own provincial administration and was under the direct control of the central government of Nanking. Wallis hired a rickshaw to take her to her appointment with Mr. Ku since the streets in this section of the city were too narrow for a car. When she had arrived in China, the idea of one person acting as a form of transportation for another had made her uncomfortable. Now, this mode of travel seemed natural. She leaned back in the chair. The rocking motion eased her tension and allowed her thoughts to wander.

She was not sure what Mr. Ku could do for her. After all, Nancy had suggested his name in relation to his help in obtaining a divorce. Instead, she needed the purchase of travel documents (known to be available in the black market), which she could not afford. Still, it seemed not improbable that Mr. Ku might be helpful. Lawyers knew many influential people. And he had been exceptionally polite on the telephone.

"Is the matter referred to a marital difficulty?" he had asked in clipped but adequate English.

"No, another personal matter," she replied. "I would prefer speaking to you in person about it."

"It shall be arranged," he agreed, and an appointment was set for two P.M. the next afternoon.

She glanced down the road that the rickshaw boy was traveling. A stranger could easily be lost in the narrow crooked lanes of this section. They passed few Caucasians other than a group of tourists standing with a native guide, in front of the Wu Ding Tea House. There was a profusion of teahouses in Nantao; a profusion of everything, for that matter. One street was given over entirely to bird dealers; wicker cages were stacked high outside shops and the cawing of the caged creatures was an assault to the ears. Most roads were crowded with small stores and street stalls selling only Chinese goods—porcelain and crockery, clothing, herbs, tea, rice, vegetables, game and dried and smoked meats. The odors were pungent, the sounds strident as deals were struck; every item seemed to be up for auction.

Her rickshaw turned into a more sedate street dominated by the large offices of the Doo Ka Say where rice was brokered. This was obviously the financial center of Nantao. Mr. Ku's offices were in a building that abutted a bank. Wallis felt instantly reassured.

His secretary (or receptionist or wife or servant—Wallis could not be sure which) was a tiny woman in Chinese dress with a startling purple scar that started at the corner of a sagging right eye and ran to her delicate chin. Wallis guessed she must be about fifty; although youth had faded from her face, old age had not yet withered her skin. She spoke no English but seemed to be expecting Wallis and ushered her directly into Mr. Ku Ling Yong's private office and then, bowing several times, backed out of the room.

Mr. Ku was surprisingly young, about thirty-five, a slight man, elegantly dressed in Western clothes. He had sharp eyes, tight, almost waxen skin and over his narrow mouth was a thin mustache elaborately curled at the ends.

"How can I be of service?" he asked after the traditional pleasantries had been exchanged.

"I wish to go to Peking," she said.

"The way is dangerous."

"Yes, I know that, but I still want to go. The problem is that I have a passport but no further travel documents."

"If stopped by soldiers—either side—you would be turned back."

"I am aware of that."

"And you remain determined?"

"I do. You see, I have good friends in Peking."

"Perhaps you should return to your country. There will be worse times here soon."

"I came to China to go to Peking and I would like to complete my journey."

Mr. Ku smiled wanly and for the first time. "Ah, I see."

Wallis was certain that he thought she had a romantic rendezvous planned in Peking. She did not enlighten him, believing he might be more inclined to help her under those circumstances.

"Your passport is American?"

"Yes, of course."

"Documents can be secured. A letter of safe conduct be arranged for American citizen traveling to their legation. It would help with soldiers but not bandits."

"I understand the dangers," she ventured.

"You are prepared to pay?"

"I expect there is a price, yes."

"You have money?"

"I will have it as soon as I arrive in Peking," she lied.

"To persuade official is a serious and costly business. I could lose my certificate. Perhaps go to jail. The price must be high."

"How high?"

"Two thousand American dollars; one half before you leave, the rest to be delivered forty-eight hours after you arrive Peking."

"I've told you, I won't have money until I reach my destination."

Mr. Ku shrugged his shoulders.

Wallis rose from her chair and he instantly stood up. "You very good friend Mrs. Nancy Armstrong?" he asked.

"I believe so."

"We make trade. In exchange first half, you agree to get for me certain information in Peking."

"What sort of information?"

"Oh, easy. Help our cause. The Chinese people suffer much," he answered enigmatically.

She was unable to pinpoint in her mind what exactly he wanted. It seemed he might be asking her to spy for him, an idea that was too wild for her to conceive. Yet, she could not interpret his words otherwise. Who, in Peking, could she possibly secure information from? The U.S. Legation? He was mad if he thought she would betray her own country. She wondered if Nancy had also come to Mr. Ku for help and, if so, what she might have agreed to give for it. Certainly, Nancy would not have been involved with anything like spying. And she had written down his name for her, without any warning. She must have believed he was an honorable man. Times had changed since her friend resided in Shanghai. China was now engaged in a civil war and the city, specifically the Chinese section, was a hotbed for revolutionary and anti-revolutionary activities.

"I have to think about it," she said, hoping to delay a reply.

"No time think. Yes or no?"

This urgency for her answer rather startled Wallis and she began to rise from her chair.

"There will be fighting here, in Shanghai, in days," he warned. "No travel documents then."

"When could I leave and how?" she asked.

"The *Express*. Eight-thirty, this night."

"So soon! But I can't get a ticket *that* quickly."

"Ticket, too," he said, his gaze razor-edged.

"You mean you will *include* the ticket—*first class*—in your price?"

"That is correct."

Wallis sat down. Mr. Ku took writing materials out of a desk drawer and slid them in front of her.

"You will write. I will dictate," he said. He leaned forward. He wore a peppery scent, unusual in a Chinese, and his nails were manicured. She had not yet agreed and he waited for her to lift the pen—her signal that she did.

"What is it you want me to write?"

"A pledge."

"What exactly does that involve?"

"You receive first-class ticket and papers to Peking. Man named Fu Looog will contact you there. You do as he asks."

"And if I find I cannot?"

He straightened. His look was glacial. "There would be a price, of course."

"Which would be?"

"Set then."

"And if I could not pay?"

"You *will*," he said, "one way or another. Now, you write." He lifted the pen to hand it to her and then put it down near the paper again when she did not take it from him.

"I . . . I . . . must think about it," she hesitated. "I could come back tomorrow."

"Too late."

She paused and made a search of her handbag for a

handkerchief before she replied, trying to gain time to figure things out. He waited patiently, his expression unyielding. "You mean you would not help me once I leave this office if I don't agree to your terms now?" she finally asked.

He nodded his head.

"Give me half an hour so that I can go to a teahouse and think about it."

"I prefer you consider here."

"But I can hardly decide anything in your presence."

"You may sit with Wang Lu. I will wait your return."

Wang Lu, she assumed logically, was the scarred woman. Wallis had been fully in control until this point. But the thought of sharing the small outer reception area with Wang Lu caused her considerable discomfort. Even now, she could not help but wonder how the woman had received that horrifying scar. The image of Wang Lu's distorted face filled her thoughts. It had been a mistake, a terrible error in judgment to come here. She prayed the rickshaw boy, whom she had hired for the afternoon, had not disappeared. She would telephone Mr. Ku from the Palace and tell him she had changed her mind. If she had not received a ticket or any papers, there surely would be nothing to which he could hold her even if she signed a pledge. She lifted the pen. "What shall I write?" she asked.

She wrote as he slowly dictated a paragraph with the same terms as he had previously set forth. She paid little attention to his awkward grammar and stilted phrases and transcribed his words exactly as he spoke them. If ever a problem arose, she reasoned, she could convincingly prove that she would not write in such a manner and that the pledge was, therefore, a forgery.

"Sign, please," he requested.

She did so but left the *i* in "Wallis," undotted, feeling this might also give credence to a future claim of forgery.

He picked up the paper and read what she had written, not recognizing anything was amiss. He folded the paper in half and slipped it into a small box on his desk and then locked it with a key attached by a gold chain to his vest pocket.

"Return to hotel and pack," he said. "You will receive papers soon." He bowed stiffly and rang a brass bell next to the locked box. Wang Lu instantly appeared. "Good-bye, Mrs. Spencer," he smiled and Wang Lu bowed her head as she escorted Wallis out of Mr. Ku Ling Yong's presence.

To Wallis's relief, the rickshaw boy stood waiting on the street. She paid little attention to the route he took or the lanes they passed through on the way back to the hotel. She was apprehensive about what had just taken place in Mr. Ku's office. Somehow her call and her request had come at a fortuitous time for him. It was not difficult to believe that the man was part of an intelligence operation, although whether it was for Sun Yat-sen or the Nationalists, she could not speculate. She understood little about China's internal problems or the politics involved. In fact, she wanted to have nothing to do with either party. How she could help Mr. Ku was, therefore, a complete mystery.

Upon her arrival at her hotel, she went directly to her room. To her dismay, an envelope with a first-class reserved ticket on the *Shanghai Express* for that evening was under her door. She tried ringing Mr. Ku, but received no reply. The time was ten minutes past six. The train departed at half past eight. Well, what was the good of the ticket if she had no papers?

There was a knock on the door. The maid who brought Wallis her breakfast tray every morning bowed low. "My packee he chop-chop walkee," she said in pidgin English, which Wallis understood meant that she would help her pack in a hurry for a trip. Then, without Wallis's approval, the maid took down her suitcases from a high shelf and began to empty the drawers and wardrobe, swiftly and smoothly folding and packing the contents.

"Now look—" Wallis began and stepped in front of her to stop her.

The girl smiled toothily and took a folded piece of paper from inside her sleeve and handed it to Wallis.

PAPERS AT STATION WITH MAN IN GREEN HAT, it said.

She could not possibly go along with such utter madness. And yet, she now possessed a ticket to Peking and a promise of travel documents before she boarded the train. She let the girl go on with the packing and crossed to the telephone.

"I would like to send a telegram," she said. "COLONEL LOUIS LITTLE, U.S. LEGATION, PEKING. WILL ARRIVE PEKING VIA SHANGHAI EXPRESS THURSDAY 9:10 A.M. STOP PLEASE RESERVE HOTEL ROOM STOP MANY THANKS WALLIS SPENCER."

15

The railway station was across Soochow Creek on the edge of the International Settlement. The car Wallis hired drove along the banks of the muddy Whangpoo River, which flowed with deceptive lethargy into the great mouth of the Yangtze. Large and small steamers, freighters, tugs and barges crowded the Whangpoo. A junk fleet pulled into port. As she glanced back, factory smokestacks belched black clouds into the chiaroscuro sky. Shanghai looked no different than on her day of arrival. Nothing indicated civil war raged nearby.

Because of the weight of the baggage, the car had difficulty navigating the steep hill that led to North Szechuan Road. Her nervousness returned. She wished she had a flask like the one Nancy carried for she sorely felt the need of a strong stimulant. The night was cold and bitter; yet beads of sweat marked her forehead and reappeared almost immediately after she had wiped them away.

How was she to find a man in a green hat in a crowded railway depot? It was surely all madness. Her uneasiness increased when she reached the station. It appeared that half of Shanghai must be going elsewhere, although she knew there were only a few departing trains. "The *Shanghai Express,*" she told the coolie who had strapped together her suitcases and heaved them onto his back.

"My walkee chop-chop," he replied from under his load.

She stepped lively in order to keep up with him as he wove his way expertly through the milling people to the gate from which the *Shanghai Express* departed. To her amazement the man who collected the tickets wore a green silk hat. She handed him the envelope with her ticket.

"Moment please," he said, and disappeared into a small shed on the platform. A few moments later he returned with the envelope, which now felt considerably fuller. He gave the coolie a command in Chinese, obviously telling him to take her and the baggage to their proper car, for he pointed at the track where her train was waiting. "Follow please," he told her.

Not until she was in what she assumed was to be her private compartment on the train did she open the envelope. If the papers weren't there, she knew she would be forced to disembark. Whatever fears she had were quickly dispelled. Mr. Ku had kept his end of the bargain.

A rather plump, middle-aged American soon joined her. "Larry Dean. I live in Peking. Work for the China Import Company as an international sales representative. We are the major agents for Chinese porcelain and tapestries," he told her. "Sorry about this. I suspect you have a ticket for this compartment. So do I. The Chinese habit of selling space twice is pretty infuriating, but since the train is packed I suggest we accept the situation." He began immediately to organize her luggage so that they had more room.

"I also suggest we go into the dining car and grab a bite before it's too late. God knows what we can expect by morning," he said.

The train gave a tremendous heave as it started forward and Wallis grabbed hold of his arm to keep from falling. "What do you mean?" she asked after thanking him for his support.

"Lady, there's a nasty war going on in this country. Didn't anyone tell you?"

"No one had to tell me, Mr. Dean," she replied testily, "I've been in China since September. And my name is Mrs. Spencer."

"Call me Larry." He had merry eyes and an open smile

and Wallis decided she might as well make their traveling time together as pleasant as possible.

Dinner was enjoyable and well served. The car was crowded with an international mix of people although they seemed to be the only English-speaking diners. "Why Peking?" he asked.

"I have friends there. Colonel Little of the U.S. Legation and his wife and Mr. and Mrs. Herman Rogers."

"Top drawer," he grinned.

She asked him to tell her about Peking, which he was pleased to do. Larry Dean was from Trenton, New Jersey, and he firmly believed he had been given "a chance in a million. When I was a kid," he laughed, "I once tried to dig my way down to China. Some other kid on the street told me this was possible. I dug up a bone our neighbor's police dog had buried and he nearly tore off my arm. I still can't believe I'm in China." He then launched into a long description of Peking's wonders.

"You'll want to see the Temple of Heaven and the Lama Monastery, the Great Wall, the Ming Tombs—and of course, the Imperial City if you can. It takes up about two square miles in the center of the city. A pink wall, at least twenty feet high, surrounds it. Then, inside the Imperial City are more walls surrounding the still more exclusive Forbidden City. Until the Boxer trouble in 1900, foreigners were not permitted to enter it. Since then foreign ladies have been allowed in if they have enough pull. You should speak to your friend Colonel Little."

"I'll do that," she agreed.

After dinner they returned to their compartment. The facing seats had been made up into two beds. "Don't worry," he grinned. "I once taught Sunday school, and I'm a happily married man. I'll sit up fully clothed. I suggest you do the same. Stay dressed, I mean. There's a nasty patch we're riding through during the night. We might have unexpected visitors."

The lights went off almost as soon as he said this. "No use being a glaring target," he commented, and settled back. Moments later he was snoring.

Larry Dean's presence was reassuring. He was a touch of home and the sequence of this day's curious events had become unreal. As the darkened train hurtled through the night, Wallis's anxiety resurfaced. *What if—What if*—the train wheels ground out. What if this Fu Looog in Peking turned out to be a drug dealer? What if drugs had been stuffed into one of her suitcases without her knowing it? What if he threatened her harm if she could not pay the two thousand dollars? She recalled Lu Wang's scarred face and she shuddered.

"I just can't think about it," she told herself. "Some how, I'll get through it." But her troubled thoughts would not leave her.

The train came to a sudden halt sometime in the middle of the night. Voices rose outside her window. Wallis pulled up the shade slightly and peered out. A man holding a lantern was standing with his back to her. They were not in a station. A group of armed, uniformed men marched past and she jerked the shade down.

"Larry, Larry—Mr. Dean!" she called and touched his shoulder to awaken him. "We've been stopped by soldiers."

He came to attention just as the lights went on again.

Footsteps and voices inside the train now. The door to the compartment slid open. Two armed Chinese soldiers in ragged uniforms stood poised in the doorway.

"We're Americans traveling to Peking," Dean offered. "Do you speak English?"

The men had an exchange in Chinese. Finally, one turned back and said something to them.

"I believe he wants to see our papers," her traveling companion advised.

Wallis took the envelope from her pocketbook and handed it to Dean, who in turn presented it with some papers of his own to the soldiers. The uniformed men went out into the corridor. The terrifying thought now occurred to Wallis that if the soldiers were not satisfied with her credentials, they might turn her out right here in the middle of nowhere with hostile forces both before and behind her. Pains gripped her stomach and she let out a small gasp.

"Are you all right?" Dean asked.

"Scared," she admitted with a small, forced smile.

He reached for her elbow and supported it with his hand. The soldiers returned. For a dreadful few moments neither of them said anything. The man who held the documents flapped them abstractedly against the butt of his rifle, which was slung over his shoulder. Pain seized her again. She fought hard to control her reaction. The soldiers were studying her with magnifying intensity. Quite suddenly the one holding the papers relaxed and handed them back to Dean. The uniformed men departed.

Wallis collapsed onto her bed-seat as Dean closed the door to their compartment. "You better ease off if you can," he warned her. "This could happen a number of times before we reach Peking." He took a hip flask from his pocket and offered it to her. Wallis refused it. "I think you should take a swallow," he pressed. "You're white as a ghost."

She did as he said and was glad she had done so, for in a short time the alcohol dulled the waves of pain. The train lights were once again doused. Harsh voices exchanged angry words outside the window. Wallis was just about to lift the shade when Dean restrained her.

"They've taken some people off the train," he told her.

"What will happen to them?"

"I'd rather not speculate." The train lurched forward and five minutes later he was snoring again.

About dawn, Wallis finally dozed off. When she awoke, her new friend was handing her a cup of cold tea. "The problem with a rebel army," he said, "is that they have to eat. The stores in the dining car have been looted. Drink this. I have some oranges with me. About noon, some of the enterprising Chinese in the not-so-*luxe* cars will come along with rice cakes or fruit that they have fortuitously brought with them and for which we will have no other choice but to pay highway-robbery prices." He peered closely at her. "You okay?"

"Yes, I'm fine, thank you. If it happens again I won't panic, I promise." She had actually awakened with new assurance. If the soldiers the previous night had accepted her documents as valid, there was no reason to doubt that the papers would see her through to Peking. At least she would not be taken off the train.

Several times during the day the *Shanghai Express* jerked to a violent stop; tense armed men in shabby uniforms climbed aboard, pushed their way through crowded vestibules and peered into their compartment. Imitating Larry Dean's attitude, Wallis assumed an air of utter indifference. They were not asked again to present their documents and after a fifteen-minute delay the soldiers would disembark and the train would once again be on its way.

"They want food," Dean explained.

They were traveling through relatively flat, uncultivated land. The day was cold, the car poorly heated. Wallis sat wrapped in two coats staring out the window. As the *Shanghai Express* pushed its way through to Northern China, burned villages and fields became a frequent sight. There were lines of refugees, small figures carrying huge loads on bowed backs. When the train reached the Shantung Province, the terrain became hilly. Mountains rose in the distance. At the approach of nightfall they crossed the famous Yellow River bridge, one of the longest in the world. Below was the treacherous Yellow River which so frequently flooded the surrounding land and villages that some people called it "China's Sorrow."

"Twenty-seven years ago, fifteen villages were devastated by that river," Dean told her. "Only twenty years earlier a million people died when it flooded its banks. It says something for the spirit of these people. They never have controlled this river, but they clean up and rebuild their villages and start again."

Dean had great respect for the Chinese people and an admiration for their culture. "Their politics—that's another story."

They reached Tientsin, the capital of Chihli Province, at eleven o'clock that evening. There, at Central Station, the *Shanghai Express* ended its journey. They were scheduled to change to the connecting Tientsin-Pukow Railway and travel the remaining eighty miles to their destination.

Wallis was met on the platform by a tall man with a beak nose and a ruddy face. "Stanley Becker, ma'am," he introduced himself, a distinct trace of Texas in his voice. "I'm the American Consul here. Colonel Little has asked me to advise you of the dangers ahead if you proceed. There's active hostility in the area, not to mention some bandits."

"Do I understand that you are only advising me not to continue and not *prohibiting* me from going on?" she inquired.

"I have no authority to stop you, ma'am. But if you don't mind my saying so, I think it would be a damned fool thing for you to do. And you could get yourself involved in an international incident that would make it mighty difficult for our legation."

"Well, I think it's safer to continue for eighty miles than to backtrack six hundred miles, or however far we've traveled," she answered stubbornly.

"There are U.S. boats anchored here and you are the wife of a naval officer. I have already requested that the Navy see you safely back to Hong Kong." His face grew stern. "I'm afraid if you don't agree I will have to report to the Navy that you have disregarded the advice of the U.S. government's representative."

"Having come so far, Mr. Becker, I do not propose to be stopped by a civil war. I'm from the South and I can tell you it never stopped my ancestors either."

"That may be so, ma'am," he replied stiffly, "but this is not your country or your war." Unable to back Wallis down, the Consul escorted her to a nearby hotel where she was to remain for the night since the train for Peking was not due to leave until the following morning.

Wallis found comfort in Mr. Becker's reappearance early the next day to see her off and to say that an assistant in his office had been sent ahead to hold a seat for her. The train she was to travel in was anything but *luxe*. "Well," the Consul said, as he helped her aboard, "if it should be your bad luck to run into trouble, I can bet my Stetson the bandits will be the ones to regret it. You won't be an easy hostage, that's for sure!"

Larry Dean was also on the train and managed to trade a seat to sit beside her. Wallis told him about her contest of wills with Mr. Becker. "Do you think I did the wrong thing?" she asked anxiously.

"Mrs. Spencer," he smiled, "it's the inalienable right of American travelers to make life impossible for their consuls."

Twice during the journey, bandits halted the train. They were surprisingly polite and not nearly as frightening as the soldiers had been. They did not ask Wallis to open her suitcases. Following Dean's example she gave one group the Chinese money in her wallet and the next ten American dollars, and the men quickly disappeared. The train stopped at Hanku. Fighting was taking place on the line ahead. Shots filled the air. There was shouting, loud screams, but the passengers on the train sat passively, eating oranges and spitting out the pits. Two hours later the train continued its journey. People crowded to the windows to see out, and Wallis, who had a window seat, was almost crushed.

"Why do they want to look?" she asked Dean, her eyes averted from any sign of the massacre that might have taken place.

"Maybe they are searching for family members," he replied seriously.

Colonel Louis Little strode down the platform to meet her when the train finally arrived, eight hours late, in Peking. Wallis could not mistake the Colonel's Marine training. A sixty-year-old man, he was extraordinarily hardy for his age, his stride forceful, his bearing rigid, and although he was a big man with broad shoulders and a barrel chest, there seemed to be no excess fat on his large frame.

"The undauntable Mrs. Spencer, I assume," he said with unmistakable leatherneck grimness.

"Oh, Colonel Little," she replied, in a voice suggesting the frailty of Southern womanhood, "have I really done a terrible thing in coming here?"

"You should not have come," he scowled. Then, thawing slightly, he added, "But you're here, and what might have happened is no longer important."

Her first glimpse of Peking from the window of the U.S. Legation car was of high brick walls and the city gate, topped with a tall tower that stood out starkly against a gray twilight at the southeast corner of the Tatar City. Troops guarded the gate. "Last night, there was a case of *ping pien,*" the Colonel told her, "a mutiny of troops in the northern section of the Tatar City. How-Meu—that's the gate you see—is closed. Some of the more affluent residents of that area have been flocking into the Legation Quarter all day and have been taking rooms at hotels. Not the Rogerses, however. They are quite used to these things by now. Mutinies often occur. But only three weeks ago, the railroad station and telegraph offices were occupied and telephone communications were cut off." He said this in a stern fashion, so that Wallis assumed he was still annoyed that she had not taken his advice and returned to Hong Kong, and from there home. (She also understood now why she had not received an immediate reply to the letter she had sent him from Shanghai.)

The day was sharp with wind. Thinly dressed people huddled under papers in doorways of buildings built during Peking's glorious imperial past. Armed soldiers loitered on the streets to recall the present.

She was driven to the Grand Hôtel de Pekin, near the Legation Quarter. Larry Dean had disappeared almost immediately after they had arrived, having said good-bye to her on the train. Thankfully, Mr. Fu Looog did not appear and there was no message from him at the hotel. Wallis did not let this lull her into the false illusion that she was home safe. She suspected that Mr. Ku was not a man in the habit of giving anything on which he did not expect a return.

Flowers and an accompanying note from Gerry Green were waiting in her pleasant hotel room. "Welcome! And please let me escort you to a dinner-dance tonight. Eight P.M., your hotel. With great anticipation—Gerry."

The telephone rang.

"Wallis! Is it true? I've just heard from Louis Little that you're here!" Kitty's melodious voice. "There must be a story. You can tell us all about it later. You and Gerry will join us at our table. It's Thanksgiving, you know? The U.S. Legation makes a big thing about it every year. Look, Herm and I have discussed it and agree that you must come here and stay with us."

"I couldn't possibly, Kit."

"Of course you could—and you will come. You stay at the hotel tonight. Meanwhile I'll have your room readied for you. We'll move you over at lunchtime tomorrow."

"I never expected . . ." she began.

"I'm sure you did not or you would have written you were coming. That was naughty of you, Wallis. But all's forgiven. Now I won't take no for an answer and that's that!"

Quickly, miraculously, her life was changing. In a matter of hours she would be with old friends and tomorrow she would be a guest in what she was certain must be a palatial and gracious home. It would be impossible for her not to be included in Peking's most prestigious international group. As Larry Dean had said, Kitty and Herman were top drawer. Her fear of Mr. Fu's sudden appearance, endangering her life and her aspirations, did not desert her. She drew strength from the people to whom she could now turn. She would not ignore her obligation to Mr. Ku and his associates. Whatever price was put to her, she would, of course, negotiate. She was more than willing to pay "interest" on what had been advanced on her behalf. It would have to be paid off by monthly installments. If she signed a note of some kind for a two-hundred-dollar monthly payment, Mr. Ku would have his initial investment returned in a year. She would, she decided, offer to extend these payments for an additional year. Fair profit to the lender, she thought.

This meant she could not divorce Win for at least two years or the allotment check would stop. A way to supplement her income would also have to be found. Money problems had always worked out for her in the past and Wallis saw no reason to doubt that they would do so in the future.

Because this was an American holiday, she chose to wear a red chiffon dress from her Washington days, navy shoes and a white silk shawl, purchased in Shanghai. Gerry was waiting for her when she came down to meet him in the great white-marble lobby made dazzling by the crimson, blue and gold brilliance of the patterned carpets and a colonnade of carved white elephants with gold gilt trappings.

"Wallis! My God!" In the short time since they were together in Paris, Gerry had somehow become more distinguished-looking. A sprinkling of gray now touched his dark hair and he wore a hand-tailored suit that gave his short, wiry figure an illusion of some stature, increased by lifts on his shoes, which added about two inches to his height. He kissed her lightly on the cheek. Then, laughing, he gave her a quick hug and with his arm still around her, led her through the lobby to a private dining room decorated with red, white and blue bunting and with small American flags on tables set for at least a hundred. As Wallis entered she spotted Kitty and Herman, who immediately crossed from the bar to greet her.

Always a beauty, Kitty was now strikingly handsome, her figure slimmer than ever, the golden hair cropped in a soft bob around her lovely face, the slate-blue eyes emphasized by the brilliant blue of her satin gown. (Wallis quickly learned this color, peculiar to the local silk factories, was called Peking blue). Herman, lean and handsome, wore his brown wavy hair with a center part, which gave his tanned, well-boned face an additional theatricality.

The women embraced and Herman kissed Wallis's hand. They all laughed out of sheer happiness at seeing one another again.

"Has it really been three years?" Kitty asked, quickly answering her own question. "Well, we've been away from the States for that long, so it must be! You see, when we were married we thought we would travel the world and decide where we wanted to spend time. Somehow, we struck roots in Peking. After six months, when we went back to Herm's home in Hyde Park, we found we were bored. There was not much to do there except play bridge and visit friends and relatives. Herm's family were not a *bit* pleased when we decided to return here. They just couldn't believe anyone in their right mind would want to leave America to go to China because they think that Hyde Park, New York, is the finest place in the world. They thought Herm had wandered enough and should take his place, like his brother, in a Wall Street firm.

"We really *do* love Peking," she continued, "although our paradise is running out of time. We always believed Peking would be immune to the war. Now, after last November fifth, we know we were being naïve."

Noting the concerned look on Wallis's face, Herman interjected, "Americans are quite safe here. I don't think I would want to be English, though."

"We recently came back from Europe," his wife went on. "Now we think if things do get difficult, we might go to Florence or the South of France. Herm has this great yearning to write a book and France is filled with so many talented artists and writers from all over. Now! Enough about us. Tell us about yourself."

"Well, for a start, I have left Win," she began.

"Good!" Kitty exclaimed, and then was instantly apologetic. "I'm sorry, Wallis. I never liked that man and I don't think he is equal to you in any way."

Colonel Little and his wife, Eleanor, her unrouged face flushed from excitement, now joined them. "Mrs. Spencer! I've been so anxious to meet you. There aren't many people, male or female, who can say no to Louis." She leaned in conspiratorially to Wallis. "He isn't as tough as he'd like people to think, though." She winked, her clear brown eyes displaying an open, happy nature. Eleanor Little was squat and square-built with a face which, although not pretty, was agreeable. She had the look of a woman who had no time for cosmetics or clothes; and Wallis, having known many service wives in her time, spotted her as the sort who filled up her days with charitable works and legation niceties.

Lighthearted conversation dissolved into more serious discussion as the evening progressed. Wallis learned that on November fifth, the imperial family had been ordered to leave the Forbidden City and was under house arrest. The British Legation had refused them refuge. A plan, it was understood, was under way to get at least the Emperor safely to the Japanese Legation Quarters. The "haven" to which Wallis thought she was coming, although not presently under siege, was dominated by the presence of bands of soldiers.

"There's no danger to us," Kitty insisted.

Wallis unsuccessfully searched the room of Legation personnel and U.S. businessmen and their wives for Larry Dean.

She noted that the women, except for Eleanor Little, all were fashionably dressed. Kitty gave her brief biographies of the ones who came over to their table. When dinner started, the assemblage raised their glasses "to the good old U.S.A.—long may her flag wave!" Duck was served in place of the traditional turkey and plum jam for cranberry sauce. Apart from that, Wallis felt she could be on any service post in America.

"Do you know a Larry Dean with the China Import Company?" she asked Gerry.

"Don't recall the name. Friend of yours?"

"He was on the train coming here."

After dinner, they danced to popular American music played on a gramophone. Wallis felt a kind of affection for Gerry. But almost as soon as she was in his arms on the dance floor she knew that she could never feel anything much more than that—which did not mean that adventures were not still to be had in Peking. The room contained far more men than women, many of them quite attractive, although Wallis paid them little attention. For the present, romance was far from her thoughts.

The only man out of her past whom she could imagine might arouse her interest now would be Espil. The thought occurred to her that, perhaps, she should write him. She instantly dismissed the idea. "I'm over him," she mused. Without knowing when it had happened, she realized she had lost her feelings for him. An extraordinary sense of freedom was liberating her. Reminders of Win were being swept away along with those of Espil. A new life stretched before her and she was eager to clasp it to her.

It did not affect her, any more than it seemed to impress the Rogerses, that she was in a country in the throes of great agony. She had adapted quickly to this small, narrow-minded circle of American expatriates. They had very little in common with the missionaries and Red Cross workers from their country who were dedicated to helping China's great impoverished masses. Some members of the Thanksgiving party were here simply because the U.S. government had sent them to China. Their main aim was to do their jobs and to re-create as much of the ambience of home as possible. They were a close, cohesive group. Few actually knew any Chinese people except for their servants, whom they taught to cook Western-style food. This was equally true of the rich Americans like the Rogerses, who regarded Peking as a perennial vacation spot where with dollars one could live in princely luxury.

"Do you play bridge or poker?" Herman asked Wallis when they were dancing.

"Both."

"Splen-did!" he replied.

Gerry saw her to her room. "If I can help with the move to the Rogers house tomorrow, let me know," he offered, and kissed her on the cheek. "Glad to have you aboard, Wallis. I was about to sink until you arrived."

Exhaustion hit her as soon as she closed the door. The past two days had been exceedingly trying. She kicked off her shoes and headed for the bedroom of her comfortable suite. Suddenly, to her surprise and confusion, Larry Dean stood in the doorway.

"Sorry to drop in on you like this, Mrs. Spencer. It seems we have some unfinished business," he said.

"Look, I don't know how you got access to my rooms, or what mistaken ideas you might have, but I suggest you leave immediately or I will call both the management and the Marines!" Anger overcame her. Why, she thought furiously, do men assume a shared experience meant you would also want to go to bed with them?

"I assure you, it will be better for you to deal with me than with Fu Looog," he replied.

A cold shiver worked its way up her back and settled like an icy hand about her neck. When she spoke, she hardly recognized her own voice. "How do you know about Fu Looog?"

"He is my direct superior." He walked into the sitting room and to a tray with glasses and poured a drink from his flask and then offered it to her.

"This time I would rather not," she said sharply. He shrugged his shoulders, a gesture of his she now interpreted as revealing an arrogant nature. "You are a spy," she said. "Worse! You are a liar and a fake!"

"I like the order in which you said that," he laughed.

Things began to clear in Wallis's head. Larry Dean's presence in her compartment on the train had been no accident. Whatever the need for him to gain safe passage to Peking, she had provided it for him and Mr. Ku and their confederates.

"Well, all right, Larry. You and Mr. Ku used me as a front for you. God knows what kind of danger I was *really* in when those soldiers took our papers. Luckily, they assumed you were with me. I never saw your papers, but I have an instinct they claimed you were my husband."

"Clever girl."

"Okay. I've paid for my trip here, so now you can go."

"That was the down payment. I was told there was a matter of the second half to be settled."

"You can tell Mr. Ku and your Mr. Fu Looog that I consider the jeopardy they placed me in payment in full."

"We do not."

"We?"

"Let me just say we do not support the Red Christian Army. Now, since you have passed the test—you have a lot of nerve, you know—we feel certain you can help us one more time. That would clear up your debt and we would disappear from your life."

"You forget my connections with Colonel Little," she warned.

"To the contrary. We have taken this into careful consideration. Your affiliations guarantee that you would not want the U.S. Legation to learn that you have helped a spy—and not one of theirs—slip into Peking. I can assure you this would quickly end any of your social aspirations here, and further, that if you do not cooperate we will have proof of your confederacy in the Colonel's fist very quickly."

"I *will not* be blackmailed or intimidated," she snapped. "I pledged to pay two thousand dollars for safe passage here. I will do so."

"I suspect that won't be as easy for you as what we ask."

"Which is?"

"We will tell you when the time comes."

"As I said," she insisted, "I will pay the debt I owe as agreed and that is all."

"You have no money, Mrs. Spencer. You will do as we say," he insisted.

"Get out of my room," she demanded.

He crossed to the door. "We shall be in touch," he smiled, and left.

Wallis was shaken but she strongly believed that Larry Dean, or whatever his name *really was,* could not force her to do something against her will. He was trying to frighten her. Recalling Wang Lu's scarred face, she was grateful he had not threatened violence. She had been so naïve. She should have realized that Dean's appearance in her compartment on the train was too much of a coincidence—the only other American. And why had she been so stupidly gullible and accepted his story of the double booking?

She made sure the bolt on the door was locked before she got into bed. As she lay there, unable to sleep, she went over and over the bizarre events of the past few days. She decided she would write Nancy Armstrong—just a chatty letter to say she was safe in Peking with Mr. Ku's kind assistance—and to see if this roused any reply. She would not say one word about Larry Dean.

Her tension eased. Okay, she had helped a spy on his way to Peking but, at least, she did not know why he was here. That was proof enough that she had been innocently enmeshed in his travel arrangements. Dean and his superiors were trying to frighten her into helping them further. When they saw they could not, that would be all there was to it.

16

The city Wallis was in might well have been the Peking of the fifteenth century. Not only had the architecture and the city plan remained unchanged, Peking's soul was unaltered, and political intrigue, treachery and conquest were rife.

Peking was considered a safe harbor for foreigners because of the political power of the legations situated there, most of whom occupied substantial compounds within the Legation Quarter. The United States, Britain, Japan, Netherlands, France and Italy also kept military guards. Although the international community lived in a protected environment, the very nature of their security—the numerous nations that had representation there—created a complex web of intrigue. Spies from almost every major country had made their way to Peking and were existing in the shadows of the recently vacated Inner Forbidden City.

With its massive surrounding walls, Peking, when approached, looked like a giant box. Few of the many temples, pagodas and palaces were higher than the city's walls and the houses behind them were mostly one story. Built in an exaggerated thickened T-shape, the northern end of Peking, known as the Tatar City, where Kitty and Herman Rogers lived, was protected by still another solid wall and fortified with guardhouses positioned at equal intervals.

A chauffeured car was sent to transport Wallis to her friends' home. The traffic in Peking was unlike that in the other Chinese cities she had visited. Double-humped camels with heavy freight strapped on their backs were a frequent sight on the wider thoroughfares, along with mule-drawn carts. Bicycles and rickshaws were often ridden ten abreast. The air was filled with the intricate cries of the street hawkers. What little modern transport could be seen most often bore embassy crests, and the cars made their way slowly like elephants in a circus parade. The vehicle in which Wallis was riding—a Rolls-Royce Herman had had imported from Britain—entered the Tatar City near Ha Ta Men Gate and then awkwardly negotiated a series of narrow, crooked lanes. All Wallis could see on either side of her as she stared out the windows were pitted gray walls of mud and plaster. Pedestrians, oncoming rickshaw drivers and bicyclists pressed against the barricades to allow her car to pass. If another automobile had approached there would have been an impasse.

This did not seem to her to be a section of palatial homes. She would learn soon that in Peking the magnificence of a house was always concealed from the street; the finer the residence, the seedier the walls. The chauffeur drew up before a wrought-iron gate and helped her out. Through this opening she entered a spacious cobbled courtyard dominated by an ancient gnarled yew and a sunken lily pond.

Her host and hostess rushed out of a rambling one-story structure roofed with old gray tiles arranged in an intricate herringbone fashion and crossed the courtyard to greet her.

"Welcome! Welcome!" Herman called.

Kitty linked her arm through Wallis's and led her inside. Rooms were connected by doors cut in the shape of large keyholes. Gray-stone floors were covered with magnificent, thick, brilliantly colored Peking rugs. Antique Chinese tapestries and paintings decorated the walls. An ancient vitrine held a vast collection of valuable carved ivory and jade. Wallis had an immediate feeling of being in a home where the occupants had both wealth and good taste.

She was given two connecting rooms, her own maid, Sulan, and, also for her personal use, a handsome black rickshaw with rubber tires and a rickshaw boy named Li. Wallis accepted her new luxuries without serious struggle. Her financial worries suddenly faded. That evening Kitty and Herman had dinner guests and later Herman asked her to join them all in a game of poker.

"You've played before, haven't you?" he asked. "You know what a straight is? And a full house?"

"Oh, yes," Wallis replied. "I learned the game from the Navy."

"That should make you almost a professional gambler," he laughed, his dark eyes glinting. "You just play. If you lose I'll assume your losses."

By the end of the evening she had won exactly $225, the same amount as her monthly Navy allotment.

"Wallis," Herman said, after his guests had departed, "you don't need a protector at poker! From here on, you're on your own."

Thereafter, she played frequently and won consistently and her new source of income gave her an independence previously unexperienced. With Kitty's guidance she bought Chinese antiques that were a good investment. Larry Dean had sent no word. As the weeks flowed into months, Wallis felt more and more certain that his threats had been a bluff. Her apprehensions faded; her original instinct to visit Kit and Herman was validated. Unlike those in Hong Kong or Shanghai, Peking's international colony was essentially a diplomatic enclave that centered around the *corps diplomatique* of the Légation Quarter, and Wallis, with her Navy background and her year in Washington, fit right in.

For foreigners like Wallis and her friends, Peking, despite the dangers of the war that raged beyond its gates, offered an exotic and luxurious way of life. Servants were cheap; Western food—because of the legations—was always available and the rarest Oriental fruits, vegetables and condiments plentiful at an amazingly small price. At night, the gates of the great walls would lock, separating the city from the outer world. As Mr. Ku had predicted, Shanghai had experienced several bloody riots since Wallis's departure. Elsewhere in China the war pressed on. But with the removal of the Royal Family from the

Forbidden City, Peking—at least for the foreign community—had returned to the pleasures of the past.

"Peking," Wallis wrote Aunt Bessie, "is an ideal place for a woman with time on her hands and a secret sorrow in her heart. Bachelors outnumber unattached women by a ratio of ten to one. Of course, there are some honorable men with dishonorable intentions, but if prudently recognized in advance, they are readily manageable."

Experience had taught Wallis that it was not difficult to get any man for one night. The trick was to find a rich one and to make him want her for life. Wallis was convinced that if she set her sights on a millionaire she would find one, and that if she concentrated on one day living in a palace—or at least a home as opulent as Kitty and Herman's—she could make it happen. She did not think of herself as avaricious but she believed that having money was the most important thing in life and absolutely essential for happiness.

Men appreciated her bonhomie. She was not one to moan about her past bad luck. She had learned her lesson in Pensacola years before. In accordance with her new list of rules, she would win over the wives and daughters of the men in her circle, never encourage a married man's attentions and make herself noticed and talked about—nothing, however, of a scandalous nature. Scandal, perhaps, made a woman grow stronger but it weakened her potential to marry well.

She dressed more and more with confident originality and with the intention of catching the eye of both men and women. Her necklines were modest, her hemlines many inches below the current fashion for short skirts. At one legation affair she surprised and pleased everyone by attending in a white coolie suit, her dark hair drawn back with white camellias. The only color to her outfit was several giant strands of bright lapis beads bought with her poker winnings. And she fought a winning battle to remain slim.

"Men may say they like a woman they can get hold of," she wrote Aunt Bessie in a letter confiding that she had placed herself on a rigid diet, "but it's a lie. The men I've met mostly marry thin women and then cheat on them after a while when they begin to put on weight."

Marriage was not a serious concern; she was, after all, still legally Win's wife. No word had come from him since their parting, and she hoped he would not contact her. What she wanted was to meet a man of Herman's position and wealth who would be satisfied for the time being to function as her adoring protector and swain. But despite the many available and attentive men in Peking, she had not met one whom she considered worth pursuing. And so she relaxed and enjoyed the admiring company of Gerry Green and several other men in her circle.

The days passed pleasantly. She drifted in an exotic time warp. She roamed among the crumbling ruins of Taoist and Lama temples, their stone gods severed from their pedestals, the sound of temple bells only occasionally breaking the silence. Often in the late afternoon she would walk along the broad parapet of the Great Wall around Peking and look down over the crowded city below. But she never got closer to the real Peking and the Chinese people than her daily encounters with servants, shopkeepers and the tailors and seamstresses who made her clothes from patterns she supplied from magazines or from her own designs. The Chinese were never invited to the legation parties. Nor for that matter was the international community welcomed in their social activities.

Herman had an office in the Legation Quarter, where he spent his days writing a book on Chinese temples, while Kitty, when not accompanying Wallis, took various eclectic lessons. Their friendship flourished. Wallis liked to talk to Herman about his work and encouraged him to continue; and she felt the warmest regard for Kitty, who proved to be as generous as she was caring. The fact was that if Wallis admired Kitty, this admiration was returned several times over. Wallis had great éclat and a sense of independence that her hostess respected.

Herman and Kitty had appropriated an abandoned temple in the Western Hills about fifteen miles from Peking and furnished it with Oriental bed platforms and camp chairs covered with colorful brocade rugs. An enormous Buddha presided over the central chamber; two other rooms were used to accommodate men in one, women in the other. Weekend parties were held for as many as twenty people. They ate around an open fire, spent long evenings in candlelight and rode the saddle horses brought up by a convoy of servants before they arrived.

In the mornings, during the week, Wallis would ride with Kitty and Herman along the esplanade that surrounded the Legation Quarter. On warm days she had her breakfast in the courtyard, took a swim before lunch at the American Legation pool or played tennis at the British Legation. Afternoons, traveling by rickshaw, she shopped at the permanent markets and bazaars for porcelains and bits of brocade or added to her growing collection of "lucky" elephants—tiny figures carved of ivory, amber, jade, turquoise and rose quartz—colors that were now her favorites. For bargains she would rise shortly after daylight to see what could be found at the "Thieves Market," which took its name from the supposition that stolen merchandise was sold there. She attempted lessons in Chinese with a gentleman named Mr. Wu, but was unable to progress past his second visit. Three times a week there was polo to watch at the Polo Club. Evenings were filled with dinner parties and dances.

The happenings of the world beyond her current life of leisure came only as faint and implausible echoes. What was real was the dream-like passage of her days. She felt young, and with three ardent admirers—Gerry, Salvio Marininni, an Italian naval officer, and Lieutenant Gordon Breakshaw of the British Legation—she could be the Southern belle of her childhood fantasies. She went to bed once with each (without the others knowing) and refused to allow such an "impassioned slip" to happen again. Gerry proposed. Softly smiling she reminded him that she *was* married. Salvio, who bore a strong resemblance to Rudolph Valentino, wrote her poetry; and Gordon gave her a gilt and leather volume of Chaucer which she had not yet opened.

Few of her set attached great importance to China's increasing inner conflict. Dr. Sun Yat-sen had died and the revolution he had begun was gathering momentum. Wallis shrugged off even fleeting concern for either her guest country or herself. Her treacherous journey from Shanghai had been shuffled into the long ago. She had happily exchanged illusion for reality. And in this way, a year passed.

One morning when she was having her breakfast in the courtyard at the small table just outside her apartments, Su-lan appeared with an envelope. Overhead, pigeons with bamboo whistles ingeniously fastened to their tail feathers turned the air to reedy music. Kitty could be heard practicing for her weekly lesson on the bells. Wallis smiled to herself. The sounds, the scents, even the texture of the air filled her with contentment.

"Missi-lady, this now come," Su-lan said, bowing as she presented what looked like an invitation.

"Does a boy wait for a reply?" Wallis asked.

"No, Missi-lady. Hab puttee in rickshaw. Hab go way."

"That's curious. Well, thank you, Su-lan."

Mrs. Earl Winfield Spencer, Jr. was written in a precise, even hand across the face of the small square envelope. Wallis carefully slit it open with her breakfast knife. A white card fell onto the table and she picked it up to see it better. For a moment she could not believe her eyes and squinting to block out the sunlight, stared at it again. The name *Fu Looog* was engraved on the front. Her hand trembled as she turned the card over.

Come alone 9 tonight. S.E. corner Ha Ta Men Gate.
Bring $2,000 or other currency equivalent.

There was no signature.

She sat rigidly, her long neck stretched until it hurt. For a moment she stopped breathing—or was she just holding on to her breath? She could feel the strain on her heart and she let out gasps of air in sharp fragments. Kitty was still playing the bells. The pigeons circled and sang a strident accompaniment. Only seconds had passed since she had experienced an overwhelming sense of well-being. Now she teetered over an abyss of fear.

"Life is perfectly mad," she whispered soundlessly and told herself that, if only she had had the sense to refuse Mr. Ku's help, she would not now be faced with this predicament.

She began to regret having come to China at all. Yet, why should she not have come? How could she have known that a revolution would coincide with her arrival?

The abdominal pain that had been recurring with irritating frequency suddenly seized her. She grasped the edge of the table. Her knuckles were white. She was cold, her head giddy. She was not sure she could make it back to her apartment but she knew she had to try. Su-lan had disappeared and she did not want to see Kitty at this moment. What could she say was wrong? She slipped the fateful card into the pocket of her morning robe and managed to get up. She had less than fifteen feet to walk. Slowly, shuffling her feet, she made her way to her door. Once inside she collapsed on the floor.

Time seemed to have stopped for, although she was certain she had remained in this ignominious position for ages, the hands on her wristwatch had scarcely moved. The pain was softer, moving off, but she did not have the strength to stand up. She crawled on all fours across the room and lifted herself with much difficulty onto the bed. *I don't have time to get sick,* she thought. *I must decide what I am to do.* She rang for Su-lan, and when she appeared told her to tell Kitty that she had her monthly "woman troubles" and would not be able to join her in the day's activities. Conversations with Su-lan held in pidgin English were difficult enough; to get her to deliver a verbal message that was accurate was almost impossible. But she could not manage a written note. The girl, her smile at least indicating that she understood what she was to say, bowed backward out of the room.

Wallis spent the day in bed, rising only once to drink some tea Su-lan brought. She could not sleep and lay staring wide-eyed at the ceiling. Her thoughts were feverishly agitated, circling and tangling in her head like string in a cat's paws. She would not meet Mr. Fu. After all, how would he know if she actually had received his card? But if she did not go to see him, might he not come here? No, that would never do. Well, if she went what could she say? She had been extravagant on her shopping trips recently and had only two hundred dollars stuffed in the ginger jar on the bedside table.

Perhaps if she asked Herman for a loan—or Gerry? But

how would she explain her desperate and immediate need for such a large sum? Telling the truth was not among the options she gave herself. The truth distressed her. She had been unforgivably stupid both in accepting Mr. Ku's assistance and in her handling of the entire situation. The idea of exposing her lack of wisdom stunned her and she knew with startling clarity that she must not, *could not,* reveal her incompetence. Her public image meant far too much to her to jeopardize it. It was her trump card, her opportunity to score and upset the odds of the poor hand that she had been dealt.

By the end of the day she had been unable to form a plan of action. At five P.M. Su-lan came in with another pot of tea. Wallis got up. The room was stuffy and she opened a window and let in a sweep of warm air. The courtyard was empty; even the pigeons were gone. The blinds were drawn and there was no sound from the main house. Except for the servants she was alone. She thought how easy it would be for her to slip into the sitting room and take a piece of expensive carved jade and bring it in payment to Mr. Fu. She turned guiltily away from the window and viewed her own collection. The entire lot was not worth two thousand dollars.

She sat down at the tea table, lighted a cigarette and for the first time calmly considered what she must do.

Every third summer day of the foreign calendar, a night fair was held on Ha Ta Men Street. At nine P.M. it would be in full swing and crowded. Wallis did not know how she would find Fu Looog, but she was certain he would somehow recognize her.

Kitty, looking her loveliest in a pale blue dress, diamonds sparkling around her slim, white neck, stopped at her apartment at half past seven to see if she would be joining them for a dinner dance at the Polo Club. Wallis asked to be excused and Kitty was understanding. She did not dress until Kitty and Herman had left for the evening. She chose her outfit carefully: the print dress she had brought with her to China, no jewelry except her watch. She rang for Li to bring the rickshaw round at eight-forty and waited for him at the courtyard gate. Despite the fact that he chose to take the most deserted route, she remained cool—reassured by the rhythmic sound of his slippers slapping against the pavement as he trotted through the dim streets and by the *clack-clack* of the watchmen's wooden clappers as the men patrolled past the homes of well-to-do owners.

It had never occurred to Wallis that Li's work was degrading or that it was a harsh way to make a living. She had been surprised when she learned that he was only nineteen years old; his nine years as a rickshaw boy had aged him so that he looked like a man of thirty-five. Although she had observed that he seldom smiled and that frown lines burrowed deeply into his forehead, as she sat back in the chair, soothed by the rocking motion his trotting created, she realized she would have a difficult time describing Li to anyone for she saw him mostly from the rear. Sudden shame for her lack of sensitivity overcame her, but she quickly dismissed it. This was China, not America, and rickshaw drivers, who—like mules or horses—pulled people in carts, were part of its everyday life, just as segregation was accepted, at least by the white population, in the South.

Li had turned onto Ha Ta Men Street. Colored lanterns were strung across the wide thoroughfare. Wheelbarrow coolies cried out their wares, jugglers performed in the middle of the boulevard, and on an improvised platform a contortionist twisted his body grotesquely. The sweet smell of candied apples filled the air. The crowd was so great that Li had difficulty in getting through. He let her off at her request at the corner of Ha Ta Men and Legation streets where she ordered him to wait for her. The designated meeting place was only fifty yards away. She recognized a man from the British Legation mingling with the crowds and prayed he might not see her. As she walked with averted face past him, he called out someone else's name and she hurried on. She saw no one waiting at the southeast corner of Ha Ta Men Gate and nervously positioned herself to one side to be less conspicuous, for it would seem odd that a woman was out alone at night.

"Mrs. Spencer," a man's clipped, Chinese-accented voice rasped so close to her ear that his warm breath prickled. Wallis wheeled around. The man had moved back into the shadows of the wall and she could not see his face. "Come with me," he ordered.

She edged her way along the wall behind his dark figure. They were in a small park square directly behind the Legation Quarter. The American flag atop the lighted U.S. building helped quiet her fears. The man motioned for her to be seated on a stone bench.

"I'd rather not."

"I am Fu Looog," he said. She could see a cadaverous face still half hidden by shadow. His head was shaved with a long pigtail left in the back but he wore Western clothes—a white vested suit—which surprised her.

"Do you have identification?" she asked.

"I am Fu Looog," he repeated, his expression grim.

"I refuse to talk to any underling," she insisted.

"I am Fu Looog," he said again, his tone knife-sharp. "Mrs. Spencer, in China it is most serious when persons do not pay their debts."

"I'm afraid I don't know what you are talking about."

"The ticket and papers secured for you by the Honorable Mr. Ku Ling Yong. Our cause is right and just and we cannot take money from it without gaining more in return."

As he spoke his left hand remained in the pocket of his jacket. Wallis was certain a knife was concealed there. She tried not to think about Wang Lu's scarred face but she knew that Fu Looog would not hesitate to do her an injury if her plan should go awry, and she gathered together all her courage so that her voice would not betray her fear.

"Does your cause validate blackmail and larceny?" she questioned. Before he could answer, she hurried on. "You have already used me as a cover for your agent, Mr. Larry Dean, to whom I paid two thousand dollars. Now you have the mendacity to demand more from me. Which brings me to question if your Mr. Ku is as honorable as you claim."

"You lie! You pay no money," he said, the lines around his narrow mouth twittering in anger.

"I certainly do *not* lie!" she countered.

"You send money to Mr. Ku?"

"No. I gave it to Mr. Dean." With that she opened her

purse and took out an envelope, the same one that had contained her letter from Mr. Ku. "I have the receipt right here. I made Mr. Dean write it out when I gave him a check almost a year ago. He insisted I make it payable to cash and I did. Although it made me several hundred dollars overdrawn, my bank paid the full amount six weeks later. The check was signed by Larry Dean and the money credited to a bank account in Geneva."

Her voice was entirely confident. Fu Looog was taken aback. Wallis now withdrew from the envelope the receipt that had taken her two hours and at least six attempts to forge.

"I will give you the receipt if you take your hand—empty—out of your suit pocket," she bartered.

"You are a clever woman," he said as he pulled his fist free and upturned his open palm.

Wallis backed up slightly so that the moonlight fell directly on her. "Here it is," she said, and held it up for him to see. Fu Looog stepped forward into the brighter light.

She did not move. Silently she counted to five, then took a small breath. She must give the impression that she was not concerned so that he would not doubt the validity of the receipt. "I made Mr. Dean sign it with a carbon," she said, her voice fully collected, "which is with my lawyers in Washington. You can, therefore, take this one and present it to Mr. Ku. If you have not received the money from Mr. Dean, I can only surmise that it is still in his possession, unless he has already spent it."

Her last statement was not a wild shot. She knew there was no way Fu Looog or his organization could verify this with their agent. Gerry Green had recently asked if she was still interested in Larry Dean of the China Import Company whom he recalled her inquiring about when she first arrived in Peking.

"Only out of curiosity," she had replied.

"Last night he was found floating facedown in Tungshow Canal," he told her.

Fu Looog carefully folded the receipt in quarters and placed it inside his vest pocket, bowed his head courteously, turned and in a matter of six or seven long strides disappeared into the darkness. Fearing he might be standing in the shadows and watching her, Wallis struck an even, unhurried pace back to Ha Ta Men Street. Dozens of rickshaws were lined up where she had left Li and it took her a moment to find him. When they reached home she gave him a sizable tip. "No talkee," she said.

"Can do, can do!" he vowed.

The next day Wallis told Kitty and Herman that, hard as it was to leave them, it was time for her to return home and to file for a divorce from Win. Herman made travel inquiries that afternoon. A Navy ship was leaving from Tientsin for Japan in two days' time and would arrange space for her. From there she could take a passenger ship to Seattle. Su-lan helped her pack all her Chinese mementos. Colonel and Eleanor Little, Gerry, Kitty and Herman bid her an emotional farewell at the train. This time the journey was free of bandit raids. Stanley Becker met her in Tientsin and escorted her to the Navy ship that was to take her on her first lap home.

She stood in a warm summer breeze on the upper deck along with two missionaries and a small American girl, whose missionary parents had been murdered in a rebel ambush, and watched as China slipped away. She and the child had seen two sides of the country. For the little one scars were certain to remain. For Wallis, the illusion of her lotus year would soon fade and she, too, would be left with her own wounds.

17

Light fell through the opened door of the darkened room that Wallis occupied. She could not tell if it was day or night because the blinds on the window were tightly shut. She was in a bed with a steel railing, covered by a white sheet and was numb, cold, unable to move—but she forced her eyes to open and tried to focus on her surroundings. A faint medicinal odor indicated she was in a hospital. More with sheer determination than strength of body, she lifted her arm from above the cover and probed beneath with her hand. Bandages bound her from waist to groin.

Her piercing scream—not from pain but terrible fury—rocked the hospital corridor with the force of a six-point earthquake. Two nurses and an intern appeared almost immediately at her bedside.

"I can't die!" she shouted. "I have too much I have to do!"

"You aren't going to die, Mrs. Spencer," the intern, a wiry, red-haired, bespectacled youth, told her. "You have been very sick. So ill, in fact, that we had to call your next of kin. You were operated upon yesterday morning by Dr. Esnard, the head of our gynecological department. I'll call him now and tell him that you are awake. I'm sure he'll be by to see you shortly."

"Would you like me also to call Mr. Warfield?" the older of the two nurses asked. "He left word that he could be reached at his hotel."

"Sol Warfield?" Wallis asked with surprise.

"Yes, I believe so."

"He's here?"

"Yes, certainly. He gave permission for the operation."

"Where am I?"

"Why, you're in General Hospital, Seattle, Washington."

"Mr. Warfield was listed as next of kin on your passport," the intern explained. "Dr. Esnard called him right away. I understand he arrived last night."

Why, of course, Wallis thought, and then wondered why she had not given her mother's name as next of kin. But then, she had obviously chosen rightly for Uncle Sol had apparently taken things into his capable hands.

The young nurse, shaggy-browed and makeup-less, brought out a hypodermic needle and lifted Wallis's arm. "This won't hurt. You have very good veins," she stated, rather smugly, "and it will relax you."

Wallis pulled back. "I do not want to relax," she said. "I want you to open the blinds so I can see what time of day it is and I want you to tell Mr. Warfield when you call him that I need a nightdress that does not look like a cook's apron!"

Early morning sunlight streamed into the small room with its dull green walls as she waited for the doctor and Uncle Sol to explain what had happened and what sort of operation had been performed on her. As she lay there, weakened even further by her outburst, she tried desperately hard to recall the sequence of events that had preceded her present condition.

The pain—the same one she had suffered after Win's abuse and intermittently ever since—had seized her again at sea two days away from Seattle. This time it was relentless. She had no memory of remaining in the ship's infirmary for forty-eight hours and then being transferred to the hospital by stretcher and ambulance. Nor could she remember how long she had been in the hospital, obviously in a semiconscious or unconscious state. The bright sun seared her eyes and she lowered her lids. The action brought back another memory.

* * *

She was at one end of a long, long tunnel and at the other there was a light that drew her to it. Beyond were cloud-like formations in a sea of soft blue. A voice—*was it her mother's? No! it belonged to Grandmother Warfield*—called out, "Go back, Bessie Wallis! Go back!" The voice had faded into the distance and then was gone. Something was over her face. She had felt icy cold. "Wallis," a man had said. "Keep breathing. Come back. There's the girl."

* * *

The door opened and a large, ruddy-faced, dark-haired man of Mediterranean background entered her room. He wore a green hospital gown and he looked bleary-eyed and tired. Still, he was an extremely handsome man and Wallis was immediately conscious of how terrible she must look.

"Well, I'm glad to see some color in your face, Mrs. Spencer," he said.

Strange, she thought, *it's Mrs. Spencer now!* For even before he introduced himself she knew he must be the doctor who had called her "Wallis" during her operation.

"I'm Dr. Esnard," he continued. "You've had a tough time, but you're a survivor. In a few weeks you'll be dancing the Charleston."

He eased himself onto the edge of her bed and despite his considerable size it remained firm.

"Are you ready for the medical prognosis?"

"Of course."

He leaned slightly forward. "The good news is that I was able to avoid a complete hysterectomy although you did miscarry. I understand your husband is in China, where you have just left him. Since it was impossible to contact him, I discussed the situation over the telephone with your uncle, Mr. Warfield." He straightened and his voice mellowed. "I had to explain to him that the wall of your uterus had been severely bruised, perhaps in a car accident a year or so ago, and that your kidney was also damaged. I had to remove your uterine tubes, which means you can never have another child."

Her head was spinning. It seemed he must be confused,

that he was discussing another patient's diagnosis. "Did you say I had a miscarriage?" she asked.

"Yes. I am sorry."

"I didn't know I was pregnant," she confessed. "Could you possibly be wrong?"

"No. The fetus was about nine weeks." He stood up. "Well, that makes it easier, I suspect."

Wallis struggled to recall whose child she could have been carrying. She had had intercourse only three times in Peking; Gerry, Salvio and—yes, of course! Gordon Breakshaw—last but certainly not least!

"You will have to remain at General for another two weeks. I understand you are on your way to your family in Washington. I would not recommend you travel by train for a further two weeks. You have had major surgery. We almost lost you on the table, but thank God! you fought back. I will want you to remain under a doctor's supervision for a time when you get home. I don't anticipate any complications but you have had extensive damage to several organs and it is likely that you will have some aftereffects that could be lasting."

"Such as?"

"Stomach spasm, back pain. You'll need to rest at those times. Tell me, Mrs. Spencer. *Were* you in a car crash?"

"No, Dr. Esnard, my husband beat me up," she replied candidly.

"I'm afraid that is what I suspected. I'm sorry."

"And I'm damned mad," she answered.

"With good reason," he assured her as he left the room.

She had allowed Dr. Esnard to believe that she had been carrying Win's child. Wallis did not think of herself as promiscuous, nor was she ashamed of her sexual freedom. After all, it was the time of jazz babies, champagne baths, midnight revels, petting parties in the purple dawn and "red-hot mamas" and lovemaking. Women were no longer a mixture of honeysuckle and barbed wire. In view of what she had read and what she had seen in Paris and Shanghai, Wallis considered herself fairly conservative, a young woman with moral fiber, discreet, a lady in public and in private. She had never gone to bed with a man she did not know well or whose credentials weren't strictly upper-class and whose discretion wasn't totally reliable.

She had learned to use sex, not to be readily available, but as a means to secure a relationship with a man. Intimacy broke down the usual barriers between men and women, and she had found men (except for Win) to be better friends after they had slept with you.

Fear of getting pregnant had never beset her, perhaps because it had not happened during her active married life and she had therefore thought herself to be infertile. And, since she was one of the many women who often missed a period or two, she had not realized that she had been "caught." Dr. Esnard had expected her to be distressed over her future inability to bear a child. As she considered this, she realized that she was, instead, elated. Children changed things in your life, became a persistent restraint, an encumbrance. Remembering her almost maternal love for her childhood pet, Bully, she thought, "I would rather have a dog. They don't ask for more than you want to give."

Low voices rumbled outside her door. Her heartbeat quickened; the idea of preferring a dog over a baby suddenly seeming culpable and unclean.

A moment later Uncle Sol entered her room.

"Well, Wallis, you certainly made a botch of things this time," he said.

Son-of-a-bitch! Wallis thought.

He walked around to the foot of the bed and stood looking down at her. The bracing scent of a spicy cologne clung to him and a small rust spot on his chin proclaimed that he had nicked himself while shaving. He had aged considerably and lost weight since she had last seen him. His mustache was entirely gray, and pucker lines pleated the exposed part of his upper lip. His eyes had retracted into a warren of lines and a gray pallor dulled his once-vital complexion. Nonetheless, the aging process had not run Uncle Sol to seed. He remained unbent. The pupils of his eyes were just as blue, his studied gaze no less penetrating. His hands, as he folded them in front of himself, were steady; and his voice had retained its sharp, biting tone.

"I left some personal things for you with the nurse. Your luggage still has to be cleared through customs."

"Thank you, Uncle Sol. And thank you for coming to my aid," she said, her exhaustion forcing her to slide more comfortably back into her childhood attitude toward him. *Thank Uncle Sol for your shoes, Bessie Wallis.*

"You need not worry about the medical expenses," he added, "and I have asked the staff to get you a private nurse."

"Thank you."

"Oh, for Christsake! Stop thanking me!" He whipped away and strode over to the window, his back to her as he stared out across the rooftops of Seattle. "Wallis, you and I have to talk turkey. You are damned lucky to be alive. But take a hard look at what it has cost you and those who love you."

When he turned back into the room Wallis had the uncomfortable feeling that he might be fighting tears. Could it be that Sol Warfield really cared for her after all? That he had feared she would die? He came closer to the bed and took hold of the iron rail as if to steady himself.

"You will never have a child," he said. "Did the doctor tell you that?"

"Yes."

"That means your mother will miss the joy and immortality of having a grandchild."

"I haven't thought about it in that way. But, of course, you are right."

"Dr. Esnard says he believes you took a brutal beating. Did that bastard Spencer abuse you?"

"Yes."

"Can't you say anything but *yes*?"

"I don't know what you want me to say, Uncle Sol, or why you are so angry with me. I have just been through a terrible ordeal. I nearly died. I have been told I will have physical repercussions for the rest of my life. I am exhausted and I hurt—I hurt *awfully*." She could not control the shake in her voice. Tears rose in her eyes and she lowered her head to avoid his gaze.

Sol was instantly at her side and, as difficult as the gesture must have been for him, he reached for her hand and held it tightly in his own.

"Wallis," he began, in an unfamiliar, almost tender voice, "I have something important to say to you, something I have steadfastly believed I would never reveal. It is about your mother and myself."

"You don't have to say anything. I've always known how much you love her," Wallis replied as she dried her tears on the sleeve of her white hospital gown.

"Look at me, Wallis," he commanded.

She turned her head grudgingly toward him. As soon as she did so, he glanced away—his eyes, as if in meditation, peering into the unseeable. Instead of pressing him to speak, Wallis listened to his restrained breathing, fascinated as he pressed his lips together to suppress even that little sound. Finally, he turned, visibly moved, close to tears himself. He eased his hand away from hers. He was lost for a moment in his thoughts. When he did begin to speak, his voice—though lower, gentler—was clear and steady.

"Please hear me out until I finish," he requested. "What I have to tell you is not easy for me and may even be more difficult for you. I have been in a state of confusion ever since I received Dr. Esnard's telephone call. 'Mr. Solomon Warfield?' he inquired. 'Yes,' I replied. 'You are related to Mrs. Wallis Warfield Spencer?' he continued. 'I am her uncle, why?' I asked. 'I am Dr. Raoul Esnard, chief of staff of gynecology at Seattle General Hospital. Your niece is unconscious and in need of immediate surgery. We cannot operate without your authorization as *next of kin.*'

"After he had filled me in as well as he could as to your condition, I told him he must do whatever was necessary to save your life. I also asked him how he came to assume I was your next of kin.

"'It is so stated in Mrs. Spencer's passport,' he told me.

"Now, I had twenty-four hours to think about this on the flight out here."

"You took an airplane?" she asked with surprise.

"I said not to interrupt me, please. Otherwise, I might not be able to say what I feel must be said. Yes, I traveled by air—

quite an experience I should add—and all the time the words *next of kin* kept drumming themselves into my head. Why would you write in my name? Surely your mother's would have been the proper one. Or, considering the time frame of the issuance of your passport, Spencer's name. It came to me with some pangs of pleasure that perhaps you looked upon me as a paternal figure and that your feelings for me might go deeper than I had been led to believe."

He cleared his throat and once again walked over to the window. This time he did not look out but studied her from a distance. "This supposition made me happier than I supposed it would. Once upon a long ago time, I had hoped I might be a father to you—that is—a true, acting, accepted, involved parent. I had wanted your mother to marry me. As you might well know, she refused my proposal. I have not told her that I am now discussing our intimate dealings with you and I would appreciate it if you kept this just between ourselves, as well."

Wallis was unmoved by Sol's recitation of his feelings toward her and Alice. She wondered what the purpose was of this long monologue which dredged up the past; and she was irritated that he did not realize the state of her exhaustion, how hard it was for her to concentrate on his words and how desperately she needed simply to be permitted to go to sleep. She now regretted not having taken the hypodermic the nurse had offered her.

"I am not pleased with the knowledge, but I am aware that you are a woman of the world," he relentlessly continued. "You have dealt with love and desire and, most probably, desire without love. I don't know how the child you lost could have been Spencer's, but I prefer you never tell me otherwise despite the loathing I feel for the man."

He paused and, glancing sideways, said, almost under his breath, "The sins of the fathers." For a moment he was lost in his own thoughts. "Wallis," he said, when he had turned his attention back to her, "my brother Teackle was *not* your father. I am."

She thought she might not have heard him correctly. "What did you say?" she asked.

"I am your father," he repeated.

She lay there too stunned to speak. It seemed she might be listening to a crazed man. But Uncle Sol appeared perfectly sane, if somewhat mellower than usual. The room spun. She knew if she lifted her head or tried to say anything she would become violently ill and so she remained mute and perfectly still.

"I am only telling you this because I am old now and you have been close to death. I do not want you to die without knowing the truth about yourself and the circumstances of your birth." He moved away and stood beside an ugly, green-painted chest of drawers. In the mirror above his head, Wallis could see her own reflection glancing over his shoulder and back at her. She scrutinized the two faces but could find no resemblance.

"I have always loved Alice and always will," he continued. "She was the first woman who shared my bed. I begged her to marry me and she refused. I believe she did love me but simply could not see herself as my wife. Then, she discovered that she was to have my child. She still refused to marry me. But I insisted she not allow our child to be born a bastard. Teackle was ill, dying. We took him into our confidence and he willingly agreed to marry your mother and, therefore, render you legally a Warfield. The rest you know, except that I did try through the years to change her mind so that we could be a proper family. She remained adamant in her refusal."

Neither of them spoke for a time. A pigeon perched on the sill in her room and she watched it with fascination. She wondered what floor she was on. At least the fifth or sixth because she saw rooftops beyond. *It must be wonderful to just take flight whenever you wish,* she thought as the bird lifted its wings and flew off.

Her thoughts were tangled and confused. She had just been told that what she had believed was her history was untrue. Her entire life had been undermined. She kept seeing the gaunt face in the gold locket she still kept with her. She stared at Uncle Sol. High waves of anger flooded over her. If he was her father, why had he always been so cold and critical of her? She felt unable to cope with the rush of her puzzled thoughts. More desperately than anything else at this time, she wished she was alone.

"Uncle Sol," she said, "—if I may still call you that—could you please leave now." Sol studied her quizzically. "Don't be offended, *please*. Everything is going around and around in my head—too much. I think I have to rest. I think—" Her words faded away; her eyelids lowered.

Sol thought she had drifted off to sleep. He approached the bed and leaned over her as if he meant to kiss her on the forehead. Inexplicably he straightened and hurried from the room.

A few moments later Wallis rang for the nurse to give her a sedative. When she awoke there was an expensive but discreet silk nightdress at the foot of her bed. A large bouquet of flowers was resting on her bedside table. With it was attached one of Uncle Sol's engraved cards with no written message. Miss Gomez ("Call me Lorette"), the nurse he had hired, told her Mr. Warfield had returned to Baltimore.

"You certainly are lucky to have such a nice uncle," she added.

Her hospital stay was extended an additional two weeks, and then Wallis took the train to Washington where, for the next three months, she would be with Alice.

Even with the passage of many weeks the impact of Uncle Sol's confession did not fully hit Wallis. She said nothing to Alice about his disclosure, but the secret knowledge had placed an indefinable wall between them which her mother attributed to the circumstances of her illness.

Upon waking one morning in her mother's room (Alice having taken the sitting-room couch for the duration of Wallis's stay), she silently watched her retrieving some lingerie from a bureau drawer. Even in this mundane task, Alice exuded a sympathetic composure. "How could she have lied to me about something so important as the identity of my father?" Wallis wondered. She felt betrayed, cheated. She understood why Alice had agreed to marry Teackle. She accepted the advisability of her true parentage being concealed from outsiders. But, surely, she had the right to know that Sol Warfield was her father. She would not have felt so humbled through the years when she had had to turn to him for financial assistance. They might even have had a different, warmer relationship. No matter what Alice's private reasons were for hiding the truth, they did not justify the unfairness to herself.

Alice straightened and pushed in the drawer, which squeaked badly. She held an eggshell-white silk undergarment in her hands. Her eyes, Wallis noted, were as blue and sparkly as ever. "Oh, Wallis," she said. "Did I wake you?"

"It's all right. This is your bedroom, after all," she replied, somewhat caustically.

"I never was much good at tiptoein'. Always in too much of a hurry, I s'pose." She approached the bed. "Are you okay, darlin'?"

"I'm fine."

"You seem . . ." she began.

"I'm fine, Mama," Wallis curtly repeated.

"Well, that's good." Her fingers absently caressed the slip she held.

Wallis considered the idea of telling her that she knew now that Sol was her real father, that Alice could end the secrecy and deceitfulness. She wanted to confront her and to say, "I trusted you and you lied to me." Instead she remained silent and when her mother's softly smiling face became too unnerving to look at, she closed her eyes.

"That's right, darlin', you get a little more sleep," Alice soothed, and did her best to leave the room quietly, although she remembered, just before stepping out into the hallway, that she had forgotten her stockings and had to return. The drawer creaked open and shut again before she finally disappeared into the front room.

Wallis lay listening to the even tick of the bedside clock. She tried to recall if there had ever been any indication in the past that would have given away Sol's true idenity. Images like sand drawings sifted through her mind. He had always looked at Alice with great devotion and admiration. No woman had been able to erase her from his heart. Tears filled Wallis's eyes. Was not at least a share of that devotion rightfully hers? The years were slipping away. Soon she would celebrate her thirtieth birthday. There was no time to waste if she was to seek out her own devoted lover.

It was at this moment that Wallis decided to file suit for divorce as soon as possible. She had learned from Corrine, who was now the wife of Lieutenant-Commander George Murray, that if she established residence in Warrenton, Virginia, for one year, she could obtain a divorce for only three hundred dollars.

"Dolly Fletcher jus' got hers there," Corrine said when she visited Wallis, her new marriage having brought the old glint back into her wide blue eyes. "You remember Dolly, don't you? She was married to that nice Lieutenant Fletcher in Pensacola. Well, actually, he turned out not to be so nice. The very mornin' of their ninth anniversary he left the house to buy a package of cigarettes an' nevah came back—*nevah*! Seems there was this older woman, very rich—well! that's another story.

"Mind you," she continued, "I don't like to interfere, but if you really want to get on with your life, you hafta get a divorce an' Warrenton's only a short hop an' skip from Wakefield Manor an' it has a mos' sociable atmosphere. Dolly had an apartment at the Warren Green Hotel, which was formerly a private estate—*très grande*!" She laughed. "How do you like that, Wallis? I'm speakin' French!"

Two weeks had passed since that conversation, and as Wallis stared up at the low, white ceiling in her mother's bedroom this morning and listened to Alice singing out of tune to a distant gramophone, she decided to take immediate action. By that afternoon she had focused all her strength on the steps she must take. She wrote letters to Dolly Fletcher, a local lawyer whom Corrine had mentioned and to the Warren Green Hotel.

She felt instantly reborn, redeemed. Life offered infinite hope and the sun that shimmered through her open window transformed the dowdy room into a shining place. By the next summer she could be free to set forth into a glorious new world.

PART THREE

MRS. ERNEST SIMPSON

1927–1933

18

Wallis glanced sloe-eyed over the tops of her cards at her attractive bridge partner. "Four no trump," she bid. The man, who was about her own age, smiled and she looked down to plan how she would play out her hand. She and Ernest Simpson had been bridge partners several times and she now was convinced that they were a pretty unbeatable pair.

Ernest, who was employed in the New York offices of the ship-chartering firm controlled by his British father, was a tall, well-built, dapper man with sharp blue eyes, wavy brown hair and a small, trim mustache. His mother, from whom his father had been separated for years, was American; although Ernest had been born in New York and was a graduate of Harvard, at twenty-one he had become a British subject and, during the last year of the war, joined the Coldstream Guards as a second lieutenant.

Riding to hounds with the local horsey set of Warrenton's surrounding country estates had not been to Wallis's taste. The people she met were provincial, and to alleviate her boredom she often visited New York where she stayed with Mary Kirk and her French husband, Jacques Raffray, in their charming Greenwhich Village apartment, on the ground floor of a converted mansion on Washington Square North which, in contrast to other parts of the Village, was striking for its dignity, with its row of impressive early-nineteenth-century red-brick Greek Revival homes. Wallis's room overlooked a large garden in the rear. She did not much like Jacques Raffray, who, she was certain, had married Mary for her money and to attain American citizenship. She found him a dark, Mediterranean type with sly eyes and an all-too-familiar attitude with women. Nonetheless, she had to credit him with being a good host and spending his wife's money with great panache.

With the Raffrays as escorts, Wallis came to know New York well. She liked riding in the large checkered cabs to the glittering theaters of the Great White Way, its midnight streets as brilliant as a bright morning in July; or dining at fashionable restaurants like the Twenty One Club, hidden behind the grilled fence of the old Hockstader estate, the Onyx, where black tie was mandatory, or Tony's, New York's most famous speakeasy.

Under Wallis's direction the two old school friends would shop the sales at the many small boutiques that carried designer clothes and afterward would stop at Roseland Ballroom to tango with a graceful tightly trousered gigolo. Along with her sense of style, Wallis had sharpened her appetite for adventure. Although Mary gladly followed Wallis's lead, at heart she was parochial. It was Wallis more often who could be seen dipping and bending to a tango rhythm. Determined to play the matchmaker, Mary organized bridge games, always including an available bachelor as a fourth. ("Infinitely more acceptable than meeting a man over a cocktail," she proclaimed.)

Ernest was actually not unencumbered. He was married to an American society woman and they had a daughter. Because the marriage was in difficulties, he had taken a *pied-à-terre* in the city away from his wife and child, who lived in Connecticut. Reserved in manner, yet with a gift of quiet wit, always impeccably well turned out, the only son and heir of a successful and respected businessman, Ernest was attractive to Wallis on several counts. His European demeanor most impressed her: his fluency in French and Italian, his cultivated English accent, his knowledge of art, theater, literature, wine and good food.

However strong the appeal, each of them was caught up in a personal dilemma of some complexity. Their relationship remained on the teeterboard of flirtation, but after each meeting Wallis returned to Warrenton, where her divorce was becoming more imminent, with an optimism she might not otherwise have had.

What was very much on her mind was how she was to support herself once the divorce was granted and Win's allotment check stopped coming. She no longer heard from him and was certain he was gone forever from her life. He had agreed to her lawyer's request for a future monthly support of one hundred dollars until she remarried, a figure that would not even cover her basic expenditures. To her confusion and bitter sense of new rejection, Sol had refused any help at all if she persisted in her endeavor to secure a divorce. He would assist her if she remained separated, but divorce—unlike adultery or illegitimacy—was against his moral and religious belief. Grimly she realized nothing had changed between them.

Her divorce was granted in June, although she would not receive her final decree until December; but it was Alice who remarried a few weeks later. The wedding was held at Wakefield Manor with Wallis as her mother's matron of honor.

"Here on the Fourth with my third!" Alice wrote in Cousin Lelia's visitors' book. Wallis's new stepfather, Charlie Allen, was a cheery-natured widower who worked for the Veterans Administration. He was what one might refer to as a "good sort." Alice could retire from work, but her life would not be one of many comforts.

"Why Charlie, Mama?" Wallis, perched on the veranda rail of Wakefield Manor, asked her the day before the wedding. The sound of a lawn mower buzzed nearby. Through an open window she could hear Cousin Lelia giving instructions to a maid. The breakfast bell had not yet rung and Wallis and Alice were having a one-to-one talk.

"You could say I'm on my last lap!" Alice laughed, her old gaiety undiminished.

"You can joke if you wish, but you must realize that marrying Charlie means make-do clothes and beer instead of wine. He's a nice enough man, but maybe, just *maybe*, you've set your sights too low," she warned.

"Oh?" Alice stared up at her with wide blue eyes. She was wearing a pale-pink, loose cotton peignoir and was seated in a white wicker chair. The smell of fresh-mown grass filled the air.

"If you want security—and I don't blame you a bit for that—you had other options." Alice's eyes grew wider. "Well, *one* other option anyway. Uncle Sol." Wallis said his name with slow deliberation.

She had spent many hours debating whether to confront her mother with the knowledge that she now knew her true father. When she finally decided to do so, Alice wrote that she was to remarry and Wallis abandoned her plan. Instead, she would try to convince Alice, before it was too late, to consider another idea—the possibility of becoming Mrs. S. Davies Warfield.

"Lord knows Uncle Sol has always been in love with you," she continued. "All you ever had to do was take the first step toward him. Even now I'm sure if you wrote him, if you met him privately, he would propose. Charlie can't possibly love you as much as Uncle Sol. And just think of it—you could have it *all,* Mama—an apartment on Park Avenue, a fine country home near Baltimore, travel, a name that *means* something!"

"I was a Warfield once an' so were you. Can't see how it brought either of us much good fortune," Alice said. For a moment she was lost in memory; folding her hands neatly in her lap, she glanced out to the familiar Virginia hills. "Your Uncle Sol is a man who is not capable of real love. He only knows how to possess an' that can end up a mighty unhappy thing. Yes, I could have married Sol years ago—before—or after—Mr. Rasin—God rest his soul. But I've always been the kind of woman who needed a loose hand an' who didn't feel ashamed that I enjoyed the commoner things in life." She looked Wallis straight in the eye and nodded her head as though agreeing with herself.

"I often thought you should have been Bessie's daughter, not mine. You talk the same language, put stock in the same values, an' you both have high hopes. You see I nevah would feel right in that mausoleum of Sol's on Park Avenue or playin' hostess to his grim-faced banker friends. He loves opera. I don't understan' a thing about it. I like a livelier kind of music, the kind you can dance to. I can see you would have benefited more if I had married Sol. But our life together would have been hell. I'm sure of it." She leaned back in her chair and stretched her body with cat-like grace.

"Maybe I'm a selfish woman. Or, maybe, I'm an honest woman," she smiled. "I'd rather think the latter is the case. I don't believe in reincarnation. I believe we are given only one life an' that we should enjoy it. I also don't believe we should live our lives to satisfy others. An' I guess the truth of it is—I jus' prefer beer to wine."

Wallis composed her expression beneath the shadow of a wide-brimmed straw hat as she watched her mother, who wore a flouncy pale-blue organza dress, and Charlie Allen, his full face flushed and perspiring, his beige suit limp in the heat of the summer day, exchange vows. She felt a curious mixture of regret and relief. She had always wanted more for Alice than Alice had wanted for herself. Well, she could at least say her mother was the wife of a man in government.

After the newlyweds had gone off in a shower of colored confetti for a three-day honeymoon in Atlantic City, Aunt Bessie sat Wallis down in the deserted living room where the wedding had taken place, the altar of roses wilted, petals strewing the floor.

"What will you do now?" Aunt Bessie asked.

"The same thing I would have done if Mama hadn't married."

"Which is?"

"Find a place to live and a way to support myself."

"You mean get a job in a store or an office?"

"I suppose so."

"That might be all right for some women, Wallis—not you."

"You work."

"I had no alternative."

"Mama was self-supporting."

"Alice was always a fool. You know what you need, Wallis?

You need time. You mustn't rush into anything. It could be a great mistake if you went to work as a salesclerk or some such thing. It's bad enough that you are a divorcee. People never forget it if you've been a shopgirl or a secretary. What you have to do is concentrate and develop your strong points. And believe me, Wallis, you have many. You are a Warfield. You are good-looking, possess style, humor and intelligence. You are a sophisticated woman. You would do much better, I am sure, abroad than here."

"Better at what?"

"Finding a suitable husband."

"Aunt Bessie," Wallis sighed, "I am divorced but I won't have my final decree for six months. What am I supposed to do in the meantime?"

"Accompany me on that European trip we've always talked about," Bessie grinned.

"You *really* mean it?"

"If you say *yes* we can sail to Trieste in two weeks, travel by car across Italy to Monte Carlo, on to Nice, the Provence and then up to Paris. I'm meeting Mrs. Smith there and arrangements have been made to lease a townhouse through next spring."

Wallis bounced to her feet. "Oh, Aunt Bessie!" she shouted, and then fell to her knees before her.

"I take it the answer is *yes,*" her aunt laughed.

Aunt Bessie proved to be an ideal traveling companion, amusing, incorrigibly independent and fiercely enthusiastic. Almost before their ship had been led out of New York Harbor, the women had found a willing shipboard escort, a young homosexual lawyer from Philadelphia who then accompanied them on their journey by train and car from Trieste to the south of France. He and Wallis introduced the Black Bottom to Villefranche and demonstrated the Charleston in Juan-les-Pins before he met a French beachboy who carried him off.

The two women continued on alone to Paris where, while her aunt waited for her employer to arrive, they had rooms at the elegant Hôtel Lotti. Wallis missed the carefree gaiety of her previous visit with Corrine. This time there were no attentive young men to take her to bistros or the cafés along the Boulevard Montparnasse. Aunt Bessie did manage a window table at the Tour d'Argent, where they drank champagne and watched as night gently cloaked Notre Dame just opposite.

Her aunt remained a devotee of the pictorial press, which featured photographs of leading society figures and celebrities. "Look at those jewels—diamonds and emeralds—*and* those furs!" her aunt commented one morning as she studied the weekly rotogravure. Her eyes had caught on a picture of former showgirl Peggy Hopkins Joyce who, the caption said, had taken up residence at the Ritz to select her next season's wardrobe. "Now that's what you call a success story. Once a chorus girl and now a courtesan who would have given Madame de Pompadour a real run as a royal favorite!"

"You mean she's a kept woman?"

"One thing you learn in Europe, Wallis, is the difference between a kept woman and a courtesan," her aunt advised.

"And that is?" Wallis inquired.

"The company they keep, the salons they host, their good taste, their discretion and their ability to be a wonderfully entertaining companion."

"I sometimes don't understand you, Aunt Bessie. You are scandalized by divorce, impressed by people's genealogies but admire a well-rewarded courtesan," Wallis said, shaking her head.

"One takes special talent; the other shows a lack of good judgment."

"Which does what?"

"*Really,* Wallis!" her aunt sniffed and went back to perusing the newspaper. "Look here. Freda Dudley Ward is in Paris and being seen in the company of Rodman Wanamaker—you know, the department-store heir? Our rich American boys all seem to go for foreign women. However, Mr. Wanamaker hasn't a chance with Mrs. Ward. She's the Prince of Wales's lady friend."

"How on earth do you know that?"

"Oh—from reliable sources."

"Housemaid's gossip, you mean."

"Well, this one worked for Lady Cynthia Asquith before

she married an American sailor and came to Washington to work for Mrs. Smith."

"I once saw the Prince of Wales," Wallis said wistfully.

"You did? When? You never told me about it!"

"It was one of the worst nights of my life. The Prince was on his way to Australia—I think it was in 1920. Mama was visiting. A large reception was held at the Hotel del Coronado and Win and I were to be presented to him. With his usual good timing, Win got drunk and we left early so I never did get to see the Prince up close. Still, I was rather surprised."

"At what?"

"He was such a little man."

When Mrs. Smith arrived in Paris, Bessie left the Lotti, and Wallis, who could not afford to stay there despite her aunt's assistance, moved to the more modest Left Bank hotel where she had stayed with Corrine. Of course, she could have returned home had she come to a decision where that might be. Until she did, Paris seemed as good a place as any in which to wait for her final decree.

The window of her small room looked bleakly across a dark stairwell; and the bath was three flights down, off the courtyard. Still, the man at the reception desk was always friendly, there was a charming entrance foyer with vases of fresh flowers beautifully arranged and a grand piano that no one seemed ever to play. Around the corner was Orlov's, an inexpensive Russian restaurant where she could have blinis and vodka and listen to balalaika music for a small sum when Aunt Bessie or the friends Wallis had made at the American Embassy were otherwise engaged.

Coming out of Orlov's one evening she picked up a copy of the early edition of the Paris *Herald Tribune,* the newspaper that kept Americans in Paris in touch with home. As she waited at the front desk for her key, she glanced at the front page. Her eye traveled to a narrow column on the side that contained late dispatches.

"Oh, my God!" she exclaimed.

"Par-don?" the pleasant young man at the desk inquired, noting a tone of distress in her voice.

"It's—it's—" She took her key without finishing the sentence and ran all the way up the three flights to her room, spread the newspaper out on her bed and smoothed the front page. She had to make sure she had read the item correctly. There it was.

> Baltimore—Tuesday—Financier.
> S. Davies Warfield died
> suddenly last night.

She rushed down the stairs again to call her aunt. A cable had just been delivered and the desk clerk handed it to Wallis. It was from Alice and confirmed the story in the newspaper, adding that Uncle Harry Warfield had been with Sol when he suffered the fatal heart attack. The funeral service was to be held that coming Friday. Even if she was able to sail that night there was no way Wallis could arrive in time for the interment. She decided to wait before calling Aunt Bessie and walked aimlessly through the streets of Paris, the lights of the city flickering in the deepening dusk of evening.

She wanted desperately to cry as one should, she thought, for a lost father, even one who had been lost for many years before he had been found. Memories flooded her heart *("Thank Uncle Sol for your shoes, Bessie Wallis")*. Images reeled in her head like spiraling film projected on a screen. She could see brief flashes of Sol during all the stages of her life—lecturing, condemning, cajoling; judge, jury and prosecuting attorney. She had not known what a father's role should be. Perhaps, after all, Sol Warfield had been a father to her; perhaps fathers did expect their daughters to live their lives as they ordained and were cold and unjust when their authority was crossed.

There had been little communication between them since his confession to her in Seattle. What had she done to earn his constant disapproval? She remembered "Carmen" and the gallery of women in his New York apartment. "Hypocrite!" she had shouted. Would she have said this if she had known at the time that he was her father? "I should have been told!" she cried, the tears coming as she stumbled on, not quite sure of where she was going.

The neighborhood cafés bristled with activity. A warm summer rain began to fall, and she stopped to have a coffee at a table under a yellow canopy. People ran for shelter from the rain. Umbrellas bobbed above bowed heads. Lovers strolled unconcerned. Streetlamps on the Quai d'Orsay were lit and their reflection shimmered like silver fish on the surface of the Seine. Across the river, domes and rooftops glistened. The rain stopped and she paid for her coffee and continued on. The old irregular streets of the Left Bank had given way to grander boulevards and she found herself on the doorstep of Mrs. Smith's rented townhouse.

Aunt Bessie had also received a cable from Alice.

"Did you know?" Wallis asked, still terribly distressed.

"If he was ill, you mean?"

"No—that—" She could not complete the sentence.

"I think you should return as soon as possible. I can make the arrangements. You should be there for the reading of the will."

"Why, Aunt Bessie, why?"

"Because you are a blood relative and Sol was a very rich man."

Wallis sailed home two days later, then took the train to Washington where Alice, looking wan and suddenly much older, met her at the station. "You've lost too much weight, Mama," Wallis said with concern.

"I thought you told me a woman can nevah be too thin," Alice laughed, the gaiety somehow missing from its tone.

"Or too rich," Wallis added.

Alice informed her that Sol's will had already been read to the family. The bulk of his estate, over four million dollars, had been left to found and support a home for impoverished gentlewomen. It was to be named after Grandmother Warfield. Alice was bequeathed nothing. Wallis was left a fifteen-thousand-dollar trust fund from which she was to receive only five hundred dollars a year—to cease in the event of her remarriage. Sol's harsh censure was to continue from the grave.

The taxi moved slowly through the heavy midday traffic. Neither woman spoke for a while. "Your Uncle Harry would like to talk to you," Alice said, breaking the silence.

"Uncle Harry? What on earth about?"

"I don't really know. I guess jus' 'cause he's got somethin' to say to you."

"It certainly has taken him a long time to say it. I haven't seen Uncle Harry since my wedding to Win."

"Well, I'm jus' passin' on the message as he asked me to do," Alice replied.

Wallis remained overnight with her mother and Charlie and then took another train to Baltimore to see Sol's only surviving brother, her Uncle Harry, with whom she had never been close.

Uncle Harry had been Adjutant General of Maryland during the World War and was known by most people as "the General." He and Wallis's Aunt Rebecca lived at Salona Farms, an estate in the lush Dulaney Valley just north of Baltimore and close to Uncle Emory's old place. When Wallis was a child she had twice come to Salona Farms with Cousin Henry and his parents. She had slept in the second-floor guest room, from which she could see the luminous waters of Loch Raven, off to the east, and played tag with her older cousin Mary, Uncle Harry's only child, on the broad sweeping lawn among the boxwood hedges of the large rambling white frame house. She had not been overly fond of Mary, jealous because Cousin Henry found her to be a very good companion.

Even as a youngster, Wallis had suspected that the reason Uncle Harry so seldom visited Preston Street was because he and Uncle Sol were not on the best of terms. The General had not had as notable a career as his older brother; but he had been President of the Baltimore County School Board and a successful insurance broker, and his home reflected a more than comfortable standard of living. A chauffeured car had picked her up at the railroad station and she stood now in the impressive reception hall, Warfield family portraits glaring censoriously down on her.

"Well, Wallis," her uncle said as he came out of his library, "you certainly have developed into a handsome woman."

Wallis was startled by his appearance. Although he was a large man, she realized suddenly the uncanny resemblance he bore to Uncle Sol. "How's Aunt Rebecca?" she asked.

"Oh, I'm very well, thank you, dear," her aunt said as she

came down the stairs to greet her. A petite woman, she wore her gray hair in soft waves about her small, oval face. She kissed Wallis lightly on the cheek. The scent of lemon verbena lingered as she stepped back. "It's so sad, isn't it? Sol's death. We hadn't seen him in eons. But then—when was it when we last saw you? Seems decades. Of course it can't be, you bein' as young as you are. But it shouldn't take a death in the family for kinfolk to see one another. John!" she called to a black servant hovering in a nearby doorway. "Fetch some ice' tea for Mrs. Spencer!" She took Wallis by the arm and led her into a sitting room furnished with antiques in the style of her grandmother's house. "You are still called Mrs. Spencer, aren't you?" she asked.

"Becky, don't badger the girl," her husband admonished.

"Oh, I am thoughtless, aren't I? I s'pect you might be tired an' would like to rest a bit," she said.

Wallis sat down uneasily on the edge of a settee. "No, I'd rather hear what Uncle Harry wants to talk to me about," she said frankly.

Husband and wife exchanged nervous looks.

"Well, in that case, I'll see how cook's gettin' on with the dinner." Aunt Rebecca left the room in a swish of summer voile, trailing the whiff of lemon verbena behind her.

"Wallis, I'm not sure how to even start this conversation," her uncle began.

"My mother indicated it might have something to do with Uncle Sol's will," she said.

"Indeed, indeed!" he exclaimed. He paced back and forth, hands behind him, his chin tucked in as he concentrated on what he must say. She noted that his hair was balding in the back of his head in the same way as his brother's had. John came in with the iced tea and a few minutes were occupied with the business of "sugar or lemon or perhaps both?" Finally, they were alone again.

"There's no way to do this but straight out," he said, and sitting down in a wing chair opposite, took her hand, patted it absently and then released it. "Shortly before he died, my brother Teackle wrote me a note asking if I would come to see him at a time when he thought he would be more or less alone. There was an urgency in the letter's tone and although I had recently had an angry disagreement with Sol and did not want to encounter him, I went. After all, I could not very well refuse a dying brother's request.

"It was Sunday morning and my mother and Sol were at church. Alice ushered me in. How is your mother by the way?" he digressed.

"Happy," Wallis replied, and then immediately wondered why she had not said her mother was well.

"Good, good. She has not had an easy life. Well, to continue," he said and cleared his throat. "Teackle waited until your mother was out of the room and then he made me vow that I would carry out his death wish. Of course, I agreed. Teackle was always the most sensitive member of the family. Long illnesses do that to people, I s'pect. I was uncommonly fond of him. He was my little brother, delicate—well, I said I would do what he asked.

"'If Sol dies before you, I want you to tell Bessie Wallis—,'" her uncle paused, stood up. "This isn't easy," he said.

Wallis decided she would not confess that she knew what he was about to say. She honestly believed she was not being dishonest. She just wanted to hear his story straight through without allowing him to skip anything.

"I'll try to say it as simply as I can," he continued. "Teackle grabbed my hand. 'You tell her that I am not her daddy. That Sol is her real father.' I thought these were the words of a fevered mind and I didn't want him to get upset. He was very frail. I remember even after all these years being able to see the gaunt look of death on his face. 'Sure, I'll do that,' I promised, 'but, if this is true, shouldn't Alice be the one to tell her daughter?' Oh, it was true, he insisted. He had asked Alice to vow to tell you, but she had refused his request and so he was counting on me. 'Why should the child know at all?' I asked. 'Because I'm poor and can't provide her with a legacy. Her real father can.' 'Sol?' I asked again. 'Sol,' he repeated. 'And tell Bessie Wallis, it was too late for Alice and me, but I loved her mother, too. And that I was proud to claim her as my daughter.'"

He took a large white linen handkerchief from his pocket

and mopped his brow. In the movement, she had caught a glimpse of Sol's watch chain attached to his vest. The nail clipper seemed to be missing.

"Thank you, Uncle Harry. Thank you for telling me this," she said quietly.

"I know it is a shock. But it is true, I assure you. Before Sol died I told him about Teackle's claim and my vow to him and he admitted it was true. 'Why in blazes don't you tell the girl!' I demanded. 'Because I'm rich and she is not and I would never know how she really feels about me.' Sol was a pigheaded fool at times. 'Well, you'll never know if you *don't* tell her!' I shouted at him. Seems like Sol and I never could have a civil conversation. 'You won't have to carry out Teackle's request,' he finally said. 'I've taken care of the matter.' 'You swear you've done this, Sol?' I asked him. He swore he had.

"When I heard the damn will being read, I couldn't believe my ears. Not only did he not reveal his kinship to you, he cheated you out of a sizable inheritance. I do believe he meant to change it. At least that's what I'd like to think."

Wallis got up and walked over to the window. Outside, rolling fields and pastures stretched away for a mile or so in the distance. She knew she should tell Uncle Harry that Sol had confessed the truth to her, that there had been no need for him to say it again in his will. But if she did this she might forfeit the General's help. For, from his attitude, it seemed to her that he had some plan in mind to compensate for his brother's "ill deed."

"I guessed," she lied. "I don't know how, but I guessed the truth. Maybe there was something that bound us, or maybe it was his constant involvement in my mother's and my own lives. He did not approve of my divorce," she added. "He made that very clear to me on several occasions."

"Well, I figure he owed you a lot more than what you got. It's a matter of Warfield honor. And for that reason I suggest that you allow me to hire you a lawyer who, *very privately,* I assure you, will talk to the trustees of Sol's estate and see that you will be better provided for." She had turned back into the room. The light behind her formed a muted halo. "You will let me do that for you, won't you, child?"

"Do you really feel that is what I should do?"
"Most certainly."
"Then, of course, go ahead."

Before she left Baltimore she learned that Ellie had died and left her $836, her entire lifetime savings, mostly in old one-dollar and two-dollar bills, the full amount stuffed into a large envelope with Wallis's name and her address in Warrenton. Although they had always exchanged messages on holidays, it had been years since they had last seen each other. Ellie's legacy had been forwarded from Warrenton to Alice who, in turn, had sent it on to Wallis at Salona Farms.

During the last years of her life Ellie had lived on the meager money she had received from the sale of her little house. It was ironic that a poor black woman should leave her what to Ellie must have been a fortune and her own father, who was rich, had been so miserly. Ellie's death brought back all the difficulties of her childhood, the hard times, the constant reminder of being the poor relation. Ellie had been the only truly selfless person Wallis had ever known.

Much saddened, she went to the black cemetery in Baltimore where Ellie was buried to place a wreath on her grave. Wild grass and tangled weeds marked the section where she was buried. It would have been difficult to find the marker, a stone no more than a foot high, except for the fresh earth of the recently dug grave. Ellie's real name was Eleanora. Wallis had never known that. And once she had been the wife of Alonsius Adams, 1868–1893. She had not known that either.

The plot was so narrow and the graves on either side so close that she was certain the caskets beneath the earth touched. Ellie had bought the cheapest burial she could so that Wallis would have an inheritance. Tears burned her cheeks. Ellie deserved a better resting place, a hillside, a peaceful meadow, flowers, trees. She marched the long distance back to the shambling frame cemetery office. And after an hour's negotiation, and a payment of $836 in cash, she arranged to have Ellie's remains moved to a larger and better site on a hillside overlooking the town that the black woman had loved, but which Wallis hoped she might never see again.

19

"It was at the Belgravia house of Ernest Simpson's sister, Maud Kerr-Smiley, that the Prince of Wales first met Freda Dudley Ward," Kitty said.

Kitty and Herman had moved from Peking, which had become increasingly perilous, to Lou Viei, a villa on a hill behind Cannes in the Côte d'Azur. Wallis was spending the spring of 1928 with them. She had heard nothing from the General about the matter they had discussed in Baltimore. Six months had passed, and she had about lost any hope of enlarging her share of Sol's estate. In this time, both she and Ernest had received their final decrees.

Ernest had taken up permanent residence in England and was employed in the London office of his father's firm. With Wallis on the same continent he was urging her to come to London. He was, he claimed, in love with her and wanted her to marry him.

Until this exchange with Kitty took place on Lou Viei's terrace Wallis had been assailed with doubts. Temperamentally, she feared, she and Ernest were at opposite poles and she wondered if, with an introduction from the Rogerses, she might not meet a European who was not only rich and well connected, but a man more passionate of nature—a man, perhaps, like Felipe Espil.

She knew now what she had not known when Ernest had been her bridge partner at the Raffrays. Ernest and his father did not get on well, and there was some question whether the reins of the company would eventually pass to him. Also, he had very little money of his own. His wife had been rich and his father was not known for his generosity. She had also learned that his sister held a solid position in London society and that Mr. Simpson senior's company was internationally powerful.

"Maud," Kitty continued as she adjusted her sunglasses and turned her deck chair away from the sun, "is married to the brewery heir, Peter Kerr-Smiley, who was once part of the Prince of Wales's set. The way Maud tells the story, she was giving a party for the Prince, sometime toward the end of the war, when there was an air-raid warning. Mrs. Dudley Ward and her escort—*not* her husband, of course!—happened to be crossing Belgrave Square and took shelter in the Kerr-Smileys' open doorway. They were led with the rest of the guests down to the cellar.

"A young man came up to Mrs. Dudley Ward and began an animated conversation. She had no idea who he was and joked easily with him. 'Where do you live?' he inquired. She told him and asked, 'Where do you live?' 'London,' he replied, amused, 'and sometimes Windsor.' She still didn't get it. Or maybe she was being dense on purpose. The Prince of Wales, it turned out, desperately wanted to be liked for himself.

"After the all-clear sounded, they danced in Maud's ballroom and they seem to have kept on dancing together ever since, although one hears gossip all the time. Maud says he never can seem to say 'no' to a willing partner and, God knows, there must be *hundreds* of them!"

"Why a married woman?" Wallis asked.

"Safer, I imagine. I don't think he's ever been involved with a single woman. Of course, that's perfectly all right over here. And in England to have been a mistress to one or other of the Royals is the key to social success. Ambitious husbands even *push* their wives into such liaisons. I figure Mr. Dudley Ward considers it quite an honor to be cuckolded by the Prince of Wales, his future king."

"Sounds perverted to me."

"Well, Wallis honey, if you plan to stay around Europe you should take a crash course in European sexual behavior." She squinted over the tops of her dark lenses. "You better get out of the sun, Wallis. You're turning lobster red."

Ernest had said very little about his older sister, Maud. Now, Wallis plied him by mail for information. (Maud still had the house on Belgrave Square and she would be pleased to meet Wallis. Yes, she knew certain members of the Royal Family, a Lascelles cousin, one or two of the Mountbatten clan, but her husband was ill and a recluse and she no longer gave large parties.)

Toward the end of May, Wallis took the train to Le Havre and a boat to England. Ernest had rented a small London flat for her. It was, he laughed, tiny; but the Prince of Wales, who lived nearby at St. James's Palace, was almost her neighbor.

Maud, a small attractive gray-haired woman with hazel eyes, introduced Wallis to quite a few titled friends. Not wanting to make a faux pas, Wallis bought a book that explained who had precedence over whom. Throughout the early summer Ernest never gave up asking her to marry him. Wallis did not say "yes." On the other hand, she did not say "no" either.

Her hopes were growing ever slimmer that she would hear from Sol's executors that she was to be a rich heiress. Finally Uncle Harry wrote that nothing could be settled until the will had gone through probate at the end of the year. "I am sorry to say I have met with much resistance," he wrote, "but, my dear, they don't call me the General for no reason. Please understand I will wage a hard-fought battle on your behalf."

She wanted to believe in Uncle Harry, but she knew that Sol's righteous banker friends who were the executors of his estate would not easily be moved by sentiment. Soft hearts like soft mattresses led to weak backbones. They would think her mother was a scandal and to acknowledge Wallis would be to disgrace the good name of Warfield.

After reflecting on the degrading years as Win's wife, the rootless years on her own and with the specter of a future that might parallel her mother's life of hard work and few rewards, she found the security and respect she would receive as Mrs. Ernest Simpson more appealing. And it was not as though she did not find Ernest attractive or even endearing, just that she wished he was richer and more exciting.

They were returning in a taxi from the Savoy Grill where they had dined with a Greek shipping executive and his mistress when Ernest, once again, proposed. He had from the start regarded her with the highest respect and had not even attempted to lure her to bed. His attitude had always been—this is the woman I want to marry.

"Yes, Ernest," she said coolly, as though he might simply have asked if she was comfortable.

He was so surprised that for a moment he sat silent in the darkness of the cab's interior, too shocked to speak. Then he took her gently in his arms and cried as he held her close to him. "Wallis, you won't be sorry," he repeated over and over. "You won't be sorry."

> *Dearest Mother [she wrote Alice the next morning], I've decided definitely that the best and wisest thing for me to do is to marry Ernest. I am very fond of him and he is* kind *which will be a contrast. We will be married this coming Saturday. It is simple here, we just go to a Registry Office and the deed is done in fifteen minutes.*
>
> *Mummy, I shall miss having you with me terribly but the second time doesn't really seem so important. I can't go wandering on the rest of my life and I really feel so tired of fighting the world all alone and with no money. Also 32 doesn't seem so young when you see all the really fresh youthful faces one has to compete against. I hope this hasn't upset you darling—but I should think you would feel happier knowing somebody was looking after me—*
>
> *All my love to you—and do please give your wishes for success this time.*
>
> *Wallis*
>
> *P.S. I sent Uncle Harry a cable and have written a note.*

Wallis, however, was not resigned to a future as merely a

supportive wife. She recalled the success she and Ernest had as bridge partners. They were a winning team as long as he let her play out the hand. And he had been dealt some formidable trump cards: his father's connections with men like Onassis and Niarchos in Greece and the Cunard family in England; Maud's contacts; and his own educational background. She would have to get his father to loosen up the purse strings, but she felt she was clever enough to do so.

They were married on a perfect, sunny July morning, attended by Maud, whose otherwise conservative outfit was topped by a large cartwheel hat that overwhelmed her small, compact body; Maud's twenty-two-year-old son, Peter, who would obviously have rather been elsewhere; and Mr. Simpson senior, his white goatee freshly trimmed, his squat figure cloaked in a gray frock coat that, Wallis thought, made him look like a parading penguin. The bride wore a bright yellow dress and a cerulean-blue coat. "You are the sun and the sky," Ernest said when he met her on the steps of the Chelsea Registry of Marriages. The ceremony was performed in a cluttered office by a harried official standing beside a battered desk. Wallis clutched a small bouquet of heliotrope and white freesia, and the flowers' strong scent, mixed with the mustiness of old leather-bound books, almost overcame her.

The service was brisk, a rattle of words.

"Do you agree to this marriage willingly and freely of your own accord?"

"Yes, I do," said Ernest, looking dapper in his pinstripe suit, a white carnation in the buttonhole.

"And you?" the registrar asked Wallis in a bored tone.

"Yes."

"This marriage is therefore legal and binding."

The newlyweds kissed tentatively and then fled from the room, down the grimy corridors of the gloomy old Victorian building and out into the glowing warmth of the July sunshine. There was a wedding breakfast with vintage champagne at Mr. Simpson senior's austere West End flat. Then Ernest and Wallis, in a recently purchased Vauxhall saloon car driven by their newly employed chauffeur, Hughes, very smart in gray and black livery, left for the Channel ferry and a honeymoon in Paris. They stayed at the Hotel St. Regis on the Rue Jean Goujon, just off the Avenue Montaigne with its luxurious shops and couturiers.

Ernest did not buy Wallis any jewelry from nearby Cartier's, but he knew Paris well, spoke French fluently and with a good accent, and was knowledgeable about French history and art.

He listened attentively to what she had to say and, more than any other man she had known, made her feel intelligent and valuable. Unfortunately, he was at his best out of bed, unable for three nights to achieve an erection. On the fourth, Wallis became the aggressor, slipping out of her clothes first, speaking to him provocatively as she stood nude before him, and then moving his hands over her body. She undid his suspenders, the buttons on the fly of his trousers. "Let me see how hard you are, Ernest," she said in a low, breathy voice, her hand moving downward. "My God, how firm!" she said and took his hand and led him to the bed.

He tried to please her, but they had not made love before and his anxiety and the excitement she had provoked in him caused him to rush things. He came before she did and then was consumed with guilt. Almost as an offering, he placed his hand between her legs. "It's all right, Ernest," she said in a soft voice. She kissed his brow and turned away.

The next morning she told him how wonderful he had been, how she loved him more than she thought. She was not lying. She had felt a gentle caring for him. Their love life might not ever be thrilling, but she was unthreatened by it. Ernest would never force himself upon her.

Shortly after returning to London they moved into a furnished house on Upper Berkeley Street near Portman Square where some of London's great homes were located. Although her new house was considerably smaller than its neighbors and lacked a personal touch, after her years of living in hotel rooms, it felt like a palace; and in addition to Hughes, she was able to engage a butler, a cook and a housemaid.

"You'll find that it will make quite a difference in the attitude of a new staff member if you carefully drop a few titles into your initial interviews," Maud advised her.

In order to "drop" a title, Wallis had to have one ready at hand. To begin with she borrowed a few names from Maud's guest lists. But her sister-in-law's circle consisted mostly of older aristocrats, no longer in the mainstream of London's social whirl. Perhaps even more distressing was the icy feeling that came over Wallis when she was in the company of Maud's friends, who, she felt, looked upon her as an ethnological curiosity.

Most Mayfair drawing rooms were kept as safe as was possible from the slang and characteristic impulsiveness of England's former subjects from the colonies. Wallis knew she would have to cultivate her own, younger contacts, those people who were, perhaps, on the fringes of the Prince of Wales's set.

She formed the daily habit of studying the Court Circular, which recorded the engagements and appearances of each member of the Royal Family with extensive lists of those in attendance. Ernest enthusiastically joined her in her voracious appetite for gossip about the Royals and was as much under their spell as most of the English seemed to be. Queen Mary's name was spoken in a hushed tone, the King's with manly respect, and there would be an indulgent smile for the Prince of Wales, whom Ernest admiringly referred to as "a gay blade."

Ernest was extremely meticulous, a frugal man, but he understood Wallis's need to make a place for herself in English society for he had fought a lifetime to be accepted by his father's countrymen. Wallis started giving a small fortnightly dinner party, carefully budgeted but always luxurious, with some dish on the menu to arouse an exclamation of delighted surprise. Remembering Alice's attention to detail back in the days of her catering career, Wallis did all her own shopping, starting on her rounds at ten in the morning the day before a party and sometimes not finishing until four in the afternoon.

She had fixed ideas about food. Whenever she was serving fish or fowl, each item had to be exactly the same size so that no guest would have a smaller portion than another. Beef was seldom on her menu unless it was the tenderest of fillets or ground as steak tartare, for women did not look attractive in the act of chewing. Soup was never included. "Too much liquid after cocktails," she proclaimed. She liked to combine two extravagant items: smoked salmon and caviar, avocado and prawns, pheasant and brandied peaches; and to include one—but *only* one—American dish that her dinner guests were unlikely ever to have encountered. Maryland crabcakes made their appearance as a first course, chicken—fried or in a deep-dish pot pie—as a main course, and apple pie à la mode or angel-food cake and fudge sauce for dessert.

The recipes were sent to her by Alice, and she supervised every step of their preparation by the cook. Her spectacular floral arrangements took hours. Her Chinese treasures had been shipped: a brilliant Peking carpet covered the house owner's threadbare dining-room rug; her collection of jade and ivory elephants was displayed in a glass-fronted vitrine. From her many bolts of brocaded Oriental fabrics a dressmaker had fashioned several slim-lined mandarin jackets with skirts that slit decorously at the ankle.

Their first guests were mainly shipping executives from Scandinavia or Greece to whom Wallis would add an English couple who invariably could be relied upon to discuss the evening with friends. The Simpsons soon received frequent and prestigious invitations. Wallis now knew the who's who of London's social world and could recognize a name at first meeting. A short time later, that person would receive an invitation from the Simpsons.

"I don't give a hoot if Maud thinks I'm a social climber!" she told Ernest when he discussed his sister's attitude toward her. Wallis knew full well that her own social success was more important to her than any help she might give Ernest in his career. Until she became a woman of consequence, she would never be able to exorcise the humiliation she had suffered in Baltimore in the home of Mrs. Kirk and her rejection by Felipe Espil. Her natural powers of good reasoning told her dwelling so much on the past was foolish, but she could not do otherwise.

"Well, that's how I am," she told herself. "It's a matter of pride, the conflict of the Warfield and Montague blood in my veins." And when Ernest asked her why she spent so much time in the preparation of her parties—he always thought of them as *hers,* not his—she had replied, "Because I want to show the world I have no equal." To Wallis, "the world" was now circumscribed by the names she saw printed daily in the Court Circular.

One overcast day, Hughes was driving her past St. James's Palace when she noticed the scarlet-coated sentries at the entrance had suddenly stiffened to present arms. A chauffeur-driven black Daimler emerged and within a few moments drew into the next lane to her car. Hughes slowed to allow the crested vehicle to pass. Wallis caught a fleeting glimpse through the side window of a delicate boyish face staring straight ahead.

"That was the Prince of Wales," Hughes said, in awed tones.

She did not reveal that she had seen him once before, but something in her heart lurched. "One day," she mused, "I won't see him from afar. He will be a guest in my home." She laughed at herself for having such a grandiose idea.

"What was that, madam?" Hughes inquired.

"Nothing, Hughes, nothing. Just a private joke."

"So sorry, madam."

"It's okay," she said, immediately realizing that she had once again slipped and used an American slang expression that her sister-in-law and her friends would consider as crude as if she had dropped an "h."

To her amazement, with Christmas came the remarkable news that she was to receive $37,500 from Sol Warfield's estate. She signed a paper stating that the payment would acquit the estate of any further claim. The dollar was exceptionally high in London at the time and could purchase many times its value. Wallis felt rich and it gave her such a marvelous glow that Maud came by especially to ask if she might not be pregnant. The possibility of her having a child had never even come up between Ernest and herself. Ernest did not know she could not conceive, but since he had a daughter, she had not thought it mattered.

That evening Ernest asked what Maud had come to talk about.

"She thought I was pregnant," she replied.

His face turned deep red. "Are you?"

"No, of course not. I can't have a child."

A puzzled look clouded his eyes. "What do you mean?"

"I was very ill once and they had to operate. Something about my kidney. Anyway, afterward I was told I could no longer become pregnant."

The color faded from his face. He smiled, came across the room and kissed her. "I'm not unhappy about it, if you thought I might be," he said. "Children change things."

"Yes, I know."

That night, for the first time, Ernest played the role of aggressor. The next day they went looking for a large mansion flat rather than a house, so that the building staff could augment their own.

It did not take them long to find the right place, a charming apartment at 5, Bryanston Court on George Street only a few blocks from Upper Berkeley Street. It had a commodious, high-ceilinged drawing room, an attractive dining room large enough to seat ten comfortably, a modern kitchen, three bedrooms, two bathrooms, a cloakroom, and—in another part of the building—four staff bedrooms. For the first time in her life Wallis had the means and the opportunity to create the setting for herself that she had always wanted and she plunged into its decoration with enormous energy and excitement.

Then she received the crushing news from Aunt Bessie that her mother had suffered a thrombosis and was seriously ill. Ernest was needed at the office and so Wallis took the first boat out alone. Mary Kirk met her at the pier. From her expression and even the choice of the drab colors she wore, Wallis guessed the news was not good.

"Oh, Wallis," she said, and removed her glasses to wipe her eyes with a handkerchief. "It's terrible, terrible. I've just heard from your Aunt Bessie. Your mother is in a coma."

They drove directly to Pennsylvania Station where Wallis boarded an express train for Washington.

* * *

The bedroom was well heated and papered in a small cornflower design, the color of her mother's now closed eyes. The smell of disinfectant, eau-de-cologne and waste body matter assailed Wallis. Aunt Bessie stood on one side of the bed. Charlie was in the kitchen drinking beer. Wallis came close to the bed. "Mama," she whispered very softly. "Mama, it's me, Wallis." She lifted Alice's limp white hand, which rested outside the covers, and held it firmly in her own.

"There's something I must tell you, Mama—something . . ." She thought she discerned a tremor of movement and she leaned in closer and began to talk rather wildly. "No, Mama, I want you to tell me about all the deep things you've ever thought about in your life. I want to know everything there is to know. Mama, I love you so. I've always loved you so much. And I wanted you to be so proud of me. Oh, please, Mama, don't die now. Please."

"Stop it, Wallis," Aunt Bessie said gently.

"I can't. I want her to know I am here."

"She knew you were coming."

"Did she?"

"She tried to hold on to consciousness. She was just too weak. She always avoided going to the doctor. When she finally did, the blood clot had traveled too far."

Wallis took Alice's frail hand, tucked it under the bedclothes and then stroked her forehead.

"We thought she was doing fine. Then it started to travel again," her aunt continued. "I think she called your name but it was so faint, a whisper really. I told her you were coming, to hang on, and she has."

Wallis was by her side when she died the next day. She refused to let them draw the curtains. She remembered how fearful she had been as a child waiting in the dark for her mother to return. Her mother had brought gaiety into her world. She could not at this moment imagine life without her. For all the years of separation there had been something that had bound them closer than the normal bond of mother and daughter. Alice had understood her as no one else ever could or would.

Not until she stood by her mother's grave a few days later did her anger and frustration surface. She had never had a chance to confront her mother about Sol, to tell her that she, Wallis, felt cheated, that Alice had played with her life unfairly, that if she had conformed just a little bit more, if— Then, suddenly, she was thoroughly ashamed of herself and she began to cry uncontrollably, "Mama, mama, I'm so sorry."

"You have nothin' to be sorry about," Aunt Bessie soothed, "nothin' at all, darlin'." For a moment Wallis was almost certain it was Alice who had spoken.

20

Wallis returned from Washington in a mood of quiet despair. Figures in her past moved slowly and untouchably through her dreams and she would wake up in the middle of the night feeling like a frightened child.

Within one year she had lost three of the most meaningful people in her life; and their deaths, rather than freeing her, plagued her with unanswerable questions. She now felt she might never have known any of them, that who they really were had eluded her as did the phantasmagoria in her dreams. To add to her depression, home had always been wherever Alice lived. Now she had no place to which she could return.

Nothing was going well at the new flat. London was gray and cold. There were few parties to attend while her friends nervously awaited an indication of what effect the recent panic in the New York Stock Exchange would have on their own economic futures. Evenings, Ernest returned home exhausted, tense and concerned about their own finances and the stability of his father's company. Her inheritance was by now almost totally depleted on the expenditures on the new apartment. Wallis was fighting an ineffectual battle to keep up her spirits when, to her delighted amazement, Corrine appeared, her husband, Lieutenant-Commander George Murray, having been assigned as Assistant Naval Attaché at the American Embassy.

Suddenly, through Corrine, Wallis and Ernest were swept into the lively doings of London's American colony led by Ambassador Charles Dawes and his wife. Among its members were the U.S. Air Attaché, Mike Scanlon, an attractive bachelor, and the First Secretary, Benny Thaw, who, since his Coronado days, had married the former Consuelo Morgan. Also in the group were Consuelo's twin sisters, Thelma, wife of Viscount Furness, known as "Duke," and Gloria, widow of Reggie Vanderbilt. The twins were spectacular beauties who had captivated London. Both women had enormous brown eyes, dark hair, camellia-like skin, slim figures that suited all the finest of Paris fashion; and they shared an American gaiety that Englishmen found refreshing.

With the prospect that she and Ernest might become an integral part of this new social group, Wallis threw herself, with renewed enthusiasm and with Corrine's help, into the business of readying the apartment. She soon realized that if she wanted to compete with the Morgan sisters she would need a more professional eye to decoration than either she or Corrine possessed. She turned for help to Syrie Maugham, author Somerset Maugham's divorced wife, who had startled everyone ("Imagine Syrie in *trade,* dear!") by opening an interior-decoration shop on the King's Road.

Syrie was American, an enchanting eccentric who, like the minister at the Brexton Hotel when Wallis was a child, dressed in white from tip to toe. Syrie's establishment was filled with an astonishing assortment of old bits and pieces: French Provençal armoires, Biedermeier sofas and nineteenth-century chests that had been pickled and tarted up, and furniture of undetermined age painted with flowers, scenes or trompe l'oeil. Syrie might personally have preferred white, but her shop glowed with color.

Wallis took immediately to Syrie. She was lively, she was elegant, she was witty—and you never knew whom you would chance to meet in her establishment. Smart London was entranced with her American ingenuity. Trompe l'oeil and painted furniture had found their way into the drawing rooms of Noël Coward, Gertrude Lawrence and Cecil Beaton, as well as into homes of the Thaws and the Furnesses, and—one heard—the bedroom of the Prince of Wales. Syrie sold Wallis a dining table of uncertain origin that was a blue-green color and a dozen matching chairs with tall backs, upholstered in white leather and studded with hammered nailheads, extremely *avant garde* by the standards of London's mahogany and plush-velvet dining rooms. Still, when Syrie saw Wallis's dining room complete for the first time, she was not satisfied.

"All the light fixtures must go," she ordered with a sweeping gesture that made her look like a great white-winged swan. "Candlelight will soften the effect—and, anyway, my dear, at thirty-*odd,* a woman looks considerably better in *blurred* light." The electrified chandeliers were soon transformed to hold thirty-six candles.

In Wallis's bedroom, the desk and armoire (which *might* have been French Provençal) were painted off-white with tracings of aquamarine and pink to match the rest of the room's decor. Ernest had his own bright tartan bedroom, to which he strongly objected.

"Not to the tartan! *Surely* not to the tartan!" Syrie cried with dismay, her strident voice lingering in the upper register.

"To separate bedrooms," Wallis explained.

"Well, my dear, it is not as though he has to climb over a wall! And it is really gauche to share a room as though you were traveling players. No, no! It won't do. I'm sure Ernest would feel most uncomfortable in pink and aquamarine, and somehow, I cannot feature you in tartan!"

To placate Ernest, a wall of bookshelves was built in the drawing room to accommodate his vast collection of books. Two large sofas and several man-sized chairs were added for a solid, masculine look, although the colors were kept light and airy—beige, off-white and a willowy green.

Wallis was entirely satisfied with the effect Syrie had created. The overall impression of her new home was one of cheerful informality and ease that were novel to social London. She added an American social invention, the casual cocktail hour. From six to seven P.M. people could drop by for a drink and Wallis's unique cocktail canapés—deviled crab, bacon wrapped around Chinese chestnuts—before they went off to the theater or a dinner party. She had practically memorized the entire *Savoy Cocktail Book* and, using a low coffee table and several small shakers, mixed and served the drinks herself. She could estimate the correct proportions as accurately as the barman at the Savoy; and once she had poured, the glass was brimful and the shaker empty. She served American fashion, over ice and in largish glasses. The generous cocktails did wonders for the liveliness of the hour, and soon the flat became a gathering place for Americans and English to intermingle at the end of the day. Friends would ring up and ask if they could bring a guest.

Cocktails at the Simpsons' became an "in" thing, like shopping at Syrie's, or being on the guest lists of Elsa Maxwell's large parties. (An unpublished song of Cole Porter's, written that season, was making the rounds of Wallis's circle. *"I'm dining with Elsa, with Elsa, supreme—I'm going to meet princesses—wearing Chanel dresses—Going wild over strawberries and cream—I've got Bromo Seltzer—To take when dinner ends—For I'm dining with Elsa—And her ninety-nine most intimate friends—"*)

One gloomy day in November 1930, Consuelo Morgan Thaw (who was known to her friends as Tamar, short for her middle name, Tamara) rang up Wallis in some agitation to ask for her help.

"Look, Wallis," she confided, "this is a very awkward situation. You know of course that Thelma has been seeing the Prince of Wales? Well, who doesn't! Even my aristocratic but foul-mouthed brother-in-law, Duke Furness himself, knows. *Droit du seigneur*. Nonetheless, these things have to be handled with a certain finesse."

Wallis could not imagine how she could help in anything involving Thelma and her Royal romance but she waited eagerly while Tamar, as usual, went on and on in her distinctive nasal voice. Wallis could visualize her caller's narrow crimson mouth stretched in a smirk, the pointed chin bobbing in exclamation. Tamar did not have her sisters' beauty; but a certain exotic quality to her looks, almost Eurasian, made her even more distinctive. Corrine called her "Madam Chan" or, on occasion, because of Tamar's long, lacquer-red fingernails, "Lady-drippin'-blood."

"This weekend there is to be a small hunting party at Duke's country estate, Burrough Court. Duke is remaining in London, as he always does when the Prince and Thelma have a weekend in the country planned. Benny and I usually play chaperon; the presence of a married couple in such a delicate situation is absolutely *de rigueur*. But Benny and I have just found out we have to be in Paris. *Sooooo,* dear, Thelma and I were hoping you and Ernest might take our place."

Wallis was stunned. "Tamar, I wouldn't know what to say to the Prince of Wales or what to do as a chaperone."

"Don't be silly, dear. You don't have to *do* anything but be present. And as for what to say, just remember that Royalty must lead the conversation and that politics and controversial matters should not be discussed."

"How will I know what might be considered controversial?"

"I wouldn't worry about that. The Prince is never stuffy. May I tell Thelma that you will do it?"

"I just can't, Tamar," Wallis insisted rather weakly, even while she was aware of her vow that she would one day meet the Prince of Wales. Now, faced with the opportunity, she felt terrified at the prospect, although she could not understand why.

"You won't be alone," Tamar explained. "There will be other guests. But you will officially be the chaperons. And the Prince of Wales's youngest brother, Prince George, will also be there."

"Tamar," she begged, "how can I manage two curtsies?"

"One at a time," she laughed. "Now be a dear and call Ernest and tell him I want you to do it as a favor to me."

To her surprise, Ernest was not only delighted with the idea, he insisted they accept. "Of course we'll go," he said firmly. "It's really a great honor."

Wallis practiced a curtsy for days with Ernest's enthusiastic coaching. "The trick," he explained, "is to put your left leg well back and behind your right one."

They arrived by train at Melton Mowbray on a Friday at about five o'clock in the afternoon. Wallis, having spent the entire morning deciding upon the proper ensemble, had worn a blue-gray tweed dress with a cape of the same material edged with nutria. When she stepped off the train, she shivered with the cold. The outfit was not nearly warm enough, and she hurried to the waiting limousine that met them. The drive to Burrough Court was a matter of only a few miles. She hardly spoke to Ernest. Her eyes were fastened on the passing countryside as she waited for Burrough Court to loom into view. When it did, she was struck by the magnificence of the grounds and the dignity of its sprawling ivy-covered brick façade.

Thelma and the Royal guests had not yet arrived. Tea was laid on a large round table in the drawing room before a roaring fire. Wallis and Ernest were the lone guests in the vast high-beamed room. "Oh, Lord, I'm sorry we came," she murmured to Ernest under her breath, hoping one of the servants did not overhear her. "I've got a cold. I just know it. My throat is sore and I can hardly breathe."

"Drink your tea," Ernest suggested. "You're just nervous."

They sat and had their tea and made small conversation. Ernest glanced down at his watch. It was seven o'clock. Then, suddenly, there was a rush of activity in another part of the house, a sound of gay voices in the hallway; and Thelma, looking spectacular in a scarlet riding jacket and a matching skirt slit to the knee (*Just like the girls in the singsong house,* Wallis thought) entered, a prince in very loud-checked tweeds on each arm. Trailing behind them was a tall, rakish-looking man with one arm, who, it turned out, was Brigadier-General "G" Trotter, Groom-in-Waiting to the Prince of Wales.

The Heir to the Throne was not much taller than Wallis remembered, only an inch or so more than she—five feet six at the most. His golden-blond hair was slightly wind-rumpled, his skin was hairless—as though he had not yet been through puberty. His nose was turned up, rather like the illustrations for *Tom Sawyer.* What struck her most were his eyes which, when they finally turned to her, held a strange, wistful, almost sad look. The youngest of the four Royal brothers, George,

Duke of Kent, was considerably taller, with neatly brushed brown hair, aquiline features and insinuating dark-blue eyes. Although he gave the impression of gaiety and *joie de vivre,* she had heard that he was a heavy drinker and took drugs. At this moment she found it hard to believe.

"Sir," Thelma said, and led the Prince of Wales forward into the room. "This is Mr. and Mrs. Ernest Simpson."

Left leg well back and behind your right one. "Sir," Wallis managed, her voice weak, her heart pounding, as from one corner of her eye she saw Ernest flush madly as he bowed.

"I understand you are from the southern part of America," the Prince of Wales said.

"Baltimore, Maryland."

"Home of Mr. Henry L. Mencken and burial place of Edgar Allan Poe, I believe."

"Why, yes, that's right!" Wallis said with some surprise.

"I hope that didn't sound like an epithet," he laughed easily, and turned to Ernest. "Lady Furness tells me you attended Harvard. I always thought I might enjoy one of your extraordinary college football games—Harvard and Yale, is it, who are such fierce competitors?"

"Yes, Sir. But, of course, I am British. 'Fraid cricket's more my style."

Thelma stepped forward with the younger Prince. Wallis did her curtsy for the second time. A fresh tea tray was brought in; and after tea and some small talk, the Prince of Wales excused himself and Thelma disappeared into the hallway with him and his brother. Wallis and Ernest talked generalities with Trotter. A butler appeared a few minutes later and led them to a suite of rooms that had been prepared for them. There was a fire burning and the heat was on as well (Burrough Court was one of the few country houses with central heating; Thelma's American influence in evidence), and Wallis felt as though she had a fever. They would be expected in the tack room for drinks before dinner at nine, the butler informed them as he departed. Their clothes had been unpacked and pressed, their toiletries placed in the bathroom. Their penchant for single-malt whiskey had been noted, and a decanter and glasses were set out. Wallis, instead, took two aspirins and had a long soak in the tub, her cold still nagging at her; her sense of pleasure rising in anticipation of the evening.

She had expected a number of neighboring estate owners to join them in the evening's festivities. A young male friend of Prince George's was the only addition. Wallis felt considerably overdressed in her high-necked, long-sleeved gold-silk jersey gown, for Thelma's shimmering blue-satin bare-shouldered dress was as brief as a slip. She appeared to be wearing no undergarments and her painted toenails protruded from her high-heeled gold mules. On the thin spaghetti straps of the dress was a pair of magnificent diamond clips. She would absentmindedly touch them and then smile at the Prince of Wales, who looked quite handsome but who was dressed, surprisingly, in a paisley smoking jacket. He seemed somewhat nervous and fussed noticeably with his tie.

Wallis was conscious of an uncontrollable fluttering of her pulse, a vague sense of anticipation. She attributed her heightened excitement to the fever she was certain she had. Being American, she was not prepared for the feeling of awe she experienced in the presence of the two princes. She did not know what she had expected, but to find that Royalty lights a cigarette in much the same way as other people do and employs much the same gestures and mannerisms was to her an astonishing revelation.

With only two women present, Thelma sat Wallis and herself at the two ends of the table. The Prince of Wales was on Thelma's right, Prince George on her left, while Wallis had "G" Trotter and Prince George's untitled friend Ned on either side of her. Ernest sat between Prince George and Trotter. Positioned as she was, Wallis did not have much opportunity for a personal exchange with the Prince of Wales, who held forth amusingly. Then he rose and excused himself. His brother and his friend departed as they were staying elsewhere. The Prince of Wales was down the corridor from Wallis and Ernest. Thelma occupied the master suite that led off the top of a handsome curved stairway.

"I don't understand how Duke can agree to such an arrangement," Wallis said when they were undressing.

"You're too American in your ideas," Ernest replied as he got into the large swagged and canopied bed. "In England husbands and wives often go out on their own. And there's nothing wrong in one's wife having a royal liaison. In fact it's rather an honor, I'd say."

"I wouldn't. I'd call it adultery." She could see him in the mirror of the dressing table. He was propped up against the quilted headboard, his blue eyes staring at her back.

"Yes, I suppose it is. But that is the closest most men will ever come to royalty," he said.

At Ernest's instigation (a rare occasion), they made love almost as soon as she turned out the lights and joined him in bed. He asked her to create an aura of fantasy in their lovemaking. "Call me Sir," he requested.

"Yes, sir," she obliged.

"No, with a capital *S*, with *reverence*."

She followed his lead and then took it, knowing instinctively the game he wanted to play. He was the Prince and she was Thelma. He fell asleep almost immediately after his orgasm. Wallis lay in the dark, hearing every creak in the old manor house. She thought she detected footsteps in the outside corridor. Then she was certain she was right. They went stealthily past the door of her bedroom and up the hallway. It could only have been the Prince of Wales because Trotter was in another wing. She expected to hear someone descending the stairs, but the footsteps stopped. There was a knock on a distant door, a creak as it opened, a click as it shut. The Prince of Wales had gone into Thelma's bedroom.

Wallis wondered why on earth he had not been given a connecting room if this was the plan. *Propriety has to be preserved,* she told herself. *What would the servants think!* She mulled over the hypocrisy of it all for a time, feeling extremely irritated. Then her thoughts traveled into the room Thelma and her royal lover now occupied together. Thelma would be nude. She had not had much to remove anyway! And the Prince—Wallis unsuccessfully tried to switch her thoughts elsewhere. She felt feverish again. Then she became chilled. Her throat was sore. Her cold was getting worse. Perhaps she needed some tea and honey, but how did one get such a thing in a country house at this late hour?

"Ernest," she called, and shook him lightly on the shoulder.

He grumbled under his breath and moved away, still asleep.

Her mind went back again into Thelma's bedroom and filled with sensual images: Thelma's supple, white flesh, the Prince's golden hair, the slightly petulant mouth, the sad eyes suddenly keen. *Sir! Sir!*

Ernest grumbled again and Wallis turned on her side away from him. To her overwhelming surprise she had experienced alone the satisfaction their earlier lovemaking had not achieved. And as she drifted off to sleep, she thought, *Well, it can't be adultery if the sex is imagined.*

21

An almost uncontrollable sensation of being in the hands of something stronger than herself had seized Wallis. Since her meeting with the Prince of Wales she moved in a suspended state, as if by autosuggestion. While her conscious mind directed her day's activities, another part of her was dominated by a thought that she normally would have considered preposterous; the Prince of Wales would tire of Thelma and she would become his mistress.

The events of the weekend revolved over and over in her mind as she struggled to find any one incident to give credence to such a wild possibility. On the second day at Burrough Court she had not seen the Prince of Wales until everyone met for cocktails. Breakfast had been served to her in bed, and when she came downstairs, nursing a full-blown cold, the men, including a deliriously happy Ernest, had gone hunting at a neighboring estate. There were no additional guests that evening and conversation had centered around the day's shoot. Thelma wore the diamond clips again, this time with a more decorous but equally flattering filmy creation of black chiffon, while Wallis was dressed in a simple soft green gown and her Chinese jade jewelry. She had brought classic, underplayed outfits at Syrie's suggestion. She was conscious of the striking contrast she made to Thelma and was not sure she had brought the right outfit.

By the time dinner was served, she had almost lost her voice and managed only the briefest of gravelly comments. Later that night, Ernest was content enough with memories of the day's heady Royal shoot to dismiss the idea of sex with a sniffling wife. The Prince's late-night perambulations down the hallway were repeated. The same knock on Thelma's door, the creak when it opened, the click when it closed and—*yes*—a repetition of her own sexually gratifying fantasy.

Sunday had brought guests from all over the county, sixteen for lunch and ten for cocktails and dinner. Thelma seated the Prince and herself at the two ends of the long dining table and Ernest and Wallis were lost in the lower ranges of the spectrum of precedence. After coffee the guests were divided into two groups—one to play poker with the Prince. Wallis joined three others as a fourth for bridge, but her eyes kept straying to the Prince's table. Ernest was losing more than they could afford. The Prince played spiritedly, groaning with disappointment if he lost a hand and exclaiming with delight when he won. At midnight he rose from the game and made his way through the room to say good night.

"I see you are feeling better," he said to Wallis; and noting the pound notes that had just been paid her, added, "Winning helps." Then he was gone.

That night there was silence in the upstairs corridor.

At luncheon the next day she was seated beside him for the first time. Tamar's enjoinders conveyed to her over the telephone about what one said and did not say to royalty in conversation censored all of Wallis's lighter impulses and she sat through two courses fairly speechless.

"I hope you are not now suffering from laryngitis, Mrs. Simpson," the Prince finally said.

"Oh, no, Sir. But listening can be so much more informative than talking, don't you think?"

"It depends on the subject and the speaker, I would say. What have you learned today at this table?"

"That in addition to the Quorn and Cottesmore Hunts, Melton Mowbray also has the Belvoir which, I did not realize, has a silent *l* and so I've been saying *Belver* instead of *Beaver* all weekend."

He laughed. For a moment his face was illuminated. Then the look of sadness in his expression quickly returned.

During dessert he inquired as to if she ever had been to Hollywood. "I am most fond of the movies," he admitted.

"No, although it's odd, because I lived in California once."

"And where was that?"

"Coronado."

"Ah, yes. Lovely port. I've been there years ago."

"I know. I attended a reception in your honor. Although I am sorry to say I wasn't presented to you."

"Pity," he said, "pity." His expression was wistful.

Except for a polite "good-bye" in parting, that was the sum and total of their exchanges.

Despite her private discomfort on the weekend, which she attributed to the strangeness of royalty to an American, Wallis decided that the Prince was one of the most intriguing men she had ever met, half boy, half mature man. While seated next to him she had studied his face and concluded with astonishment that he had never shaved for there was not even the smallest evidence of a stubble. His soft-waving golden hair added to his boyish look. And yet there was a strong maleness about him: the manner in which his pensive glance focused on a woman, the way his voice (*Pity—pity*) in the most ordinary conversation could evoke a sudden and deep current.

On the way home, with Ernest talking on and on about the glory of the weekend, she wondered about the strange, melancholy expression that so perpetually haunted the Prince's face.

"Do you suppose he's a really happy man?" she asked.

"Well, when you think of the kind of life he has to lead—the business of always being on show, the boring civic affairs he has to attend, the foreign tours and all the rest—it's hard to imagine that he can have much to be happy about," Ernest replied.

"Do you think he'll ever marry?" Wallis pressed.

"Of course! Part of his duty is to secure the Monarchy. He's expected to give the Empire a future heir."

"He seems anything but the marrying kind, taking into consideration the women in his life."

"There you go again, Wallis, slipping on your American attitudes. With Royalty, marriage does not negate mistresses, or the other way around. Just think about Edward the Seventh and all his lady friends, especially Mrs. Keppel. Even Queen Alexandra recognized her."

But Wallis wondered how the Prince ever overcame the formalities that isolated a Royal person. It seemed to her that others could never be altogether at ease with him. She had detected a barrier even between Thelma and the Prince that, at least in public, had been unbreached during the entire weekend. Did Thelma, as Ernest obviously assumed, actually call him "Sir" in bed. Did she curtsy first? Did she avoid anything controversial (*Sir, you must be quiet about it. Remember the servants—and my husband*)?

Shortly after the weekend at Burrough Court, the Prince set off for a tour through South America to help bolster British prestige and combat the cut-rate German and Japanese competition that had so undermined Britain's current economy. The press lavishly covered every inch of his journey and Wallis assiduously followed the accounts, clipping all published photographs of him. He belonged to her dream world, a world utterly outside her life as Mrs. Ernest Simpson. Still, her fantasies continued, her sense that she was being inexorably drawn into a second life born of her own creation. She came to recognize in his pictures each small nuance that revealed (she believed) his state of health and mind.

She kept her deepest feelings about the Prince to herself, not chancing the possibility of ridicule or of being thought quite mad. She was especially reticent with Maud, who was in a jealous pique that Wallis had spent an entire weekend in the company of the Prince.

"Serves her right," Wallis told Ernest. "Maud has been impossibly rude to Thelma and Gloria and says terrible things about them behind their backs. She calls them the 'Morgan Money Whores' and the 'Whoopsy-Daisy Girls.'"

From Syrie, she heard stories about the Prince. He was headstrong, impetuous and independent in "a rather unroyal way." On tour he seduced the wives of local officials. There were rumors that King George and he were at loggerheads and that Queen Mary had a short list of names, with Princess Ingrid of Sweden at the top, from which she was insisting, obviously unsuccessfully, that he select a wife.

"It's all awfully unfair," Syrie said over lunch alone with Wallis in her office behind the shop. Syrie was a devoted follower of a health faddist and their plates were filled with organically grown greens and sprouts accompanied by tall glasses of combined vegetable juices. "Things would not have reached this impasse if it wasn't for those greedy bitches. They take his jewels, every advantage his Royal favor has to offer, but not one of the Prince's mistresses has ever been even ordinarily faithful to him. Which has to make the poor man feel absolutely wretched. No wonder he keeps moving on from one woman to the other."

"What about Freda Dudley Ward?" Wallis asked, rearranging the food on her plate with her fork to make it look as if she had eaten a bit of the unappetizing salad.

"Well, Dickie Mountbatten told me the Prince was madly, *abjectly,* in love with her for years. Had that not been the case he probably would have married. Then about three years ago he learned Freda had been unfaithful to him. He has never been the same. There have been various women in his life since then, like dear Thelma, but when he is in London he sees Freda every day at five P.M. and she can always get through to him on the telephone no matter where he is—or with whom."

A few days later Wallis recounted the story over the telephone to Corrine. "Wallis, you are gettin' progressively obsessive about the Prince of Wales," Corrine commented scornfully.

"That's not true," Wallis said defensively.

"It is too true! Why, you're practically sniffin' up Thelma's skirts."

"I find that most offensive, Corrine."

"Well, you can't wag a bitch's tail for her, an' that's the truth!"

"Corrine, I have never hung up a receiver on anyone in my life, but I am about to do so now!"

"Jus' remember Win, Wallis, an' how you wouldn't listen to me then. You're hell-bent for trouble. The Prince won't give you the time of day an' Thelma will soon catch on an' *Whoops!* there goes all your fine social connections."

Her feelings toward Corrine began to chill from that moment. Although she believed that her cousin was overreacting, Wallis, nonetheless, became more cautious when conversations with others touched on the Prince, which they invariably did, and she showed a little more outward affection for Ernest. He still adored her. She did not question that, and she remained comfortable and secure in his presence. They enjoyed the theater, seldom missing a new play. With his knowledge he stirred her mind and her imagination. She felt pride in his intellect and her respect for him went deep. He liked parties, was a good dancer, attractive, possessed a quiet charm and never prevented her from doing whatever she wanted, seeing whomever she wished or entertaining as often as she liked, although her inheritance had now all been spent (some of it lost in a bad stock investment) and his father's company was suffering some serious reverses.

More and more, American society figures frequented her dinner parties. Theater people were sometimes included. Craps was incorporated into her after-dinner entertainment. She would slip to her knees and, producing a large pair of dice, would blow on them and then proceed to bounce them off the wall. "I can't shoot craps alone, now can I?" she would say, and soon there was a semicircle of guests squatting on the floor beside her. She was a very good crapshooter, fast and accurate. "Deliver me a pair of shoes," she would say to the dice in her softest, most caressing Maryland tones. In twelve throws, she was known to roll four naturals and make her point seven times before a pair of boxcars finished the run. Many evenings she won back a good part of her dinner expenses but neither her guests nor Ernest found this gauche. Wallis's parties were such fun and Wallis so contagiously peppy that they seldom broke up until three in the morning.

She wrote Aunt Bessie a weekly account of her activities and her financial difficulties. Mrs. Smith had died and left her aunt a comfortable inheritance. Aunt Bessie frequently enclosed a check when she replied, helping Wallis to maintain her life-style. In return Aunt Bessie, not without her niece's gleeful agreement, had the pleasure of telling their Baltimore relations and others who had been cool to Wallis as a young woman that she was traveling high and had been at a house party with the Prince of Wales and mention was made of the fact in Amelia Love's society column in the *Baltimore Sun.*

The middle of March passed. In spite of the sudden patches of yellow daffodils and forsythia in Hyde Park and London's hundreds of grassy squares, spring was late. The Prince of Wales had returned from Argentina. Wallis often suggested to Thelma that she bring him to cocktails at her apartment. The answer was always, "It's not quite as easy as all that," or something similar. Wallis was beginning to believe she might never see him again, when, to her great excitement, Thelma invited her and Ernest to a large afternoon reception at her home on Grosvenor Square at which the Prince was to be present.

As Wallis entered Thelma's magnificent drawing room filled with London's most stimulating people, she could not help but think how Thelma had it *all.* For she was born a beauty and a Morgan, had married a wealthy viscount, gained a title (*Lady* Furness), a husband who was a confidant of members of the Royal Family, and had won the attentions of the Prince of Wales. *Yes,* Thelma definitely had it *all* and Wallis could not help being envious.

Laughter mingled with cigarette smoke in a swirling cloud in the high reaches of the cathedral-like interior. At an enormous baroque piano in the far corner of the oak-panneled room, surrounded by enthusiastic listeners, Noël Coward, a red rose in the buttonhole of his white dinner jacket, a droll expression on his keen, angular face, played and sang one of his newest songs.

> "In Bangkok
> At twelve o'clock
> They foam at the mouth and run
> But mad dogs and Englishman
> Go out in the midday sun."

"Noël can be a headache, on occasion a splitting one," the

writer Beverley Nichols was saying, "but he is never a bore. Even if the Last Trump were to sound he would have something apposite to say about it—probably that it was flat."

"There is peace from twelve till two.
Even caribous
Lie around and snooze
For there's nothing else to do.
In Bengal
To move at all
Is seldom, if ever done.
But mad dogs and Englishman
Go out in the midday sun."

There was a burst of wild applause and high-pitched laughter. Slim and elegant, Noël rose. A young man slipped into his place and began to play a Jerome Kern melody. The group around the piano slowly dispersed.

"Oh, the Simpsons, how good to see you both," Tamar Thaw said as she approached Wallis and Ernest. "Does Thelma know you're here? Of course not!" she answered herself. "She's gone to greet the Prince before he joins us."

Tamar had her arm linked through that of an exotic, dark-haired young woman, dressed dramatically in a heavily embroidered cossack shirt, trousers and huge gold earrings. "You've met, of course?"

"I'm afraid not," Wallis said, although she had recognized the woman. "Nada, this is Mr. and Mrs. Simpson. Wallis and Ernest—Nada, the Marchioness of Milford Haven."

The woman smiled benignly at Ernest, then turned to Wallis, her almond eyes flashing. "The lady of the wicked cocktail," she said in a thick Russian accent.

Nada was married to Dickie Mountbatten's brother, the Marquess of Milford Haven, and therefore was related through marriage to the Royal Family. Wallis was about to enter into a small exchange with Nada when she became aware of a tall man staring at her through a monocle from the doorway, a distance of about twenty feet.

"Could you excuse me, please," she said. "I've just seen a

very old acquaintance." She gently prodded Ernest who picked up the conversation with Tamar and the Marchioness. Nada's eyes followed Wallis as she made her way through groups of people to the doorway.

"Wallis," the man grinned and took her hand. "You look marvelous."

"Felipe, this is a surprise."

"A happy one, I hope."

"It's always nice to see old lovers when one looks well."

"And has been so successful, eh?"

"Well, I'm merely married. You, I understand, are to be Argentine Ambassador to the United States."

Because of the crush of people surrounding them they stood quite close to each other. Paunch now saddled Espil's face. He had thickened and aged. Wallis's lack of great emotion in seeing him had little to do with his changed appearance. So much had happened in the years since that last bitter good-bye, he no longer held any allure for her.

The young pianist struck a few thunderous chords. Heads pivoted. Thelma, in a seductively draped white jersey afternoon gown entered with the Prince of Wales dressed in a dark suit. Conversation stopped. Everyone stood and he began to move through the room, Thelma at his side. Wallis happened to be nearest to the entrance.

"How nice to see you again, Mrs. Simpson. I trust you have been well since our pleasant weekend at Burrough Court," he said, his blue eyes a bit fatigued but his voice sincere.

"Oh, yes, Sir. Quite well."

"Sir," Thelma said, "this is Señor Espil."

"I've just returned from your beautiful country," the Prince acknowledged. "Beautiful women and beautiful horses."

Espil laughed and after a short exchange about the wonders of Argentina, the Prince moved on.

"Well, you *have* made it, Wallis," Espil said. "It makes me very happy."

"Believe me, Felipe, that was never one of my goals," she replied. She turned abruptly aside and joined Tamar and a small group of people. Espil stood smiling cynically for a moment and then walked away.

The Prince did not return to talk to Wallis. He left no more than half an hour after he had arrived. *Thelma is wrong to expose him to such a large gathering,* she thought. *He looks finely drawn as if this last tour has exhausted him.*

"Why so silent?" Ernest asked on the ride home. "You don't have those stomach pains again, do you, darling? You really should be careful with what you eat at these cocktail parties." Recently Wallis had experienced recurring abdominal spasms. She had never told Ernest about how she came to have them. Her discomfort, she informed him, was caused by a gastric ulcer.

"Oh, no. Just wondering," she said.

"About what?"

"Silly thoughts really—if the Prince of Wales still sees Mrs. Dudley Ward at five every afternoon."

"What made you think about that?"

"Because he left at exactly four-forty-five *without* Thelma."

It was Maud who first gave Wallis the idea that she should be presented at Court. "A presentation always helps one socially," she told her. "Although, dear, you certainly appear to do well on your own." A faint smile of disdain passed over her face. "Since you are only British by marriage, you have to be presented by an Englishwoman and not through the American Embassy, as is the usual case with citizens of your country."

"I believe it was *your* country once as well, Maud," Wallis snapped.

"A long time ago."

"Yes—*ages,*" Wallis said.

"Well, I would, of course, help if I could," Maud continued, ignoring the sarcasm in her sister-in-law's voice, for the two of them had been locked for months in a tongue-sharp game of *snipes.* "Court etiquette, however, does not permit me to make more than one presentation in three years and there's young Peter's fiancée to be considered."

Wallis immediately consulted Syrie. "Whom do you think I can get to present me at Court?" she asked bluntly.

"Mildred Alwyn," Syrie responded without hesitation. "She dotes on *any* excuse to be seen at Court. Now don't take that wrong, Wallis dear. It's meant with the very best of intent. Millie has impeccable credentials—father a well-known barrister, husband a prominent banker. But she is not connected at Court and is mad for the pomp and posh of it. I'm sure you could find *droves* of presenters, but Millie is perfect, she truly is."

Within moments Syrie had rung Mildred Alwyn and it was all agreed.

The date of the presentation was set for June 10, only two weeks hence. "Whatever will I wear?" Wallis complained to Tamar over the telephone.

"We're about the same size. Come right over and try on the gown I wore at mine," Tamar offered.

When Wallis arrived at the Thaws' exquisite Farm Street flat, Thelma was already there with the additional necessary items for the event: the train, feathers and fan worn by her the previous year. Nada Milford Haven, dressed in trousers and a poet's tunic, her raven hair sleeked back from her high forehead, a single golden hoop earring on her right ear, was stretched out on Tamar's bedroom chaise longue when Wallis went in to try on the clothes being lent to her.

"You will need a tiara," Nada said as she watched her dress. "You have?"

"Afraid not."

"I have several." She studied Wallis intently, her dark eyes narrowed, her thick brows arched. "They come from my father, the Grand Duke Michael. The Grand Duchess Elizabeth smuggled them out of Russia just before the murders. You know *which* murders of which I speak?"

"Yes, of course."

"I never wear the rubies. They remind me of the blood shed by those unfortunate people. You want you can wear the rubies."

"Well," Wallis hesitated, somewhat overwhelmed.

"No! Not the rubies! They will know they are mine," she

said, changing her mind. "Something simple. I have a bandeau of diamonds and aquamarines. From some Hungarian cousin, I believe. You will wear it, yes?"

"Thank you. That would be swell," Wallis said.

"Swell? What is swell?"

"American slang. It means marvelous."

"You will look *swell* then."

Wallis started out of the room, pleased that Tamar's dress fit her so well and that she would have a tiara to wear.

"Wallis," Nada called after her, "in July—Tamar, Gloria and I are going for six weeks to the Riviera. You join us, yes?"

"I'd love to but there is Ernest to consider."

"Husbands! They appreciate a wife's absence now and again. Believe me. I know this to be true. You do not ask. You say, 'Beloved, I go with my friends to France for a holiday. I shall be desolated with loneliness for you and return with even greater passion.' He will say—*swell.*"

"I'll go," Wallis agreed.

This rash decision caused her much anxiety over the next ten days. Ernest looked white and wan. Business was in a slump, their income severely cut back. The car had to be sold and Hughes let go. It seemed no time for Wallis to be thinking about a Court presentation or a vacation to the South of France. Yet she looked upon both as a necessary investment in her own and Ernest's future.

"The closer the contacts with the truly influential people, the better your business opportunities will be," she countered when he told her he did not see how they could afford her proposed journey. "I'll ask your father for the money if you like," she suggested.

Ernest paled. "You are not to consider such an idea!" he ordered.

So she wrote to Aunt Bessie—not to *ask* for money, just to tell her of her difficult situation. Within a week she received a reply with the required sum and more. With it, Wallis bought a wardrobe for her trip, settling, with Nada's suggestion, on several pajama suits along with a few summer outfits.

"Pajamas!" Corrine huffed. "With your little ol' bosoms you already look like a boy! An' I have heard things about Nada Milford Haven. She's one of those."

"One of *who*?"

"*Those*. Like Virginia Wolff an' Gertrude Stein. One of *those*!"

"Well, if she is, she certainly isn't after the Morgan sisters."

"Maybe no, maybe so. An' maybe it's *you* she's afta!"

Wallis looked at Corrine with disbelief. "It's just like you, Corrine. Lately all you ever do is try to ruin things for me. This is an innocent holiday which I am much looking forward to, both as a change from all our financial problems and as a step up in my social life."

Corrine screwed up her face in disdain. Her youth has gone, Wallis observed, and her soft-blown beauty with it. At forty, Corrine was a middle-aged woman, her skin, though still milky white, turned to flab and the golden halo of waving hair, graying and frizzy. "Why, she's jealous!" Wallis thought. Remembering back, she wondered if Corrine hadn't always been envious of her.

After a cold *good-bye,* Corrine departed.

"Corrine is really very selfish," Wallis told Ernest later.

"Well, both she and her husband are odd ducks," he replied. "They never go anywhere anymore. Maybe it's for the best that he's being transferred back to the States."

"I think so," Wallis agreed.

The sun shone fitfully the day of the Court Presentation. The night before there had been a heavy rain and the pavements were not yet dry when Wallis and Ernest set off for Buckingham Palace in a hired car. They had hoped to arrive before the steady stream of presenters, presentees and their guests had begun. When the car swung into the Mall it joined a slow-moving caravan of other limousines, taxis and private cars.

"Oh, Lord, it's going to be *mobbed,*" Wallis moaned.

"Don't worry, darling," Ernest consoled, "the feathers on your headdress will show them who's chief."

Wallis did not find this amusing and turned to look out the window. Sun filtered through the upper branches of the plane trees in St. James's Park. A car, hooting impatiently, pulled around her side of the limousine and nosed before them into the queue.

"Hughes would never have permitted that," she muttered.

A narrow strand of onlookers rimmed the edge of the park. Heads craned to see if any of the passengers in the moving vehicles could be identified. As their car finally made its way through the Palace gates, Wallis heaved a sigh of relief.

This was the first time she had been to the Palace. She believed, being an American and sophisticated, that she would feel no differently than one did in arriving at Covent Garden for a spectacle: great expectation at what was to come, a heightening of spirit and curiosity about the performance and the performers. Therefore, she was not prepared for the sense of awe that overcame her when Ernest and the chauffeur helped her out of the car. She walked a few feet ahead of Ernest, her train folded over her arm as she entered through the guests' door.

"Ah, Mr. and Mrs. Simpson," General Trotter said as he approached them at the entrance to the Throne Room where the ceremony was to be held.

"I'm so pleased to see you, General Trotter," Wallis sighed. "It's all a bit more than I expected."

"Well, look, you follow me." He led them inside and to seats in one of the front rows. The scene before Wallis was from a distant age. The scarlet and gold room was immense. Wearing white-plumed hats and crimson and gold uniforms, Gentlemen-at-Arms flanked the gold thrones—over which the great Indian Durbar Canopy was raised. Deep purple hydrangeas and massive red and white roses were banked high on all sides of the room. An orchestra behind a gold brocade curtain was playing the music of Sir Arthur Sullivan.

Wallis glanced around at the many other women to be presented, probably close to a hundred and all in white with the traditional three-feather plumed headdress. Never had she seen such a display of diamonds. Tiaras sparkled like a full constellation of stars beneath the elaborate crystal chandeliers. She recalled how vulgar she had once thought it was to wear jewels in the daytime. Now she wished she had more than Nada's bandeau.

Equerries politely hustled people into their seats. The orchestra struck up "God Save the King." Everyone stood. King

George and Queen Mary entered. The Queen was in a beaded, blue, crepe de chine gown and glittered brightly with her breathtaking array of jewels. She wore five diamond necklaces around her extraordinary long neck. A majestic diamond and pearl tiara topped her abundant gray hair. On her full bosom were pinned several spectacular diamond brooches. Her wrists and fingers dazzled with the refracted light from brilliantly cut gems.

"She certainly has bagged all the best," an American woman seated to Wallis's left whispered.

The Prince of Wales entered a few moments after the King and Queen and was seated on a throne on a lower dais.

Wallis was to be the seventh woman to be presented. An equerry signaled her to rise and stationed her ten feet behind her predecessor. She saw the Queen smile, then nod her head as the woman was being presented. The King only nodded. The woman swept into a deep curtsy, rose and then moved on, a footman with a long, gilded stick straightening her train.

"Mrs. Ernest Aldridge Simpson," a herald announced.

Wallis stepped forward and curtsied low (*left foot far behind the right leg*), first to the King and then to the Queen, whose smile had not altered. Wallis straightened slowly. For a brief moment she stared up at Queen Mary's face. The blue eyes were ice. Her thoughts spun crazily back to the time she had defiantly faced Mrs. Kirk. Her pulse quickened and she turned away and to the Prince of Wales, who seemed about to doze, but came to life when he recognized Wallis. He smiled warmly. Wallis returned the gesture.

The presentations took over an hour. Everyone kept their seats until the Royal Family had departed. As the Prince of Wales passed by her row, Wallis overheard him mutter to a man to his right, "Something ought to be done about the lights. They make all the women look ghastly."

Thelma had arranged a small party to celebrate Wallis's presentation. About twenty people were there, including Thelma's bulldog of a husband, Duke. The Prince of Wales, still in full regalia, arrived with General Trotter. Thelma and Duke greeted them. Small talk was exchanged. Then the

Prince addressed Wallis, who had been conversing with Tamar a few feet away.

"Your gown is most attractive," he smiled.

"But, Sir," she replied with a straight face, "I understand that you thought we all looked ghastly."

He was startled. "I had no idea my voice carried so far," he said.

He left the party with Trotter after a short while, explaining that he was on his way to his country place, Fort Belvedere, and was late. Wallis noted that he and Thelma exchanged a glance. "Ah," she concluded, "Thelma is meeting him there." Thelma then disappeared for a longish time.

To Wallis's irritation Ernest had dismissed the car once they had reached Thelma's, feeling it was too great an extravagance to keep it idly waiting when they were paying for its use by the hour. They left Thelma's about half an hour after the Prince with the intention that Ernest would hail a taxi. To their surprise the Prince and Trotter were standing by the side of the Royal car.

The Prince stepped forward. "Could we give you a lift?" he asked.

"Thank you, Sir, that would be very much appreciated," Wallis replied. She had left the train from her outfit at Thelma's and she entered the car—the same one in which she had fleetingly seen him on St. James's Street—with some ease. The Prince sat beside her, Trotter and Ernest opposite them. Wallis turned her head so that she would be looking at the Prince.

"You must come down to the Fort some weekend," he said. "It's a bit of a ruin right now, but I've wonderful plans for restoring it. Tomorrow morning I want to put in two or three hours in the garden. Are you much of a gardener, Mrs. Simpson?"

"I'm afraid not, Sir," she laughed. "Cut flowers are more in my line."

"Do you like roses?"

"Why, of course, Sir. Doesn't everyone?"

"Lady Furness claims they die too fast when cut."

"Perhaps she is right. But beauty should be captured while it lasts, don't you think so, Sir?"

"Yes, I suppose so."

He helped her out of the car when they reached Bryanston Court.

"Would you care to come up and join us in a drink, Sir?" Wallis asked.

"I'd like very much to see your flat one day," he replied. "I'm told it's charming and seeing it might give me some ideas for brightening up the Fort. But I have to be up early. Still, if you would be so kind as to invite me again, I'd like to do so." He turned away and reentered his car.

"Quite a day!" Wallis said as she and Ernest entered their apartment.

Ernest was staring at her from a distance of about five feet. "Wallis," he said, "the Prince of Wales was waiting at Thelma's for you to leave."

"Don't be ridiculous!"

"I'm not. Whether he's a commoner or a prince, as a man I can see when another man is intrigued with a woman."

"His being outside when we left was just a coincidence. He must have been detained with Thelma," she protested.

"He said he would come to the flat."

"He only said he *might* visit us."

"*Us?* He said nothing about us." Ernest went over to the bar and poured himself a scotch. "I just think you ought to be prepared, Wallis, that's all," he said, and then took his drink, leaving her standing alone in the lowering shadows of the afternoon light.

22

Wallis stood on the balcony of her suite at the Hotel Miramar in Cannes attempting to memorize all she saw. The fashionable Boulevard de la Croisette which brimmed Golfe-Juan and the small harbor of Cannes was directly below. In the distance were the deep-red, craggy Estérel mountains. To the southwest lay the radiantly blue Mediterranean. On the horizon a mirage of white sails blurred in the bright morning light and an ocean liner, looking like a sleek white whale, came into sight. Steps led down from the hotel under the boulevard to the beach. A man in a striped bathrobe had just stepped onto the sand. As he neared the water, he took off his outer garment, tossed it aside and ran to meet an incoming wave, his red bathing trunks bobbing up and down like a flag of distress. The nearly deserted beach was flooded with white sun. It was only eight A.M. She had arrived with Tamar late the previous night, Gloria and Nada having preceded them the day before.

Ernest had not been enthusiastic about her taking the trip. His father, he said, would not understand her spending so much money at such a difficult time. "It's not *his* money," she reminded Ernest. "It's not even your money. It's a gift from Aunt Bessie." Now that she was here she was glad she had come. She desperately needed a change from all the problems in London. And, of course, to be included in the company of Gloria, Nada and Tamar was a remarkable experience.

"Wallis, is that you prowling about out there?" Tamar called from inside.

It had been arranged that Wallis and Tamar would share one accommodation; Gloria and Nada, another. Gloria had been going through the dreadful ordeal of a custody battle with the Vanderbilts over her small daughter in America. On the way down in the train, it was all Tamar could talk about. She was furious at her sister's in-laws for what she called "an evil conspiracy" and she was concerned that Gloria might not be able to cope with the strain of the court case that appeared imminent.

"Gloria left a message that she would see us for lunch," Tamar said when Wallis came back into the bedroom. "Poor dear has been so frazzled she needs as much rest as she can get." She glanced up at Wallis, seeing her really for the first time since she had entered the bedroom. "My God! Wallis! You're completely dressed! Have you had breakfast?"

"No. I couldn't sleep."

She had never seen Tamar without makeup and was surprised how very attractive she was. Prettier, she thought, far prettier and more feminine. She wore a pale-pink bed jacket with marabou down the front. An eye mask was pushed back from her forehead in bandeau fashion, and the dark mass of her hair formed a halo on her propped-up pillows, softening the sharp lines of her angular face. "Well, darling, don't think I'm antisocial if I have mine served in bed. Morning is just not my best time. What hour is it, anyway?"

"Eight."

"Oh, my God!" She slipped the eye mask back in place and slid down under the covers. "I'll need at least two more hours," she mumbled.

They lunched with Kitty and Herman at the Eden Roc in Antibes. Later they lazed on the deck of Herman's boat, *Shady Lady,* which was docked nearby. Herman seemed delighted to be the only man among five attractive women. Nada received his most open admiration. Even Herman, who remained slavishly devoted to the lovely Kitty, found himself drawn to her exoticism.

Nada exuded excitement. She moved panther-like, laughed with white teeth flashing, a hard sparkle in her cat-like eyes; raised herself to the sun prayer-like, a supplicant with such a look of ecstasy that one expected a sudden miracle to occur. Nada possessed more than beauty: a kinetic oneness with life's energy, and Tamar's disclosure that her accent was fake (she was born in England) did not dim her appeal.

"I've always had these sexual fantasies," Gloria was saying to Wallis. "Thelma was the one the boys were mad about. It was something I never could understand. We are identical twins and as children even our parents found it difficult to tell us apart. Boys, however, always could. I tried to figure out what was different about Thelma. I never succeeded. So to compensate I would have these really torrid sexual fantasies." She paused dramatically.

"Thelma and I had this divine riding instructor when we were about thirteen. I imagined that we rode to the top of a mountain and he did all sorts of racy things to me on the soft earth. I could actually feel the heat of the sun on my naked body. I had no idea how one made love. And my projections were pretty bizarre. I was always thinking about sex."

"What are you girls whispering about?" Herman called from the bow of the boat.

"Sex!" Gloria shouted back.

Nada turned onto her side. "Just like schoolgirls," she laughed.

"She is an amazing woman," Wallis commented.

"Nada's unique," Gloria agreed.

"I never see her with her husband."

"Well, the Marquess prefers to stay in the country and be the squire of the manor. He's not terribly well, either. Nada married him when she was just nineteen. It seemed a good match. Except for the Royal Princes, he and his younger brother, Dickie Mountbatten, were the most eligible bachelors in England at the time. Nada's father was the Czar's cousin.

He wasn't killed by the Bolsheviks, but almost everyone else in her family was."

Gloria rearranged herself in the deck chair. She lacked Thelma's grace, the well-tuned, neat curve of body.

"Does Thelma talk to you about the Prince?" Wallis asked.

"One thing one learns in a Royal liaison is not to talk to *anyone* about it," Gloria laughed.

"Not even your twin sister?"

"Well, Thelma's going through a lot just now. She's decided to leave Duke."

Wallis could not control her surprise.

"Now, you are not to breathe a word—"

"Of course," Wallis vowed.

"We've all told her not to be too hasty about it, that she's a fool. Duke can be crude and a bit of a boor and a bore. He is rich though and the title is real enough. 'You Americans and your divorces,' Nada is always saying. She's right. Marriage is a woman's best defense. However, nothing anyone says does any good. Thelma is going ahead."

"Maybe the Prince has proposed," Wallis prompted.

Gloria laughed cynically. "He could never marry Thelma. Too many insurmountable obstacles. Not that Thelma ever dreamed he would. The problem is that he might think it was too delicate a situation to be seeing or be seen with a woman in the throes of a divorce. And once it's done with, she'll be single—not easy from his point of view either. Anyway, by then he could be married to some dumpling of a Balkan Princess!"

Wallis could concentrate on little else for the rest of the afternoon. The women dined at the Rogerses' that night with several other guests. The days that followed were idyllic. They prowled Antibes, had picnic lunches on the nearby islands and swam off the *Shady Lady*. Men were scarce and "four women terrifying," she wrote Aunt Bessie.

Antibes once had been a Roman city with baths, an arena and an aqueduct. Gloria and Nada were not much on ruins ("One old rock looks much like another," Gloria insisted). Wallis and Tamar, therefore, went alone to look at the remains. They brought lunch to the grounds of an ancient monastery, high above Antibes. From here there was a view of the sea; of the Riviera's string of coastal cities gleaming like pearls around a beautiful woman's neck, and of the distant Italian mountains capped with snow. To the east was Nice, beyond it, Monaco on its high promontory. In the bay, directly below them, the sailors of Antibes, barefooted, wearing white shirts, walked the decks of their small and large vessels.

One day they drove to Nice in a hired car. The lunatic driver whipped around the dangerous curves of the lower *corniche,* his hand steady on the horn to announce his approach, terrifying his passengers into silence. Once miraculously there, they visited the flower market and trooped through the old fortifications. Nice had numerous acceptable hotel ballrooms where tea dances and graceful gigolos abounded. Wallis preferred to spend her days with the sun and the sea and her friends. This was not as quixotic as it seemed. Wallis knew that this vacation was an important occasion for her, in some ways the most important in many years. From Tamar, Gloria and Nada she was learning all about the various members of the Prince of Wales's Set, the ins and outs of Royal protocol and, perhaps even more valuable, where all the bones were buried.

Early one windless morning, the sea quite still, Herman took them on the trim white *Shady Lady* to Monaco. The yacht crept slowly beyond the breakwater, through the Golfe-Juan. The Riviera glided past in endless spectacle. They reached Monaco at noon and went ashore to meet friends of Herman and Kitty's in Monte Carlo for lunch at the Hôtel de Paris. Wallis had been to Monte (as the smart set called it) on her trip years before with Aunt Bessie, and the fashionable shops and hotels were not new to her.

"Why all the secrecy, Herman?" Wallis asked, as the taxi circled the port and began its ascent up the steep road to the hotel. "Who are we lunching with?"

"You'll soon find out. It's a surprise," he said.

The brightness of the midday sun made it difficult for her to see as they entered the dark interior of the grandiose lobby. They were all dressed in their sailing clothes. "Quite a crew I've got," Herman boasted, as eyes turned their direction.

A tall man and a petite woman had advanced toward them.

"Well! This is a jolly fine treat!" the man said as he stepped in close to Wallis and bending forward kissed her lightly on the cheek.

Gordon Breakshaw stood beaming down at her, balding and leaner than ever, an exclamation point of a man, his head somewhat too small as punctuation to his elongated body. His cheeks were as pink as a young boy's. His eyes danced merrily. Wallis could not recall if she still had the book he had given her inscribed with a rather moving sentiment. How well she remembered that her poet admirer had become the bumbling schoolboy in bed.

"This is my wife, Irina," he said proudly. He drew the small woman forward. She was pretty in a lace and scent fashion, blond hair framing a powder-puff face, long lashes veiling chalk-blue eyes.

"My pleasure to meet you," she said in an accented voice. Viennese, Wallis supposed.

The round of introductions continued. Wallis sat across the table from Breakshaw, feeling numb. It was too ridiculous. She didn't care a fig about him. Nonetheless, the thought that she had once carried his child, no matter how briefly or unknowingly, startled her. What if it had been a full pregnancy? Like it or not, she would have been tied to Breakshaw for life. What had Espil once said to her? "Another career lost between the bedsheets." Well, she could not say she had a career, but any aspirations she had to take her place in society would have been lost forever.

"Irina and I are here on holiday before being transferred again," he said. "This time it is to be Calcutta."

"Whatever came over you," Herman asked when they were on the boat once more. "I thought you would be pleased to see old Gordon. You know, I always suspected he had a yen for you in China." He laughed merrily. "Sorry, Wallis. Bad joke," he admitted.

When you spend day and night in close contact with three other women, there is not much they can hide from you. Nada was a fascinating and complex personality. This woman of the world could be tenderhearted as a child, frank to the point of dubious taste, bold yet haunted by fears. The suite she shared with Gloria adjoined Wallis and Tamar's rooms. One night Wallis awoke startled at the sound of a woman screaming. Tamar was fast asleep in the other bed. Through the wall, Wallis now heard feminine sobs. It had to be either Gloria or Nada. After a moment of hesitation, Wallis decided not to awaken Tamar, who required eight to ten full hours sleep, and to investigate herself.

She made her way in the dark, slipping into her robe as she crossed the sitting room. Leaving the door slightly ajar, she went into the corridor and knocked on the door to the next suite. Except for the distant sound of a woman weeping, there was no response. Wallis tried the door, and as it was unlatched, she entered.

"Nada? Gloria?" she called. "Are you all right?" Muffled sobs came from the bedroom. "Gloria!" she called again.

"It's all right, Wallis," came Gloria's assurance from the next room. "Nada's had a nightmare."

Wallis was not sure at that point whether she should leave or see if she could assist Gloria. Deciding on the latter, she crossed the sitting room and tentatively entered the bedroom.

Nada was still sobbing. A bedside lamp was lit. Gloria was holding her against her bare breast as a mother might cradle a frightened child. Nada appeared also to be nude. From the waist down they were under the covers. The second bed had never been slept in.

"It wasn't real, Nada," Gloria was saying. "Only a bad dream. You're here safe with me." She looked up and saw Wallis, unperturbed, it appeared, at the impression the lurid tableau must have made. "She often has these nightmares. Some stupid idiot once showed her a picture of the room where the Czar and his family were murdered. She dreams sometimes that she is in the room with them. She'll be fine in a little while."

Wallis left without saying a word. The images of the women, nude, clinging to each other, the un-slept-in second bed—kept her awake for most of the night. She had never known any lesbians, or at least not to her knowledge. If she thought about their existence at all, it was with fleeting and not prurient interest. Her conception of one of *those,* as Corrine had euphemistically referred to lesbians, was of an unattractive, mannish woman. Neither Gloria nor Nada fit this description.

Although she wanted to believe the incident was entirely innocent, too many other pieces of evidence, no matter how circumstantial, were involved. Perhaps two women could sleep in the same bed without sexual implication if one was frightened of something. But not in the nude. There was Nada's penchant for trousers, the glances the two women so often exchanged, the way they always arranged time alone. Gloria and Nada were lovers, of that she suddenly was certain. How that affected her own life, Wallis was not immediately sure.

Her old friends from Washington, Ethel and Willmott Lewis, were visiting the Côte d'Azur for a few days before going on to Paris. Wallis and the others were to meet them for lunch at the Eden Roc. At the last minute Gloria announced, "Nada needs some rest," and Wallis and Tamar went on alone.

As soon as the taxi pulled away from the hotel, Wallis nervously began the inquiry which she was determined to make. "Tamar, last night, I heard Nada screaming—"

"Yes, Gloria told me."

"Well, it isn't just *that.* Tamar, I have to ask you this. Do you think Gloria and Nada are—"

"Lovers? Yes, they are. Mind you, I don't think Nada is bad for Gloria at this time," Tamar said, thoughtfully. "Nada is a loving woman and Gloria could do with a bit of tenderness."

"Maybe Gloria needs professional medical help," Wallis suggested.

"She's been seeing a Viennese physician by the name of Steiner who practices psychoanalysis. He says she has a *Minderwertigkertcomplex*, the *Minkos* for short. That means an inferiority complex. Our mother did a great job on all three of us girls. People always thought we were from the rich side of the Morgans. We were not. Mama was determined we would all marry into the great families. To accomplish this she kept us believing we could not trust our own judgment and, therefore, must trust hers.

"Gloria not only had to cope with Mama, she had to compete with Thelma, then deal with Reggie and the dear, dear *poisonous* Vanderbilts," she continued. "Now there is this beastly court case facing her and the possibility that she might lose little Gloria whom she really, really does love. It's been hell for her. I don't know how much I believe in this new fad of discussing quite blandly with a doctor one's darkest thoughts, anal-erotic impulses and all that. Most women pay the ten-dollar-an-hour fee just to have a cultured, intelligent man listen to them talk about themselves because, quite frankly, the men they know all seem to want to talk *only* about *them*selves." She glanced out of the window in private thought.

"Dr. Steiner has, at least, helped free Gloria from some of her inhibitions," she said as she turned back. "No one should feel guilty for having honest sexual desires whatever the gender of one's partner."

Tamar had delivered this short, somewhat shocking, treatise without any awkwardness. What she said was sensible on the face of it. Nonetheless, Wallis found accepting it a moral struggle. They had reached the Eden Roc. The conversation was ended and Wallis did not wish to reopen the subject. She was now suspicious about Tamar's leanings, for she seemed too conversant with Nada's sexual proclivities. The thought that Tamar might also be one of *those* alarmed her. They were, after all, sharing a bedroom. The danger was not so much that Tamar might make an unwelcome advance, for she could certainly let it be known that such a thing was completely out of order. What concerned Wallis was the possibility that *she* could be labeled one of *those* merely by her close association.

First there had been the specter of Gordon Breakshaw—now *this*. Seeing Ethel and Willmott somewhat buoyed her declining spirits. By the end of lunch a sense of anger at Tamar and the two other women had flourished. It did not take much intelligence to see that she had been used as a *beard* for their erotic activities.

Ernest knew no more than that she had come back from holiday in an agitated mood, having cut it abruptly and unaccountably short. Oh, she had told him that she felt a pig lolling in the heat and sun while he was stuck in dismal London where it was raining nonstop and business was so foul. Her distraction from the moment of her homecoming made him doubt that this was the case. He preferred not to dig any deeper. Since the night of her Court Presentation an invisible wall had distanced them. Wallis was a woman entranced.

He could not claim to have ever completely understood Wallis. Yet, curiously, now that they had settled into a relationship of studied consideration, he felt he knew her better than when sex determined their emotions. Wallis had elected the change. One night her bedroom door had been locked to him. It seemed to him to be as simple as that; no degrading discussions or backbiting recriminations. The next day they moved onto a new plateau in their marriage. They were now best of friends. A silent agreement had been struck allowing each to go a separate way, respect for the other being tacit. It never occurred to him that she had come to feel their lovemaking was an ordeal. Nor could he have faced himself with the irrefutable truth that Wallis now felt confident she could get what she wanted from him without the bother of pleasing him in bed.

He contented himself with lascivious thoughts, at times shocking even to him. They were not directed at Wallis. What he felt for her now was love, not lust. If Wallis had her fantasies, he had his, as well. He was sacrificing Wallis, pure and untouched, to the gods. The idea filled him with sinful delight.

She had telegraphed him from France that he need not meet her at the train. Before she arrived, he came home from the office with a fragrant summer bouquet. Wallis loved flowers. His arms were too full to manage the key and he rang the bell. Blane, the housemaid, was due to be on duty. After several moments, Ernest put the flowers down in the vestibule and opened the door. The flat was silent and dark. He switched on the hall light and brought in the flowers.

"Blane?" he called. There was no reply. "Damn!" he swore. "I'll have to arrange them myself and I'm no good at such things!"

He placed the bulky parcel, blossoms poking out from the paper they were wrapped in, on the hall table. His reflection in the mirror above surprised him. Disembodied, framed in the ornate gilt rectangle, it stared out Van Goghish, eyes haunted, face gaunt, the ruff of brilliant bloom throwing streaks of yellow and blue across his pale, tired features. He had aged, looked middle-aged. Of course, he was over forty, no longer a young man.

"Blane!" he again shouted hopefully. The room smelled of stale Turkish tobacco. With Wallis away he had slipped into old habits, leaving cigarettes half burning in ashtrays. Blane had apparently not been in since morning.

A light flashed on in the kitchen area and the harried housemaid, her wiry red hair flying, burst into the hallway.

"Oh! Mr. Simpson! You startled me!" she said.

"It *is* six P.M.," he answered sternly, "I *always* return from the office at this time." He pressed the flowers into her arms. "Here, put these into a vase and bring them back here. The sitting room needs airing. Mrs. Simpson will be home in less than an hour."

Blane hurried off and Ernest went into the tartan bedroom that he had always abhorred, to dress for the evening. There was nothing in the house for dinner. He would take Wallis to the Savoy. That would be festive. He was very much looking forward to her return. The house was gloom without her. Wallis had this incredible ability to fill a room. She was a remarkable woman, so sure of herself. She could sometimes be pigheaded and she had the American woman's irritating tendency to reform her husband. She moved and spoke with authority, was never dull, always quick on the verbal trigger.

He studied the photograph he kept of her on his bureau. Wallis never took a picture that did her justice, he thought. She had the length of face, the high, well-poised forehead that was much admired in nineteenth-century portraits. Her slim, flawless figure had always pleased him more than it did Wallis, as did the distinctive mole on the right side of her mouth that had become more prominent in recent months. Wallis hated this spot on her otherwise ivory-smooth, vellum complexion and had only been convinced not to do away with it medically after he had shown her paintings of Marie Antoinette with a mark positioned exactly where hers was.

When he was dressed he walked through the flat making sure everything was how she would want it. Of course, Wallis could never be satisfied with the way others arranged things. She was demanding of him and of the staff, who minded where he did not. It was not just that Wallis was a perfectionist. She had innate style, an ability to turn the commonplace into the unusual with a flick of her wrist.

He was standing in the doorway to the dining room when the doorbell rang. Blane brushed past him, cap now tightly secured to her head, her hair drawn neatly back, her uniform wrinkle-free on her generous frame. "Madam's home," she called over her shoulder. Then Wallis entered.

He noticed the slight nervous shake of her head instantly. "Flowers!" she said, turning over all her parcels to Blane's care. "Ernest, what a glorious choice! Yellow and blue!"

"The sun and the sky, remember?" he asked.

"Yes, of course." She spread the stems a bit apart, giving the arrangement a freer look. Then she met him halfway as he came toward her. He kissed her smooth, cool cheek and then stepped back.

"My, aren't you tanned and healthy-looking," he said.

"And you—oh, *poor* Ernest! You look so white and wan. It's time *you, too,* had a holiday. You really must speak to your father. At least he could contribute *something*. If you had your choice, where would you go?"

"Scotland, I think," he smiled. "Car sightseeing with you." A vein in her neck pulsated slightly.

"If we could drop in on a castle or two, I suppose that would be all right."

"How was the trip?"

"Lovely. Everyone sends love to you. I brought you a presie. When Blane unpacks I'll give it to you. Nothing grand. I'm sorry now that it isn't."

"I've made a dinner reservation at the Savoy," he said.

"Did you? I told Kitty and Herman that you're the most considerate husband—and you see? I was right." She whizzed by him and disappeared after Blane into her bedroom. "How long do I have?" she called back.

"Two hours."

"Then be a dear and fix me a whiskey and soda and I'll have a soak first."

Ernest hastened to the bar to do as she asked. For the first time in three weeks, since Wallis had departed on her journey, he felt energized.

Once back in London, Wallis walked a thin, dangerous line. She had decided she would not see Gloria or Nada again, if it could be tactfully avoided. Tamar was another matter. She and Benny were key in her social world and extremely close to Thelma, perhaps her only confidants. Wallis admitted to herself that Corrine had been right, yet again. She *was* obsessively interested in the Prince and Thelma. She did not know why she felt compelled to develop the friendship, maybe only to be invited to the Prince's private estate, Fort Belvedere. And although Thelma helped him to arrange his weekend guest lists, Wallis and Ernest had not been included.

There was the possibility that Thelma had suggested their names and the Prince had vetoed their inclusion, but this did not seem too likely in view of how pleasant he had been to them the day of the presentation.

She rang Thelma one morning and invited her for lunch at the Ritz. "Just us two girls," she said.

Not until coffee was served did the subject get around to Thelma and the Prince of Wales.

"Thelma, maybe I shouldn't bring this up—and if it is off base, please say so. But I can't help noticing how much weight you have lost and how pale you look and Tamar mentioned that you were considering divorcing Duke," she said sympathetically.

"Oh, Wallis, Tamar was right. I have already left Duke and I never should have made the move," Thelma said softly, her lovely brown eyes clouded with unhappiness. "Duke is blustering and hurtful, impossibly self-indulgent. The Prince is shy, gracious, meticulously considerate. We have a special rapport. I thought, despite Tamar's warnings, that he would be pleased. I had this notion that he would arrange a suitable townhouse for me. The one on Grosvenor Square belongs to Duke's family."

"And was he pleased?" Wallis asked.

"Well, yes! He took me in his arms when I told him and *said* I had made the right decision. But that was weeks ago and nothing has been done about an arrangement."

"Surely Duke will give you a settlement that would be sufficient," Wallis declared.

"That's not the point. I'll know—and so will everyone else—that the Prince has not made a commitment. If I was recognized as *Number One* I could deal with the sex problems. There would be compensations. I would *never* look elsewhere as that bitch Freda did." The waiter brought a small silver dish of pastel petit fours. Thelma pushed it away. "It's all too depressing," she said. "I have this sinking feeling, just like when I was a child and I broke something truly expensive and I knew Mama was *bound* soon to find out. I'm going to lose both of them, Wallis. I just know it."

Wallis leaned forward confidentially. "Don't be foolish, Thelma. The Prince loves you and I'm sure if you wanted Duke back all you would have to do is snap your fingers," she consoled.

"You really believe that?"

"I do and so should you."

"I suppose you're right. It's just been so unsettling lately—all this business with Gloria and the Vanderbilts. We've always had this strange psychic bond, almost like we were Siamese twins without the connection. When Gloria's in a traumatic state, no matter *where* she is, I become absolutely manic. It works that way with her, too."

Wallis, seeing that Thelma had lowered her guard, figured *what-the-hell* and took the leap. "What kind of sex problems, Thelma?" she asked in a soft puzzled voice untouched by salacious interest. Wallis had not become her own charming social invention without a considerable talent as an actress.

"What?" Thelma inquired, still distracted.

Wallis cast a cautious side glance to make sure no one could overhear their conversation. "You mentioned sex problems," she said.

"Oh, *that.* Well, the little man has problems rising to the occasion, if you know what I mean. It can be dreadfully tedious and any silly thing can ruin his concentration. He's not *that way*—or at least I don't think he is. But he's built small and he is always apologetic about it. I loathe that in a man. I just want them to get on with it and *out*." She absent-mindedly reached forward and drew the small cake dish closer to her and after a moment of casual study of the contents, selected a bite-sized cake and popped it into her wide crimson mouth.

"Poor man," Wallis said honestly.

"Poor me!" Thelma corrected, as she dabbed the corners of her mouth with a large overly starched white serviette.

"No, Thelma," Wallis gently contradicted. "One has to feel the most sympathy for the little man because he has to measure up, so to speak." She looked directly into Thelma's quizzical eyes. "Maybe he needs some extra stimulation. A distraction. Why don't you ask him?"

"Are you mad, Wallis?" Thelma asked incredulously.

"Thelma, do you or do you not want to hold on to the Prince of Wales?"

"Of course I do!"

"Then *ask*," Wallis insisted.

"Well, I'll think about it. Wallis, no one must ever know about this conversation. *Never*. You must *swear* you will never discuss this with anyone, even Ernest." Thelma looked at her with an odd, embarrassed stare as she waited for Wallis to reply.

"*Never*," she vowed.

"Thank you," Thelma said, her voice quavering.

"How are all the renovations going at the Fort?" Wallis asked, in what seemed to be an attempt to divert the conversation.

"The work on the Fort isn't the worst of it. Freda was put in charge of overseeing things two years ago. It gives her an excuse to be in constant contact and is probably the reason it's taking so long! Besides that, it's costing a fortune and it's a terrible mess. But the Prince is determined to turn the Fort into his own retreat. Royalty always has to live with other people's taste—usually from an obsolescent age."

"I'd love to see the place," Wallis said casually.

"You haven't been there, have you? Well, I think that could be arranged."

When they were in the cloakroom waiting for their wraps, Thelma took Wallis by the arm and drew her aside.

"Remember, you swore? Not a word *ever*."

"You have my promise," Wallis said, and led the way to the lobby.

23

Fort Belvedere's mock bastions loomed into view. The center triangular tower and hexagonal turrets rose in the soft purple twilight in misty beauty—an ancient castle surrounded by forest. Wallis felt as though she were being propelled into a mythical kingdom where, unlike Smudge the Cat of her childhood, she was an invited guest of the castle's Royal resident. Ernest sat beside her in the rear seat of the Prince's car which had brought them from London. As they drew closer, they noticed a strange flag flying from the staff on the topmost tower. The car turned into the gates, the three feathers of the Prince of Wales on either side. A smooth white stone driveway led to the arched entrance. Suddenly, the Prince was coming toward them, a small, bounding figure, looking for all the world like a youth.

"Hallo!" he called. His blond hair fell over his forehead as he waved enthusiastically. He wore tweed plus fours and held a matching cap in his hand.

The chauffeur assisted Wallis out of the car. She quickly took up the attitude of a curtsy. The Prince placed a restraining hand on her shoulder.

"Please, don't," he said. He pointed up to the flag, which she could now see was an inverted pyramid of fifteen golden balls on a black background. "That's the flag of the Duchy of Cornwall," he explained. "I fly it to show that this is to be regarded as a private house, not as a Royal residence."

He led them into the domed octagonal entrance hall. The black-and-white marble floor was inlaid with a giant star as the center. Overhead, there was a handsome cut-glass chandelier and in each corner of the room stood a bright yellow leather chair. The look was spare and elegant. If this was Freda's hand showing itself, Wallis thought, she was a woman of striking good taste.

"I'll show you the house on the way to your room," he said eagerly and then kept up a spirited commentary as he led the way. They were the first to arrive. He thought she might not mind helping him set up a cocktail table similar to the one at her flat. Thelma was coming with Tamar and Benny Thaw. Lady Diana and Duff Cooper were to join them. Trotter was here, already having a Turkish bath. Ernest might like to have a go later. It was a new addition. Unfortunately it was in the basement, there had been no other place to install it.

His bedroom and study, both done in red chintz and furnished with Chippendale, were on the ground floor looking out on to the garden. The Fort was not as large as the façade led one to expect. There were really only six good bedrooms besides his own in the main building. They went up a newel staircase to the second story. Thelma was to occupy the first bedroom. It was called the Queen's Bedroom, he laughed, but there was no record of a Queen ever having slept in it. The legend went that George IV had enlarged the room for one of his favorites.

He opened the door so they could look in. There was a lovely bow window with a dressing table before it and an oversized bed with a draped canopy all in deep blush pink, as were the linens, blinds and rugs. Freda had not made the room for the comfort of a visiting male.

He took great pride in guiding them around. They were shown every room, told how he had installed central heating, had a bathroom with a shower built for each bedroom and had converted the former lily pond into a swimming pool. Tomorrow, if there was sun, they could swim. First though, they would have to see the gardens. They were his special passion. He had as many varieties of roses as had been exhibited at the last Chelsea Flower Show.

Their twin-bedded room, called the Blue Room because it was done in handsome delft-blue tuiles, was next to the "Queen's Bedroom." To Ernest's discomfort, the Prince himself lifted one of their bags onto a luggage stand. They were to rest, but not for too long. Wallis was to remember her agreement to help him with the cocktails. Then he left. On a French chiffonnier was a large silver bowl filled with roses of brilliant red and mauve hues, their strong scent exhausting the air around them. Beside the fragrant bouquet was a handwritten note on a card embossed in red with three feathers: *These blooms are my personal welcome. Edward P.* Wallis took the card and slipped it into her jewelry box. "I'm made," she said under her breath.

Since her lunch at the Ritz with Thelma, Wallis and Ernest had seen the Prince of Wales several times—at a Christmas party given by the Thaws, New Year's Day cocktails at Thelma's and, finally, at a dinner party they had hosted at Bryanston Court two weeks later. The Prince had enjoyed himself enormously and the evening had not broken up until four A.M. She had served what she told him was a typically American dinner: Maryland crab cakes, grilled lobster, fried chicken, black beans, stuffed tomatoes, for dessert a cold raspberry soufflé and, as a concession to her English guests, a savory of marrowbones. There had been ten people: themselves, the Prince, Thelma, the Thaws, the actor Raymond Massey and his wife and Lord and Lady Sackville.

Wallis could not have known her impact on her Royal guest. He had told Thelma that the Simpsons had a charming flat, that everything in it was in exquisite taste and the food, in his judgment, unrivaled in London. What he did not confide was how witty and crackling he found the conversations that Wallis led. Unlike Thelma's gatherings and, before those, Freda's, gossip and small talk were soon left behind for new ideas and opinions on current events.

For weeks beforehand Wallis had boned up on all subjects she knew to be of interest to him. She read four daily papers front to back and had made a chart of his public engagements published in the Court Circular so that she would know what organizations he backed, where he had spoken and what he had said. She had read the most recently reviewed books and had Ernest take her to the theater's new hits. She placed the Prince at one end of the dining table, with her at his right; Ernest at the opposite end with Thelma at his left. On the other side of the Prince sat the quiet, unassuming Lady Anne Sackville. She was determined not only to have the Prince's ear but, this time, to make the most of it.

That afternoon the Prince had returned to London from Manchester where, in an address in Free Trade Hall, he had warned a large audience of hardheaded businessmen that British industrial prestige was no longer what it was. In the company to which he was accustomed, this disclosure by him would have inspired a sympathetic response such as, "Oh! Sir, how boring for you. Aren't you terribly tired?" Wallis brought up the subject herself and wanted to know if he did not think important markets were being lost through the failure of British manufacturers to alter their designs in line with new trends. She quoted figures, made some astute comments, disagreed with his projections, and made a witty observation about the "George Arliss look-alike" who had introduced him.

She had this marvelous talent for keeping her attention entirely focused on whomever she was speaking to. It was, in fact, something he and all his siblings had been drilled in by their mother as part of royal demeanor and it greatly impressed him. By the time dessert was served he knew he wanted to see her again—and soon.

"What does a Royal day consist of?" she inquired with true interest.

"Do you really want to know?" he had asked, amazed.

She had laughed. "I don't ask superfluous questions," she said.

He went into such detail that they did not move into the drawing room for coffee until thirty minutes later.

"Mrs. Simpson," he said, before rising from his chair, "you are the first woman I have ever known who was interested in what I do."

* * *

The drawing room at the Fort was, like the hallway, octagonal. Yellow velvet draperies were drawn across the tall windows; the walls, which were paneled in natural pine, were hung with Canalettos; Wallis's experienced eye identified the furniture as mostly Chippendale, except for a baby grand piano and a gramophone; and opposite the fireplace on one wall were shelves filled with finely bound books.

As Wallis entered wearing a simple evening gown in the deep-plum color so complimentary to her complexion and hair, she was surprised to find the Prince dressed in a gray and red tartan kilt checked with black. A silver-mounted pouch hung about his waist and from it he took out a slim cigarette case. Ernest hurried to light his cigarette for him. Two Cairn terriers, Cora and Jaggs, bounced about at his feet. Cora snarled at Ernest, and the Prince snatched her up, spanked her rear and explained, "Cora is always this way when anybody new appears."

Thelma and the rest of the guests joined them a few minutes later, giving Wallis just enough time to check the cocktail table for her host to make sure all the necessary ingredients were on hand. This was the first time Wallis had met the Coopers. Duff was a newly elected member of the House of Commons and the author of the successful and recently published *Talleyrand*. Lady Diana was startlingly beautiful and her stage appearances in aid of charity had made her a celebrity. She had mystical blue eyes and the profile of a madonna. There was an aura of fantasy about her. She had a piquant style, a manner of speaking that reminded one of Noël Coward's sophisticated heroines. Once she had been a contender for the Prince's hand in marriage, and as the daughter of the Duke of Rutland, she had been eminently qualified. She had, however, fallen madly in love with the charming Duff Cooper and from the way she looked at him was obviously just as captivated by him as when they were first married.

From the time Thelma came in, dressed in clinging white jersey, the shape of her breasts, Wallis noted, clearly defined, she kept up a running conversation about Gloria's latest problems, the horror of divorce, and the beastliness of the English weather. Her voice was a bit strident, but otherwise she seemed in very good humor, was attentive to the Prince and appeared confident that all was well between them. Not once was the Prince questioned by her as to his activities that week. Wallis had read that he had been in Tyneside where tens of thousands of men were out of work.

"Sir, it must have been grim for you," Wallis said, when they were seated in the pine-paneled dining room; paintings of horses by George Stubbs hung on the walls; below them, two handsome Georgian sideboards displayed crested, ornate silver. The Prince had placed her on his right.

"I'm afraid my father's depression-ridden realm is a sad sight," he replied, his eyes unhappy. "Throngs of idle men everywhere, with no place to go. Men aimlessly milling in the streets or standing about outside the labor exchanges and in front of the pubs they lack the means to patronize. It makes my heart exceedingly heavy." He launched into a discussion of how he had talked to local officials about establishing social centers so that these men would have some escape from the defeatism of the streets.

"What a wonderful idea," she agreed.

The first course, oysters, which he explained came directly from his own oyster beds in the Duchy of Cornwall, was served. Excellent roast beef, salad, chocolate mousse and a cheese savory followed. "Not as inventive a menu as you might have conceived," the Prince commented to Wallis.

After coffee in the drawing room, he organized a game of Red Dog, a form of rummy unfamiliar to Wallis. "I'll coach you," he offered.

"Must we play cards?" Thelma complained. "I've never been good at them and it is dreadful *always* to lose." She and Tamar retreated to a long table in front of the main window where the pieces of an extremely difficult jigsaw puzzle had been scattered. After a short while, Thelma got up, apparently bored, and went over to the gramophone and leafed through the records. "I feel like dancing," she said.

The Prince rose from his chair energetically. "Perhaps we all do," he suggested. Thelma put on "Tea for Two," and as the lilting music filled the room, she swayed seductively from side to side, the nipples of her unbound breasts at attention beneath the soft white jersey bodice of her gown. A look of pleasure swept over the Prince's face. He moved toward her with outstretched arms. Thelma kicked off her high-heeled shoes, an act that brought her closer to her partner's height, and shimmied forward into his embrace. With her head inclined on his shoulder, her dark hair brushing his cheek, the Prince danced her out of the room and into the octagonal hallway.

The record was halfway played before the other guests got up to join in. Wallis watched through the wide drawing-room doorway as Thelma and the Prince circled and dipped. The Prince was a graceful figure; Thelma a sensuous partner. Later, he danced once in turn with each of his female guests, Wallis being the last. He was cautious that their bodies did not touch, but she was aware of the pressure of his hand on her back. As soon as they were done, he excused himself. "Stay up as late as you want. Get up as late as you wish," he said before retiring. "I go to bed early and get up early so that I can work in the garden."

Five minutes passed. Then Thelma said good night; the others lingered for an additional twenty minutes or so. Wallis was already in her room when she realized her evening purse had been left on the card table in the drawing room. As she returned from retrieving it, she passed by the closed door of the Prince's study. The soft sound of a woman's muffled laughter came from within. No need to listen for footsteps in the hallway this night. Thelma had gone to her lover's apartments for their nocturnal rendezvous.

By eight the next morning, Wallis was up and dressed in a well-tailored white blouse, navy-blue culottes, flat shoes and a bright calico bandanna folded neatly to hold back her hair from her forehead. She left Ernest sleeping soundly and made her way downstairs to partake of the morning buffet set up in the small dining room off the terrace. Thelma's door was closed but the door to the Prince's study was open and the maid at work cleaning the room.

She found him alone and just finishing his breakfast. As on the day before, he wore baggy plus fours. His hair was tousled from the morning wind and a thick sweater was tied loosely by its sleeves about his shoulders. He had already been out working in the garden.

"Ah, Mrs. Simpson. Dressed exactly right," he greeted her. "I take it you would not be averse to helping me clear away some of the tangle of undergrowth that has overwhelmed this property during its many years of disuse and neglect."

"I'd be happy to, Sir. Sounds like good exercise."

"You ever use a billhook?"

"I'm afraid I don't even know what one is!"

"It's a sort of machete. I use it to cut down the brambles which I have sworn to annihilate if it costs me my last guest. Eat your breakfast and then I'll equip you with the necessary weapon."

"I think it would be smarter if I exercise first and eat after," she said.

"Well, at least take some fruit," he advised. "Can't have women fainting on the lawns from hunger. Gives the Monarchy a bad name. I'll show you the grounds before you go to work, if you like."

She took a glass of orange juice instead and drank it while he waited. Then he led her out onto the terrace. She heard sounds behind them and glanced back toward the breakfast room. It was only Trotter, and he looked as though he was settling in for a full meal.

She stood beside the Prince looking southward where the land sloped gently toward a lovely, clear lake. "The Fort is only a short distance from Windsor," he explained. "And when I was a child my sister and my brothers and I used to paddle in rowboats on this lake. It's called Virginia Water."

Just below them, the emerald lawn ended in a semicircular stone battlement that held thirty-some eighteenth-century cannon (Belgian, he informed her), muzzles pointed in the general direction of London. To the left of the battlement was a huge swimming pool, and to the right, a hard tennis court.

"Would you like to see the flowers?" he asked.

"Of course!" The morning was cool and she shivered

slightly as they stepped off the terrace and away from the protection of the building.

"Here," he said and, untying his sweater, placed it around her shoulders.

They took a flagstone path with a wide herbaceous border, then some steps to a long, secluded walk with ancient cedars, giant rhododendrons and azaleas collaring their trunks. His pace was brisk, always a step or so ahead of her. From time to time he stopped abruptly to point out the improvements he had made, explaining that *here* he had felled yew trees in order to open the view and *there* he had unearthed three fine granite George III plaques, which were now set into the back wall of the pool area.

"It's certainly not a beautiful place, as houses in Britain go," he said, glancing back at the irregular shapes of the turrets. "But on a clear morning, from the top of that center tower, one can see London and with a spyglass make out the dome of St. Paul's Cathedral, which is twenty-five miles away. My father always speaks of the Fort as 'that queer old place,' as if it were still some deserted ruin. But for me it has unusual charm, and I've found more pleasure in fixing it up than—" He checked himself. "I shouldn't bore you with this," he finished.

"I don't find it the least bit boring," she insisted.

"Something took possession of me when I came here," he confessed. "The landscape gardener displaced the fox hunter. I like to do things with my own hands—and here I have. I planted, moved shrubs, mowed hay, built the rock garden. I've been in such a hurry to see it all come together that not only do I begrudge any lost daytime hours but I'm afraid I press all my weekend guests into pretty arduous physical labor to which most of them are unaccustomed. I even commandeer my brother Bertie, who lives nearby in the Great Park at Royal Lodge, to lend a hand when no guests are here. That doesn't set too well with my sister-in-law Elizabeth. She's of the notion that Bertie, who has never been too robust, should conserve his strength. I have three brothers, you know—Bertie, Harry and George. If I were struck dead, Bertie would one day be

King; a strong reason why Elizabeth wishes me especially good health."

"I'm sure everyone does, Sir."

"Please don't call me 'Sir' if we are alone, Wallis. I loathe and despise such constant reminders that I am not like other people." The shallow lines around his mouth deepened and his face set in a look of great sadness. He had called her by her Christian name for the first time but she made no comment.

Voices came from the direction of the terrace.

"My family name is David," he said. "In private I like to be called that. I have already taken the liberty of calling you Wallis. I trust that was not presumptuous of me." Thelma, Tamar, Benny, Trotter and Ernest were heading toward them.

"Of course not," she smiled, and then added: "David."

"Ah! here you lazy-ducks are!" he said as the group drew closer. "As you can see, right over there is a particularly bad stretch of brambles." He raised his arm and waved and a gardener with a wagon full of tools approached. "Everybody choose their weapons and follow what I do." He took a vicious-looking billhook from the wagon, strode toward the untidy enemy bushes and, stooping, began to hack away at the underbrush with fierce, practiced strokes.

"This is strictly men's work," Thelma announced. "Come on, ladies." She took Wallis and Tamar by the hand to lead them back to the house. For the first time she noted the sweater around Wallis's shoulders and stopped to remove it. "We'll leave this here for you, Sir," she said, as she hung it on the branch of a tree. "We wouldn't want you to catch a chill."

The Prince paused in his labors and watched the three women stride up the incline to join Duff and Diana Cooper on the terrace. "Your wife is a most intelligent woman," he said to Ernest.

"Thank you, Sir," Ernest replied. "I'm sure she would be flattered to hear that you think so."

24

Thelma knew her hold on the Prince's affections was beginning to slip. She blamed her decision to divorce Duke. Divorce was not recognized by the Church of England, of which the King, as Defender of the Faith, was titular head. Even as late as the reign of Edward VII, the Prince of Wales's grandfather, no divorced person, even if the innocent party, would be received at Court. That rule had been relaxed somewhat and the innocent party was now allowed to continue to enjoy the social distinction an invitation to Court bestowed. The guilty parties, however, suffered what amounted to excommunication from Court and were not allowed to attend presentations, Royal garden parties, or the Royal Enclosure at Ascot.

As Thelma and Duke prepared for their divorce, it had yet to be decided who would be marked the guilty party. In order to receive the settlement she needed to live well, Thelma might have to concede. For Duke, as an English peer, stood to suffer a more lasting ostracism than his American wife. To Thelma's consternation these delicate negotiations had continued for more than a year and her dealings with Duke had become acrimonious. There seemed to be no way back.

To keep the Prince involved, she organized more frequent weekends at the Fort, theater parties and nightclub soirees. Benny Thaw had been unexpectedly transferred to Oslo, and Thelma, much bereft by her older sister's absence, saw Wallis more frequently and included her in the activities she arranged for the Prince, who appeared to enjoy her company. Thelma gave this no further thought. Wallis was neither beautiful nor seductive. The Prince told her he found her witty, intelligent: "a clever woman." Never in Thelma's experience had she known a woman described by a man in such a fashion to be a threat.

While Thelma was beset with her struggle to hold on to the Prince's affections, Wallis fought simply to hold on. The past months had been difficult. Ernest's business affairs had gone steadily downhill. A proposed and much looked forward to trip to visit the States and Aunt Bessie was canceled and there was the possibility that if things did not improve, they would have to sell the flat. Added to these concerns, serious recurrences of Wallis's abdominal condition had put her in the hospital for several days.

Except in her letters to Aunt Bessie, she confided her difficulties to no one. Ernest spent much time away from home, traveling to Germany, Scandinavia and Greece for the firm. Wallis could not entertain on her former scale. This had its advantages, for as old friends began to fade away or be transferred, she spent more and more time with Thelma and the Prince, taking over Tamar's former position as "chaperone." The Prince was now in the habit of dropping by Bryanston Court for cocktails to discuss his views with her. Through her friends in the American Embassy, she had a great insight into her country's economic situation and how it would affect Great Britain. He found Wallis continually stimulating. And, despite the gloom that had settled a restraining hand over England, she made him feel that they were living in exciting times.

In June she celebrated her thirty-seventh birthday. The Prince presented her with a set of fox furs. Four days later he was thirty-nine. She gave him a silver matchbox engraved with his emblem. Ernest had remained "understanding." The bedroom door stayed closed between them. Yet they had a rich life together. Ernest was her confidant, her best friend, her most enthusiastic supporter and her kindest critic. She loved him now as she never had before.

For Christmas, Thelma gave her a set of three rings, one of sapphire, one of ruby and one of diamonds, and the Prince presented her with a fine Chippendale occasional table. Thelma was grateful as she believed Wallis to be a stabilizing factor in her royal relationship. The Prince was a man who did not like change, and he had burrowed into his life at the Fort. Wallis made weekends there homey yet glittering occasions. She contributed menus, gave the chef her recipes, helped arrange the flowers. The pool was a long way from the house. To avoid trooping back and forth for lunch during the warm summer days, she had instituted an outdoor barbecue, a picnic table and a cocktail bar.

Wallis frequently found an envelope in her bedroom at the Fort with fifty or a hundred pounds, accompanied by the Prince's card and a message suggesting she might want to select something for herself as he was not good at women's wardrobe styles. Wallis did not find this in the least bit demeaning. She only wished he were more generous.

All Wallis could see from her drawing-room window was a moving flare. For three days the fog had been so thick that one could not make out a hand before them. The flare was to direct the few cars foolish enough to be on the street. London was at a near standstill. Ernest was in Germany and would be gone until the end of the week. She was going mad in the apartment. Day had been turned into night. Black dust and grit seeped under sills, covering everything and returning moments after being wiped away. She was in exceptional ill humor when the telephone rang.

"Wallis," Thelma said, "I *must* see you!"

"Well, do come over if you can make your way," Wallis suggested.

"No. It's much too difficult. Meet me for lunch at the Ritz."

"I don't see how I can, Thelma. It's black as pitch and the news broadcast—"

"The Prince has offered his car."

"Then why can't you be driven here?"

"This ghastly weather has me so depressed I thought the Ritz would be a relief."

"All right. Is anything seriously wrong, Thelma?"

"Oh, no. It's just important that I see you."

The ride in the car to the hotel was bizarre. One man with a flare walked before the vehicle, another behind. The Royal crest was not visible and even had it been, the journey, a distance of a little over a mile, could not have taken less time than it did. All the driver could do was crawl at an ant's pace. Wallis could see nothing out of the window and only realized that she had arrived at the hotel when the doorman in his tall silk hat, a handkerchief across his mouth to keep from breathing the foul, acrid air, helped her out of the car. Together they inched their way up the steps to the Ritz's gold and mahogany front door.

It was only one P.M. but the lobby was ablaze with light. All the guests were milling about not knowing what to do with themselves. Everywhere you looked there were bowls of magnificent flowers. Gilt door handles gleamed, the satin curtains shimmered and the many mirrors reflected a blinding display of crystal, light and gold. The contrast with the blackness that shrouded everything outside was dramatic.

Thelma was waiting for her at a secluded corner table in the dining room. For the first time Wallis was struck by the real difference between Thelma and Gloria. Thelma had a petulance to her features. From Gloria she now recalled hearing that Thelma had been the favorite child in her family and, more than her two sisters, was accustomed to getting her way.

"Gloria needs me in New York," she said as soon as they were settled. "I'll have to be gone five or six weeks. She's going through the most shocking time with this case coming up soon and Tamar can't leave Oslo just now, so it's up to me. Mama's no good. In fact, she has Gloria in a constant state of terror. According to Mama, if Gloria loses this case the Morgans might as well end it all!"

"Oh, Thelma, the little man is going to be so lonely," Wallis said.

"Well, dear, that's exactly why I just had to speak to you. Things with Duke are finally coming together. I feel sure by the time I return the divorce will all be amicably arranged. I'll have to give up a good part of the settlement, but Duke has *almost* agreed that he will allow himself to be photographed in a hotel room with some hired lady so that I can become the injured party."

"That, at least, is good news."

"Is it? I hope so, Wallis. I hope the Prince will think so, too."

"What is it you want from the Prince, Thelma?" Wallis asked gently.

"I'm not sure. I've never thought about it really," Thelma replied, her lovely dark arched brows slanting quizzically. "Well, it's no secret how ill the King is. It can't be too long before the Prince is called to the Throne." A smile broke through the shadowy clouds in her face like the sun after a summer storm. "I would very much like to be the King's mistress," she said.

"Why on earth would you want *that*?"

"Because it's—*historic,* I guess, a kind of perverse immortality." They paused in their conversation as the waiter brought them their first course.

"Do you love the little man, Thelma?" Wallis asked when he was gone.

"I'm not sure I know what love is. Do you, Wallis?"

"Yes. I love Ernest. I wouldn't want to lose him."

"I don't want to lose the Prince either. That's why I need your help." She shuffled her chair forward and leaned in close. "With me away he will be lonely, as you say. So what will he do? I'll tell you. He'll revert to the familiar—which is that wretched Freda. She keeps coming up with new projects for the Fort and he still sees her every afternoon when he is in London. I cannot imagine what the tie is. Sometimes I think they had a child together, or lost a child. But that's madness. You see—I shouldn't tell you this—but—well—just take my word for it—I'm positive he could *never* make a woman pregnant. Which is just fine with me, but does present problems for him as Heir to the Throne."

Thelma was toying with her food, her mind elsewhere. Wallis did not know how to interpret what she had just been told and decided to put it aside for the time being. "How can I help you, Thelma?" she asked.

Thelma gazed across the table at her. "Just by keeping him well occupied and cheerful and from turning to Freda for consolation. Perhaps you could organize a few weekends at the Fort and maybe cocktails or dinner once or twice at your flat. He likes your company so much. You could have Fruity Metcalfe and his wife, Lady Alexandra. The Prince is very fond of them. And Prince George and his current friend, Princess Marina. And there's Trotter and the new equerry, Major Aird, who's a bachelor, and, of course, Lady Diana and Duff Cooper."

"I'll do what I can, Thelma," Wallis promised. "But, of course, the Prince will have the last word."

"Not if I know you, Wallis," Thelma laughed. "Just keep him out of mischief." She breathed a deep sigh. "Well, I feel a lot better now. Can I bring you anything back from the States? Or call anyone?"

"Stockings from Kleins on the first question. Beige colors, please. Size eight and a half. Mary Kirk Raffray in New York on the second. You met her last year when she was visiting with me. She's also going through an unpleasant divorce. I'll call you with her number."

The weekend after Thelma left, Wallis and Ernest returned to the Fort. She brought along her own recipes and put the Coopers in the pink-sheeted, pink-blinded Queen's Bedroom. At dinner she asked their host to play the bagpipes for them, an instrument Thelma hated. He donned his Scottish cap and evening kilt and, with his stalwart piper behind him, marched around the table as they played and sang "Over the Sea to Skye." Wallis encouraged him on and for an encore he sang a Scottish song of his own composition.

Ernest had business abroad the next week, and Wallis twice arranged cocktails at the apartment for the Prince with Noel Coward and some other theater friends and members of the American Embassy. After the second such gathering, Blane came running into Wallis's room. "Madam, the Prince of Wales wishes to speak to you on the telephone." It was the first time he had ever called in person. He thanked her for a marvelous time.

By now Wallis had taken an active interest in the Fort. Besides suggesting menu additions, she rearranged the furniture and introduced various small innovations including a folding tea stand which allowed the Prince to have tea wherever he wished. She made friends with Cora and Jaggs, taking them for walks when the Prince was gardening or playing golf.

One afternoon he turned up at Bryanston Court unexpectedly with a Cairn puppy under his arm. "This," he said, "is Slipper. He is yours."

It rained nonstop the first weekend in April. Plans were put aside to go to the Fort. Saturday morning the Prince rang.

"Could you have dinner with me here at York House tonight?" he asked.

"I'm not sure if Ernest is free," she replied. "He has a client arriving from Germany."

"Well, if he could spare you, I can send the car round to fetch you about eight."

Ernest was standing in the hallway as she prepared to leave. "So this is it," he said.

"What on earth do you mean?"

"You are dining with the Prince of Wales without me at York House, St. James's Palace."

"You are busy with Herr Berringer."

"True, true."

"The Prince could not have possibly known that."

"Did he say who else would be there?"

"No. Nor did I inquire. You don't request a guest list from the Prince of Wales."

"There will be no one else," Ernest said flatly.

"Don't be ridiculous!"

He took her loosely by the shoulders and gazed steadily into her eyes. "It has been heading this way and was to be expected," he said. "But, Wallis, I want you to be very sure of what you are doing. I will be here for you if you need me. All right?"

"You are making far too much of this, Ernest. Look, cancel your dinner with Herr Berringer and come with me. I'm sure the Prince will be pleased."

"I can't. Berringer is an important client."

She kissed him on the cheek. "Then win him over tonight," she said.

He watched her as she walked to the door. She looked just right, he thought. Wine colors were most flattering to her and the dress was discreet and chic at the same time, the soft folds of the crushed velvet perfectly setting off her slim figure.

"The same to you, Wallis," he said, as Blane held the door open for her. "Win him over."

She laughed and in that instant both of them understood the stakes of the game.

Ladbrook, the Prince's chauffeur, brought her to the Palace's entrance on to the beautiful Tudor Friary Court. As the car drove over the stones laid there during the reign of Henry VIII, Wallis glanced out the rear window to the historic Clock Tower with Henry's and Anne Boleyn's initials carved boldly upon it. The King had been besotted with love when he built St. James's for her.

Liveried servants rushed to help Wallis out of the car and to guide her through what the Prince had once told her was no home, just "a rambling, antiquated structure. Good only for romantic intrigue." One could never have found one's way alone. Passages led to unexpected steps, which in turn took one through unsymmetrical hallways and rooms. She followed a footman up a stone stairway to the first floor. How unlike life at the Fort this was! No wonder he had such a driving need to make the Fort his private domicile.

The Prince stood, dressed in an evening suit, at the top of the stairs to greet her. "That will be fine, Sanderson," he said to the man. "I will show Mrs. Simpson the way from here." He took Wallis by the arm and they turned the corner into a reception area with access to another staircase. Suddenly the decor had taken on an entirely different mode: Persian carpets, handsome vitrines filled with rare porcelain, massive cachepots with flowering plants. *Freda's hand again.*

The drawing room, large and well-shaped, was dominated by two walls covered with maps of the world with the British Empire colored red. An elegant Empire desk was placed between the floor-to-ceiling windows on a third wall. Comfortable red and gold quilted-chintz sofas faced each other in front of the marble fireplace, over which hung a portrait of Queen Mary in a white evening gown wearing the Order of the Garter, a magnificent diamond tiara on her head and a fabulous diamond necklace around her neck. A cocktail table was set up to one side.

They were alone.

"I have taken the liberty of ordering dinner here, but if you prefer we can go out. I've also alerted the Hotel Splendide. The food there is good and they have a Viennese orchestra." He stood looking sheepishly at her. A perfect fire burned in the hearth behind him. His mother, the Queen, glared down over his shoulder.

She stood paralyzed, the unreality of the moment seeming to trap her. "You're an awfully sly fellow," she said, forcing her voice to sound perfectly natural. She gave him a warm smile. "We'll eat here," she agreed.

He crossed to her. His hand brushed her cheek. It was the first time there had ever been any real intimacy between them. "Please be nice to me, Wallis," he said, with not the slightest whimsy or self-consciousness in his voice.

Out of the tail of her eye she could see an opened door on one side of the room and through it, in dim lamplight, observed the edge of a bed. She moved to the cocktail table. "Shall I make us a drink?" she asked.

He talked all the while she prepared the cocktails, never taking his eyes off her.

"Forgive me if I have done this clumsily," he said. "Royal persons live in strange isolation from the rest of the world. However much they wish to encourage intimacy with another person, a wall of deference exists between them and most people. But I have felt with you, Wallis, a familiarity I have seldom experienced before. In childhood there was a natural camaraderie with my sister Mary and my brothers Bertie and Harry. I can be myself with my youngest brother Georgie. But seldom with a woman, even those I greatly respect or desire." She handed him his drink and he took the opportunity to hold her hand. "And even those to whom I make love."

"Has no woman ever made love to *you*?" she asked.

The question took him aback. "I'll answer you frankly, Wallis," he said after a moment. "Women tend to believe a Prince requires service, not love. I have been well serviced by many very good ladies. I don't think it is self-pitying of me to say, I doubt if ever I have been loved." The old look of melancholy crossed his face and settled in his thoughtful blue eyes.

"Everything in life has a price," she said softly.

"And yours?" he asked.

"That I have the opportunity to love the man, not the Prince." She stared at him with eyes blurred with emotion. "David," she whispered. "What a beautiful *eanum* name."

"Eanum?" he smiled quizzically.

"It was a special word that my mother made up. She created stories for me as a child and sometimes they had make-believe language in them. *Eanum* was a secret word for what can be felt and not said." She could feel his hand ever so lightly smoothing her hair. *"Eanum,"* she repeated.

He traced her lips with his fingers and took the cocktail from her hand and put it down on a table along with his. When he turned back, Wallis stood in the doorway to the bedroom. For a bewildered moment, he was not sure of what he should do. He had come to this stage of their relationship believing he was in control of what might happen, how far it was to go. And now he was frankly scared. There he stood, midway between the icy disapproving glance of his mother and the *eanum* warmth of Wallis's unique violet eyes.

She was poised erect, a proud woman of good breeding. Her head was held high and her face was raised so that the ceiling light fell across it and cast the rest of her figure in shadow. The deep red tones of her dress spiraled out like a spreading flame. He felt drawn to her, unable to break their magnetic connection. He walked over to her and took her hand and led her into the bedroom, closing the door after them. He sat down on the edge of the bed. She stood there, looking down at him. He slipped off his jacket and undid his belt.

Wallis had not moved. Not one small flicker. And her eyes never left his face even as her hands moved behind her making small, hidden motions as she undid the buttons at the back of her gown. The dress was not allowed to slide all the way down. For a moment she held it tightly around her narrow waist, a rich, burgundy pillow for her bare torso. Her skin was the color of cream bisque, her nipples were magenta points. She was almost flat-chested and the smoothness of her skin made the top part of her body look like that of a young boy. Quite deliberately, she swayed from side to side to ease the dress down. The flames fell to her ankles, binding her there. She wore delicate flesh-colored silk panties. These she rolled down as far as she could without bending. And still her eyes had not left his face.

He saw the narrow purple scar that cut across the soft curve of her stomach and it brought tears to his eyes.

"Oh, my poor *eanum,*" he cried and to Wallis's amazement, he slid off the bed and onto his knees before her and kissed the length of the scar and buried his face in the dark silk of her pubic hair.

Wallis had not known what would happen when she entered the bedroom, nor what had impelled her to act as she had. Whatever she had done had been instinctive. Even at the height of her excitement she experienced an uncomfortable fear that things had gone crazily askew. The Prince was on his knees to her, sublimating himself to her. In that moment when he had removed his leather belt, she had experienced a flash of déjà vu and the specter of Win had seemed to be in the room with them. But to the contrary, he was set on pleasuring her. When she had the breath finally restored to her and could glance down, she saw that he had apparently pleasured himself as well.

She crumpled to the floor beside him and he cradled her in his arms and they both were silent for a while. Then he got up and went into the bathroom. Wallis climbed into the canopied bed and drew the fine linen sheet with his crest on it up to her chin. Her head was spinning and she knew she must clear it. He returned wearing a gray paisley silk dressing gown. Over his arm he carried a pale lavender silk negligee which he laid across the foot of the bed. "This is for you," he said. He removed his robe and slipped into the bed beside her so deftly that she saw only a tan streak of bare flesh and tight muscular thigh.

He talked almost nonstop as they lay, their bodies touching, her head on his shoulder, telling her what he could of his past with all its terrors, follies, despairs and small triumphs. He talked about his childhood and the nanny who had sexually abused him when he was only two and three and who would pinch him before he was taken to see his mother at tea and how it took ages for her to realize why he howled so when he was brought to her.

His mother was cold to all her children. "It sounds mawkish, I'm sure. But I wanted so for her to let me love her. She never would. I don't recall that she ever kissed me.

"My father has never approved of me or my friends," he said in a matter-of-fact voice. "He is a difficult parent but a good King and I suppose that is what, in the end, truly counts."

There were sounds in the drawing room. "That would be our dinner," he explained. "When it is quiet again, we'll go in. No one will bother us. I've asked to be left alone."

A table for two had been set up with a heating tray on a sideboard. There was lobster, roast duck and a steamed bread pudding and he ate ravenously. "My brother Georgie has a suite on the second story. I moved him here a few years ago because he was in dreadful shape and addicted to drugs. I never thought we'd bring him round again. For three years before I met Thelma, I was doctor, jailer and detective combined. We tried every cure. During the critical stages I would sit doing needlework, which I learned to do from my mother, in his sickroom as I watched over him. It was a terrible and terrifying thing to happen to anyone and far worse to one's brother. He slipped back into taking drugs just last year. Mama refuses to discuss the situation. Papa barely acknowledges it existed. Thank God for Princess Marina. It looks as though she will marry him and that should take a bit of trouble off my hands. He's been drug-free since he met her. Freda has been a great help through all this. It was she who introduced Marina, who is a friend of hers, to Georgie."

"Your family seems like many others," she said, "holding together their own scandals."

"And are there skeletons in the Montague-Warfield attics?"

"Numerous ones." She did not know what possessed her, but she told him about Alice, Teackle and Sol. He leaned across the table and took her hand. The sharing of this secret in her life had endeared her to him.

"Royal households are not without similar situations," he said, his look soft. "One never knows whether a current lover might not be one's unknown relation." They laughed. "You'll stay the night, Wallis?" he asked, coming around and placing his hand gently on her shoulder.

"I'll stay," she said.

They listened to music on his gramophone—Noël Coward's "Room with a View," Irving Berlin's "Always." He was a romantic, he confessed. He did not like opera and never had the patience for long classical pieces. They went back into the bedroom. This time he was more brazen in his exposure of himself. His testicles, Wallis noted, seemed trapped within his body. This must have given him a great deal of sexual difficulty through the years and was probably responsible for the lack of hair on his face and chest. An erection could not be easy. She recalled what Thelma had told her and this time, when they made love again, Wallis returned the favor he had given her.

The next few weeks were filled with excitement for Wallis. Thelma was still abroad; her royal affair continued, and she now was expected to be at the Fort every weekend. Whether Thelma's return would alter things remained to be seen. At present her main concern was finding the money for the additional wardrobe required for her Fort Belvedere weekends and to keep Ernest in good humor.

"I think I'm the only poor one he has ever had," she

wrote Aunt Bessie, confessing that she and the Prince were now lovers. "Am dying to be asked for Ascot week even if I have to steal to pay for an appropriate new outfit, and am hopeful he will take me on the Continent with him in August." Aunt Bessie reciprocated with a check and a mild warning to her niece not to lose Ernest in her pursuit of a royal adventure.

Ernest did not seem to mind that his wife and the Prince dined together alone at St. James's twice a week, and he accompanied her to the Fort every weekend. "God knows what Aunt Bessie would make of that!" she wrote Mary Kirk in a confessional mood.

Wallis was trying to keep a cool head. She *believed* David was in love with her. She *knew* he found her sexually satisfying. Aunt Bessie's former discussions on what constituted a courtesan had remained with her all these years. At the same time, she was reminded of Thelma's statement about the historic value of being a King's mistress. Immortality did not so much intrigue Wallis as how her royal affair might affect her mortal life. Two words repeated themselves in her mind: *money* and *power.* The problem was a third word, one that beat a strident note—*love.* For try as she had to avoid it, she had found David to possess much *eanum.*

"We don't want to be disturbed for any reason," Wallis told Blane when she showed Thelma into the drawing room the Monday after she had returned from the States. "Please answer the phone." The door was closed. The two women were alone.

"I had to see you, Wallis. I don't know what has happened between the Prince and myself but something is *drastically* wrong."

"Now calm yourself, Thelma," Wallis said compassionately, "and tell me all about it."

"Well, as you know I got back last Friday. Of all things, Prince Aly Khan was on the ship, too. I could hardly help that. After all, there were two thousand other passengers as well! I told the Prince of Wales and you know what he said—*nothing*—just dead silence." Thelma's crimson mouth set in a petulant frown.

"Start at the beginning, Thelma," Wallis prodded.

"Aly is *impossible*. Every time I said *no,* more baskets of red roses arrived. I had no idea he would be in New York when I was, and until the ship sailed for Southampton I didn't even *guess* he was aboard. When we were approaching England I told him my car was meeting me. He asked me for a lift. Naturally, I said *yes*. How could I refuse?

"Saturday morning I went down to the Fort," she continued. "It was just a small, intimate group, darling, that's why you weren't included," she apologized, unable to know that Wallis and the Prince had planned it that way.

"We were in the Prince's study—the two of us—when suddenly he said to me, 'I hear Aly Khan has been very attentive to you.' I nearly fell over. I don't know how the news got to him so fast. It really did catch me off guard, because I was planning to tell him myself and make a joke of it. The fact is, I know only too well what kind of reputation Aly has and that he could be off and wooing someone else in a matter of *minutes,* so when I dropped him off at his hotel, I told him I absolutely would not go to bed with him. He took it almost *too* philosophically for my ego.

"Anyway," she continued, crossing her shapely legs, "I rather flippantly replied to the Prince of Wales, 'Are you jealous, darling?' He didn't answer and was in a black mood the entire weekend, formally cordial and personally distant. It was ghastly, and I was terribly grateful no one important was there—only Trotter and Jack Aird and Fruity and Alexandra. I mean, Wallis, he did not make even the most *casual* overture. Now, I can't believe this was because of my small flirtation with Aly. He could see well enough that it wasn't serious. Aly's already in Paris! No, I'm sure there is another woman. Probably the tenacious Freda again. I was certain you would know if there was someone else."

Wallis looked across the coffee table at Thelma and, with a small reassuring smile, replied, "Oh, Thelma, you know the little man loves you very much. The little man was just lost without you."

Thelma breathed a sigh of relief. "If you say so, it must be true. Look, Wallis, he *has* asked me to come to the Fort next weekend. It's Easter, you know? Would you and Ernest care to come down? It might help."

"Well, I'm not sure of Ernest's plans," Wallis responded slowly.

There was a knock on the door and Blane, somewhat flustered, poked her head in. "You're wanted on the telephone, madam," she said to Wallis.

"I told you that I did not want to be disturbed, Blane," Wallis retorted irritably.

"But, madam," she said hesitantly, half in a whisper, "it's his Royal Highness."

Wallis got to her feet, a perplexed look on her face. "Excuse me, Thelma," she said, "I'll be right back." She followed Blane into the hallway where there was an extension, leaving the door open so that she was in full view of Thelma. "Yes, Sir, I am very well," she said into the telephone.

"Wallis, I must speak with you," he said.

"Thelma is here," she replied, noting, as she spoke her name, that Thelma had risen from her chair, assuming the call must really be for her.

"Then I will call later," he said. "But you should know that Thelma has insisted on coming here this weekend and I would like you and Ernest to be here, too."

"I think that could be arranged, Sir. I will have to speak to Ernest, if you can wait for an answer," she said. She rang off and returned to the sitting room. "He called to invite us to join you for Easter," she informed Thelma. "I thought you would want to talk to him at a more private time."

"Yes, that does seem the wise thing," Thelma agreed.

An hour later the Prince called Wallis back. "I know I will be putting you in an awkward position, Wallis, but Thelma is more knowing than she appears. She will understand when she sees the two of us together, straightaway, and it is better that she leave of her own accord. Will that be too terrible for you?"

"No, of course not," she replied. He had not mentioned Aly Khan or even that he suspected Thelma of having a flirtation. "She thinks you are jealous of Aly Khan," she ventured.

"One can only be jealous when feeling exists," he responded, and then added in a tender voice, "Good-bye, my *Eanum.* Until Friday."

At dinner at the Fort that evening, Thelma could not help but notice how intimate Wallis was with the Prince and that they had their private little jokes. At one point, he picked up a leaf of his salad with his fingers. Wallis playfully slapped his hand. Thelma, aghast at such a lapse of decorum, caught Wallis's eye and shook her head. Wallis, she thought, should know that, no matter how friendly the Prince appeared, such familiarity was not permitted for his image of himself was always framed by the Royal three feathers.

Wallis smiled blandly at her from her position to the Prince's right. Then, suddenly, it was clear to Thelma. Wallis, of all people! She went directly to her room after dinner with the excuse that she was not feeling well. The following morning she left while everyone else was on the tennis court.

A light tap on her door awakened Wallis on Easter morning. Ernest no longer shared a room with her when they were at the Fort. She leisurely stretched and glanced at the bedside clock. It was only seven A.M. She rose sleepily from the bed and, putting her morning robe on, went to the door. No one in the corridor but a small gift-wrapped box stood on the threshold and she took it back to bed with her. Inside was a hinged cardboard Victorian Easter egg with lace trim and a painted scene of four children in a rowboat on Virginia Water, obviously a memento from the Prince's childhood. Wallis opened the egg.

The radiant sparkle of finely faceted diamonds met her glance. Attached to a small square of burgundy velvet was a magnificent brooch in the shape of the three plumes and the crown of the Prince of Wales, pavé set with circular and baguette-cut stones. It was the most expensive piece of jewelry Wallis had ever owned, but it was not the extravagant cost of the gift that brought tears of great delight to her eyes. She interpreted the brooch as being a pledge of his Royal protection. She thought about the story she had read as a girl of the ring Elizabeth had given Essex. Under the velvet there was a note:

God bless Wallis
With eanum love
David—Easter, 1934.

She wore the diamond clip to Ascot on a handsome new navy-blue ensemble. To her disappointment, the day she visited the Royal Enclosure, the King and Queen did not attend.

The Queen was not one for idle gossip. Still, her oldest son's interest in Wallis could not be ignored. The idea of an American woman who did not understand the delicacies of being a Royal mistress having a hold on David was worrisome. She had not feared Freda Dudley Ward's influence; for, like the legion of like women through the years of the English Monarchy, she had been content to stay out of the public eye and could be expected to encourage the Heir to the Throne to do his duty and marry a suitable wife. But here was this Mrs. Simpson, with no sense of propriety or the order of things, being photographed at Ascot and at various nightclubs in London with the Prince of Wales, wearing this indiscreet gift he had obviously given her.

Still, as long as Freda Dudley Ward remained a presence in his life, there was no reason to think he might do anything as untoward as making Mrs. Simpson his established and only mistress. The Queen and Wallis saw eye to eye on at least one issue: as long as Freda was in the picture, she—Wallis—would never be entirely secure.

One day in June, only a month after Ascot, Freda placed a call to St. James's Palace at five P.M. to speak to the Prince of Wales as she had done every day for ten years when he was in residence and they were not together.

"I have something so terrible to say, I don't know how to say it," the telephonist on the Palace switchboard answered in tones of great distress.

"What can it be? You *must* tell me," Freda pressed.

"I have orders not to put you through."

"Well, I shall call tomorrow then."

"Not then, either. Oh! Mrs. Dudley Ward, I am *so, so, so!* sorry! My orders are *never* again."

PART FOUR

ROYAL MISTRESS

1934–1936

25

Wallis lay back on her chaise and studied the Prince—dressed in what she called his Robinson Crusoe clothes: shorts and sandals, torso bared—as he stood looking out to sea from the terrace of their lovely Spanish-styled villa in the secluded outskirts of Biarritz. He had opened the gates for her to a new and glittering world. Nothing in her life had ever excited her as much as being within the radius of his powerful orbit. His slightest wish seemed always to be translated into the most impressive kind of reality. Trains were held, yachts materialized, the best suites in the finest hotels were flung open, aeroplanes stood waiting and all this was brought to pass without apparent effort—the calm assumption that this was the natural order of things, that nothing could ever go awry. It was incredible to her, that she, Wallis Warfield, who had fought so hard throughout her life for just the smallest acceptance, could be part of this enchanted world.

"David," she said, sitting up. He turned instantly. "Let's have dinner alone tonight. Maybe at some small bistro on the waterfront."

They were by themselves at this moment, having just finished breakfast. Both of them knew, however, that in a short time they would once again be surrounded by the other members of the Royal party, as they had been for the past three weeks. "That's a marvelous idea," he responded. "Of course we shall!"

As Wallis had hoped, she had joined him on his trip to Biarritz, where he had rented a villa for the month of August. Although Ernest had been invited to accompany the Royal party on this holiday, he had decided instead to go to New York to see his daughter and to transact some business for his father's firm. Aunt Bessie had taken his place as "chaperone," and from the moment she had met the Prince, they had gotten on famously. The other guests included the Prince's equerries Jack Aird and "G" Trotter, his Assistant Private Secretary, Hugh Lloyd Thomas, and an old school friend from his days at the Royal Naval Schools at Osborne and Dartmouth, Lieutenant-Commander Colin Buist and his wife, the ebullient Gladys.

Wallis was aware that nothing she could do would ever endear her to them. They were all in Freda Dudley Ward's camp and had not accepted Thelma either. Wallis knew that they talked about her behind her back. She was an American, a rank outsider whom they did not understand or trust. Freda could be expected to keep her place; not Thelma or herself. *Pax Britannica* was their tribal chant. Wallis heard a different refrain.

She considered herself to be daring and ambitious. Perhaps she was a social climber, as were so many of the Americans she knew, a fact which had been true since Victoria's day. Like those of her compatriots, her dreams may well have been an invention of a foolish romantic mind. Ernest had often quoted the expatriate Henry James's list of flaws possessed by fellow Americans: "No sovereign, no court, no personal loyalty, no country gentlemen, no palaces, nor manors, nor old country houses, no Oxford, nor Eton, nor Harrow, no literature, no sporting class—no Epsom nor Ascot." She agreed in part with James although she did not think of herself, because of these lapses in her culture, as being inferior to any English person including the members of the Royal Family. If this made her vulgar in the eyes of English society and the courtiers, or not to be trusted by them, then so be it. She saw right through their pretensions.

She had not yet met an upper-class British subject who

would not have given his soul to the devil to be accepted in Royal circles. And the courtiers' world revolved around the particular Royal person they served. That person was their sun and where they stood in Court circles was entirely dependent upon their precedence in his or her life—who had the Royal ear and on whom the Royalty relied the most. In this tight little social island, the Prince of Wales's circle was the golden ring.

Even David's best intentions could not ward off this pack of Royal wolves. He did not fully understand his position in their lives, how they fed off him, nourishing their arrogant egos. He was as much the open sesame to their social prestige as he was to hers. The difference was that they were so blinded by their vanity that they could not see the truth. To get into their good graces would have been harder than pulling a rope through a needle's eye and she wasn't foolish enough to try.

She smiled with satisfaction as she viewed herself in the mirror as she dressed for their private dinner. Elephants would have to roost in trees before the courtiers could outwit her. She had spent a lifetime toughening herself to the bruising glances and open attacks of those who thought they were her superiors.

Fear was on her side. They feared her because she did not, and would not, conform. Freda would never have dined alone with the Prince in a bistro. She would not have contradicted him in public if he was wrong or voiced her opinion when it had not been petitioned. She would have listened to the contrived advice and comments and acted accordingly. Through Freda they once had an extra input into the Prince's confidence. Wallis looked after herself, and so they treated her with chilled elegance. In battle it pays to know more about the enemy than he knows about you. Wallis had been immune to their form of ammunition since Mrs. Kirk had used it against her twenty years earlier.

"They've kept the place half empty on purpose," she said with annoyance when she and the Prince entered Le Bistrot. "Jack Aird's doing, I'm sure," she grumbled.

Le Bistrot was not the unpretentious small restaurant one would choose for a romantic evening. It was a colorful, glamorous establishment that attracted many of Biarritz's visiting celebrities. Its presence on the busy waterfront was barely noticeable: a small door and name plaque were the only clues. Inside, along the far wall, the brilliantly candlelit premises opened up to the sea. The night was warm and almost still and most of the diners were seated beneath the stars on the gaily lanterned outside patio.

Wallis and the Prince were led past a lineup of bowing waiters dressed in native Basque costume to a table in the dining room encircled by a large number of fully set unoccupied tables, glasses and silverware gleaming on impeccable shell-pink linen. Perhaps it was Aird's plan that their conversation not be overheard, but once seated she and the Prince would be visible to everyone in the restaurant and their dinner would be anything but private. Wallis stopped suddenly. "Sir," she said as a command. The Prince turned to her. "May I suggest we dine alfresco?"

The Prince cast a glance around the room and saw instantly why she had proposed this. "Yes, of course," he agreed. "On such a perfect night, it would be a crime to remain inside."

They stood a short distance apart waiting for the stout, mustachioed proprietor to sort out the problem they had just created for him. Obviously, Aird had arranged to pay for the empty tables. Therefore, the man had seated his guests on the patio and no table appeared available. Since he could not possibly request his other customers to move inside, he had to make room for His Royal Highness among them. Finally, it was decided to take out a large center service buffet, replete with a tank of lobsters and an enormous arrangement of shellfish and flowers, to accommodate another table. There was frantic activity as waiters and busboys removed it. Diners ducked their heads, hoping not to be in the way if a live lobster should somehow be cast their way.

By the time the proprietor was ready to seat them, everyone in the restaurant was aware of their presence. It should have distressed the Prince: all this commotion, the knowledge that the other diners would be sure to talk about the dark-haired American woman and the Prince of Wales. But as he watched Wallis being seated, his heart missed a beat. He was in love as he had never been before, and whatever Wallis did or suggested they do seemed right and perfect to him. Whereas he had always cared what people thought before, now he wanted only to please Wallis.

He was not sure when his feelings for her had passed from attraction to real love—sometime during the last few days, he thought, perhaps the afternoon they had gone swimming off a boat. As he sat down across from her now he could see her once again as she rose out of the deep sea water, her dark head with its sleeked-back hair breaking the surface, her bare wet shoulders gleaming beneath the sun, her hands grasping the side of the boat as she lifted herself out of the water to him, radiant and laughing.

She was laughing and radiant this very moment, pleased that she had had her way.

Or had he crossed the line only this morning, which had seemed brighter, purer, cheerier than any morning in his memory? For Wallis had shared his bed the entire night and he had slept a kind of safe, comforting sleep such as he had never known. The other women in his life had all left discreetly and shortly after the lovemaking ended. He wondered now if it was an unwritten law: the Prince of Wales is always to wake up by himself in a room void of any feminine traces. Or perhaps, Aird and his long queue of predecessors had advised the ladies in his past of special rules where their Prince was involved. If so, Wallis had been unreachable—although not to him.

He could even now, as he brushed her hand with his, recall with full sensation the flower scent of her skin as he had awakened, the feeling of warm security as they clung together spoon fashion, "in the buff," as she called it.

"People are shameless," she said. "You would think that once having taken a good look at you, they would stop staring."

"You get used to it," he told her.

"Why should you have to?"

"It comes with the job," he explained.

"Poor David," she murmured. "It's not fair."

Wallis had come to some conclusions about her attraction to the Prince. In part, she had decided it was her American independence of spirit, her directness, her ability to make him laugh and have fun, her breezy and honest curiosity about him and everything concerning him. She had also recognized his tremendous sense of aloneness and had somehow found a way—and even she was not sure exactly what she had done—to penetrate it.

Later they walked barefoot along the palm-shadowed beach, the limousine following a discreet distance behind them. "I don't think I can bear for this to end," he said.

Without realizing it he had played directly into her hands. The blond and vivacious Posy Guinness, a member of the famous brewing family, was also vacationing in Biarritz on Lord Moyne's yacht, *Rosaura*. Lord Moyne, Posy had told Wallis just that day, would be pleased if the Prince of Wales and his party joined them for the remainder of their cruise. Wallis stoked up her courage and now mentioned it to him. "We could spend ten days traveling down the coast of Spain and Portugal and then some time in Cannes with my good friends the Rogerses before continuing on to Italy."

"That's a wonderful idea!" he agreed.

They paused. Nearby, the night tide slapped against the dark sand. He took her in his arms and kissed her with the passion of a familiar lover. "Wallis, I am in love with you," he confessed when they had drawn apart. "You have to understand, real love is a new experience for me. The emotion I feel for you is something I cannot define. I don't know how to say this without sounding ridiculously maudlin, but I am quite sure no woman has ever truly loved me. Not even my mother. Everyone has seen a symbol where I feel you have found the man. Your lips tell me this—your touch confirms it."

They kissed again, clinging long. Arms entwined about each other's waists, they walked up to the road where the car was waiting. They drove in stirring silence back to the villa. As they were about to enter, he took a narrow velvet case from his inside pocket and slipped it into her hand.

"Open this later," he said, adding softly: "Come to me in an hour."

"No, David, this time you come to me," she replied.

He smiled and nodded his head.

Aunt Bessie was sitting by herself in the lounge working

on some embroidery when Wallis entered. In her hand was the velvet case still unopened. Her aunt glanced up. "Another present, Wallis? Soon you'll be receiving the Crown Jewels!"

Wallis snapped open the box. It contained a superb diamond and emerald bracelet. A card carried the message—*With eanum love, David.*

"Isn't all this very dangerous for you?" her aunt asked. "If you go any deeper, you're going to be dissatisfied with everything you've ever known. What will you do if you lose *both* the men in your life?"

"I know what I'm doing," Wallis said testily.

"Do you, Wallis? I wonder. Wiser people than you would have their heads turned by such lordly admiration. Look at that bracelet. It's worth more than Ernest can make in a year."

"Don't be an old hypocrite, Aunt Bessie. You thought it was perfectly grand that Peggy Hopkins Joyce received jewels from her rich lovers."

"She wasn't married at the time and they weren't the Prince of Wales. I can't crawl into your head to learn what you are really thinking, Wallis. But I believe I know you as well as anyone does. *Must have—will get.* This time I'm not so sure you aren't courting disaster. Suppose Ernest leaves you?"

"He won't."

"What makes you so certain?"

"I am, that's all."

"And the Prince, who I have to admit is a charming fellow and certainly generous—suppose when you get back to London he has a change of heart?"

Wallis went over to her aunt's chair and sat on the armrest. "All my life I have had this fantasy—that one day I could look down on everyone in my past. Oh, not you, darling, or Ernest either. He has been good to me and I promise I won't hurt him. But I *must* have this time with David."

"Do you love him, Wallis?"

"I am very *fond* of him."

"Could you let him go if you had to?"

"Yes, but not now."

"Wallis in Wonderland," her aunt smiled.

"I'm afraid I've gone further than that. I've traveled right through the Looking Glass." She got up and started out of the room. When she reached the door she glanced back. "We're going on a cruise in a few days. We'll be gone about three weeks," she announced.

"Oh?"

"I was thinking that you might prefer spending some time in Rome or Venice. You do get a bit peckish on small boats."

"I see."

"What does that mean?"

"That you don't want an interfering old lady to spoil your good time."

"That's not exactly it."

"Of course it is! But remember, that pack he travels with are set to devour you, so you better be certain that you can defend yourself."

"Don't worry about me, Aunt Bessie."

"Wallis," her aunt laughed, "I have been doing it for thirty-seven years and it's rather comforting. Makes me feel less alone." She picked up her needlework and folded it neatly. "Rome and Venice. Yes, that does sound like an interesting itinerary."

"Good night, Aunt Bessie," Wallis said gently.

"Good night, darling. And remember, keep your wits sharpened and always be prepared."

A full gale was blowing when the Royal party went on board the *Rosaura,* assuming that the boat, a converted Channel steamer fitted with great luxury, would not be put to sea until the weather had calmed. Her owner and captain, Lord Moyne, a beak-nosed Irishman with thinning gray hair and a bombastic personality, had a pet monkey who had the run of the boat and chattered endlessly. "The *Rosaura* can ride out any Atlantic storm," Lord Moyne boasted to the Prince after he had welcomed him on board and then ordered his crew to get the vessel under way.

Before the *Rosaura* cleared the harbor, it was struck by the full fury of the winds which shrieked through the rigging. The yacht buried her bows deeper and deeper with each pitch. Wallis staggered to her cabin and threw herself down on the bed. The storm's violence increased and a short time later a steward looked in on her. "His Royal Highness wanted me to be sure you were not ill," he said.

"I'm all right," Wallis insisted. "And the Prince?"

"A bit green, I fear," he confessed.

"How soon will it be before we make it back to port?" she inquired hopefully.

"I've yet to see the storm that would keep Lord Moyne in port," the steward replied, "and I've never seen him in finer fettle. He's just ordered caviar, grouse and a bottle of champagne for Mr. Aird and himself. Everyone else seems to have gone to their cabins."

Finally, the Prince summoned his last reserve of strength to go up on the bridge himself to convince Lord Moyne they must head the yacht into the near port of Corunna. Faced with a Royal command, Lord Moyne finally gave in.

By the next morning the sea was calm and the *Rosaura* once again headed down the coast of Spain. What followed was a magical idyll. Lord Moyne, as though to compensate for the dismal beginnings of the cruise, charted a course that kept his boat out of the way of curious eyes. Each day he would put in to a new and enchanting bay or inlet. The speedboat was lowered and the group was off for glorious hours of sunbathing, swimming and exploring rarely visited shores. Wallis and the Prince were seldom apart.

No one seemed aware of the bitter passions that were so hideously being brought to a boil beyond the shores of their idyll and that would in only one year's time erupt in the Spanish Civil War. Nor did they see the country's rural poverty or urban squalor, nor discuss the fact that only three years earlier the last of the Bourbons had bowed himself out of the chaos and had given in to a left-wing Republic.

They glimpsed, instead, the castles that stood overlooking the sea, castles so grand that they were what the ambitious Crusader dreamed of when he went off to war. They swam in cool waters and lunched in sandy sheltered coves on Lord Moyne's best stores from Fortnum & Mason picnic baskets equipped with crystal glasses and fine porcelain plates.

After dinner on board the yacht, Wallis and the Prince often sat alone on deck in the soft evening air sharing a closeness magnified by the immensity of the sea and the sky. The Prince was a man drunk with love and Wallis glowed alluringly in the knowledge. That haunted look had left his face. He seemed more boyish than ever. He believed Wallis was the most beautiful woman he had ever known and, indeed, the sea air had endowed her with a dazzling brightness.

She was entirely relaxed. Her eyebrows would arch with surprise when she laughed at one of his jokes, for he was not by nature an amusing man. The wolf pack did not let any of this pass by them. They had not come to like her more, but familiarity had caused them to fear her less. These great minds had now decided that she was perfectly happy with the way things were and that, although they did not sincerely care for her, she was no threat to them.

They cruised for eleven days before they reached Cannes. During all this time Wallis thought very little about Ernest. Yet, she was pleased to find several letters waiting for her. "Maybe this rendezvous with the Prince is nothing more than a shipboard romance," she confided to Kitty.

"Maybe for you," Kitty replied, "not the Prince. That man's wild-mad for you, Wallis."

"Well, it won't be the same when we get back to England," Wallis said with sincerity, then added: "He's asked if you and Herman could join us on the rest of the cruise, and I'm hoping you'll agree. It would be such fun."

"Yes, it would," Kitty agreed. "Who would have *thunk* it, Wallis, back there in Coronado, that I would be a *very* rich matron and you would be—" Kitty hesitated.

"A Royal mistress?"

"Well, yes, but *much* more."

"Hey, Kitty," Wallis laughed, noting her friend's glazed look, "don't forget this is *my* dream!"

September was nearly over before the cruise came to an end at Lake Como. Kitty and Herman returned to Cannes. Wallis, the Prince and the rest of their party spent a week at the lake before motoring to Arona to board the *Orient Express* for Paris, where she was to meet Aunt Bessie and do some shopping while the Prince returned to London. Two private cars had been attached to the rear of the train to accommodate the Royal party. The station officials were being presented to the Prince when Wallis became aware of a short, stolid woman on the platform waving frantically to her. As she advanced, Wallis called out, "Nancy Armstrong!," unable to control her surprise at seeing once again the neighbor who had nursed her to health after Win's brutal attack.

The Prince glanced her way and then back to his welcoming committee.

Nancy threw her arms around Wallis. "My God, girl! I never expected to lay eyes on you again!" she exclaimed as she stood back and viewed her. "You look great. Just great!"

Wallis introduced her to Posy Guinness and a few of the others, and when the Prince was finished with protocol, she turned to him.

"Sir, I would like to present Mrs. Nancy Armstrong, a friend of mine from China. Nancy, His Royal Highness, the Prince of Wales."

"Yowhee!" Nancy said as she stuck out her hand. The Prince laughed as he shook it.

"Where in America are you from, Mrs. Armstrong?" he asked.

"Soda Falls, Kansas," she replied. "How did you know I was an American?"

They all laughed.

Arrangements were made for Nancy to join them in the Royal car for drinks before dinner.

Seeing Nancy had brought the past vividly into focus for Wallis. It had been years since she had thought about Win or her distressing experience with Mr. Ku Ling Yong, Larry Dean and Fu Looog. She was sorry now that she had introduced Nancy to the Prince. She could as well have gone over to her on the platform, said a few words and then let it go at that. But Nancy's openness of personality and her natural candor were refreshing. She regarded her as a quintessential American and deep inside Wallis a love of her native country remained.

Nancy appeared in the door of the Royal railway car at the exact minute of the appointed time. She had reapplied her makeup and tidied her wispy gray hair; otherwise she was unchanged—her simple beige cotton dress, neat and serviceable for travel, her brown oxford shoes, buffed and sturdy, the alligator pocketbook (the one touch of elegance to her costume) large and practical for touring documents. Not exactly what one would wear for cocktails with the Prince of Wales, yet, somehow, the American woman's lack of artifice was endearing.

"There's no way I can curtsy," she whispered to Wallis who had come to greet her. "It just seems un-American to curtsy to an English Prince."

Wallis laughed and taking Nancy by the hand led her to where the Prince stood talking to Colin and Gladys Buist. "Mrs. Armstrong's husband Fred is a Navy man," she said, after introductions had been made.

"Was," Nancy corrected.

"Oh, I'm so sorry," Wallis instantly apologized, assuming Nancy must now be a widow.

"No, Fred hasn't died," she said. "He's retired. Or is just about to. He's been stationed in the Mediterranean for the past two years. We'll be going home in a few weeks' time and I thought it would be swell to go to Paris and do some shopping and looking around before it's back to Soda Falls and the Ladies' Saturday Afternoon Garden Club. I can't speak more than three words of French so I hope I don't get myself into difficulty. Of course, one can always count on the folks at the American Embassy to help you out."

By now Wallis was certain it had been a mistake to ask Nancy to cocktails with the Royal party and at the first opportune moment said, "Well, Mrs. Armstrong and I have some reminiscing to do, Sir, if you will excuse us." Taking Nancy by the arm, she drew her to a nearby corner where they could sit down and have a fairly private conversation.

"I don't mean to pry," Nancy said, "and you can just say it's none of my business—*but*—what exactly is your position here?"

"Position?" Wallis asked puzzled.

"Yes, are you a secretary or some such thing?"

"No," Wallis smiled. "The Prince and I are friends."

Nancy looked over at the Prince and back to Wallis. "Oh, boy! Now I'm in trouble! Are you *good* friends?"

Wallis nodded her head.

"I knew you were plucky the first time I saw you despite all the gaff you took from that bastard Spencer," she said. "Incidentally, I heard through the Navy grapevine that you divorced him and good riddance! Still—I can't quite figure it out. How the hell did you get from *there* to *here*?"

"It's a long story. Briefly, I married a British subject, moved to London, made some friends and was introduced to the Prince."

"And your husband?"

"Ernest Simpson. He's in the shipping business. Oh, well—*droit du seigneur*." Nancy stared at her uncomprehendingly. "Never mind. Let's just say he is understanding."

"Let's just say Simpson's a simp!" Nancy snapped and then was instantly contrite. "There I go! Damn! I don't ever think of myself as being insensitive. That's always been my problem. I charge into other people's lives because I'm interested and I have no business doing so."

"You keep your sense of humor, at least," Wallis smiled.

"Yeah, I guess you could give me credit for that. I try hard to keep up my spirits. I can tell you after all the marvelous places Fred and I have been, I'm not much looking forward to Soda Falls."

The bartender approached them and asked for their orders. "Tomato juice," Nancy said, and in an aside to Wallis confided, "I'm on the wagon." There was no tomato juice and she settled for orange. "I almost didn't recognize you when I first saw you at the station," she continued. "You look *that* smart. I thought, 'Well, there's a woman who looks like Wallis Spencer.' And then I looked harder and even from where I was I could hear you laugh and I knew it was you." She shook her head as she glanced around at the luxurious appointments in the car and at the style and obvious affluence of the occupants.

"You've gone up in the world, Wallis," she said. "However you've done it, I give you marks. Me? Sometimes when I catch a glimpse of myself in a mirror—I'm fifty-two, dreary lines in my face, my hair's lost its color, my looks, whatever they were, are going, my health's not so good either—I wonder what it's all been for. I'm taking home an empty suitcase. You're lucky you left the Navy, Wallis. There is nothing as redundant as being the wife of a retired Navy man." She got up. "Am I supposed to back out of the Prince's presence?" she asked.

"Just be yourself," Wallis advised.

"Good-bye, Sir," Nancy said to him on her way out. "It's been a real pleasure meeting you." To her surprise, he took her hand and shook it.

When she was gone, Wallis realized that she had not asked Nancy what she knew about Mr. Ku Ling Yong. Then she decided perhaps it was for the best. That part of her life was better buried forever. No use digging up old bones.

They arrived in Paris late the next night. Wallis had not seen Nancy again and had pushed her out of her thoughts. More pertinent was the imminent departure of the Prince to England and then Scotland for the christening of the new ocean liner *Queen Mary*. They would not reunite for three weeks; for he was then to go to Balmoral to be with the King and Queen, who would have heard about the cruise of the *Rosaura* in detail from either Trotter or Aird, she was sure.

As the porter assisted her from the train, Wallis happened to glance sideways down the platform. Nancy was waving to her. Slowly Wallis raised her hand and returned the acknowledgment.

"Wallis, this way," Trotter was saying. She turned to follow him. The Prince walked on ahead surrounded by station officials. A crowd of the curious had formed about them; and when Wallis looked back over her shoulder through the mottled green light, Nancy was gone, and the locomotive, having dispersed all its passengers, stood motionless, steam still rising at its base. Wallis recalled the train in Tolstoy's *Anna Karenina* and the hunched man who had moved ominously along the track testing the wheels. She shivered and paused for a moment.

"Are you all right?" Trotter inquired.

"Fine. Train stations depress me, that's all."

"Ummm. Understandably," he replied. "Dingy, disagreeable interiors most usually."

They continued on past the tall, palm-like pillars along the tracks to brighter light in the huge, domed waiting room and then to a private entrance where a team of chauffeured cars was lined up in attendance.

26

While Wallis waited restlessly for the Prince to return to London from his royal and familial duties, she suspected he was being exposed to forces that could jeopardize her future. She did not doubt his love for her, but she was well aware that his parents and his country wanted to see him married. The subject was bound to arise during this time, and breaking his current liaison would seem a proper start. He would, she feared, be vulnerable without her and, in the charged emotional atmosphere of Glasgow and Balmoral, perhaps unable to resist.

From the reports in the press, Glasgow's awful little temperance hotels were filled to overflowing. The launching of the *Queen Mary* had become for many a religious pilgrimage, a symbol of everything dearest to the arrogant humility of the British heart. The abandonment of its construction, because of a lack of funds, three years earlier after only nine months of work had been regarded as a dreadful moral defeat. The resumption of its building and, now, its completion had become, for Britain, an emblem of all that their land stood for: a sturdy vessel, the brightest, biggest and bravest in the world.

The day of the launching the front page of every newspaper in England carried a picture of the King (in admiral's uniform), the Queen (in a toque higher than the grandest crown) and the Prince of Wales (handsome and healthy from the cruise), standing behind a glass enclosure (it was pouring with rain) and flanked by an impressive group of officials, top hats in hand, as the Queen stepped up to a microphone to give the command to crash the bottle of christening wine (Australian Burgundy) against the giant side of the mountainous ship.

Full radio coverage was given, the BBC announcer describing in ministerial tones how the ship had begun to move, swaying slightly, and how all the top hats had been waved as it slid past. "She's off!" the crowds shouted. Tugs, specially brought from Liverpool and Southampton, surrounded her and began the difficult job of maneuvering her into the dock.

"It's like launching the Harvard Stadium into the Charles River," Ernest said as he and Wallis sat in their living room listening to the tug-by-tug description. "Peter Pan certainly knows when to appear in public and with whom," he added as the voices of a hundred thousand people singing "God Save the King," accompanied by interfering static, came roaring through the loudspeaker.

Lately Wallis had noted a small decline in Ernest's British allegiance. And he had begun the irritating habit of referring to the Prince as Peter Pan. (*So much for droit du seigneur,* she thought.)

"I wish you wouldn't refer to the Prince that way," she commented.

He got up and left the room, and she turned off the radio. The ship-shaking rumble of the *Queen Mary* seemed to her to have been an unmistakable alarm. Not only was the Prince under baleful influences, Ernest would no longer be the complaisant husband.

What Wallis did not understand were the natures of these two men, both of whom loved her and to neither of whom was she able to give her whole self. Why she could not do so was also unfathomable to her, and yet it was right there on the surface ready for her to grasp—*the truth.*

She had never been able to believe in anyone except herself. All the strength she had as a child and as a woman had come from within. Her ambition had been her one security.

And perhaps that was why she took what she could and went after the things she wanted in what might seem to others a ruthless fashion. She had given her complete love to Grandmother Warfield only to be rejected. She had turned to Alice for loving tenderness, for the warm safety of a real home, but her mother had always placed her own needs first. Even Aunt Bessie had used her to fulfill her personal fantasies. If Wallis accepted money from her aunt without conscience, it was because she felt everything in life did have a price and that Aunt Bessie was paying a low cost for a dream—the daughter she did not have, the woman she could never become.

The circumstances of her life had given Wallis a strength, vitality and initiative few women possessed. Her driving demand to be important so that she could control her own life (feeling there was no one to fall back upon) had drawn her to men who required the strong hand of an authoritative woman. It had been her misfortune that beneath her sturdy masculine inclination lurked the deeply feminine Southern coquette she had had to sublimate in order to survive. She desperately wanted to be spoiled and protected, given her way and made to feel no guilt for expecting, as a woman, to be taken care of.

She had another conflict. The idea of a married woman having a lover was an entirely European concept, one that was foreign to her culture—as an American (and especially an American from the South)—and did not rest easy with her principles. Yet she had known very soon after she married Ernest that she could never be happy simply being his wife; and after the difficulties of her divorce from Win and her terror of being alone once again to fight the world, leaving Ernest had never been an option. Then the Prince had entered her life. History had always regarded a Royal mistress as an honorable position. Ernest's compliance had substantiated this. Why then did she now detect a growing resentment in his attitude?

It never occurred to Wallis that Ernest might really love her, that he was also in conflict. His continual struggle to achieve his father's approval always met with rebuffs. His mother had never had the slightest maternal concern for him. His first marriage had been a dismal failure. He had clung stubbornly to the belief that everything would be different when he found a place for himself in England and was willing—eager, really—to fit in. If he once thought that Wallis's romance with the Prince of Wales could establish his own position, he now knew he had miscalculated the situation. For while his wife's honor remained untarnished and her social prestige was ascending because of her Royal liaison, he, as a cuckolded husband, was barely tolerated.

Wallis did not comprehend the reality of what was happening in her marriage. For the moment she could not see beyond the sense of exhilaration in her royal affair—the hotel suites and yachts, the jewels. "Two more bracelets and a smart diamond for my hair were waiting for me when I returned to London," she had written Aunt Bessie that very day. "Ernest complains we won't be able to afford the insurance."

The Prince's favor had cast a growing radiance over her life. New doors were opening. There was a heightened interest and attention to her most casual remarks. Invitations to the best social affairs came daily through her mail slot. She felt as though she were being borne upon a rising wave that was carrying her ever more rapidly and ever higher. Her instincts told her that if the Prince returned and she was still in favor, she would really begin to savor the true brilliance and sophistication of London society.

The trouble was that little word—*if*. When it was coupled with Ernest's small hints of dissatisfaction, the ground beneath her feet suddenly seemed to contain quicksand. Aunt Bessie's words rang in her ears—"What will you do if you lose *both* the men in your life?"

She left the door to her bedroom open that night and although she called out to him, Ernest did not come in. She lay sleepless, seeing the photograph that had appeared in all the afternoon papers—Queen Mary, standing tall and majestically, giving the order that would send her namesake ship out to a life of British service, the King and her eldest son, the future King, behind her. If Wallis was taking a chance that she might lose Ernest by continuing her affair with the Prince, then, by God! she must make sure she did not lose her Royal lover. As she saw it at this time, the Queen was her greatest adversary.

Wallis did not try to understand the deep and difficult relationship between the Prince and his mother. She could not know the tremendous insecurity the Queen had endured as a young woman who, like Wallis, had always been the poor relation in her family, her parents in perennial debt and often only one step in front of the bailiff. Nor the store her parents had set on her marrying well up in the Royal Family to save themselves. Little had been written or was said about her first disastrous engagement to her present husband's older brother—the man who was born to be king, but who, because of his degenerate ways and mental illness, could never be allowed to ascend the throne. She had been sacrificed to the image of the Crown. That her fiancé had died, or perhaps been murdered, before the marriage had saved her from much heartache and suffering. Her sacrifice had, in the end, bought her the Queen Consort's crown and she wore it now with the pride and defiance of a dedicated and grateful woman.

Wallis was astute enough to see that the Queen was a dominating woman with a masculine, no-nonsense nature, a martinet who expected her children, and no doubt her husband as well, to live by her high standards.

"David needs a strong mother's hand and the soft touch of a compliant mistress," Wallis thought. "I can be both." Suddenly, she felt relieved. "And I'll be nicer to Ernest." There was something of the lost child in this reasoning, the Bessie Wallis who was confident that she could keep her grandmother's and her mother's love. She fell asleep before any doubts put an end to her renewed sense of self-confidence.

The blue-eyed charmer, as Wallis referred to the Prince in her letters to Aunt Bessie, returned to London, and to her relief their affair resumed its familiar pattern on an even deeper level. One problem was keeping up with two men, for she was determined not to let Ernest slip from her grasp. This meant entertaining numerous shippers with their wives at Bryanston Court between the Prince's visits and her weekends at the Fort. Her other concern was financial.

Despite the magnificence of the gifts the Prince heaped upon her, Ernest's salary had not increased, but their expenses had. She had dropped small hints to the Prince about "the terrible cost of good clothes these days," and he had given her money for a leopard-skin sports coat to be made along with some fashionable ensembles. Still she found it difficult to balance the budget. To Ernest's strong disapproval she took to accepting, as *gifts of gratitude,* sums of money from friends and acquaintances who wanted desperately to be included on a weekend at the Fort or a social event that she and the Prince were attending.

"It's disgusting," Ernest told her. "Cheap and vulgar."

"I'm only trying to make things easier for you," she consoled. "I know how you hate going to your father for money. The truth is, he is grossly underpaying you."

"You might not have noticed, Wallis, but we are in the midst of a depression and I am damned lucky to have the job I have," he retorted.

"That's the worst of it with you, Ernest. You underestimate yourself so. I am very much aware of the country's serious economic situation. But just because a forest is on fire does not mean every tree in the country is in danger of burning down. Your father's firm is doing well, especially with those new German contracts, and he seems to be living a lordly life with that new French mistress of his. *She* gets an apartment in Paris and you have your expense account cut."

She came over to where he sat and balanced her slim body on the armrest of the club chair. "We shouldn't have these ugly discussions, Ernest. It's all wrong. I know you're doing your best. I'm just trying to contribute whatever I can."

Ernest looked up at her quizzically. "You really believe that, don't you, Wallis?"

She kissed him lightly on the forehead and bounced to her feet. "Some people are coming over for cocktails," she said, avoiding an answer. "Posy Guinness. You *do* like her. And Jack Aird. A touch of politics on my part. Winning over the opposition. You know his father died and he is now *Sir* John Aird. Imagine that!! Sir John!" she laughed and disappeared into the kitchen to supervise the making of the cocktail bits.

Ernest picked up the Paris edition of the *Herald Tribune*

which he had sent to him. Inside was a featured article on the sensational Vanderbilt case. Gloria was seeking to recover custody of her daughter from her sister-in-law, Gertrude Whitney. Both Tamar and Thelma had given evidence and Wallis's name was mentioned in connection with the holiday she had taken with Tamar, Gloria and Nada Milford Haven several years back. The two latter women were now alleged to have taken part in homosexual acts at that time. Ernest's hand shook as he turned to the next page where the article was continued.

An extra paragraph had been added to the story, identifying Wallis as the Prince of Wales's current good friend and suggesting that divorce proceedings between him and Wallis appeared to be set for the near future. "Damn it!" he swore and, taking the paper with him, strode angrily into the kitchen to confront Wallis with this new, distressing problem.

"This kind of gossip is not what any of us needs," he told her, after bringing her into his study and closing the door. "We must talk about this, Wallis—you and me and the Prince of Wales. If father even *whiffs* scandal brewing he'll send us jobless back to New York so fast your precious jewels will have to follow!"

"Your father! That old hypocrite!"

"That is probably true, Wallis, but he is still our only bulwark between *this* life and the queues of unemployed."

The Prince remained after the rest of the cocktail guests had departed and the three of them had a long talk. The Prince was suitably shocked when he read the article in the *Herald Tribune*. "None of the English papers would dare carry such a story," he declared.

"That may well be the case, Sir," Ernest agreed, "but gossip like this travels fast enough by word of mouth."

"So it does. So it does," the Prince concurred. "Perhaps you should have accompanied Wallis and me on the cruise. However, once burnt we should beware of the flames. It would be good of you, Ernest, if you could come to the Fort whenever Wallis does and escort her to the various social events that gain press attention. Which brings me to a more joyous discussion.

"As you know, my brother Prince George is to be married soon at Westminster Abbey to the Princess Marina of Greece. There will be many gala events held in their honor culminating in a grand state reception given by the King and Queen at Buckingham Palace two days before the wedding. I will see that Mr. and Mrs. Ernest Simpson are invited and presented to my parents. Then you shall have seats at the Abbey for the wedding. I believe that will do more to quash these ridiculous rumors than anything else."

Wallis was in a cloud of euphoria for the next four weeks as she prepared her outfits for the two historic events. The dress she had designed for the state reception was made of violet lamé that turned her eyes to a deep, startling purple. Simply and elegantly draped, the gown had as its only ornamentation a vivid green sash that hugged the waist and fell down the back of the dress like a train. Wallis had searched through hundreds of fabric samples for the color of green that was closest to the emeralds—bracelets, earrings, ring and pendant on a diamond necklace—she had newly acquired. What she did not have was a tiara, which she knew the titled guests at least would all be wearing.

"Well, of course," Syrie Maugham suggested, "you could borrow one from Posy Guinness or someone like that. Still, I think that would be a bit tacky, don't you? People might recognize the piece. But I bet Cartier's would loan you one."

"Cartier's?" Wallis repeated with surprise.

"Yes. I heard they are loaning half the minor Royalties *and* the Ambassador's wife pieces for the affair."

"Syrie, that's inspirational! I'll give it a try."

The manager of Cartier's, who was well informed on his Royal gossip, took not one but three tiaras from the safe in his private office for Wallis to make her choice. "As your own emeralds are a deep, deep green, may I suggest this one." He eased his selection onto Wallis's head and she looked at herself in the hand mirror he then held up for her. "It makes a definite statement," he said. "Simple, expensive and *soigné*. Not too many diamonds, a clean, modern line and most flattering to your coloring and the shape of your face."

"Mr. Simpson is terrified that it might be lost or stolen," she admitted.

"It will be fully insured," he guaranteed her.

"And there will be no cost to me?"

"Well, we would be grateful if in descriptions of your attire, mention be made of your *Cartier tiara.*" He glanced down at the jewel case she had brought with her. "And you might remind His Royal Highness of our continuing gratitude for his patronage."

In the weeks before the wedding, and while Princess Marina was in Paris with her parents selecting her trousseau, the Prince of Wales hardly let "Georgie" out of his sight. This meant that Wallis saw a great deal of him. They had fun together shopping and gossiping and the prospective bridegroom was on his best behavior. The Prince of Wales had been Georgie's "caretaker" for years; their brother Bertie being too involved with his own family, his wife Elizabeth and their two young daughters, Elizabeth and Margaret; and their brother Harry being somewhat frail of health.

Wallis now knew all about the homosexual appetites, drugs and scrapes that had dominated Georgie's life. She found him pleasant company, artistic, and objected only to his use of a strong, musky perfume. Georgie had a particular penchant for the blond good looks of German boys, and there had been one indiscreet episode only two years earlier when David had had to pay a large sum to recover some passionate letters his brother had written to a young man from Vienna.

The Royal bridegroom seemed, however, to be sincerely in love with the beautiful Greek Princess, and Wallis was conscious of how relieved David and, she supposed, the entire Royal Family were that he was getting married.

The night of the state reception in their honor, Wallis dressed nervously. The weather was miserable. Rain the entire day, the streets all looking as though the Thames had overflowed. The almost gale-force winds concerned her the most and she secured the tiara to her head as best she could, fearing it might come loose and land in a swirling pool of gutter water to be swept away into the sewers of the city.

Ernest stood in the doorway to her dressing room wearing the obligatory knee breeches. "It's about time the Court came into the twentieth century," he complained.

"I think you look distinguished," Wallis said.

"The car is here. So whenever you are ready."

Wallis rose from her chair. Ernest stared at her with fascination. "My dear," he said softly, "you look like a queen."

The reception rooms at the Palace gleamed with sparkling crystal chandeliers and gold gilt. The massive bouquets of flowers gave off a heady scent. Wallis had never seen so many diamonds before. Many of the women's gowns were beaded with real jewels. Nonetheless, she felt she was dressed correctly and enjoyed the looks she received when she and Ernest entered.

Trumpets sounded as the King and Queen and all the other Royalties, including the Prince of Wales, approached the wide reception doors. Wallis and Ernest took their places in one of the lines of guests that, by custom, must form on either side of the Royal procession, bowing and curtsying as they passed. Wallis glanced up through the tops of her eyes so that she could get a good look at the Queen in her white and silvery splendor, diamonds like a shower of giant ice chips seeming to cover her. On her face was a serene expression that commanded the room.

The Prince of Wales, his aunt, the spinster Princess Victoria, on his arm, followed; the engaged couple behind them. The Prince caught Wallis's eye, smiled and continued on, a gesture that did not go unnoticed by those near to her in the line. Later, he brought over Prince Paul of Yugoslavia, the brother-in-law of the bride-to-be. "Mrs. Simpson," Prince Paul said extravagantly, his medals and ribbons dazzling on his brilliant uniform, "there is no question about it—you are wearing the most striking gown in the room."

Both her lover and her husband beamed. After Prince Paul left them, the Prince of Wales led Wallis and Ernest over to where his parents were standing. "Ma'am," he said to his mother, "I would like to present Mr. and Mrs. Ernest Simpson."

"From America, I believe," the Queen said perfunctorily as Wallis curtsied. The King, who, Wallis observed, looked like a frail old man, merely nodded in recognition when they were presented to him. Heads had turned the moment Wallis and the Queen stood face to face. Wallis felt a chill as the Queen's—and then the King's—eyes rested briefly on her. The icy menace in their glances startled her. The rest of the evening she had to struggle against an invading sense of foreboding.

Two days later, wearing a handsome, subdued aquamarine gown and very little jewelry, she attended the wedding in the Abbey. Ernest wore the crimson uniform of the Coldstream Guards, in which he felt very grand. Festive crowds packed the foggy, damp streets. Streetlights burned despite the morning hour. As each car went by a rousing cheer was raised.

They had excellent seats on a side aisle and an uninterrupted view of the altar and of the Royal pews, where the Prince of Wales sat with his family. Wallis's glance slid their way. A startling thought came to her. Would a time come when she might sit beside David in a Royal pew? A premonitory shiver ran through her, for she suspected that only the King's death could bring that about. And that would mean David would be King.

27

Wallis closed her eyes, unable to pull away from the dream she had been having before being awakened by the sound of cowbells. She and David were in a suite at the Grand Hotel, situated at the edge of the ancient town of Kitzbühel in Austria. It was February and the winter sports season was at its height. They had come with a small party: just five others, friends rather than courtiers.

Since the Royal wedding, David had been rather pensive. He appeared outwardly happy and there were times when the passion in their lovemaking reached an almost unendurable brink of emotion. Still, Wallis glimpsed on occasion that sad, haunted look that would slide across his face, possess it briefly and then, by dint of his determination, disappear. He seemed to be reaching for something that was as yet unknown to him, although Wallis could guess at its genesis.

With his brother Harry also soon to wed, he would be the only one of the King's four sons to be unmarried. The Queen, he had confided to Wallis, invariably raised the question of his bacherlorhood whenever he dined with his parents. It was time, his mother insisted, he marry and settle down with a "suitable" princess. This pressure upon him had become increasingly uncomfortable and his visits to his parents were now infrequent. Georgie was involved in his new life; David had never been close to his brother Harry; and Bertie, who was only two years younger than David, had always followed a different drummer.

Bertie was like an injured child. The closer you were to him the more dependent he became. At least with Georgie, David had been able to take a course of action—a doctor's advice for a drug cure, money paid out to escape a scandal. Bertie's scars were deep, and his older brother could do nothing to lessen his paralyzing stuttering or to ease the insecurity that caused his drinking. He was relieved that Bertie's wife, Elizabeth, was an understanding and forbearing woman. But seeing Bertie and his family, with his two lovely little girls, only made David sadder and so he saw them less and less.

His alienation from his family brought him closer to Wallis, more demanding of her time. This had made her life with Ernest progressively difficult. Despite the agreement that had been struck among the three of them, Ernest was now outwardly hostile. He managed to find reasons why he could not join her and the Prince for dinner or at the Fort for a weekend. He would not listen to what she had to say about the Prince's life. When she told him they had been invited to Kitzbühel, he had refused to go.

"But you know what will happen," she pleaded. "If you aren't with us, people will talk."

He laughed harshly. "Really, Wallis, you are not such an innocent as to believe they aren't already gabbing their heads off!"

"I mean the press."

"The American papers are filled with pictures of the two of you."

"Not here, though."

"It won't take long and my going on a ski party, when I have never been on a pair of wooden slats in my life and don't intend to chance breaking my neck on them in the future, is not going to stave off the advancing army for long. You want to stop the talk—don't go to Kitzbühel with the Prince. Come with me to New York where I have business to conduct."

"You know I can't do that."

"I know nothing of the kind."

They stared at each other in brutal silence, neither able to give an inch. Then Ernest left the room, and for the first time she heard a door slam shut between them.

She wanted to push all these unpleasant thoughts from her mind, to return to the warm comfort of the dream still within reach. The bed was empty beside her. David must have gone back to his own room. She recalled now that he had fallen asleep in her arms. There were times when she felt almost maternal toward him.

In her dream she had been a child again, resting in her small iron bed in the sunroom of Grandmother Warfield's house. Voices rose up to her, the plaintive tones of a Negro spiritual. She had taken her precious corncob doll, Sally, with her as she walked over to the window to look out. There in the yard below were almost all the people from her past. They were looking up at her and their voices swelled with the music. She raised her hand and waved—and then—and then—there had been the sound of the cows in the nearby valley.

The dream had vanished and with it all those shadowy figures of her life. Suddenly she realized that no one in her dream had acknowledged her greeting. She sat up in the bed feeling a chill and drew the mammoth eiderdown that had slipped to the foot of the bed up tight around her. She could hear David in the next room. He would be dressing to go skiing. She had not yet had the courage to try even the gentlest of the nursery slopes. For her, the best part of the day was when their little party rendezvoused in the afternoon in a village inn and they sipped hot chocolate before a blazing wood fire as they watched the sun fall behind the mauve peaks.

She had been spending the early hours of the day reading the new American books Aunt Bessie sent her—a novel about China by Pearl Buck and Douglas Southall Freeman's fine biography of Robert E. Lee. This morning she decided she would go with David and take her first lesson on the lower slopes while he navigated the upper ones.

She slipped into her negligee and, after listening to make sure she heard no voices, knocked lightly on their connecting door. To her surprise he opened it dressed in a traveling suit. Behind him she could see that his suitcases had been packed.

"David, where are you going? Has anything happened?" she asked with concern.

"I feel like waltzing," he replied, "and Vienna's the place for that. Our train doesn't leave for several hours so I thought I should let you sleep as long as you could."

His eyes told her that he was wrestling with some deep currents of emotion. "I'll get dressed and packed right away," she said. "Vienna sounds just swell."

He managed a small smile. He had never ceased being amused at her use of American vernacular.

Once in Vienna, he decided that, although a Strauss waltz was wonderfully tender, it could not match the fire of gypsy violins and so, three days after their arrival, they continued on to Budapest, where, in the same amount of time, he was struck again by the desperate need to move on.

They had just returned to the hotel from an evening at a tavern lit by flickering candles, where they had drunk sweet Hungarian wine as they listened to the soulful music of half a dozen gypsy violins.

"Wallis," he said, when they were alone. "Perhaps it would be better if we returned to London."

"Of course," she agreed. "When?"

"Tomorrow morning."

"David, is there something you aren't telling me?" she asked. The blood rushed suddenly to her head, for she had the dreadful thought that perhaps there was someone else. After all, he had turned away from Thelma to her. The attractive faces of the two women in their party flashed in her mind's eye. They were both English, more socially acceptable than she. She could see their graceful figures in stylish ski clothes as they had accompanied him to the upper slopes in Kitzbühel, recall them whirling romantically in a waltz with him in Vienna and laughing prettily in a tipsy fashion just this evening.

"Oh, my darling!" he cried and grasped her to him in a wild embrace. "No! No!" he protested, guessing from the hurt, dazed look on her face what she had been thinking. "I love you with an eanum love that is my entire being." He kissed the lids of her eyes, the bridge of her nose, the edge of her lips and then buried his head into her neck.

A shudder of relief caused her to tremble and he held her tighter. She could feel his heart beat hard against her chest. Placing her hands tightly on his shoulders, she separated them. "David, you are going to stop this childish self-indulgence and tell me *exactly* what the problem is," she demanded, now in control of the situation.

"Wallis, I am in such an awful muddle," he exclaimed. "All of Britain wants me to marry and my god, *oh-my-god,* so do I. I want to marry *you.* I want a home like Bertie and Georgie have and Harry will soon occupy with his future bride. And I want to be able to share it, as they do—and will—with the woman I love. But no! I am the Heir to the Throne—through no choice of my own—merely by being born first—and that accident of birth is to deny me the one simple liberty possessed by every other British man."

He began to pace the cavernous room with its sixteen-foot ceiling and blood-red velvet draperies and all the gold and crystal accoutrements that hotel managements believed essential in Royal suites. He looked like a man going through the worst pains of human suffering. Suddenly the youthful face was paper-white and lined, making a farce of the agility of his step, the vitality of the anger in his voice.

"It is madness! All madness!" he proclaimed. "A sham! A ludicrous sham!" He strode back to her and grasped her shoulders as she had just held his. "Wallis, you know as well as I do, and so does my mother, that I cannot give my country an heir. I damn well am not impotent, but for years the doctors have been more than clear about my sterility. Still we go on with this pretense for the image and the mystique of the Monarchy. My mother is a cake of ice, albeit one of the most amazing women I have ever known. She possesses inhuman self-control. She is *always* a Queen. Even at a family dinner she appears to be seated upon a throne. Having children was perhaps the greatest personal sacrifice she made for her country. My father finds little to like about any of his sons. Georgie has been a pervert and a drug addict, Bertie an alcoholic with deep psychological problems, Harry is a ninny and I refuse to marry someone I do not love."

She started to interrupt him, but he would not allow her to.

"No, let me continue. It's true and between us we can face the truth. All that I say is true and yet to the British people we must remain the *image* of the idealized, the *perfect* family. Well, Wallis, no family is perfect. Being human disenfranchises it. And I find it immoral as well as inhuman to perpetuate such a myth."

"David"—she moved closer to him, her hand stroked the side of his face, moved down his shoulder to his arm—"one day you will be a truly great King, and that will not be a myth."

"You won't leave me, *ever,* Wallis?"

"Not as long as you don't want me to."

She unbuttoned his shirt and then unbuckled his belt and then drew him down close to her as she lowered herself to the floor. "A little levity," she said. "Just don't ever give the order to cut out my tongue."

They both laughed at that and then they made love.

Upon their return to London Wallis entered energetically into a social regime that she thought might bolster the Prince's spirits. He had lost considerable weight. His fair eyelashes rose and fell on hollow, gray cheeks. He knew his father was failing, and how that would affect his life was causing him grievous concern. She had her own harassments.

Sooner or later, she feared, David would lose interest. She was now thirty-nine, an age when most women would expect to become chaperones to—not participants *in*—a love affair. Despite all his protestations to the contrary, she did not believe that David's love would endure indefinitely. Eventually the Ice Queen would win; he would marry.

Still, for now, he remained infatuated, almost worshipful of her, and she was determined to make the most of it while it lasted, to enjoy herself to the fullest. "I might as well finish up what youth is left to me with a flourish," she wrote Aunt Bessie, adding: "P.S. As bad taste as the clippings are do keep sending them." A picture of Wallis and the Prince while on the ski holiday in Kitzbühel had appeared in an American paper with the caption: "Nothing between them—not even a sheet."

The British newspapers' ban on mention of their romance allowed Wallis to maintain the illusion that the English public (because certainly the cognoscenti all knew) would never catch them out. And so she threw all caution to the wind. Her status in society was established. Everyone who was anyone sought her friendship. She was the talk of London, the most vied-for guest of the city's most prominent hostesses. Politicians, ambassadors, the famous in all areas of the arts and the crème de la crème of visiting Americans pursued her.

The attention thrilled her, her delight all the more meaningful in view of the dangerous situation it was causing in her home. "I'm going to enjoy it, no matter what," she thought. "It's fun to see the very best people in such hot pursuit when no one ever paid a gnat's eye to me before." She meant, of course, London's highest social set and its reigning hostesses—Lady Emerald Cunard and Lady Sibyl Colefax.

Emerald Cunard and Sibyl Colefax were—as Wallis commented to Syrie (to whom she remained staunchly loyal)—"the worst of friends." No one dared to invite them to the same dinner party, a problem always to a hostess who wanted to remain in the good graces of both. The diminutive Emerald Lady Cunard had been born in San Francisco as Maude Burke. The *Emerald* came later on the advice of a numerologist. Now in her sixties, she had taken on the painted look of the waxed figures in Madame Tussaud's: heavily *maquillée,* with a silvery powder brushed through her hair. At the turn of the century her brilliant blue eyes and delicate beauty had won her the love of the rich Sir Bache Cunard, twenty years her senior, and a few years later the admiration of King Edward VII. Then had come her two decade-long affairs (simultaneously, it seemed) with George Moore and Sir Thomas Beecham.

She gave several luncheons a week and at least one dinner party at her palatial house at 9 Grosvenor Square. The circular dining table was made of lapis lazuli, the food prepared by a superb French chef whom she had bribed away from the kitchens of the Ritz Hotel, and the conversation (led always by her) was sparkling. Wrinkles and paint were unnoticed when Lady Cunard talked, her fund of miscellaneous information was fascinating and her wit and ability to shock were much admired. To Hitler's personal envoy, Joachim von Ribbentrop, at a dinner Wallis attended, she twittered, "Tell us, dearest Excellency, *why* does Herr Hitler dislike the Jews?"

It was at Emerald's that the great met the irreverent, statesmen consorted with society, and artists mixed with titled aristocrats.

Her rival, Lady Sibyl Colefax, held as many social gatherings in her beautiful home, Argyll House in Chelsea, and her guest list was equally celebrated. "The Coalbox" as Syrie called Lady Sibyl, was small and slender, dark, shiny, metallic and younger by some years than Lady Cunard. She perhaps resembled Wallis (or perhaps the other way around) as a hostess, her parties being better known for their relaxed fun (Noël Coward, Ivor Novelo, or even Arthur Rubinstein at the piano) and interesting menus than for their intellectual exchanges. She was a skillful decorator and her outrageously expensive taste was represented in some of the smartest London homes.

The romance of Wallis and the Prince surpassed all else in interest in London society and Wallis knew it. Everyone could see how madly infatuated the Prince was by her. He did nothing to hide his love, and he would have done anything to help her storm society. Suddenly he was interested in everything American. Even his speech had taken on a curious American twang. ("One helluva lot better than the German voices of the rest of his family," Syrie proclaimed.) They looked smart together. Both were about the same size, always impeccably and stylishly groomed. The group at Wallis's cocktail parties were now the startlingly elite, the titled, the famous, and the Prince was very much the *jeune homme de la maison* as he shook and passed cocktails to *their* guests.

Ernest had been cajoled back into the fold. The haunted look once so obvious on the Prince's face had transferred itself to Ernest's. Anyone could see that he was an unhappy man. His love for Wallis had reached a desperate stage. He watched her slipping away from him. They shared less and less together, although, conversely, he came more often to her bed. (On her part, this was an attempt to keep him complaisant.) He could not do for her any of the things the Prince could; and he knew how much the acceptance of society meant to her, how she cherished her growing collection of magnificent jewelry.

She and Ernest rowed often, but both tried to refrain from saying anything that might destroy what little they had left. While Ernest was scrabbling to protect his home, the Prince grew more reckless in his possessive attitude toward Wallis, who was—after all—Mrs. Ernest Simpson, and Wallis was forced to reprimand him from time to time.

But Wallis's admonishing attitude only strengthened his love for her. They were now WE—Wallis and Edward blended into one acronym that said it all—and he was desperate to keep it so. Her rebukes, her accusations of his adolescent behavior, were counteracted by extravagant praise and impassioned love when he pleased her. He was riding an emotional teeter-totter, and Wallis was his only balance. Nothing she could have done would have bound him any closer to her. She had, as she had hoped, become the stern mother and the loving mistress.

And so, oblivious to almost all save themselves, they went through the early and late summer as England lavishly celebrated the King's Silver Jubilee with pageantry only the British could muster; and war—*war,* that awesome word, played a dissonant bugle in the background. The Prince had made an extraordinary speech at the British Legion, advocating friendship with Germany, a gesture that the King and Queen and many of the courtiers believed had been inspired by Wallis. In fact, the Prince, because of family ties, had always been sympathetic to the Germans.

If anyone had influenced him in his feelings of appeasement toward Germany, it was Emerald, who not only had welcomed Hitler's personal envoy, Joachim von Ribbentrop, to her table, but was at present hoping to seduce the German Ambassador, Leopold von Hoesch, into her bed. Emerald had brought von Hoesch to the Fort for a weekend. There, the Ambassador had engaged the Prince in vigorous discussions about Germany's wish for peace and equal recognition among the nations of the world.

During that Jubilee summer, Wallis was occupied with domestic rather than political issues. She was making some decorative changes at the Fort, an effort to erase Freda's influence completely. She redid the Prince's red room in yellow and cream with touches of mandarin orange. The pink bedroom was transformed into a light beige and aquamarine bed-sitting room suitable for married guests. A wall was knocked out and the Blue Room, which Wallis used, was enlarged into a comfortable suite. The house now had a country look. Next she removed a portrait of Queen Mary from the wall in the drawing room and replaced it with a hunting scene. The plan was to rehang it in a room at York House, but with one large painting of the Queen already on show there, it seemed not too disrespectful if this never got done.

They cruised the Mediterranean again in September. This time with Slipper, the little dog that was now the object of much affection from both of them, even though the animal had to be smuggled back into England in defiance of Britain's quarantine regulations. Ernest had been asked to join them, but declined. During Wallis's absence he made a trip instead to New York. Wallis suspected that more than business was now drawing him back to the States. Her decision was to avoid mention of it. Upon his return to London, Ernest was more cheerful than he had been in a year; and the face they maintained for the outer world seemed to her to have fallen neatly back into place.

Wallis moved restlessly around the flat at Bryanston Court, into the kitchen, back to the drawing room, to her bedroom and dressing room. Christmas was the following day, and David had just left to join his parents and the rest of his family at Sandringham.

For the past month weekends at the Fort had been occupied with helping him prepare for the holiday. There had been over two hundred presents to select and then to wrap. Even Ernest had stolidly ground out package after package with astonishing skill and artistry. Next had come a twelve-foot tree which had to be decorated, and this noon the gifts to be distributed to all the staff before David drove her back to London, Ernest having returned earlier to attend to business before his office closed for the celebration.

She was alone in the apartment. There was a small table-top tree covered with silver ornaments and artificial snow in the entry. A larger, matching tree sat in the corner of the drawing room. Tall vases of holly cheered all the reception rooms, although they did little to imbue Wallis with the spirit of Christmas. Suddenly the flat seemed small and dingy. She had come to realize her two incompatible life-styles were as different as the two men with whom she shared them.

As Mrs. Simpson of Flat 5, Bryanston Court, she still had problems making ends meet. She and Ernest were perennially in debt, always having to borrow ahead on his salary. As the Prince's favorite, she spent time in palaces, country estates, royal suites and luxurious yachts. Then she came home to Bryanston Court, the rooms seeming cramped and impossibly *déclassé*.

I'm really beginning to hate this place, she thought, as she stood in the doorway of the bedroom she had once thought so charming. Slipper had jumped up on the satin cover of the bed and was whining for her to join him. "Get down from there, Slipper," she scolded. The small puff of a dog sat up and cried louder. "Get down, I say!" she warned. The animal jumped off and scampered under the bed.

David's Christmas gift was in her hands. He had given it to her just before his departure. It was a fair-sized parcel about twelve inches square, wrapped obviously by himself, the corners sagging ominously, the ribbons tied with a knot apparently learned during his naval training days. She had planned to put it under the dining-room tree and open it in the morning along with Ernest's gift. Suddenly she had second thoughts on doing so. The shape of the package and its size led her to believe it could not be a bracelet or even a necklace. Too large. Whatever the contents, they would exceed in value anything Ernest had purchased, which would only create new tension.

Impulsively, she decided to open the package right then

and sat down at her dressing table, carefully snipping the ribbons with her manicure scissors. The paper fell off to reveal a large deep-blue velvet jewelry box with WALLIS in gold letters on the top. Inside was a complete suite of cabochon sapphires, diamonds and blue chalcedony ("To match the blue-violet of your eyes," he had written on the accompanying card) which included a striking necklace, handsome earclips and two large double-bangle bracelets all designed by the innovative French jeweler Suzanne Belperron. The truly spectacular set had cost a small fortune.

She clipped on the earrings, fastened the necklace on herself. It was ironic, she thought, that she now had a collection of jewels worth many, many tens of thousands of dollars and an overdraft at the bank. She felt she could not ask David for money; nor could she sell anything he had given her (nor did she want to!). And although designers like Mannbocher and Schiaparelli gave her clothes at cost, the wardrobe she required for her social life was nearly bankrupting Ernest.

She hoped David would like her present—a gold Cartier cigarette case decorated with a map of Europe, inscribed with the names of the various places they had been together, each represented by a diamond, sapphire or ruby, and signed simply: *David from Wallis Christmas 1935*. In order to pay for it she had sold Grandmother Warfield's tortoise and diamond combs which, because of their antique value, had been worth much more than she had ever imagined, and had also paid for a handsome pair of onyx cuff links and matching studs for Ernest.

The front door opened and closed. "Wallis?"

Ernest was home. She hurriedly removed the jewelry, placed it back in the box and stuffed it, along with the wrappings, in the side cupboard of her dressing table.

"In here, Ernest," she called.

Slipper appeared from under the bed and, curling his hairy lip, growled as fiercely as his tiny vocal box allowed.

"I wish that damned dog would realize I live here, too!" Ernest complained.

"He's just protective of me. He wouldn't think of biting you."

"I wouldn't want to wager a substantial bet on that." He studied her for a moment. "You look flushed. Any problems?"

"No. Just that we're expected at Sibyl's in an hour—and we have virtually no staff for two days." He had started out of the room. "There was a lovely letter from Aunt Bessie. She sent us a two-hundred-dollar check."

"That was generous."

"There was also a letter from Mary. Her divorce from Jacques is final."

"Oh? What are her plans?"

"Well, Mary never hurts for money. She'll do Europe in the spring. I'll write and ask her to stay with us for a time. She'll love all the new glamour."

"Sounds like a good idea. How do we dress tonight?"

"Black tie for you as usual. The Nicolsons will be there. And Dickie and Edwina Mountbatten. Sibyl's been helping them redo their flat. You can't believe the money being spent—Edwina's, of course. Priceless paintings, fabulous furniture and magnificent jade. Dickie's trained his footman, on hearing the ringing of the doorbell on the street floor, to synchronize his walk from the pantry to the apartment door with the time it takes the lift to ascend. The purpose of all this being for the man, in all his livery finery, to open the door to the apartment the exact instant the lift arrives at it. Isn't that a kick!"

"Perhaps, but not surprising. I'd better dress." He left the room. Moments later Wallis heard him run his bath and took the jewelry box out to look at her gift another time. She would have to show it to Ernest. Tomorrow, she decided, after she had displayed much enthusiasm for his gift to her. She knew it was something to wear because she had seen, in his dressing room, a box from Saks Fifth Avenue that he had brought back from his New York trip.

A shared sense of foreboding that this might be the King's last Christmas overshadowed the festivities at Sandringham. A concerted effort had been made to make it an especially happy holiday. A twenty-foot tree dominated the spacious white ballroom, scene of so many gay Christmases in the past. The King, who had seldom played with his own children, instigated games and sat lovingly watching Bertie's two daughters, his adored "Lilibet" and her sister, Margaret.

David had been the last to arrive, and his father looked up at him with such a curious expression that his eldest son was alarmed. He had this prescient feeling that the King could read his mind, that he knew how he felt about Wallis, how determined he had now become that somehow they would marry even if it meant renouncing his succession.

He planned to talk to his father before the holiday ended, to tell him what was in his heart. His father seemed to be fading even as the short visit progressed. "We are to make this a very happy time for your father," his mother warned. And so he said nothing but left early on Boxing Day. He wanted to go directly to Wallis but Ernest was home. Lately his resentment of Ernest's presence in the flat in Bryanston Court had become almost unbearable. "Something must be done," he told himself. "Something must be done *soon*."

28

Wallis could not believe her eyes. Resting on a velvet cushion in a jewelry box the same size as the one she had received for Christmas was a fabulous display of rubies and diamonds—waterfalls of them, it seemed—spilling over a necklace, earrings, bracelets and a brooch with a ruby pendant at least two inches in diameter.

"They were my grandmother's, Queen Alexandra's," he said, watching her with pleasure as she touched each piece fondly, seeming unable to lift it from the case, as though she were in a dazed spell. He picked up the necklace, the rubies—a gift from an Indian maharajah—a deep fiery red, perfectly matched, set in the design of two laurel branches with diamonds for the stems, and stood behind her as he fastened it about her throat. "It graces you even more beautifully," he said.

The weight of the piece—it must have contained over a hundred carats of diamonds and triple that in rubies—caused Wallis to stiffen her neck. "No wonder Queens hold their heads so erect," she laughed, then took hold of his hand and held it tight in her own. "David, you spoil a girl so. Such beautiful sapphires for Christmas and now these!"

"Oh, my sweetheart," he said, coming around to face her. "I know we'll have *viel Glück* to make us *one* this year."

"David, you know that is impossible."

"No, it's not. I won't believe that."

Ernest had sailed unexpectedly for America on business again, and Wallis had joined the Prince for New Year's Eve at the country home of Colin and Gladys Buist. They were now in their hosts' library, the door shut but not silencing the sounds of a household preparing for a large party. "God! to be alone for ages and ages and then—ages and ages. Wallis, we cannot go on this way much longer. I cannot do anything that is expected of me. All my thoughts are on you. If we were to marry it would be so simple—*and right.*"

"You mustn't talk this way." She looked at him with startled eyes.

"Why not? You are all I have ever wanted out of life."

"Please, don't go on," she begged him.

"I will continue and you have to listen to me, Wallis. You don't know how loving you has changed me. You don't have the slightest notion of your effect on me. When you look at me I feel ten feet tall. I could hold up worlds, universes. I know you think the obstacles are insurmountable. One by one WE can vanquish them. There is Ernest, of course. But don't you think he also is entitled to a woman who loves him?"

"That's unfair, David. I have tried to be a good wife to Ernest."

"I'm not blaming you. If anyone is to blame, it is me. I am well aware that I have come into his home and taken what he cherishes. You must agree, darling, that this could not have happened if we weren't meant to be together. I know you *care* for Ernest and because you are good and true you do not wish to do anything that will destroy him. You are wrong. Remaining with him is far more damaging to him, and it will devastate us as well."

"You don't understand. Ernest and I have a comfortable arrangement. We are good friends. Sometimes, I believe he may be the best friend that I have," she explained.

"Be that as it may, I cannot bear it knowing he is there with you at Bryanston Court. You must leave Ernest, Wallis, you *must.*"

"You can't be suggesting divorce."

"Yes, I am. Divorce from Ernest and marriage to me."

"Oh, David, you are such a boy. Do you really think your family or your country would let you marry me? It's crazy. Just crazy!"

"What is crazy is that we have a love, a oneness of soul, which is what all mortals strive for in a relationship and for some curious reason people resent it." He drew her to a nearby sofa, eased her onto it and sat down beside her. "I've never dreamed I could feel about any woman as I feel about you, Wallis. Now, be honest with me, darling, dead honest. Have you ever felt this way about another man?"

She did not even have to hesitate. Of course, she had not! There was only one Prince of Wales. The situation was unique and so she could say, without any feeling at all of deception, "Never." She saw that his hand trembled as he raised it to touch her face.

"Sweetheart," he said. There was a tear in his voice although his eyes were dry.

"But, David, you have to promise me that you will put aside these thoughts of marriage for now. You must be willing to try to be content with what we have—and that is quite a lot. I'm terrified of what could happen if I leave Ernest. The press would make much of it—and somehow we could be forced apart."

A bleak look glazed her eyes. She stared across the strange room, peering into her dead past with all its foolish decisions, the costly sacrifices, the humiliations now entombed. Could she bear to relive such pain? She thought not. She was as sure of herself as she would ever be, but she did not think David possessed the fire to melt the Ice Queen.

"We need time, David," she said. "*All* of us. I can't just walk out on Ernest. I simply am unable and unwilling to do it."

"I hate and loathe the mere thought of you being alone with him when you are not with me," he said almost as a curse.

"But now he is away and, at least for the next six weeks, you will not have to share me. Please, I beg you, be sensible, be patient for that time."

He got up and pulled her to him and took her in his

arms. "You know your David will love you and look after you so long as he has breath in this eanum body," he vowed.

He kissed her gently and then bounced back, a wide, delighted grin on his face. "Now let's see you in the entire display!" he commanded.

Her laughter came in the small, explosive bursts that were so characteristic of her. She walked over to the library table where she had left the jewel case. She was wearing a tweed skirt and a simple, tailored white blouse and it wasn't easy to attach the enormous brooch to the soft fabric. Finally she succeeded and he helped her with the catches on the bracelets, standing back and admiring her as she secured the earrings.

"I must look ridiculous," she said.

"Like a Queen," he corrected.

"Funny, Ernest said that to me once. Oh, David, they are glorious, *glorious*. No girl ever had anything to match it."

"I want you to wear them tonight," he decided.

"I was going to dress as a pirate," she chortled. "Now, I think I better go as his treasure!"

With Ernest away they spent more time together at the Fort. It was the one place they could go without prying eyes. There were always other guests but Wallis made sure they were friends of hers, like the Scanlons, and since it was the season, some of the Prince's hunting companions. On Thursday, January 16, the weather bitter cold, he went shooting in Windsor Great Park. In the entry of the Fort, Wallis was arranging flowers that had just been brought up from the greenhouse when a Royal messenger arrived with a letter to the Prince of Wales from the Queen.

"His Royal Highness will not return until late this afternoon," she heard the butler inform the man.

"Does Her Majesty expect an immediate reply?" she intervened.

"I was told to wait for His Royal Highness's answer," he told her. The man's grim face and urgent manner decided Wallis to send him out into the field to find the Prince. Less than half an hour later, David returned looking pale and anguished.

"Read it," he said, and handed his mother's letter to her.

Wallis sat down on the bright chintz chair in his study and unfolded the piece of red-rimmed paper with its embossed crown of the same color. "Dear David," the Queen had written in a cramped but steady hand, "I think you ought to know that Papa is not very well. And although I do not consider the danger immediate, his doctor, Lord Dawson, is not too pleased with Papa's state at the present moment. I therefore suggest that you propose yourself for the coming weekend at Sandringham, but do so in a manner that will not lead Papa to suspect that I have warned you of his condition."

The note was signed *Mama,* indicating an intimacy with her son that somehow surprised Wallis. She had thought *Mother* or even *the Queen* more likely. She sat silently, struck by the fact that she was holding a paper of historic importance—a Queen's private letter to her son that his father, the King, was dying. How this might affect her own life was far from Wallis's thoughts, for the Prince's distress was obvious and required immediate attention.

"He's dying," he said. "Mama would not have sent for me otherwise."

"Oh, David, I'm so sorry," she replied, realizing how inadequate were her words.

"I may never be able to confront him now to tell him how I feel about things; what I plan to do."

"I know, David, I know. When my mother was dying I felt the same emotions. There's so much anger and frustration mixed in with your grief. But, perhaps, your father will come out of this. He has been very ill and snapped back before."

"Perhaps," he repeated wistfully.

He flew in his private plane to Sandringham the next morning. His sister Mary was already there, and the two of them went into their father's bedroom together. King George sat slumped half-asleep in his favorite chair in front of the fire, dressed in an old Tibetan dressing gown, a faded relic of one of his Indian tours, and had a lap blanket about the lower half of his body. His bed, placed in one corner, was the same simple brass one in which Edward VII had slept. From the bay window across the sunken garden could be seen the square church tower from which the Royal standard flew.

The King roused himself when his children entered. For a moment a flicker of recognition came into his eyes, but he said nothing. David stood there, his mind racing. He felt as though his entire life was being destroyed right before his eyes by the shriveled figure sitting hunched, facing him. The eyes flickered open. "Have you been skating?" he asked in a rasping whisper. He was back somewhere when his children were young. The lids dropped, the shrunken head, looking pathetically small above the lavish embroidery of the collar on his robe, fell sideways onto his shoulder. His breathing was erratic, coming in small gasps.

David and his sister Mary left the room. Bertie had just arrived. His hands shook. He had trouble in speaking David's name. His brother wanted to hold him, to ease his pain in some way. But physical closeness had never been an easy thing in their family. Georgie joined them a short time later. Harry had a bad throat and did not want to risk travel with the weather so bad.

"Has anyone spoken to Dawson?" Georgie asked.

"He says it is only a matter of time. A week at the most," David replied grimly.

They were standing in the corridor outside their father's room. Through the far window a wicked wind was blowing and leafless branches scratched the panes. It was only shortly before noon, but the sky was dark and the lights on in most of the rooms. From up the hallway, familiar, sturdy footsteps approached. Their mother drew near. She wore a long black Persian-lamb coat, a tall Russian-styled fur hat and carried a black ebony walking stick. Pearls gleamed at her ears and ropes of them, choker-length, encircled her neck.

"It will do us good to get out of doors for a while," she told her sons.

A few minutes later, they walked briskly around the grounds, four abreast, defying the wind, choking back the cold. Queen Mary, surefooted on the icy paths, refused the arm of any one of her three sons. "Your father will soon be dead," she said with finely controlled emotion. "David, you will be King and as soon as possible I will vacate Buckingham Palace, Windsor and—here. I shall move back to the apartments at Marlborough House where I lived before your father became King." She had deftly, and without embellishment of soft-pedaling, put into words what they had all been thinking.

Her cool acceptance of the inevitable shocked David despite his lifelong experience with his mother's restraint. He was, as always, almost tongue-tied in her presence. He understood Bertie's problem and felt great sadness to see that his brother's old facial tics and speech impediment had returned. Once inside the house again, his mother now standing vigil in the sickroom, he took Bertie aside and poured him a strong brandy.

"Bertie," he said, emotionally, "it has never been in my scheme of things to be King."

Bertie's face reddened. He tried desperately hard to answer, but the words would not come out. David put his hand gently on his brother's shoulder. "You are a good man, Bertie. You should have been born first."

Wallis remained at the Fort, waiting for his frequent calls. She knew there was no hope whatsoever for the King's life. It was only a matter of time. David's voice was strained. He was undergoing the most terrible stress. He and his brothers were relieving their mother by their father's bedside whenever she would let them so that she could get some rest. "I love you more and more and need you so to be with me at this difficult time, my darling," he told Wallis, his voice breaking, having to pause before he could go on with their telephone conversation.

"David, dear, please take care of yourself. You will need your strength," she counseled.

"It will work out right for us, Wallis," he said, trying hard to convince himself this was the truth. "My father has never once since I've been here acknowledged my presence," he added disconsolately.

That morning, the King, semiconscious, his eyes distant, unseeing, was propped up in a chair before the open door of his room. By his side were his nurse and the Queen. His doctor leaned over the cadaverous figure and, with great effort, repeated the word *approved* over and over to him. "You must say *approved,* Sir. *Approved.* Can you hear me? *Approved.*" The King did not respond, and the doctor patiently reiterated his request.

After about ten minutes, a faint whisper was heard, "Ap—" The voice died off.

Everyone in the room breathed a sigh of relief. Lord Dawson now handed the King a paper and, holding his patient's limp hand, placed a pen in it, and guided it in the making of two little crosses. Tears filled King George's eyes, the first indication that the dying man knew he had just signed away his power as King to the Councillors of State, who were to be his wife and four sons.

At five minutes to midnight that same night the King's breathing stopped. Queen Mary glanced over her husband's stilled form at the doctor to confirm her fears. Lord Dawson nodded his head. David and his two brothers stood at the foot of the bed. His mother took a steady step toward her eldest son and, bowing, took his hand in hers and kissed it.

"God save the King," she said in a strong, unwavering voice and looked him squarely in the eye. She then stepped back with a slight curtsy and Georgie and Bertie followed her example. David looked at them, dismayed, feeling uncomfortably embarrassed. A few minutes later, he bolted down the corridor to his father's study and called Wallis.

"It's all over," he said. "Oh, God," he cried, "Wallis, my father had just died and my mother curtsied to me. I cannot bring myself to believe that the members of my own family or anyone else should be expected to humble themselves before me in this way."

"David, are you all right? Shall I continue to wait for you here?" she asked.

"Yes, *yes.* Please do. I can't tell you what my plans are. Everything here is so very upset."

An hour later, he rang her again. "I cannot believe it," he confided. "They have just read the will. Each of my brothers has been left a very large sum—about three quarters of a million pounds in cash. I was left nothing and have been precluded from converting what I have inherited, such as the stamp collection, the race horses, antiques, jewels, into ready money. I have been left the Crown without the cash. I believe my father thought he would keep me on the Throne that way. I believe he knew I did not want to be King."

"What does this mean, David?" she asked.

"It means, my darling, we will have to wait longer than I had planned *to be one.* I will have to give at least a year to the Kingship so that you will have the comforts you must have as my wife."

It was only when Wallis hung up the phone that she truly realized that David was now King. She sat there not able to fully grasp what that meant. Suddenly, his words came back to her. "I will have to give *at least* a year to the Kingship so that you will have the comforts you must have as my wife." My God! He intended eventually to abdicate! Why had she not seen this? She would have to convince him not to consider taking such a path.

Wallis awoke to the ring of the telephone. She now had two lines—one that went directly to the King's study at St. James's and her old number, Ambassador 2215. It was the latter and she sleepily picked it up. The connection was very bad, static. She could hardly hear the operator. Then Ernest was on the line. "Speak louder, Ernest," she shouted. "I can hardly hear you."

"Are you all right?"

"Yes, I'm fine. And you?"

"Wallis, the papers—" His voice faded.

"What did you say, Ernest?"

"The American papers. Nothing else except the new King. Is it to be Edward?"

"Yes, he's going to call himself Edward VIII."

"And you, Wallis? What does this mean for you?"

"I can't hear you, Ernest," she lied, for the connection was suddenly quite clear. "When are you coming home?"

"As planned. In February. Has anything changed, Wallis?"

"What's that? Listen, Ernest dear, can you call later? This connection is really bad."

"All right," he agreed. A moment later there was only a steady buzz and she hung up the receiver.

She simply had not felt able to talk to Ernest. Everything was upside down, and she was so keyed up that she had been unable to handle any of the questions that Ernest was asking. She did not know how he was going to feel about simple things like the telephone line, never mind the security detectives now stationed around the clock near their building so that the King could come visit her at any hour he might have free and feel safe. The precaution seemed unnecessary to her since, for the past few days, the King's time had been occupied with the ceremonies and formalities of a new reign.

He had arranged for her to see one of the four city-wide Proclamations of Accession at St. James's Palace from an unused apartment that looked out on Friary Court, where the ceremony would be conducted. Wallis, partially concealed, stared out from a thinly curtained window. The Earl Marshal, the Prime Minister, Stanley Baldwin, the remaining Ministers and Privy Councillors in uniform stood at the back of the balcony. The Garter King-of-Arms, attended by Heralds, Pursuivants and trumpeters, dressed in their scarlet and blue medieval costumes, flashing with silver and gold, stepped out on the balcony to join the dignitaries. The proclamation was raised, ready to be read to the massive, hushed crowd below.

A hand fell on Wallis's shoulder. Startled, she turned quickly around. David stood at her side. The others in the room, members of the King's staff, were even more astonished. One of the women made a flustered curtsy; and Wallis, although she knew he did not like such obsequious gestures from those who were part of his private life, immediately followed suit. As she rose from it, her glance met his. He looked exhausted, black circles shadowed his eyes, his face was pale. The small lines around his mouth flickered nervously. She thought how much older he had suddenly become. The boyish look had vanished.

Turning to one of his assistant private secretaries, he remarked, "This may strike you as somewhat unusual, but the thought came to me that I would like to see myself proclaimed King."

He stood beside Wallis in the window as the Garter King-of-Arms read out in a booming voice that echoed through the courtyard: "The High and Mighty Prince Edward Albert Christian Andrew Patrick David is now by the death of our late Sovereign of happy memory become our only lawful right Liege Lord, Edward the Eighth, by the Grace of God, King of the United Kingdom of Great Britain and Ireland and of the British Dominions beyond the Seas, Defender of the Faith, Emperor of India, to whom we acknowledge all faith and constant obedience, with all hearty and humble affection, beseeching God, by whom Kings and Queens do reign, to bless the Royal Prince Edward VIII with long and happy years to reign over us."

The heralding trumpets sounded. Guns in the adjoining park thundered their salute. Then one man in the reverent crowd sang the opening bars of "God Save the King." The hymn was taken up by another voice and then by a third. In a moment, the voices of the crowd rose majestically in song, punctuated by the explosion of guns.

It was almost impossible for Wallis to conceive that by the divine right of kings all this was now for David. Tears came to her eyes. He touched her hand, unseen by others. As they made their way down the stairs from the room where they had observed the ceremony, Wallis whispered, "I've just realized how different your life is going to be."

He gently pressured her arm. "There will be a difference, of course. But nothing can ever change my feelings toward you." With a brief smile, he was gone.

Wallis was restless, unable to sleep. It was the middle of the night. She got up and went to her window. The night was dark, almost moonless, and rainy. She was all alone. The servants were in their quarters. David was standing watch with his brothers at Westminster over their father's coffin. She went into the kitchen and made herself a cup of tea; then she couldn't drink it. She felt she could not stay one moment longer by herself at Bryanston Court. She dressed warmly and bundled into a coat and a rain cape, grabbed an umbrella from the stand in the entry and went down the lift to the street. As soon as she turned the corner, she knew the security detective was right behind her.

She walked all the way to the Mall. There was unrest in the streets. Thousands had already gathered to form lines on both sides to wait for the funeral procession the next day. People were selling programs. Canvas tents had been raised to cover some of the stands. There were few cars. Mounted police were struggling for order. Wallis didn't know now why she had come. It was filthy cold, the damp penetrating. There were no taxis. She wondered if there had been such crowds the night before King Charles's execution. Shivering, she started to cross the street, thinking she might be better off to go only as far as the Ritz and let them get her a car from there.

"Mrs. Simpson," a man in a brown mackintosh said as he stepped in front of her. For a moment her heart seemed to stop. He took out some identification. He was her security man. "I don't mean to frighten you. But I think you would be better off to return home. I have a car parked nearby."

She gratefully accompanied him. Neither of them spoke as he drove her back to Bryanston Court. "Thank you, very much," she said and hurried into the lift. She took a warm bath and was just getting back into bed when she heard the eerie, unmistakable sound of pipers and then muffled drums. Not until much later would she see, in film shot of the funeral procession, the even lines of sailors pulling the bare gun carriage, King George's coffin covered in the rich gold of the flag on top, with the recognized symbols of the throne: the crown, scepter and orb. And David, now King Edward VIII, in naval uniform, walking alone behind the coffin looking so small and pathetic. Behind him was the Queen's coach with its red-cloaked footmen, and behind them a dozen more golden coaches carrying the heavily veiled women of the Royal Family. In the distance was the dull sound of a minute gun. And all out of deference to one man whom history had made a King. Just as now it had touched David.

The Court was in full mourning. David could not appear in public except on official business. The weekends at the Fort continued; and during the week he joined Wallis at Bryanston Court as often as possible, but never with more than two other couples in attendance. His great devotion to her did not lessen. If anything, it increased. Yet there was a difference in their life-style, a perceptible stiffening in protocol, a heightening of formality. No longer was it possible for them to lead a private life. The red dispatch boxes containing state documents followed him to the Fort; his every move became a matter of public interest, requiring elaborate preparations; whom he saw and where he went were recorded daily in the Court Circular. Wallis's name appeared for the first time without Ernest's. Still, the English public seemed unaware of their King's passionate alliance.

Around Wallis now gathered the flatterers who wanted the King's ear or his recognition. She was the King's mistress, socially the most important woman in Great Britain. Her own desire was to help David in his duties.

Two dramatic incidents were to change the course of their relationship at this time. Wallis had hoped she could continue as before, with both men playing their respective parts of lover and husband. On March 1, St. David's Day, directly after listening to the King's first radio address to his subjects, she went off to Paris with an American friend, Foxy Gwynne, ostensibly for a fortnight of shopping and rest. Actually she had received an alarming letter from, of all people, Nancy Armstrong. Ernest had just returned to London, seeming outrightly hostile, and had, on his own, decided he must meet with the King without her knowledge.

29

On the train ride down to Paris Wallis's thoughts were on David and on what her role in his life would be. The realization that she was now the *King's* mistress had taken a while for her to absorb. She recalled once having met the elegant Mrs. Keppel, Edward VII's longtime favorite. Even after her Royal lover's death, Alice Keppel was held in great esteem by the Court; and the leading politicians, Churchill among them, came to her grand luncheons. Wallis wondered if Mrs. Keppel had advised the King on matters of state. She briefly considered the idea of inviting her for lunch or tea upon her return. Immediately, she dismissed this notion as being in bad taste.

To her utter surprise and fury, press photographers were waiting for her when she stepped off the train in Paris. They continued to dog her every movement, remaining on guard outside the hotel to snap a picture of her even if it was only as she hurried into a limousine to take her shopping. She became almost paranoid about wanting her privacy, and recalling stories of how, years before, Peggy Hopkins Joyce had the designers bring clothes to her hotel, asked Mannbocher and Madame Schiaperelli if they might oblige. To her delight, they had agreed.

Wallis had met her traveling companion, Foxy Gwynne, who now lived in London, when she and Corrine had been in Paris a decade earlier. Foxy reminded her of the film actress Katharine Hepburn, the fine-boned face, the undisciplined but glorious red hair. Foxy was rich, independent and marvelously amusing. She knew people like Cole and Linda Porter and other famous writers and artists and at the same time was at home among the *beau monde.* Foxy, who found Wallis's notoriety exciting, was much sought after, even as an extra woman guest, by hostesses who hoped to learn from her what gossip they could about the *Scandale Royal.* Foxy, however, would only smile and say, "Sorry, my lips are sealed."

At dawn, one week after the two women had arrived in Paris, Hitler ordered his armies into the Rhineland in contravention of the Versailles Treaty. This caused so much consternation in Paris that the entire city became disjointed. The general opinion in both France and Britain (and the King concurred) was opposed to the use of force to reverse Hitler's coup.

That same evening Wallis had a dinner appointment with Nancy Armstrong. A week before she had left London, Wallis had received a cryptic letter from Nancy, not from Soda Falls as she might have expected, but from, of all places, Warsaw.

"Dear Wallis—I will be in Paris on March seventh and must see you. For reasons I can't explain I can't come to London. Remember Mr. Ku Ling Yong? Write me where you will be: Mrs. Nancy Armstrong, c/o American Express, Paris. Fred is dead. Nancy."

Wallis had ordered dinner served in the sitting room of her suite. Foxy had gone out with the Porters. Nancy arrived punctually at eight P.M. On the surface she appeared unchanged. She was still on the wagon, she told Wallis. She sat opposite her at a small dining table supplied by room service. After serving them, the waiter left as Wallis requested. They were alone.

Nancy wore a gray pleated wool skirt, a matching sweater set, pullover and cardigan, and a pair of low-heeled gray suede shoes. Her only jewelry was a gold locket on a chain and a wristwatch. Her gray hair was drawn tightly back with tortoiseshell combs. The outfit was entirely fitting, colorless enough for a recent widow. Nancy would never have worn black, Wallis decided. Too theatrical. All gray conveyed the same thing without calling attention to the wearer.

Something deep inside had jolted Wallis to attention when she had seen Ku Ling Yong's name in Nancy's letter. The fact that the envelope was postmarked Warsaw also gave her pause. Wallis could not fathom what an American woman, especially one so recently widowed (for, after all, Fred had been alive less than a year before), would be doing on her own in Poland where the political situation was difficult and there was virtually no American colony.

The curious presentiment that had taken hold of her the last time they had parted in Paris returned on receipt of the letter. Now, as she guardedly studied Nancy, trying to appear as causal as she could, a cold shudder went up her spine. Instinctively she knew Nancy was not merely the Navy wife who once had filled her lonely hours with too much gin. And it dawned on her that she had never met, or even seen, Fred Armstrong. Nor to her knowledge had Win. They had been told he was on duty in the Pacific, a secret mission of some kind, and that Nancy had remained in Hong Kong rather than return alone to the States.

"Nancy," Wallis brazened, "I don't want to beat around the bush. I find the manner in which you sought out this meeting very strange. I immediately realized you knew I would see you because you included Mr. Ku's name. Now, tell me right out. What is this all about and why did you have to meet me here and not in London?"

As Wallis was talking, Nancy rose from her chair and moved around the room, eyes narrowed, her hands before her like a blind woman feeling her way, fingering the ledge of the mantel, the backs of tables, the edge of a large wall mirror. "It had to be away from the security you receive in London," she explained, apparently satisfied there were no listening devices.

"Oh-my-god, I'm right. There is no Fred Armstrong, is there?" Wallis asked, alarmed.

"Not that I've been married to."

"Who are you *really*? And what do you want?" Nancy sat down again and carefully pushed her plate aside. How could she ever have believed that this woman was merely a bored Navy wife? The person facing her had intelligence and nerve, and everything she said and did was carefully calculated. Wallis took a long swallow of the red wine she had ordered with dinner. Suddenly, it came to her. "You are a spy," she said in a calm voice that belied her true feelings. "But who for?"

"Well, in fact, I was once a Navy wife and a Navy widow," Nancy said. "My husband was with intelligence during the last war. After his death—I should say murder—Naval Intelligence approached me—"

"American?"

"Of course!" she replied with surprise. "They enlisted my help. No one at that time believed we would have a problem with Germany—at least so soon. I was sent many places, among them Shanghai and Hong Kong. The Communists were our targets. Mr. Ku was on our side. Under your innocent cover, you not only got one of our operatives out of danger; in your luggage, and without your knowledge, we managed to transport a large sum of money to pay off—*our debts*—in Peking. The man you knew as Larry Dean turned out to be a double agent. The money—American—had been slipped inside the lining of your luggage. Another agent working in the hotel was to remove it when you were out for the evening. I learned later that Mr. Dean disposed of him and took it himself."

Just before I returned to my room! Wallis recalled. *I must have caught him in the act. That was why he threatened me with blackmail and why he never tried to collect more money. He had already found what he had come for.* "What do you want now?" she asked Nancy.

"Your help. This time with your knowledge. You see—or can easily manage to see—what is delivered to the King in his red despatch cases."

Wallis jumped to her feet. "Get out of here, Nancy—or whatever the hell your name really is! I will have nothing to do with you or any intelligence agent no matter what the country!" She was consumed with fury, outraged—*yes,* and terrified, too.

"Look, Wallis, it's easy for a report of the Ku Ling Yong incident to find its way onto the desk of British Intelligence and for them to put two and two together."

I don't want to hear this, Wallis thought. She breathed deeply, hoping to bring forth her inner strength. She would not be blackmailed. She had done nothing—*nothing.*

"Our *accidental* meeting on the *Orient Express,* this arranged dinner in Paris, your note to me care of American Express, it has all been documented in a dossier with your name on the envelope."

"Shall I call the hotel manager?" Wallis warned, her eyes blazing, her tone sharp. "I will tell him you have come here to blackmail me."

"Herr Hitler is out to conquer the world," Nancy continued, unruffled. "He must be stopped. Look what has happened in the Rhineland just today. No treaty means anything to him."

A moth was flapping around the overhead chandelier and the sound was intolerable to Wallis. She walked to the door and opened it. "Get out, Nancy," she ordered.

"I must say you are impressive, Wallis," Nancy smiled.

"Not nearly as impressive as I will be if you don't leave here this very minute," Wallis cautioned.

Nancy picked up her raincoat, which was folded over a chair in the entry. "I admire you, Wallis. I admire you a great deal," she said. "You are determined. I thought you would be hard to convince. My superiors considered otherwise. They believed you would do anything rather than chance losing the King. And, of course, if he thought there was any connection between you and American Intelligence, that would be the end."

"I won't be threatened or terrorized," Wallis insisted. "If any of this false information is brought to the King's attention, I shall explain the truth to him."

There were people coming off the elevator. As they loitered, talking in the hallway, Wallis still held the door open. "Well, Nancy, it was so nice to see you. Have a swell trip home to Seltzer Falls," she said coolly.

"Soda Falls," Nancy corrected and, taking her umbrella from a stand next to the door, headed for the elevator.

Stomach pains seized Wallis moments later and she stumbled to the bedroom and fell across the bed. She had this paralyzing fear that somehow her time was running out. She was not sure of what she would do when she returned to London. Certainly becoming a Mata Hari was not a possibility. The pains came in violent waves. *Damn! Damn!* she thought, as she tried to overcome them by thinking of other things. *Nothing is ever as it seems.*

Ernest felt he had had quite enough. In the beginning of Wallis's relationship with her Royal lover, he had willingly accepted the arrangement, for it brought him into close proximity to the Prince of Wales. As the affair continued, growing more intense, his reverence for the Monarchy overcame his anguish at having to share Wallis with another man. But now the new King had constant claim to her presence and her affections. The situation was extremely complex and no less intolerable because it was the King who was in love with his wife.

The role of the injured husband was too difficult for him to play. After all, he had condoned the liaison from the start. Now his life was in limbo. There was someone whom he had been seeing, but Ernest was basically a man of steadfast loyalty. He would never leave Wallis, especially when he felt greatly responsible for their marital dilemma. In truth, Ernest still cared deeply for Wallis and he knew in his heart that no other woman could ever fill the void that would be created by her loss. All his pleas to Wallis that she sever her illicit relationship had fallen on deaf ears. Ernest was now determined to have a final go with the third interested party, the King himself.

It was a daring encounter for Ernest to engineer. He was not by nature a man who took control of a situation or who made decisions on his own. He knew Wallis would put her foot down and not allow a meeting between the King and him to take place as long as she was in London. Therefore, her trip to Paris provided him with the perfect opportunity.

He rang an old friend of his from the Coldstream Guards, Bernard Rickatson-Hatt, who was now editor in chief of Reuters News Services, and to Rickatson-Hatt's astonishment, asked him to accompany him on this mission, providing an audience was granted.

"Why me? Or *anyone*?" Rickatson-Hatt asked.

"Bernie, I need a credible witness, that's all, and I know that despite your affiliation with Reuters you are a man who can be trusted to silence. If the King approves, tell me you will see him with me?"

Rickatson-Hatt agreed, the very intrigue of the secret meeting too seductive for him to resist. The appointment was set up for a Friday evening. Wallis had been in Paris since that Tuesday. Ernest carefully prepared what he would say. He believed he had the upper hand in the situation. What he did not realize was that the King welcomed the idea of the meeting. He had thought long and hard and knew he wanted to marry Wallis. In order for this to happen, Ernest had to agree to a divorce and to be named as the guilty party.

As Ernest's car entered the courtyard of St. James's Palace, he was struck by the fact that, although his wife and the King had met often at this Royal residence for assignations, he had never stepped foot inside. Rickatson-Hatt got out first. A tall man, he had to duck sharply to clear the door of the black vehicle, hired by Ernest expressly for this meeting. Ernest, his step springy, was quickly by his side. Rickatson-Hatt, who had never considered Ernest to be a particularly vital man, was surprised at the intensity of purpose in his attitude.

A footman guided the men through a maze of rooms. The uncomfortable, dark accommodation consisted of seventy-five small, virtually sunless rooms without architectural interest. Freda Dudley Ward and a team of decorators had worked hard—but not miracles—when it was redone for its present occupant. True, it looked its best at night. Through the windows in daytime there was little more than a view of grimy London walls, while in the evening hours the profusion of crystal chandeliers sent shards of sparkling light across the rich woods of the walls and vaulted ceilings and caused the yellowing marble of the floors to gleam.

The two men were led to the King's sitting room with its vast and magnificently framed maps. Ernest could not suppress a smile as they waited for the King to appear. Despite its awesome dimensions and the museum quality of many of the antique pieces, the room had a look of masculine domesticity. Wallis had obviously not yet put her hand on the decoration.

The King entered, not from an inner door but from the same entry they had used. His face was flushed as though he had run up the stairs. He was dressed in a gray pinstripe suit and had apparently been at a meeting that had run overtime, leaving him no time to change for the evening.

The visitors bowed and after the usual exchange of greetings, he motioned for them to be seated. Ernest felt particularly ill at ease at this request because the King remained standing.

"I never could understand why, if a King can sit and stand when he wishes, his guests should not do likewise," he said in an effort to allay Ernest's discomfort.

"Sir, perhaps I should leave," Rickatson-Hatt said, making a gesture to do so.

"If it is all right with you, Sir," Ernest intervened, "I would prefer it if Bernie would remain."

"Of course." There was a tray set up with drinks, and the King went over to it. "I've asked that we not be disturbed. What will you have?"

Since Ernest had been quite used to the King mixing and serving cocktails at the Fort, his now doing so did not disturb him. He asked for a whiskey. Rickatson-Hatt took the same. The King poured himself a gin and sat down opposite the two men.

"Sir," Ernest began, "you must be aware that my position as Wallis's husband has become increasingly intolerable. I must also tell you that I have finally reached a point where I cannot continue on in this manner. The time has come, Sir, that Wallis will have to choose between us and I ask you, Sir, if it should be you, what do you mean to do about it?"

"What *exactly* are you asking, Ernest?" the King pressed.

"I love Wallis deeply, Sir."

"So do I," the King replied.

"And I believe our marriage has given her the safe harbor she has needed. Without it, she will be at sea without an anchor. She is an American. She does not understand in her *bones,* as an Englishwoman would, the discretion expected of her position and I think she even assumes that, if you wished to do so, you could marry her. American girls are raised to believe in storybook endings. They have no grasp of the reality of a monarchy."

Ernest leaned forward. His dark-brown eyes narrowed. The muscles in his face and neck tightened. This was the ultimate moment of manly strength to which he would ever rise. "Sir, are you sincere?" he asked in a steely voice. "And do you, as Wallis has intimated to me, intend to marry her if I leave her?"

Rickatson-Hatt sat up with a start and looked with shock at Ernest. The question had been simply, yet so boldly stated that for a moment he wondered if he had heard correctly. He was so taken aback by his miscalculation of Ernest's forthright qualities that his glance did not shift to the King until moments later.

The King had risen. He, too, could not believe what he had just heard, but for different reasons. Certain that Ernest would implore him to put an end to his relationship with Wallis, he had been prepared to go into battle to convince Ernest their marriage must be dissolved. Instead, Ernest had played directly into his hands.

"Do you really think I would be crowned without Wallis by my side?" he said.

Both men were shaken by this statement. Ernest turned ashen. He looked like a man who had just been told his home and family had perished. "Are you saying, Sir, that you are prepared to marry Wallis and attempt to make her your Queen if you can?" he asked, the steel melting fast as he spoke.

"I do, indeed."

"And if I do not contest a divorce and agree to become the guilty party, you will promise to marry Wallis?"

"Gladly and with all my heart."

Ernest rose to his feet and, in a curious gesture, bowed ceremoniously to the King. "It is a bargain, then?"

"Struck and to be kept," the King said.

Rickatson-Hatt followed Ernest to the door, where the latter stopped and turned. "Sir," Ernest said, "whatever outrage I may feel, as a loyal Englishman, I cannot and will not do anything to damage my Sovereign. I feel I have no other choice, not only to stand aside, but to do so with dignity and guardedness."

He did not wait for the King to reply. He spun on his heel and hurried out and down the nearest staircase. Rickatson-Hatt bowed and sped after him. He was barely aware that he had been witness to a historic meeting. As he rushed behind Ernest, through the Palace's warren of corridors with no servant as guide, his only thought was how bizarre it was, in these modern times, that a woman's life was being decided by the two men who professed to love her. *What if,* he pondered, *Wallis actually loved neither of them?*

30

Wallis stood staring at Ernest. She could not believe this was the man she thought she knew so well. He had just related to her in his own words his confrontation with the King. She was still in Paris where he had joined her directly after the meeting en route to a business appointment in Berlin. The King had called her four or five times a day, and told her his side. She was not, therefore, surprised at Ernest's news. It was his toughness in the matter that astounded her.

"Are you asking me to divorce you, Ernest?" she questioned, her shock at what had transpired at the Palace between Ernest and David and the latter's vow to marry her momentarily overshadowing her outrage that neither man had consulted her first.

"No, Wallis, I am saying—if you want to divorce me, I will be cooperative; and, as you know, the King will do the right thing by you."

"The right thing? Now look, Ernest, I *won't* be bulldozed—"

"He loves you, Wallis, perhaps even more than I do."

"Yes, I believe he does," she said softly.

"And you?"

There was a knock on the door. Ernest went to see who it

was. "A telegram," he said, and handed it to her, watching her as she read the contents.

"It's from Mary Kirk Raffray. She wants to know if she can stay with us in London for a short visit. What in the world will I do with her? Our life is so involved right now."

"You've always liked Mary, and I do, too. Answer *yes.* It would be good for you to have an old friend to talk with."

She put down the telegram, her mind set on weightier matters. "Ernest, what are *we* to do?"

"No, Wallis, not we, *you.* I will go along with the divorce. But don't think it will be easy. The King will have to fight against insurmountable odds to marry you and be crowned King. Bernie and I both felt, after my audience with him, that he would give up the throne, if it came to that."

"Oh, no, Ernest! I don't want him to do that! Lord, no!"

Ernest shrugged his shoulders. "You could break off the relationship. We could go back to New York."

"You would do that?"

"I would."

She sat down on a small gilt chair near an occasional table. She suddenly looked worn to Ernest. On the sofa was a large unwrapped box from Schiaparelli.

"And if we divorced, what would you do, Ernest?" she asked.

"What does it matter? It's not pertinent."

"Of course it is!" She glanced over at the telegram from Mary. "You should take Mary for your bride," she said. "She's always had a keen eye for you."

He laughed nervously.

"I don't know that I like the idea of your going to Germany right now," she said. "What if they intern you?"

"Why would they do that? I'm only going on business as I have a dozen times."

"There's the smell of war in the air," she replied.

"Not between Britain and Germany. They've already fought that war."

"Ernest," she said, suddenly, "I need time."

"I can't give it to you, Wallis. Neither of us have that much time left. When I come back from this trip, I will expect an answer."

On her return to London that Saturday she went straight from the train to the Fort in the Royal Daimler. The weekend proved a trying one with the King pressing her at every opportunity to divorce Ernest. Finally, there came a point where she could not tolerate any more discussion. "You can only do what you think is right for you, Wallis," he consoled, holding her in his arms, trying to soothe her soft sobs. "But if you will let me, I will arrange for you to get some legal advice."

"All right. But please, I need at least four weeks to think things through.

"Anything you want, Sweetheart. Anything you want," he said and, undoing her hair, ran his hands smoothly through it.

Not wishing finances to be a deciding factor, that next week he did an amazing thing. He began arrangements for a trust of three hundred thousand pounds to be set up for her outside England, money he had been busily converting from his various private investments since his father's death.

"Don't worry," she wrote to Aunt Bessie. "People must make their own lives. By now I should have a little experience in that line—as I wasn't able to have it arranged for me by money and position. I have had many hard times and disappointments. I've managed not to go under as yet. Never having known security until I married Ernest, perhaps I don't go along well with it because I know and understand the thrill of its opposite much better."

When Ernest returned home, he was brimming with horror stories of what was happening in Germany. "Fear, *fear* motivates everything. This question of the Jews is terrifying everyone. Hitler is turning the people against them. I can't imagine how he will succeed. After all, the Jews in Germany control the banks. They are *the* intelligentsia."

Mary arrived a short time later; and the following weekend, to her unsuppressed excitement, she accompanied Wallis and Ernest to the Fort. Ernest had relented and an agreement had been made that for the next four weeks things would go along as they always had, giving Wallis a chance to decide her next step.

Wallis could not get over the change in Mary. Her divorce from Jacques appeared to have transformed her. She wanted to go out every evening to a nightclub or the theater, which was difficult because Wallis always had to be ready if the King should decide to stop by. Then there was the problem that—unlike those in the States—English hostesses did not necessarily include one's houseguests in their invitations. To make matters worse, Mary's clothes were more suggestive than was in good taste in Wallis's circle. There were so many of them, in fact, that they could not be contained in the small wardrobe in the guest room and Mary's costumes now were jammed in with her own.

"You would prefer it if I wasn't here, wouldn't you, Wallis?" Mary asked late one afternoon before Ernest had come back from the office.

"Don't be ridiculous, Mary. It's just that I am under such terrible pressures right now." Wallis managed a reassuring smile and could not help but notice how relieved Mary seemed.

She was forced to look at her friend with a new eye. Mary had slimmed considerably and the mousy brown hair was now a dark brown, almost the same color as her own. She seemed to prefer tripping over objects in her path rather than wearing her glasses. But Wallis had to admit the myopic glaze of Mary's blue eyes and the new dark hair coloring gave her an attractive, if somewhat startled doe, look.

"Are you going to divorce Ernest?" she asked.

"I'm not sure," Wallis replied, a bit sharply.

"Don't jump at me. I'm interested, that's all. After all, our friendship goes back a lot of years."

"The rebuke is noted and filed," Wallis replied.

Mary got up from the chaise in Wallis's dressing room where they were both sitting while Wallis did up her hair, and looked over her shoulder into the mirror. Mary concentrated on their images, her forehead furrowed, her eyes narrowed to enable her to see better. Despite her improved appearance, the two faces could not be compared. Her own was winsome, yet prosaic; Wallis's was striking and enjoyed a natural exotic look. Way back, she thought, there had been Spanish blood, even Polynesian—the eyes were so wide set, the forehead high, the hair dark and lustrous. Makeup could not endow Mary's face with such uniqueness.

"I always envied you so, Wallis," she sighed wistfully. "Ever since Oldfields. You were in such iron control of your life. I know you had hard times. But you never let anything get you down. Even my mother! My, you sure made her head spin!" She laughed.

Wallis turned around in her chair so that they were facing each other. "It was not the happiest experience of my life," she grimaced.

"But you did make her sit up and take notice. You will be pleased to learn that she is an absolutely *avid* collector of all that is printed about you. She's forever sending me clippings from the papers and magazines. There is nothing that would please her more than if you found me a stray prince, even an impoverished one, so that she could say her daughter Mary has a Royal lover, as well. Not that mother would use the word *lover,* or even *think* it. In mother's world men and women keep company, hold hands and eventually exchange church vows."

She crossed over to Wallis's wardrobe and took out a very décolleté black satin gown. "I thought I would wear this to that party at Lady Emerald's next week."

"It isn't Lady Emerald, it is Lady Cunard. A woman's Christian name is only used if *she* has inherited her own title. If it is her husband's she is Lady Cunard—or whoever, just as I am Mrs. Simpson and you are Mrs. Raffray. And—no, that dress is not at all appropriate. Too naked."

"You are jumping at me again."

"I am, and I'm sorry."

A door opened and closed in the front entry.

"That must be Ernest," Mary said. Wallis did not miss the gleam that had appeared in her eyes.

My God! She's got a thing for him, she thought. Just the complication that she needed. Mary had always wanted whatever she had, which had seemed madness to Wallis, because, of the two, Mary had been the more fortunate—born a Kirk, accepted socially and an heiress to a large estate.

For the next few weeks she included her in her plans when she could, saw that Ernest escorted her to the theater or dinner when she could not. If the idea did come to her that this might become a provocative situation, she quickly brushed it aside. Mary, she believed, was just not Ernest's type. He was attracted to strong, forceful women like his first wife and herself. Mary was anything but that.

Her main concern was the decision she would soon have to make, one she knew was inevitable. Had an ultimatum not been given, she could not have gone on much longer under the awful strain of trying to please two men and to fit into two such separate lives. She was tired, nervous and irritable, and her stomach spasms had been recurring with painful frequency. She wished her life could be wound back, and like the needle on a gramophone record, she could begin anew. She recalled Win once saying that their marriage had become a scratched record. She refused to believe now that history might be repeating itself.

Whatever Ernest threatened, she remained certain that he would go on forever as things were and that, if she did let the King go, he would not desert her. She could rely upon Ernest; and, with the trust that had been set up in her name and the jewels David had given her, money need never again present a serious problem. Yet it would be difficult to go back to life in Bryanston Court as it was before.

Aunt Bessie's previous warning that she might lose both men haunted her. Well, if that happened, she decided, she would be like the Arabs and fold her tent and steal silently away to travel and find new friends.

One night when she remained home to receive the King, Ernest took Mary to a nightclub. They did not return until six A.M. Wallis was awake in bed when she heard the latch on the front door, the muffled laughter, the sounds of cautious footsteps. She avoided seeing either of them that day and then, to her astonishment, when she awoke the next morning, they had calmly gone off in a hired motor for three days in the country and had left her a simple note to the effect with no other explanations.

When she told David what had happened, he insisted they put a detective on the trail. Ernest and Mary were found in a compromising situation in a small hotel in Bray by a private investigator posing as a waiter as he served them breakfast in bed. A photograph had been taken.

Mary moved to a service flat upon their return. Until a smooth transition could be arranged, Ernest remained at Bryanston Court. As a final request, after declaring his love for Mary, he prevailed upon Wallis to keep up the status quo and to include Mary at all meals and parties. She agreed; but sitting across a dining table from her traitorous friend was almost more than she could bear, and she tried as often as she could to make other arrangements.

The scene was set for separation, then divorce. Wallis now had evidence that could brand Ernest the guilty party. At the moment he was not prepared to make the final split, wanting to be assured that, following their parting, Mary would not, in the end, reject him. Throughout the month of June, the weather was unseasonably cold, so freezing that weekends at the Fort were spent indoors. David pressed, pleaded and conspired to force Wallis to proceed legally, while Ernest had decided they should wait. Wallis was beside herself.

"I can't be pushed and prodded," she cried. But finally she went to see a divorce lawyer, who, to her shock, refused to take the case. She suddenly realized the amount of resistance they would face. Still, David did not relent. Another lawyer was found, and one early weekend in August when Wallis was at the Fort, Ernest moved from Bryanston Court into the Guards Club. Wallis was exhausted. She had lost considerable weight. She had, perhaps not wholly of her own free will, given in to events. She would divorce Ernest.

She gave as little thought as she could to what this would involve. David was constantly reassuring her that she would be beside him when he was crowned—and the Coronation was set for the following May. Had he not been able to obtain anything he wished by a simple command? Why not this? Ernest had been right; she did not understand the British in her *bones,* but Wallis did not yet know this. David was so sure, and his positive attitude eased her concern.

She could not lie to herself and say the thought of becoming Queen Consort was not madly thrilling. What woman would not have seen it as the greatest fantasy come true? Privately, she went through David's photograph albums, studying the pictures of his grandmother Queen Alexandra, so regal in her crown and jewels, and his mother—no other woman, she decided, could wear so many jewels and still look elegant. But she saw the downside, too.

There were the politicians who would fight to keep her from marrying the King, men like Prime Minister Baldwin, whom she had recently met and who had looked at her with cold, calculating loathing (she had returned his hard gaze with a frozen smile); there were the King's subjects, who loved their Sovereign and would consider her a curious choice; there were the churchmen—natural adversaries who might not recognize their marriage; and there was the entire Royal Family, who would be snide and unwelcoming, always enemies. They had shown their dislike of her all along, and lately it had intensified. The Queen Mother, Bertie and Elizabeth, Harry and Alice had refused all invitations where she would be present unless it was a Court affair. Even Georgie and Marina now snubbed her. She had not been lucky in the past with in-laws and could deal with their hostility. What it would do to the King was another matter.

Wallis was awakened by a sharp lurch of the boat. She and David had sailed off on a four-week cruise. Voices rose outside on the deck. The calm, regular rhythm of the sea as the prow of the steam yacht *Nahlin* nosed its way down the coast of Yugoslavia and Albania had stopped. That meant they had docked in the early hours of the morning at Corfu. Wallis tied the sash on her dressing gown and opened the bright nautical draperies that covered the portholes. They were anchored in a large, serene bay, ethereal mountains in the distance; the morning light so keen that everything she saw was sharp-edged. She experienced a strange sensation. It was as though she had just been roused from a long dream; all the confusion and the havoc of the past few months had dissolved into a newfound reality.

David was standing at the rail of the boat with Captain Jessel, Jack Aird and Duff and Diana Cooper. Except for the captain, they were all dressed casually. David wore tan shorts and a shirt with an open neck. His skin was bronzed from the sun, his child's hair gleaming golden. He looked terribly unkingly, she thought. She was vitalized by the idea that perhaps, here in this ancient world, they had found a place where they could be merely a boy and girl in love. Curious how they always referred to themselves in such pubescent terms. She no longer thought of David as looking boyish. It was the amazing passion and—*yes*—the innocence of their love, the great need to pleasure each other, that gave their attachment and themselves a spirit of youthfulness.

It was not yet seven A.M. but she dressed quickly, wanting to join the others up on deck. This was to be an exciting day. The King of Greece, who was David's cousin, was at his villa in Corfu and he had been invited to dine that night on the *Nahlin.* With their host country's King on hand, Wallis had hopes that Corfu would prove to be the island paradise they had been seeking in the ports the *Nahlin* had already visited. The cruise had proved marvelously relaxing when they were at sea and disappointing whenever they went ashore. There were no sheltered coves for bathing as there had been during the trip on the *Rosaura,* and the sand felt like pumice on the bare soles of one's feet.

More disconcerting were the yelling, jostling crowds wherever they docked, leaving David and her no space even to breathe when they tried to walk up the old streets of port towns to see the churches and ancient buildings. The throngs of people shouted the one English word they all knew, "Cheerio!," and surrounded them so that they could see nothing. Often the local militia had to be called out to control the mobs. To make matters worse, there had been photographers from the French, Italian and American press following the *Nahlin* in boats of their own for the entire journey and, Wallis had been told, using long-distance lenses to procure pictures of them on board ship as well as on land.

When Wallis came on deck their first morning in Corfu, a message had just been received from King George of Greece saying he was bringing six English guests to dinner. Everyone was in a bit of a dither because the *Nahlin* did not have sufficient table seating to accommodate them.

"Well, Jackie," the King told Aird, "you will have to call

on the King of Greece and see if you can't get us all invited to his villa instead."

A disgruntled Aird went off on his errand directly after breakfast to return an hour later with word that the King of Greece was also unable to seat so many people at his table (they would have been sixteen in all). Back went an overheated Aird (for the day had grown beastly hot and his temper had risen with the thermometer) with a new invitation: cocktails on board the *Nahlin.* This was duly accepted and Wallis was left to arrange the details.

The many revolutions in Greece had badly scarred the country. Ruin, not classical but modern, was everywhere. The rich villas had been mostly destroyed by the rebel forces, and King George's own Corfu residence was practically roofless. The Greek King had been a dapper, handsome man, a well-known roué, deposed more than once and welcomed in England at those times by his cousins, the British Royal Family. David had been much looking forward to seeing him and was shocked to find that he had lost over sixty pounds and a good deal of his former charm and affability. His wife had left him and he was very nearly impoverished.

"There is not one man I can trust or take advice from, and not one personal friend," he confided to his Royal cousin and then popped a deviled egg into his mouth. "You know how I've always disapproved of dictators," he finally continued, "yet, here I am, more or less a dictator despite my views. I can tell you, I am feeling the strain badly. Greece needs so much to be done to restore it. My palaces have been ravaged, and there are no more drachmas to rebuild." David's next few days in Corfu were mostly spent in discussions on money and loans. Royal families were no different from other relations, Wallis concluded. The rich members were always expected to help out the poor ones.

The *Nahlin* continued on to Istanbul. While they were in the capital city, the Turkish dictator Ataturk entertained them. Then they proceeded by train through the Balkans to Vienna and there spent five days at the Hotel Bristol, during which time the King met with the leading members of the Austrian government. It was in Vienna, Wallis now learned, that her trust fund had been deposited, although David did not disclose how he had managed secretly to transfer such a sizable sum.

The cruise had given Wallis a new slant on what her future as David's wife might be. She had reacted with panic to the crowds, whereas he had taken them in his stride. She had been bored with the King of Greece, with the dictator Ataturk and with all the heel-clicking Austrians. And she had found being charming to them an almost intolerable effort, while David, steeled to such encounters all his life, was at his peak. The journey that had been meant to relax her had instead set her even more on edge. The clear light she had experienced in Corfu—the new world she believed she was entering—now seemed to have been a warning beacon of ill tidings to come.

They parted in Zurich, David to return to London, Wallis to spend a week at the Hotel Meurice in Paris. Almost immediately she came down with a heavy cold and had to cancel all engagements. While she was nursing herself, her mail, forwarded from London, arrived. The contents of Aunt Bessie's letters stunned her. About fifty clippings fell out and covered her bed. ("I could have gone on and on snipping them," Aunt Bessie wrote, "but I assumed by this count you would have a fair idea of the commotion your cruise made here.")

She now saw the results of those long-lens cameras. There were pictures of David and her sunbathing on the deck of the *Nahlin,* of them walking through the streets of villages with David bare-chested in the tropical heat, of them holding hands by the water's edge. Their relationship and his intentions toward her had become a topic of dinner conversation for every newspaper reader in the United States, Europe and the Dominions.

"Oh, God, David," she told him on the telephone, "I can't stand this cheap, sensational attention. It's awful. And it's so degrading to you."

"I assure you, darling," he told her, "there will be no public comment in England and the furor will soon die down."

She suffered deepening misgivings. Anxiety plagued her. What she had seen as a dream took on nightmarish dimensions. The date for the divorce proceedings was set on her return. Ernest and Mary were now living openly together. There had been threats on her life and it had been arranged when she returned to London for her to move out of Bryanston Court and into a house on Cumberland Terrace in Regent's Park. She was going to lose all she had—Ernest and her home—for unknown dangers. She sat in her bed at the Meurice unable to do anything constructive. All she could think about was getting out of this deep, murky uncharted water. She tried to tell David on the telephone that they must break off. He refused to listen and immediately switched to another topic.

Finally, she took pen in hand and wrote him that she must return to Ernest because they were congenial and understood getting on together very well—which, she explained, was really an art in marriage. She added that she felt that their life once ran smoothly with no nerve strain.

"True, we are poor and unable to do the attractive amusing things in life which I must confess I do love and enjoy," she admitted. "Also the possession of beautiful things is thrilling to me and much appreciated. But weighed against a calm, congenial life I choose the latter for I know that though I shall suffer greatly now, I shall be a happier, calmer old lady. You and I would only create disaster together. I shall arrange the return of everything—the trust fund, whatever jewels belong to your family. I am sure that after this letter you will realize that it would be most unfair to make things harder for me by seeing me. Goodbye WE all say—Wallis."

No sooner had she sent the letter than she realized with a shock how demented it was of her to believe, for even one mad moment, that Ernest would give up Mary and come back to her and things could be as they once were. She was not Smudge the Cat. She could not write whatever ending she chose to her royal adventure. The reality was that Ernest would not return to the marital fold and that, if David accepted her plea to end it all, she would be alone.

She paced the floor in her room all night. Any attempts to rest failed. With morning came exhaustion and the determination to end her affair with the King even if Ernest was out of her life. She felt almost clairvoyant in believing that to continue seeing David would result in terrible consequences.

The King called her morning and evening, the Channel connection causing his voice to waver. "Wallis," he said, after he received the letter, "how can you write such hard things? I refuse to believe them. Your saying we are not right for each other is as much a flight of fancy as your supposing that you and Ernest could reconcile. You are under terrible pressure and I understand it, my darling."

"David, please listen to me," she pleaded.

"Not when you want to speak such foolish things. I promise you, Wallis, those stories will not appear in the English press and you will be safe once you return. Everything is being done here to insure that. And, my darling, I love you enough for the two of us—although that is not necessary. In my eanum heart I know you love me just as deeply, that WE are strong and will continue to be strong and that we will have our chance at a life together."

There was little she could say to dissuade him. He countered her every objection. "I should not have left you alone," he said. "I wish I never had to, that we could spend every hour of every day that God gives us together."

She disconnected with the knowledge that her fate had been sealed.

31

"Well," Syrie drawled as she surveyed the Louis XVI contents of the drawing room at Wallis's new furnished home on Cumberland Terrace, "it's reassuring to know Marie Antoinette saved her furniture even if she had bad luck herself."

"That's not funny," Wallis said abruptly. She sat down on the edge of a fringed settee, tears rising in her eyes.

"What's the matter, honey?" Syrie asked, coming immediately to her side. "Anything I can help you with?"

"I was just thinking of Mama. I don't know what on earth she would have made of all this. They chose this house for its secure situation, the ability of a detective at front and back to monitor anyone who comes in or out. Syrie, I have this scary feeling that I'm in real danger. Worse, if I go through with the divorce."

"You're not thinking of backing out?"

"I can't. I'm boxed in. There's no way to go but forward."

"Well, that's the direction we'll go," Syrie said. Then, legs firmly planted, looking for all the world like a captain at the prow of his ship, she squinted into the long distance of the room and commanded, "I'll take down the heavy brocade draperies and swag yards and yards of butter-colored taffeta over the tops of the windows and down at the side. Butter and cream. Yes! That would give the French majesty a more agrarian look."

Wallis managed a smile. "It would help," she agreed, "and flowers. I'll order massive bouquets of yellow and white to be delivered every week."

"That's more positive!"

"I'm trying hard, but I do feel as though the mobs are about to crash through the palace gates. Aunt Bessie writes that Britons abroad are ready for blood. They don't want a divorcee to marry their King. The storm will break here soon. And I can see that David is worried, although he tries to keep it from me. You know the new Buick he just gave me has shatterproof glass windows? They're for protection if someone decides to throw a brick at me! If news of the divorce leaks, all hell could break lose."

The next day she learned that *Simpson* v. *Simpson* would be heard in four weeks in Ipswich Assize, Suffolk, seventy miles from London. She would have to reside within the court's jurisdiction at the time of the hearing. A cottage in the nearby seaside village of Felixstowe was found. Chief Inspector David Storrier of Scotland Yard, craggy-faced and all business, drove down in the car with her. Slipper sat on her lap, his nose pressed hard against the window, barking from time to time at passing cars. Behind them, caravan fashion, the King's newly purchased American station wagon followed with a cook and maid from Buckingham Palace (who had both been cleared through the Yard), hampers of food from the Palace kitchens and from Fortnum & Mason, cases of wine and some of Wallis's personal effects.

Felixstowe, which was twelve miles from Ipswich, was on the North Sea, situated in a gently curving bay between the estuaries of two rivers. Its two-mile-long pebble and sand shore was fronted by sedate hotels and numerous houses built toward the end of the nineteenth century when the Victorians discovered the village's appeal. The rambling, homey cottage Wallis occupied was set back from the sea, hidden by century-old trees, from which it drew its name—Beech House. It had been built for summer occupancy and heated only by small electric fires, and a damp chill pervaded all the rooms.

Fearing scandal, David—although he called her several times a day—could not visit. Syrie came down one weekend; Foxy Gwynne another. Otherwise, she had only the staff for company. Confined by the constant rain, she read and put together a book of all her recipes to occupy herself. The gloom of the long days, thoughts of the impending divorce and inactivity conspired to increase her edginess. Her mind strayed. It was as if her thoughts were hundreds of winding roads and trails that intersected and then splintered off helter-skelter, always ending in culs-de-sac.

Because she had never questioned her decision to divorce Win, her enforced stay at Warrenton had enabled her to find a new route for her life to travel. This was entirely different. The bond between Ernest and her was hard for her to break.

They had been more like conspirators than lovers and secrets fastened themselves to such a partnership like barnacles to a ship. No one else knew as much about her liaison with the King, the ploys she had used, the small deceits, to remove Thelma and Freda from his life. Nor did anyone, least of all David, understand how tenacious had been her climb up the social ladder. With Ernest, she could, at the end of the day, be herself and be accepted fully for it. Whereas, with David, she held herself in check. She could not envision that changing even if (and despite his optimism, she retained lurking doubts) they were to marry.

By the morning of her appearance in court, Beech House was besieged by newspapermen from almost every Western country. Wallis stepped out of the cottage onto the front terrace. The rain had let up, but the smell and feel of dampness were still in the air. She buttoned the high collar of her fitted, dark-blue coat and pulled the matching felt hat farther down on her forehead. Suddenly she was aware of the masses of photographers beyond the gates of the property as they scuffled with a line of policemen. She froze, terrified.

"We will drive past them at a fast clip," Detective Storrier assured her as he came up to her side. "You will sit on the floor of the car. They will not be able to see you."

The King had sent his chauffeur, Ladbrook, down from London with a hired, unmarked sober English car because her

Buick would have been so easily identified. It was parked off the drive and on the grass only a few steps from the house. The six-foot, two-hundred-pound Ladbrook jumped out of the car and joined them on the porch. Wallis walked behind him, Storrier at her side, down the front steps to the car. Once inside, the detective helped her scoot onto the floor of the back seat.

"Ready?" Ladbrook inquired.

"Go!" Storrier ordered.

The car spun around and then sped forward. From her lowly position Wallis could hear shouting as they passed the front gates, which had been opened by the police at a horn signal from Ladbrook. As soon as they were on the road to Ipswich, Storrier helped her onto the seat.

"I thought the British press were not going to cover the hearing," she said in a shaky voice as she straightened her hat.

"Those were mostly foreign pressmen," Storrier explained. "There's still been very little that has appeared in the British papers. But be prepared for what we might encounter at the courthouse."

"Oh-my-god!" Wallis said, and leaned back faint in the seat. "I hope I have the strength."

"You will find it, Mrs. Simpson," the detective assured her.

"There's a car following us at quite a clip, sir," Ladbrook told Storrier over his shoulder. "I think the driver is intent on overtaking us."

Storrier glanced back. "Photographers!" he said with disdain. "How fast can this vehicle go, Ladbrook?"

"Faster than the one behind us, sir."

"Then press your foot to the floor."

They lost the other car after a few moments of hot pursuit.

Another gaggle of photographers was waiting for their arrival outside the courthouse. Policemen were everywhere, auxiliary officers having been borrowed from several neighboring towns. As Ladbrook slowed down to enter the garage, a photographer broke through the police barrier.

"Down!" Storrier ordered and shoved Wallis back onto the floor.

The car came to a halt at a private door in the garage. Storrier helped Wallis out and two policemen, one on each side of her, hustled her into a dark passageway and up a dimly lighted flight of rear stairs.

"You'd think I was a murderess up for trial," she said.

"I know, ma'am. We're sorry," one of her escorts apologized. "But it is safer for you this way." She was taken to a private room and greeted by her two lawyers, Norman Birkett and a man she had not met, a Mr. Frampton.

"We had no idea there would be so many reporters and, I am sorry to say, Mrs. Simpson, newsreel men as well," Birkett, a small bulldog of a man, explained. "They have tried to set up their equipment in a room that had a view of the court. Although they have been removed, the press could not be legally barred. Tickets were issued to thirty reporters; and inside the courtroom, their seats have been arranged so that all those which face the witness-box have been left vacant. Only your back will be visible. Sir John Hawke will be the presiding judge. He is not what one would term a sympathetic man. He is always vigilant as well against any signs of collusion—that is, a couple who have set up the adulterous situation. He also arrived with a beastly cold and cannot be expected to be in good humor."

"Do you think there is a chance he might not grant the divorce?" Wallis asked, alarmed.

"I simply want you to have a clear picture of what you will be met with when you enter the courtroom."

Someone took her coat. Beneath it she wore a neat blue suit and, at the collar of the ivory blouse, a simple gold pin. Her only other jewelry was pearl earrings and the bracelet of gold and jeweled crucifixes that David had given her.

She waited apprehensively for over half an hour in the anteroom, the door slightly ajar, Mr. Frampton standing guard like a nervous hen protecting her brood. Finally, he raised his arm in signal and Birkett led Wallis to the door.

"Whatever happens, do not panic," he advised. "I mean, if a reporter should get out of hand, something unexpected. There are numerous police officers and plainclothes detectives in the courtroom."

"Simpson versus Simpson," she heard a man announce from inside the courtroom. She entered on Birkett's arm and kept her gaze straight ahead in the direction of Judge Hawke, whose nose was beet red, his eyes tearing from his cold. The room was half empty. Wallis noted only two women sitting together in the gallery.

"The judge's wife and a friend," Mr. Frampton whispered.

"I appear in this case with my learned friend Mr. Walter Frampton. I call the petitioner at once," Birkett said.

Pale but controlled, Wallis went into the witness-box. A chair had been provided for her, although normally the witness stood. After she had been sworn in, Birkett, employing a gentle manner, began to question her.

"Your names are Wallis Warfield Spencer Simpson? You are now living at Beech House, Felixstowe?"

"Yes."

"Is your London address 16 Cumberland Terrace, Regent's Park?"

"Yes."

"You were married to Ernest Aldrich Simpson on July 21, 1928, at the Registry Office in the District of Chelsea?"

"Yes."

"And I think that afterwards you lived with him at 12 Upper Berkeley Street and 5 Bryanston Court in London?"

"Yes."

"Has there been any issue of that marriage?"

"No."

"Did you live happily with the Respondent until the autumn of 1934?"

"Yes."

"What was the change?"

"He was indifferent, and often went away weekends."

"On Christmas Day, 1934, did you find a note lying on your dressing table?"

"Yes." The note, which was the undated one she had been left earlier in the year when Ernest went off with Mary, was produced. Her heart pounded. She felt enormously guilty and was certain the Judge, his handkerchief over his streaming nose, was set to disbelieve any evidence, true or false, that was set before him.

"Having read the letter," Birkett continued, "did you then consult your solicitor?"

"Yes."

"Upon your instructions did they keep observations on your husband?"

"Yes."

"Did you subsequently receive information on which your petition in this present case is based?"

"Yes."

"Would you kindly read a letter which you wrote to your husband directly thereafter." He handed her a folded piece of her own stationery.

Wallis straightened the page and held it close as she read the contents: "Dear Ernest, I have just learned that while you have been away, instead of being on business as you led me to believe, you have been staying at a hotel at Bray with a lady. I am sure you must realize that this is conduct which I cannot possibly overlook and I must insist that you do not continue to live here with me. This only confirms suspicions which I have had for a long time. I am therefore instructing my solicitors to take proceedings for a divorce. Wallis."

The private investigator's report and photographs taken when Mary and Ernest were at Bray were then placed in evidence. An effort had been made to keep Mary's true identity from the court and the public. There was a buzz in the courtroom. The press had hoped the name of the other woman would be revealed. But Birkett did not introduce her name into the testimony. The papers the Judge had seen listed her as Mrs. Buttercup Kennedy. Neither did he repeat this name.

Judge Hawke looked down at Wallis with considerable distaste. On the wall directly behind him was a large portrait of the King, the one that had been hurried into completion, copied and circulated to all public offices and courtrooms. As Wallis waited for the Judge to speak, she wondered if he had any idea of who she was—beyond being Mrs. Ernest Simpson. She decided he obviously did.

"Well," he finally growled, "I suppose I must come to the conclusion that there was adultery in this case."

Everyone waited as Judge Hawke blew his nose. "Yes, costs against the Respondent, I am afraid," he said.

"Decree nisi, with costs?" Birkett repeated.

"Yes, I suppose so."

It was over. Before Wallis knew what was happening, Birkett and Frampton were on either side of her and ushering her to the door. Once in the anteroom to collect her coat she turned to Birkett. "I can't have Ernest paying the costs," she insisted.

"You can repay him, if you wish," Birkett replied. "But for the record this makes it a complete vindication of complicity on your behalf."

Chief Inspector Storrier joined them, along with the same two policemen; and the group made their way back the way they had come. To their stunned dismay, several of the reporters had managed to obtain entry into the garage. As Wallis went to step out from the dark passageway, she was blinded by the flash of cameras. Suddenly, a hand reached out and grabbed the brim of her hat and pulled it back from her face. Wallis screamed. The officers almost carried her forward and to the car. Behind her there was chaos. A photographer had been thrown to the ground. A camera was smashed against the cement floor. There were angry voices, cursing.

Storrier pushed her through the opened car door. "Get down on the floor again," he ordered and practically put her there.

Wallis began to cry. It was all so ugly, so degrading. "I can't go back to the cottage," she sobbed. "I can't. They'll follow me there."

"All right," Storrier agreed. "We'll go directly to London. The staff can pack and bring your luggage."

"Slipper!" she cried. "My dog!"

"They will bring him too, Mrs. Simpson." She was sitting next to Storrier now and her appearance startled him. *This woman is on the point of collapse,* he thought, wondering how she was going to survive the impending furor.

The divorce would take six long months before it was final. Wallis tried not to think about the future. She must concentrate on getting through each day. Her experience in Felixstowe had prepared her for what was to come. The truth could no longer be kept from the English people. She would not only be in jeopardy, she would be living in a fishbowl.

By the time Aunt Bessie arrived three weeks later, Wallis could no longer leave the house without being subjected to crowds of curious people, who even stationed themselves across from Cumberland Terrace to catch a glimpse of her coming or leaving the house. The silence of the British press was broken. There had been a terrible outburst, and members of the public were divided in their reactions. The problem was that the opposition was the more vociferous. Ugly placards caricaturing her were printed; people hissed and cursed when she appeared.

The Government's reaction further stunned Wallis and the King. Fear arose that the Government would resign, which would result in the King having to find someone other than Baldwin. A general election could be called. But then the King's plans to marry Wallis after she received her final decree would be the chief issue.

"And, Aunt Bessie, that could lead to abdication," Wallis explained. They were at the Fort for the weekend. Outside a sharp November gale twisted limbs from trees, leaves went flying in great patches and the many chimneys at the Fort echoed the wind's fury. The two women were having tea before the fire in Wallis's blue bedroom suite. "He insists on marrying me, Aunt Bessie," Wallis said. The strain of the past weeks showed on her face. She had lost considerable weight and she was gaunt, pale shadows beneath her eyes.

"And what do you want, Wallis?" her aunt asked.

"It's too late for that."

"Don't be sure. What is it?"

Wallis sat up very straight. The reflection of the flames caused one side of her face to glow red. "I would have liked to have gone on being the King's mistress. If only Ernest hadn't fallen in love with Mary! That changed everything! I don't think I will ever forgive either of them."

"What a selfish thing for you to say, Wallis," her aunt reprimanded.

"Yes, it is. And I hope God forgives me for being self-centered. That's the way I am, Aunt Bessie, and no one should know that better than you. I've always connived to get my way. And been furious with others when I failed. I don't know why I think what I want is more important than what someone else has to sacrifice to give it to me. But it's not going to do me a bit of good to hate myself for something I can't seem to control."

"Well, Wallis, it looks like this time the cat's got her tail caught in the mousetrap. How do you plan to extricate yourself from this situation?"

"The King's advisor, Walter Monckton, wants me to go abroad—*without further delay* were his words. He believes the Government is preparing for a showdown with the King. They are going to insist that he give me up. I've begged David to let me go. I used all the powers of persuasion in my possession. I tried to convince him of the hopelessness of our position. There is simply no way that I can see that the Government will let him marry me and remain on the throne."

"What does the King say to this?"

"On the throne or off, he plans to marry me. For him to go on hoping, to go on fighting the inevitable, will mean certain tragedy for him and catastrophe for me. He will be a man without a country and I will be a woman with only a shell of a man. But he won't listen. He's told me his mind is made up. If the country won't approve of our marrying, he's ready to go."

Wallis shook with sudden sobs. Her aunt stood up and, going over to Wallis, gently placed her hand on her niece's shoulder. There was a deeply maternal look on Bessie Merryman's face. Her heart was broken for Wallis. Her heart was also grieving for all the plans and future glories she had been certain Wallis would claim for them both. The crooked mouth trembled. There were tears in her eyes, but she fought hard for her composure and won. Slowly she removed her hand.

"Wallis, crying isn't going to do you a bit of good," she advised. "There is only one way to end this and you know well enough what it is. You are an American. You come back to Washington with me and you tell the King it is over, finished.

He won't be the first man, and probably not even the first King, to be jilted. He'll suffer, for that man surely loves you. And you'll suffer, too. For I can see you have a queenly glint in your eyes, Wallis, which I well understand. You would be the first American woman to snatch yourself a King and maybe even a Crown for yourself. That's a mighty hard piece of catnip to reject. But, Wallis," she continued, "now it's time to show the world just what kind of real quality the Montague women possess. Come home with me, Wallis."

"I can't do that, Aunt Bessie," Wallis said softly. She rose and crossed to the fire and took a poker and stirred up the flames to an even greater intensity.

Aunt Bessie had made a study of Wallis since she was a child. It had been her life's work. Until this moment she had believed she was responsible for Wallis's driving social ambition, her need to always reach for one more rung of power. After all, she had planted the seed as far back as the scarlatina episode. No, *farther.* For though she would never tell Wallis, it was she who had insisted Alice confess to Sol Warfield that the child she carried was his and it was she who had convinced her sister to move with her baby to Mrs. Warfield's home so that Bessie Wallis would have a proper start in life.

"Wallis, you have it in your mind to be Queen, don't you?" she asked.

"No, Aunt Bessie, that job comes with too many responsibilities and restrictions. I want to be the King's mistress. David chooses for me to be Queen."

"Once before, Wallis, I asked you this question. Do you love him?"

"I do, Aunt Bessie. I now know I do and I am prepared to go through oceans of agony for him."

"And to be Queen if it comes to that?"

"And to be Queen," Wallis replied, looking Aunt Bessie directly in the eye, her voice strong, unwavering.

"And if he was not to be King? If he should be forced to abdicate?"

"I'm sure neither a Montague nor a Warfield ever deserted ship," she said. "Neither will I."

32

The weeks that followed Wallis's discussion with Aunt Bessie were extraordinary. While she remained a prisoner in Cumberland Terrace with her aunt, the King was involved in a series of meetings with the Prime Minister, the Cabinet, his family and his own advisors. He told Wallis little about what was said, but had the talks been positive in nature, she knew he would have shared their outcome.

It was now impossible for her to go out anywhere in public. The house had become a focus of attention. The curious stood guard day and night peering up, using binoculars to see if they could get a glimpse of Wallis at a window. Her shades had to be closed and electric lights used during the daytime as well as at night.

Through the mail slot came strange and threatening letters, some signed but most of them anonymous. Then one day Detective Storrier appeared.

"I do not want to frighten you, Mrs. Simpson," he warned, "but there is a rumor of a plot to blow up this house. I am sure it is no more than hearsay. Nonetheless, for your safety we have planned for you to leave here tonight, destination unknown to any of the staff. You are to pack the barest essentials—as if you are to be gone a day or two at most."

With Aunt Bessie's assistance, she did as she was asked. Late that evening an unmarked car arrived. With Wallis holding Slipper in her arms, the women, escorted by Detective Storrier, made their way to the vehicle down the rear steps of the house. The King sat well back in the darkened interior and squeezed Wallis's hand reassuringly as she sat between him and her aunt.

"Where are we going?" she asked.

"For now the Fort," he replied.

"Won't people guess?"

"Perhaps, but it is safe." He put his arm around her shoulders. "My poor, dear eanum," he whispered and drew her closer.

Later, when they were settled at the Fort, he confessed that he had tried everything, even the plan that they had both discussed for a morganatic marriage, which would have meant they could marry but she would not be Queen. This last had been very much against his true feelings, and he seemed relieved that he had not succeeded.

The Fort was like a place under siege. Extra police had been called out to guard the gates. Plainclothesmen stood at windows scrutinizing the grounds for sight of any intruders and flares had been lighted in the front of the estate for better surveillance. The tempo of activity kept mounting. Advisors, aides and courtiers came and went at all hours. The telephone never ceased ringing.

Despite all the discussions, only two courses now seemed viable: the King's renunciation of Wallis or his abdication.

Duff Cooper urged the King to withdraw the marriage proposal from the Cabinet's consideration and proceed with the Coronation. "You can reopen the marriage issue again at a later date," he argued.

"No," the King said emphatically. Cooper left the Fort feeling the end was soon to come.

For a week Wallis was ill, the old spasms returning, and she remained in bed with her aunt in the connecting room. "Aunt Bessie," she confided, her first day out of bed, "I think I must go away for a while. Everyone here, except David, would like that. After a while my name will be forgotten by the people, and only the two of us will suffer instead of a mass of outsiders who aren't interested anyway in individual feelings but only the workings of a system."

"You are most probably right, Wallis," her aunt concurred. "But how and where?"

"I'm not sure yet. It will have to be cleverly arranged." She kept her thoughts from the King and tried to be as cheerful as possible under the trying circumstances.

That day the King had gone in to confer yet another time with the Prime Minister, feeling hopeful because Winston Churchill had given him a measure of unexpected support. On his return he went directly to Wallis's room where she and Aunt Bessie were sitting by the fire when he entered.

"Wallis, can we take a walk?" he asked. "Wrap up well," he added as he looked at her with great warmth and emotion. "It's cold outside, my darling."

A thick fog had rolled in. He held a small flashlight and led her over to the parapet where he knew they could not be overheard.

"It now comes to this," he said, as they stood close together in the chill night, the Fort, where they had been so happy together, almost eclipsed by the mist. "Either I must give you up or abdicate. And I don't intend to give you up."

"Abdication is unthinkable, David," she protested.

He seemed preoccupied, his mind far away. She could hardly make out his face in the misty darkness.

"David, I'm going to leave England. I've already stayed too long. I can go to Kitty and Herman in Cannes. I'll stay there until we can work things out. Do you think you can arrange safe passage?"

"For when?"

"Tonight, if possible."

"Yes, that would be best," he agreed, somewhat relieved. He took her in his arms and held her close. "Hold a boy tight, always, Wallis," he said. When they kissed, he tasted her tears and was very moved. "For me? Oh, my darling," he said softly. "I love you more than my life—and, I am afraid, more than my country. It will be hard for me to have you go. But, it would be harder still to have you stay. You are possibly in danger—and I cannot subject you to that. Your situation here is becoming harrowing beyond belief. Every moment I fear some mad person may take a shot at you. You are right to go. You *must* go. I must handle this in my own way alone."

They clung together for a long time. When they broke apart, both were much calmer, in control. "We'll call the Rogerses," he said as they made their way through the darkness to the house following the small beam of their torch. Once inside, he spun into action. It was decided that Aunt Bessie would remain at the Fort and return to Cumberland Terrace after Wallis was safely in France, a ploy which might encourage people to believe that Wallis was also in England. A call was put through to Herman and Kitty and the situation explained.

"Of course you must come to us," Herman agreed.

The King's Lord-in-Waiting, a former officer in the Grenadier Guards, Lord Brownlow, known as Perry to Wallis and the King, and a good friend of his, was chosen to accompany her, along with a less-identifiable Scotland Yard detective than Storrier, an Inspector Evans. Every road from the Fort was being watched by the press. Ladbrook was dispatched to London to retrieve Wallis's Buick and to drive it to Newhaven, where it was to be put aboard the night ferry to Dieppe, on the French side of the Channel. Perry Brownlow arrived at the Fort in his own car and with his chauffeur, Field. Wallis was to ride with them down to the boat, leaving the Fort as she had departed Ipswich, on the floor of the car. This meant Slipper had to be left with the King, for the possibility of the dog's giving her away was too strong.

As the last bag was being put into the luggage compartment, the King embraced her. "I don't know how it's all going to end, darling. It will be some time before we can be together again. You must wait for me no matter how long it takes. I shall never give up."

She hurried into the car. Rain had begun to fall. They had only a short time to spare if she was to make the night boat to France and the drive was long. "I am afraid I am going to have to ask you to get down on the floor, Mrs. Simpson," Detective Evans said.

She immediately complied and so she did not see the night mist engulf the Fort as they drove through the gates, past the gaping news corps and the line of police recruits who believed only that Lord Brownlow, one more courtier, had come and gone after talking to the King. Soon they were on a darkened road and Wallis was helped onto the seat. She looked back over her shoulder. There was nothing but blackness. France was to be her destination and she turned around in the seat and stared straight ahead.

She sat in silence, unable to speak, her mind on what she must face when she reached France.

"Look, Wallis," Brownlow said, as the car sped through the dark countryside, "you can still stop the King from abdication. I have a plan."

"He won't abdicate. I won't let him, Perry," she insisted.

"You won't be able to stop him once you are in France. My idea is that you come back to my house in Lincolnshire. No one will dream you are there and you can keep a dialogue up with him to influence him against taking such a drastic step." His slight frame was a shadow in the dim light.

"No. My mind is quite made up. The only thing that will stop him is my ending the relationship and I'm now determined to do so. Tomorrow he is giving a radio address to the nation. I want him to say that it is all over between us." From her purse, she drew out a small pad of notepaper with the Fort insignia on it. "Can we have the overhead light on for a moment?" she asked.

"Yes, I think we're safe now," Evans replied in a flat voice.

Wallis wrote quickly, repeating aloud her words: "Tell the country we have ended our affair." She continued writing for a moment in silence and then folded the note and handed it to Evans. "Can you get this back to the King when I board the boat for France?"

"Yes, of course," he promised. The two men exchanged apprehensive looks over her head. Both feared her message might have different repercussions from the ones she expected.

The interior of the car fell again into darkness. Wallis leaned back against the seat. Tears brimmed her eyes. She was certain that she would never come back, never see England again, that the King would be convinced not to abdicate.

When their little group disembarked in Dieppe, Ladbrook was waiting on the pier with her Buick. The press had not followed her to Newhaven and Wallis believed that she was safe from harassment and danger. But no sooner had she climbed into the back seat of the car than Ladbrook sighted several vehicles pulled into the yard.

"The press," he announced. "We'll have to drive at breakneck speed." The car jolted forward and then sped past their pursuers and onto the highway. A moment later, Ladbrook turned off the main road and followed narrow lanes through farmland and small villages. The two-day car journey to Cannes quickly became a frantic chase. No sooner had they arrived at one village to eat and refresh themselves, than the press was sighted and the exhausted group was forced to leave surreptitiously through a rear door to make still another escape.

The journey had become a ludicrous flight. Ladbrook took alternate routes, deviations and one-way dirt roads to lose their pursuers, but the chase continued. Wallis was in a state of mounting anxiety. Ladbrook proved a game and able driver. Still, there were clashes with their stalkers at hotels and restaurants along the way. Wallis made several attempts to call the King and pleaded with him not to abdicate but the Channel connections were so poor that she could barely be heard.

During the last lap of the frantic race to reach Cannes and presumed safety, rain pelted down. The windshield wipers broke and Ladbrook had to make his way blindly through the wash of water. It was two o'clock in the morning when they finally arrived at Lou Viei, the Rogerses' villa. At the gates, along with at least thirty French police officers, were the pursuing vehicles which must have arrived by a shorter route. Added to the cars belonging to the press was a large newsreel van.

"All right," Evans ordered as they approached, "Mrs. Simpson, on the floor." Wallis crouched down as low as she could. Evans covered her with a blanket and Ladbrook put his foot hard on the accelerator as they tore past the crowd, through the open gates and up the driveway. The gates closed swiftly after them. The police had been alerted and recognized the Buick.

Kitty and Herman stood at the door of their home to greet her. Wallis, her hat askew, her shoes and legs splattered with mud, fell into Kitty's arms, where she clung to her.

"It's all right, Wallis," Kitty assured her trembling friend. "You'll be quite safe here."

"Oh, Kitty, it was horrible, horrible!" She began to cry, and Kitty helped her remove her outer garments and her shoes before leading her over to the fire where she settled her in an armchair with a hand-knit afghan over her legs.

"You'll have something to eat and then you can go up to bed. You're exhausted, Wallis," Kitty said.

"No, first I must write a letter. It's imperative. Herman, when does the first mail plane leave Nice in the morning?"

"I don't know, but I'll find out," he replied.

A maid brought her a tray with soup and crackers and several small sandwiches and set it down beside her. "I can't eat, Kitty. I just want to write a letter to the King. He must receive it before tomorrow at five when he is going to see Mr. Baldwin again."

Realizing that Wallis was obsessed with writing the letter, Kitty helped her up to her room, the same one she had occupied in a much happier time. The tray with her supper was placed beside the desk. Then everyone went out, leaving her alone.

A fire was burning in the grate. Wallis still felt chilled through as she undressed before it and put on a warm robe that had been left for her across the foot of the bed. Then she sat down at the desk and, taking some Lou Viei stationery, began to write. She realized some of what she scrawled might be incoherent. She was exhausted and her thoughts refused to be disciplined, but she had a plan and she knew she must convey it immediately to the King.

The strategy she devised for him to follow (and which took her fifteen pages to write in disjointed sentences) was for him to withdraw any requests for them to marry and for her to stay abroad until the following autumn when the Coronation would be well behind him and his reign established.

What she did not tell him was her own plan to leave France as soon as the crisis was over and she was well enough to travel to the Far East, where Aunt Bessie would meet her and they could tour for several months before returning *someplace*—she could not be sure where but she thought in America. Perhaps New York or Santa Barbara. She would have time to make up her mind.

It was nearly dawn before she had finished writing. Quietly she left the room to investigate who might be about. Herman was sleeping in a chair in the drawing room by the dying embers of the fire. Gently as she could she awakened him and gave him the letter.

"I'll drive it to the airport myself," he said, and rose immediately to do so.

The torrential rains had stopped. But there was a curious sound outside. Suddenly, Wallis recognized it as the motor of a plane. She cautiously pulled up her shade. She had been right and it was circling low, almost directly overhead. "Oh-my-god!" she exclaimed, "the damned press!," and jerked the shade down again.

Not for a long while after the historic events that followed would Wallis learn the full details of what had happened after David received her letter. She spoke to him daily. He kept many of his difficulties to himself, but he refused to accept her plan for them to remain separated. She begged and pleaded with him to no avail.

On Friday morning, December 11, just five days after her arrival at Lou Viei, he told her he could not be deterred. He was going to sign the Instrument of Abdication and he had agreed to go away to some private place—he believed it would be Vienna—and remain there for six months before they were reunited.

"But, my darling, we will have the rest of our lives," he said.

The entire household at Lou Viei gathered around the radio in the drawing room that evening to hear the King's speech over the B.B.C. Wallis was lying on the sofa with her hands over her eyes, trying to hide her tears. His voice came clearly out of the loud speaker.

"At long last I am able to say a few words of my own.

"I have never wanted to withhold anything, but until now it has not been constitutionally possible for me to speak.

"A few hours ago I discharged my last duty as King and Emperor, and now that I have been succeeded by my brother, the Duke of York, my first words must be to declare my allegiance to him."

Wallis held an image of Bertie, now King George VI, in her mind—the slight eye twitch, the self-paralyzing stutter—and could not help but wonder how he would survive the arduous path before him.

"You all know the reasons which have impelled me to renounce the throne," David continued, "but I want you to understand that in making up my mind I did not forget the country or the Empire, which as Prince of Wales and lately as King I have for twenty-five years tried to serve.

"But you must believe me when I tell you that I have found it impossible to carry the heavy burden of responsibility and discharge my duties as King as I would wish to do without the help and support of the woman I love."

All the eyes in the room turned to Wallis and then quickly away. She made no gesture. Her hands remained over her face.

"And I want you to know that the decision I have made has been mine and mine alone. This was a thing I had to judge entirely for myself. The other person most nearly concerned has tried up to the last to persuade me to take a different course.

"I have made this, the most serious decision of my life, only upon a single thought—of what would in the end be best for all.

"This decision has been made less difficult to me by the sure knowledge that my brother, with his long training in the public affairs of this country and with his fine qualities, will be able to take my place forthwith without interruption or injury to the life and progress of the Empire.

"And he has one matchless blessing, enjoyed by so many of you, and not bestowed on me, a happy home with his wife and children."

Wallis struggled to suppress a small sob. She heard the rest of the speech as though it were coming through a filter. There was not another sound in the room, just David's voice, strong and yet so full of emotion, seeming to be circling over her head as the press plane had continued to do all week.

"And now we all have a new King," he was saying. "I wish him and you, his people, happiness and prosperity with all my heart. God bless you all. GOD SAVE THE KING!"

"Wallis, I'm so sorry," Kitty said. Herman took his wife's hand. Everyone left the room. Wallis was alone. She lay there, the flames snapping in the hearth.

It was over. David was no longer King. There was no escape for her now, no Far East with its exotic anonymity, no return to the States where she could make a new good life for herself, for she had been convinced that once she was out of the King's life she would soon be forgotten. She was trapped. There was to be no way out. She must wait here six long months. Then she would have no other choice but to marry the *ex*-King, a man without a country, without power, with declining prestige, a man who would be wholly dependent upon her and whom she dare not leave or she would be branded the most evil woman in the world.

Slowly she rose from the sofa and made her way out of the room. The hallway was deserted as she climbed the stairs. She had the eerie feeling that at the top there would be a guillotine. She paused, took a deep breath and continued her ascent.

AFTERWARD

(H.R.H.) THE DUCHESS OF WINDSOR

June 1937

33

Great clouds moved slowly from the west, myriad shapes, ancient beasts, mountain ranges, entire cities, the vast and mysterious vault above them. The sun shone brightly. The earth was warm. It was June and the flowers of the gardens of the Château de Candé at Montes, France, where the wedding was to take place, were in full bloom.

They had been reunited only a few weeks earlier. Kitty and Herman had driven with her to Verneuil where the ex-King, now known as the Duke of Windsor, had detrained on his return from his exile in Austria. They had hoped they could avoid the press, but of course someone had caught wind of their rendezvous. Nonetheless, such careful arrangements had been made that they did have some privacy. Herman's car had been parked in a guarded area near the track where the *Arlberg Express,* on which the Duke had traveled through the night, was to stop. He had ridden in the car nearest the engine and was the first passenger allowed off the train.

A pathway had been roped for him to pass. He beamed and waved at the press who fought to get pictures of him. He looked tan and well. Suddenly, he had stopped. He had caught sight of Herman standing beside the car and he began to run toward him, police and companions surrounding him for safety.

Someone opened the door of the car and he jumped into the back seat. The door closed. He took Wallis in his arms, unable to speak. He held her to him, kissed her face, her neck, her hands. There were tears of joy in his clear blue eyes.

"Oh, David," she finally cried. "I hope to God you will always believe it was worth it."

He laughed. "I would have paid twice the price," he said.

"That would *really* be something! To give up *two* kingdoms!" she said.

He fell back against the rear seat and stared at her. "Well," he had said, "two would have been no more bother than one."

The trip to the Château de Candé was a three-hour drive and he never stopped talking, asking questions, telling her his plans, suggesting ideas for the wedding. He looked young again to Wallis, *boyish,* and she wondered why only she seemed to age.

Now here they were preparing for a fitting end to what the press called the most famous romantic idyll of all time. But there had been some wicked last-minute blows. Bertie, now King George VI, had refused to create Wallis "Her Royal Highness." She would be the Duchess of Windsor. *Wallis Windsor.* It had a ring to it, but not the chimes of majesty. A second shock was the difficulty in getting an Anglican clergyman to marry them. At almost the last moment, the Reverend Jardine, vicar of St. Paul's in Darlington, England, a comic-looking little man with red cheeks, protruding teeth and a wide grin, had flown down to officiate amidst a roar of church censure.

Aunt Bessie joined them, Slipper in tow, and the morning before the wedding Cecil Beaton came to take photographs. Outside the château gates were the usual gaggle of newsmen and their vans of heavy equipment. Inside there was terrible confusion as the place was being readied for tomorrow's ceremony. Wallis's gown—Wallis blue, she called it—with a matching hat, a small veil attached, hung on the wardrobe door of her room, pressed and ready for her to wear. David had given her a startling diamond and sapphire bracelet for a wedding gift. She planned to wear it on one wrist, with the chain with the crucifixes on the other and one of the diamond and sapphire pins he had given her earlier at the neck of her gown.

Beaton was taking a picture of her on the balcony in a yellow organza dress, the sky deep blue above, when she heard Slipper barking on the lawns below and then let out a yelp. Silence followed. "Slipper!" she shouted over the balcony. "Slipper!" She watched as Aunt Bessie and David moved across the lawns. The way they stopped so suddenly made her realize something was wrong and she ran down the stone steps and across the grass to where they were. David was on the ground and Aunt Bessie had turned away.

"Don't look, darling," David said and tried to turn her aside.

She went down onto her knees. Slipper was dead, a small stream of blood trickling down the fur on his neck. She thought of Ellie and her superstitions. What, she wondered, would she make of this?

"It was a snake," David explained. "He tried to fight it." He took her hand and helped her to her feet and they walked slowly back to the house.

The next morning Aunt Bessie helped her dress for the wedding. The age-old custom that the groom must not see the bride before the ceremony had been adhered to. David had called her on the intercom telephone. "I love you, Wallis," he repeated.

"No man has proved it more," she replied.

An hour later the ceremony began in the flower-filled salon of the château which had been given over to them for the month by its owners, Mr. and Mrs. Bedaux, who sat proudly near the front of the small gathering as Wallis entered on Herman's arm. An altar had been set up with a large crucifix over it. On each side of the cross stood a candle, unlit, and at either side of the altar was a large candelabrum with five unlit candles, all to be lighted at various stages of the ceremony. The groom with his best man, Major Dudley "Fruity" Metcalfe, who had been with the ex-King during his exile in Austria, entered from a side door. David's hand touched Wallis's as they came together.

First they were to be married by the local mayor and then,

in a religious service, by the Reverend Jardine, in surplice and purple stole. Wallis's maiden name having returned to her with the final decree of divorce, the Reverend Jardine asked, "Will you, Edward, Duke of Windsor—Albert Christian George Andrew David—take Wallis Warfield to cherish and love as your lawful wife until death do you part?"

"I will," he replied in a clear, ringing voice.

"And will you, Wallis Warfield, take Edward, Duke of Windsor—Albert Christian George Andrew David—to love and obey, in sickness and in health as your lawful husband until death do you part?"

"I will," Wallis said, her voice soft but sure.

Fruity Metcalfe handed the groom the ring and he put it on his bride's finger with a trembling hand. "With this ring," he said, tears in his eyes, "I thee wed in the name of the Father, the Son and the Holy Ghost."

As prearranged, they did not kiss but he held her hand tightly in his until the mayor presented them with a large bouquet of flowers sent by the French premier. A champagne toast was raised: "To His Royal Highness the Duke of Windsor and his Lady!"

As she lifted her glass, Wallis smiled. Perhaps it had not ended as she might have wished, but for a girl from Baltimore with more than a few odds against her. Bessie Wallis Warfield had done all right.